MW00560347

The Tears and Prayers of Fools

Judaic Traditions in Music, Literature, and Art
Ken Frieden, *Series Editor*

Hershl the Shoemaker by Mark Kanovich.

The Tears and Prayers of Fools

A Novel

Grigory Kanovich

Translated from the Russian by Mary Ann Szporluk
Edited by Ken Frieden

Syracuse University Press

First published in Russian as Слёзы и молитвы дураков (Vilnius, 1983).

A section of this translation previously appeared in Vol. 2 of *An Anthology of Jewish-Russian Literature: Two Centuries of Dual Identity in Prose and Poetry*, ed. Maxim D. Shrayer (Armonk, NY: M. E. Sharpe, 2006), 864–74. Reprinted by permission of Maxim D. Shrayer.

Map of Western Russia showing the Jewish Pale of Settlement is reprinted from Isadore Singer and Cyrus Adler, ed., *The Jewish Encyclopedia*, vol. 10 (New York and London: Funk and Wagnalls Company, 1907), 531. Courtesy of the New York Public Library, Dorot Jewish Division.

Copyright © 2023 Grigory Kanovich
English translation copyright © Dmitri Kanovich 2023
Cover art and illustrations by Mark Kanovich used by permission of the artist.

Syracuse University Press
Syracuse, New York 13244-5290
All Rights Reserved

First Edition 2023
23   24   25   26   27   28   6   5   4   3   2   1

∞ The paper used in this publication meets the minimum requirements
of the American National Standard for Information Sciences—Permanence
of Paper for Printed Library Materials, ANSI Z39.48-1992.

For a listing of books published and distributed by Syracuse University Press,
visit https://press.syr.edu.

ISBN: 978-0-8156-1159-2 (paperback)   978-0-8156-5688-3 (e-book)

Library of Congress Cataloging-in-Publication Data
Names: Kanovich, Grigoriĭ, author. | Szporluk, Mary Ann, translator. | Frieden, Ken, 1955– editor.
Title: The tears and prayers of fools : a novel / Grigory Kanovich ; translated from the Russian
    by Mary Ann Szporluk ; edited by, Ken Frieden.
Other titles: Kvailių ašaros ir maldos. English
Description: First edition. | Syracuse, New York : Syracuse University Press, 2023. |
    Series: Judaic traditions in literature, music, and art
Identifiers: LCCN 2023006440 (print) | LCCN 2023006441 (ebook) |
    ISBN 9780815611592 (paperback) | ISBN 9780815656883 (ebook)
Subjects: LCGFT: Novels.
Classification: LCC PG3482.5.N63 K8313 2023 (print) | LCC PG3482.5.N63 (ebook) |
    DDC 891.73/44—dc23/eng/20230519
LC record available at https://lccn.loc.gov/2023006440
LC ebook record available at https://lccn.loc.gov/2023006441

Manufactured in the United States of America

To my wife
Olga M. Kanovich

Contents

Map of Western Russia showing the Jewish Pale of Settlement. Reprinted from *The Jewish Encyclopedia*, vol. 10 (New York and London: Funk and Wagnalls Company, 1907). Courtesy of the New York Public Library, Dorot Jewish Division.

A Note on History and Transliteration

While the characters in Grigory Kanovich's novel converse with each other in Yiddish, this novel is not a Yiddish classic. Written in Russian, *The Tears and Prayers of Fools* is a modern novel first published in Vilnius in 1983, and it gained an eager following of Jewish readers throughout the Soviet Union. Kanovich is regarded as one of the last Lithuanian Jewish writers who experienced Jewish life in a Lithuanian shtetl before the Holocaust.

This novel takes place in a much earlier time, in the early 1880s, when Lithuania was under Russian rule and part of a larger area known as the Pale of Settlement. A few words about the locale of this novel and its history are in order. The Pale of Settlement refers to the western areas of the Russian Empire where Jews were permitted to reside. These areas were annexed by czarist Russia after the partitions of Poland in 1772 and 1795, bringing a large population of Jews under Russian control. Jews were confined to the Pale by the laws of 1795 and 1835. While Jews for the most part could continue living in this area, they were restricted from residing in other parts of the Russian Empire. This area included modern-day Belarus, Lithuania, and Moldova, as well as parts of Ukraine, Poland, and Latvia.

From 1827, under Czar Nicholas I, Jewish communities had to deliver a quota of army recruits for twenty-five years of service, starting at eighteen years of age. Jewish boys were draftable as young as twelve to serve in "Cantonist" battalions until their official term of army service began at eighteen. Often these boys were converted to the Russian Orthodox faith and never returned home. A shameful practice of kidnapping developed in some Jewish communities whereby kidnappers called *khapers* took poor and orphaned boys to be drafted in place of sons of wealthier families. Ever present in the background of this novel is one of these lost Jewish boys whose step-father never stops hoping for his return. Against this political tableau, the other characters deal with their own yearnings—for love, for their losses, for answers, and for God.

The transliteration of Yiddish terms in this novel generally follows the pronunciation of eighteenth-century Lithuanian Yiddish, a regional Yiddish dialect. For example, in the word Torah, pronounced Toyre in Yiddish, the *oy* sound was often pronounced *ey* (as in Teyre) in this dialect. For this reason, one of the Yiddish appellations for God, *Riboyne shel oylem* (in Hebrew *Ribono shel 'olam*, Master of the Universe) could be heard in the form *Rebeyne shel eylem*. Names of the characters most often follow Yiddish pronunciation, such as "Rokhl" for the Anglicized "Rachel," but sometimes we have opted to use a more familiar spelling in English, such as "Dvora" instead of "Dveyre." The Jewish holidays *Shavuot* and *Simchat Torah* are given as *Shavues* and *Simkhes Torah*, to reflect the Yiddish pronunciation that the characters in this novel would have used.

Acknowledgments

Dmitri Kanovich

My father Grigory Kanovich often told me his wish to see his favorite novel, *The Tears and Prayers of Fools*, translated and published in the United States. It became my goal to help him realize this dream. Toward this end, I engaged the noted translator Mary Ann Szporluk, who produced an excellent English version of the novel, which to my mind captured the style and nuances of my father's text. But I was at a loss as to how to find the right publishing home for it.

At the suggestion of my brother Sergey, I consulted Barbara Kirshenblatt-Gimblett, university professor emerita of New York University and curator of the core exhibit of POLIN, the Jewish Museum in Warsaw. Barbara, in turn, referred me to Bonny V. Fetterman, a publishing consultant, editor, and agent specializing in Jewish books. Bonny immediately recognized the importance of making Grigory Kanovich's work available in English and readily committed to this project. She soon became my indispensable partner, mentor, and guide. Bonny is an outstanding professional in her field, and I deeply appreciate her exceptional skills and her devotion to this novel.

We found another champion for the book in Professor Ken Frieden, who edits the Judaic Traditions in Literature, Music, and Art series at Syracuse University Press. Ken began the process of the book's acquisition at Syracuse. I am grateful to Ken for his support and astute editing.

When I visited my parents at their home in Bat Yam, Israel, in the summer of 2022, I was able to tell my father that the English translation of his novel would be published in the United States within a year. My ninety-three-year-old father, who in recent years tended to be reticent, asked me to arrange a "thank you" call with Bonny in New York. Their short conversation in Russian and Yiddish and the happy smile on my father's face made the lengthy publishing process one of the most rewarding experiences of my life.

I am grateful to Mark Kanovich for the original drawings he created for this novel. I also want to thank Professor Mikhail Krutikov for his longtime support of my father's books. Last but not least, I want to acknowledge the steadfast moral support of my wife Olga, who is a great admirer of my father's literature, and my son David, who is just beginning to discover it. To everyone who helped this novel see the light of day in English, I extend my father's deepest gratitude and mine.

The Tears and Prayers of Fools

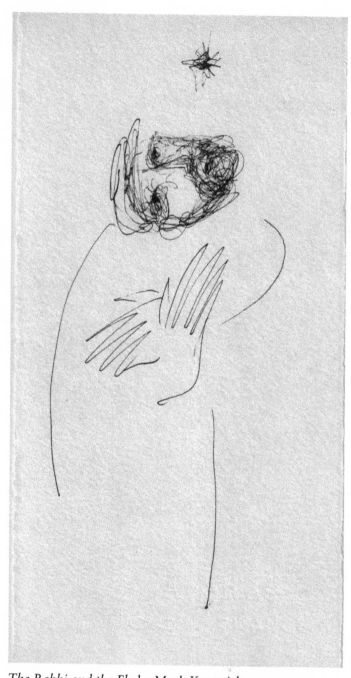

The Rabbi and the Fly by Mark Kanovich.

1

"My soul is sick," Rabbi Uri complained, and Itsik Magid, his favorite student, shuddered.

"Sick times—sick souls," Itsik countered gently, sympathetically. "The times need to be healed, Rabbi."

"We need to heal ourselves," Rabbi Uri replied quietly. He stood up from his chair and walked to the window, as if trying to make out both Itsik and himself in the clouded glass—and to see something else about the times that did not depend on his keen, old eyes. Master of the Universe, how many healers of the times had there been? How many of them had walked the earth and even passed by his window? And how would it all end? With fetters, the scaffold, madness. These sick times are incurable. We all must heal ourselves, and only then, perhaps, will the times be healed.

Rabbi Uri stood at the window and looked out at the empty street of the shtetl.

Everyone was asleep. In sleep the times seem different. There are no czars, no policemen, no madmen in sleep. No. Not until someone comes along and rouses them.

"Listen, Itsik! Can you tell me why everyone is asleep, but we're not sleeping?" Rabbi Uri asked, stroking his beard. Touching it always gave him some clarity. As if he had tossed a log onto a fire and the sparks lit up the darkness in his soul and in his home.

"Why aren't we sleeping?" he repeated, fixing his gaze on his student.

"I don't want to sleep, Rabbi," Itsik answered evasively, then remembered—it wasn't right to answer his teacher's questions with

1

such thoughtless haste. The answer should take longer to ripen than the question.

"Think it over, my son, think," Rabbi Uri muttered. "Think for a while." He stroked his beard again.

Rather than think, it would be better to lie down and fall asleep. They'd been sitting up so late into the night. The tea in the mugs had cooled, and Itsik could hardly keep his eyes open. Fortunately, because he had no wife, no one was waiting for him at home. But instead of tea, he'd find a cold bed . . . and no way to get warm.

Itsik Magid felt sorry for Rabbi Uri. If not for that pity, he would come to see him only on holidays. Rabbi Uri was approaching death—the year before last he'd already turned eighty; his soul would soon find rest and heal. The worms in the grave are the best medicine.

"Well, what did you come up with?" the teacher said, interrupting Itsik's thoughts. "Why aren't you and I sleeping?"

"I don't know," Itsik said, evading the question. He wasn't sleeping because he pitied the rabbi, and Rabbi Uri's age kept him awake. For an old person, night is a step toward death; for the young, a step toward morning.

"Someone has to stay awake, my son, when everyone else sleeps."

"Rakhmiel, the night watchman, is awake. Do you hear, Rabbi, how he's banging his clapper?"

"I don't hear it."

Itsik was surprised. Rakhmiel was walking right beneath the window. Could Rabbi Uri be deaf? He heard words but not the clapper.

"Someone who gets paid is not staying awake—he's working," the teacher said.

"What's the difference?"

"Someone who gets paid hears the jingle of money, not the cry of the soul," Rabbi Uri answered without raising his voice. "He watches over money, not pain."

"But why, Rabbi, why keep watch over pain?"

"So that it doesn't give birth."

The old man's crazy, Itsik Magid thought, and then became ashamed of his thoughts.

Whatever you might say, Rabbi Uri was not a stranger to him. And he'd done so much for him, an orphan. One could say that he had set this homeless young man on his feet. If it weren't for Rabbi Uri, he, Itsik Magid, would have become a thief, a tramp, a drifter. The old man had saved him from conscription into the czar's army by paying off the local police official, or else he would have been dragged away . . .

"Give birth to . . . ?" Itsik asked, not so much out of curiosity as out of respect. "What do you think pain gives birth to?"

Itsik Magid was not going to rack his brains over whatever it was that pain brings into the world. Now Rabbi Uri would regale him with some biblical saying, refer to the infallible Moses or the wise King Solomon, or tell one of his own bedtime parables while stroking his beard. All answers seemed to reside there.

"Pain, you should know, gives birth to death . . . madness . . . hatred," was all the teacher answered. Then, glancing at Itsik, he added, "A tired brain is like a milepost—wood that doesn't bear fruit. I see you are tired, my son. Go home."

"And you?"

"I am home," Rabbi Uri chuckled.

"It's time for you to go to bed, too."

"I'm going, I'm going," the old man assured him. "That's a simple thing to do. Unlike getting up. Go, my son, go."

But for some reason Itsik lingered. He watched Rabbi Uri while waiting for a few more words. He didn't know what the words would be, but not this bland "Go, my son, go." Those words were as nondescript as everything else in the teacher's home—the rickety walls, the kerosene lamp with its hideous shade. Behind those words, as within an eggshell, lay something else, something that tormented Itsik. He felt that their true meaning would only hatch later and would keep him from sleeping before morning came. Such things had happened to him before: he'd go home, undress, flop down on the bed, and suddenly Rabbi Uri's words would gather around him like little puppies, barking and biting. And sometimes, in the dark, the teacher's words turned crimson like the berries of the guelder rose, became unbearable, and stuck in his throat until he felt ill. At such moments it seemed to Itsik that his beloved teacher not only was immersed in the Torah, but also consorted with evil spirits. Yet Rabbi Uri swore that among Jews everything existed except goblins and vampires.

"They aren't circumcised," he had assured Itsik, as if Rabbi Uri had bathed next to spirits in the same bathhouse.

"Are there witches, sorceresses?" Itsik asked sarcastically.

"There are. My wife, may she rest in peace, was a full-blooded witch. I would wake up and reach for the saw. I'd saw off her horns at night, but by morning they had grown back. If you don't believe me, then come with me, and I'll show you the sawdust. I'd advise you—if you think of marrying, don't just look at her hair or body, look for small horns, too. At first, they're inconspicuous—small as a nail. But then . . . you'll see for yourself."

Rakhmiel, the town watchman, was aggressively banging his clapper beneath the window, fearing his own drowsiness more than thieves.

Itsik listened attentively to the clapper's even beat, then suddenly said, "Rabbi! Some strange fellow has shown up in town. He says he's a messenger from God."

"We're all God's messengers," Rabbi Uri responded indifferently. "You and I as well."

What possessed me to say that? Itsik wondered. People chatter about all sorts of things in the tavern. Just imagine—a messenger from God! What a lot of madmen this town has seen! Two years ago, before Passover, people were amused by some Napoleon the Fourth with a strange three-cornered hat on his head and a red sash. He swung his arms like a soldier, clicked his worn boots together, and swore that—if they fed him—he would abolish the Pale of Settlement, allowing Jews to live in all the world capitals for the first time. And then—if they fed him well—he would grant them complete freedom and would even lead the first Jewish state himself. The good people fed Napoleon the Fourth and gave him drinks, but he didn't abolish the Pale of Settlement. And some time before that, a Bird-Man had wandered into town! He didn't promise to end the Pale of Settlement, nor did he aspire to become the leader of the first Jewish state. In front of everyone he threatened to fly away.

"Let him fly," the tavern keeper Yeshua Mandel had said.

Bird-Man would not agree to simply fly away. He demanded that the Jews draw up a petition to God and sign it. He would deliver it, he said. When no one wanted to draw up such a petition, the madman cursed the tavern keeper Yeshua—along with everyone else in town—and then set out for Vilna.

And now—a messenger from God! Pimpleface Simeon, the son of the tavern keeper, told Itsik that the messenger hadn't asked for anything—no petitions, no signatures, no bread. Pimpleface Simeon approached him in his father's tavern and asked, "What can I do for you?" God's messenger supposedly answered, "I'd like you to stop stealing money from your father's purse!" Pimpleface Simeon threw him out of the tavern, but then, as if nothing had happened, the fellow stood beneath a window and loudly proclaimed to the entire town: "Thief! Thief! Thief! God will punish you! You'll shake from fever."

And what do you know? The next morning, Pimpleface Simeon took to his bed. His father Yeshua sent for a German doctor with whiskers and a pince-nez. The doctor examined the patient and muttered something in German—either fever or typhoid.

"Where is the messenger staying?" Rabbi Uri was curious. Now a series of questions would follow, and Itsik wouldn't be able to leave until his beloved teacher was satisfied.

"Nowhere."

"If you see him, my son, bring him to me," Rabbi Uri said, becoming strangely animated.

"To you?" Itsik was stunned and for a long time stood facing his teacher, like a maple tree when the wind blows through its leaves with a rushing sound. "Why, haven't you seen madmen before?"

"What makes you think, my son, that he's a madman? If Heaven has sent him, he can't be crazy. Don't speak irreverently of him, Itsik."

"But what if . . . if he's not pleased with you, Rabbi . . . if he punishes you with a fever?"

"What is a fever in comparison to a sick soul?" Rabbi Uri asked, but this time he was not asking his student Itsik Magid. He seemed to be addressing the kerosene lamp with the hideous shade or the hazy window glass on which the silhouette of the night watchman Rakhmiel flashed every so often. "I'm too old to look for him myself."

"But what if he won't come?" Itsik asked, with renewed energy.

"If he doesn't come, it means he doesn't care."

Itsik Magid didn't understand what his favorite teacher was talking about, yet by his voice, by the way he was staring at the kerosene lamp's smoldering wick, he guessed that Rabbi Uri was alluding to his own sick soul. No wanderer would heal it, especially not a madman. Rabbi Uri was old, and his soul was old and weak. That couldn't be helped—the twilight of life is very bitter. It's a time to resign oneself, time to gather one's thoughts, not to scatter them.

"Go, my son, go," the old man said. "And tell Rakhmiel to come see me. We'll drink some tea together."

"All right," Itsik answered. He bowed to Rabbi Uri and went out into the night.

The old man saw him to the door but didn't close it—Rakhmiel would come soon.

Rabbi Uri sat down at the table and clasped the soot-covered lamp. Heat poured out and spread through his joints, which had withered like tobacco stems. The warmth squeezed through his dry veins, moving up toward his stooped shoulders, up to his neck, which resembled a Torah scroll worn out from reading, and from there back to his heart, to his sick soul. And as a butterfly unfolds its wings, his soul spread out and soared toward the windowsill. High, so high.

Rakhmiel entered without knocking, wrapped in a woman's shawl, or something resembling a shawl, with the strong smell of someone else's hair.

"You called for me, Rabbi?"

"Yes."

"But I'm stopping in for only a minute."

"What is the meaning of a life, Rakhmiel? What is eighty-two years, exactly?"

"In my opinion, eighty-two years . . . is eighty-two years."

"No, Rakhmiel. It's only one long minute."

"Maybe," muttered Rakhmiel, who didn't understand why he'd been invited to the rabbi's house.

"You and I shall have a cup of tea now."

"I never refuse tea."

Rabbi Uri poured the warm tea into tin mugs.

"And what *do* you refuse, Rakhmiel?"

"I don't remember," the watchman said, sipping his tea.

"But I remember . . ."

"Your memory is good," Rakhmiel interrupted, complimenting Rabbi Uri.

The two sipped their tea and frowned at one another.

"They say a wanderer of some sort has shown up in town," Rabbi Uri said, "declaring himself to be a messenger from God. Have you heard about him, Rakhmiel?"

"I haven't heard. I'm waiting for Aaron, not for a messenger from God."

"How long has he been serving in the army?"

"A very long time."

"He should return soon."

"If he returns."

"And why wouldn't he return?"

"Anything can happen in so many years," the watchman sighed. "Shmuel Pyatnitsky's son returned, but I'm telling you, Rabbi, you can't imagine a greater misfortune."

"Why?"

"Because, because," Rakhmiel seemed almost offended. "He returned as Nikolai."

"What sort of Nikolai?"

What's wrong with you today, Rabbi Uri? the guest wondered. "A Russian Nikolai, Nikolai Pyatnitsky. He was baptized there in Siberia, that's what."

"Why did he come home?"

"To divide up the house. Shmuel Pyatnitsky has a two-story home in Mishkine. God forbid that my son returns as a Nikolai. My one consolation is—that I have no house. This is all my wealth," Rakhmiel pointed to the clapper with his chubby hand.

"Can I see?" Rabbi Uri stretched out his arm for the clapper.

"A clapper's a clapper," the watchman said.

Rabbi Uri took the clapper and suddenly began to bang it as hard as he could.

"What are you doing?" Rakhmiel exclaimed.

"Banging," the rabbi answered, as was plain to see. "I'm summoning death."

"Whose?"

"Is death really someone's? Death is everyone's and no one's. Do you understand, Rakhmiel?"

"I understand, I understand," the watchman mumbled. "Thank you for the tea, Rabbi Uri. It's time for me to go . . . out there, to the street."

"Nothing is happening outside," Rabbi Uri stopped him. "Stay for a while. No one robs anyone at night in our little town. Only during the day. But in daytime you're free, Rakhmiel!"

"I'm free."

"During the day you sleep."

"It depends. Sometimes I sew."

"You sew?"

"I sew. Spare money doesn't hurt. I'm putting everything aside for Aaron, Rabbi Uri . . . He'll return without a kopeck to his name."

"How old was your Aaron, when . . . ?" Rabbi Uri stumbled over the words.

"Fifteen, maybe . . . maybe sixteen . . ."

"Fifteen, sixteen . . ." Rabbi Uri suddenly started to mutter. He should have asked Itsik how old that fellow . . . God's messenger . . . was. Maybe thirty-five, forty. Thirty-five, forty . . . is the age when most of them lose their minds. The age of madmen. The age of healers, people who are trying—what vanity!—to heal the times. But what if this messenger from God is Rakhmiel's son Aaron? What if? Rabbi Uri would not recognize him. So many years had passed . . . Something formed in Rabbi Uri's head, fell to pieces, formed again, and then crumbled into dust. Words, dates, names. He fixed his eyes on Rakhmiel, who was watching the door and, looking lost, waiting impatiently for Rabbi Uri to return the clapper to him.

All at once Rakhmiel realized with acute clarity that without the clapper he was nobody—a pitiful old man in a woman's shawl, a poor and hapless being.

"Rabbi, give me back my clapper," he begged. "Give it back!"

"Here, take it," the old man said, confused. "Nothing has happened to it."

Rakhmiel grabbed the clapper and, trusting neither himself nor Rabbi Uri, began to bang.

"It's banging, it's banging," he kept repeating while moving backward toward the door. "Thank God."

After he left, Rabbi Uri walked to the window and shut the moth-eaten curtain. My God, how many years since it had been washed! But what's the point? Rabbi Uri no longer wanted to see anyone. Not his favorite student, not God's messenger, not the watchman—no one. His eyes, rich storerooms, were filled to the brim. He had seen plague and famine, had lived through three wars. He had met scores of good people and riffraff. All of them passed before his eyes now in clothes and footwear marred with dirt, blood, and vomit. Enough! From this day on he would close his storerooms. Forever. One can look and not see. Listen and not hear. One can easily go to the pantry, take out a vial intended for mice . . . and pour out eighty-two drops. One drop for every year lived and—hello, doctors, and hello, worms in the grave. But it's not right for a man to die like a mouse. A man must go out like a man.

"But when?" he asked the lamp. "When?"

The weak flame in the lamp quivered.

"When will we be snuffed out?"

Outside the window Rakhmiel was walking from one end of the street to the other, banging his clapper, most likely thinking about Aaron.

As for him, Rabbi Uri, who should he think about at night?

2

For Itsik Magid, night begins with the first star that pecks like a chick through the velvet shell of the firmament. One star pokes through, and soon after, what do you know, the whole hatch has poked through, scattering across the sky, as in a poultry yard, but each body glows. Rabbi Uri says we all have a personal star. Perhaps he, Itsik Magid, has some faint dwarf star, an ugly duckling, and it's shining out there somewhere, but what does it matter? No two stars are identical, no fates are the same. There are rich people's stars, poor people's stars, stars for the hale and hearty, and stars for the crippled. Heaven keep us from being born under a cripple's star, like the one that shone on his mother the day she was born.

Itsik Magid barely remembers his parents. His father came from somewhere near Zhitomir. After a pogrom, he killed a local policeman—my God, how many police there are in Russia! Then he fled, hid, made his way to Lithuania, became a logger, and until his death, he cut down trees instead of policemen. His father's name was Gabriel, or at least that's what he called himself. His mother worked for the timber merchant Markus Fradkin, first as a nanny, and later as a wet nurse. Every year she gave birth to a stillborn until she had him, Itsik, and five years later she died together with a baby boy, the last of the siblings he would never have. They were buried in one grave. Itsik Magid remembers standing with his father over the open pit, looking down and seeing a large May bug crawling along the grave's vertical wall. He felt very sorry for the bug, which was alive, opening and closing its wings again and again, the poor thing.

A year after his mother died, his father was found dead in the forest. No one knew how he died. One of his hands was gripping a hatchet so tightly that the dead man had to be buried with it.

"If he makes it to Heaven," the water carrier Ezer Bloom muttered, "he'll take down all the trees there."

When he was six, he, Itsik Magid, was left without mother or father. How many homes had he moved to and from, how many people had he lived with! Even with the water carrier. Bloom took in the orphan, and all day long, together, they fetched water from the river and delivered it throughout the small town. Not everyone had a well—the tavern keeper Yeshua had one; and also Shlomo Goldin, the government rabbi; the tailor Dov-Ber; and, of course, the town policeman. To the others Bloom gave water cheaply and reliably. Itsik would have become a water carrier, but one fine day Ezer sold his gray horse and barrel and headed off on foot for Jerusalem, the Promised Land. When a whim gets into a Jew's head, what remains on his shoulders is a tangled knot of nonsense. Everyone in the small town (those without a well most passionately) tried to persuade Ezer to give up his crazy idea—it was hopeless! Bloom walked out of his home at daybreak with a knapsack on his back and didn't even look back. What was there for him to look back on? The ramshackle house, the horse? Bloom beckoned to the orphan, but Rabbi Uri stepped in.

"Ezer," he said, "if God so wills, and you don't die on the road, you will be the first water carrier to drink from the river of our forefathers. But leave the boy alone. His legs are still a bit weak. Let them get stronger."

"Legs get stronger on the road, Rabbi," Ezer Bloom replied. He walked out of the house and went on his way. And after that he vanished into thin air.

The rabbi's family took care of Itsik. To tell the truth, there was no family there—just the rabbi's stout wife, Rokhl, with her double chin and dark mustache, and a cat. When Rokhl became angry, the hairs on her upper lip bristled and Itsik wanted to pluck them.

Itsik remembered the past only when he was sick. A healthy person has no time to fuss with memories. That's why Itsik thought of memories themselves as something like an illness, an unmanly ailment. Had he fallen ill? He was lying down, not sleeping, remembering someone's words, Rokhl's mustache, the crop of Ezer's horse, and the May bug on the wall of the hollowed-out grave.

What's wrong with me? he asked himself, and not finding an answer, he got out of bed and opened the window. Stillness. Not a living soul. The town seemed dead. Even Rakhmiel's clapper had stopped banging. It seemed the watchman had sat down on the steps of the Spivak brothers' hardware shop and fallen asleep.

"Rakhmiel!" Itsik shouted out the open window.

His cry fell into the silence like a leaf onto water; it didn't even make a ripple.

"Rakhmiel!" he repeated with helpless indignation, but again not a sound.

All of a sudden, he sensed that someone's shadow was rushing about near the Spivak brothers' shop.

Itsik strained his eyes and peered into the thick, tar-like darkness.

It's him, Itsik thought for some reason, and his heart started throbbing. *God's messenger!*

Itsik gulped anxiously two or three times, as if trying to push down the heart stuck in his throat. It's strange, why do I think about him all the time? Why?

He fumbled for matches in the dark and lit the wick of an oil lamp. Night moths flew in from the street, attracted by the flame. A whole mass of them. They whirled around the lamp, and Itsik didn't chase them away. He was even glad to see them. Rabbi Uri was right: we are all God's messengers—he and I, and Rakhmiel, and these moths, which reminded him, Itsik, of his own equally blind and random thoughts. His thoughts also needed someone else's fire. Then they would revive, shed the scab of laziness, and soar high into the air. In place of despair, passion would arise, a thirst for flight and an escape from self. But is Rabbi Uri such a fire? Is Pimpleface Simeon such a fire?

There *is* a fire in the shtetl—Zelda, the timber merchant Markus Fradkin's daughter, but *that* fire doesn't burn for Itsik. What shines on him are the pathetic dwarf star and this smelly lamp!

Itsik looked out the window again, but no one was near the Spivaks' shop.

But what if . . . ? What if the one who sent Pimpleface Simeon to his sick bed was a *real* messenger? Having turned up in town for the first time, how did he know about the tainted passion of the tavern keeper's son? Everyone knows that Simeon takes money from his father, but that knowledge never sent him to his bed. This pretender managed to do it in one day, which means that he has some kind of power. He's no ordinary madman. A fire blazes in him. Madness *is* fire. Most of the time it burns the madman himself, but there are exceptions, of course.

Or maybe Pimpleface Simeon's illness is just a coincidence?

There are all sorts of people in our town who could be, and even need to be, punished. Some sin can be found in everyone. Even in Rabbi Uri. Heaven knows the rabbi is a holy man, but even he has clearly not lived a sinless life. A long life can't be free of sin.

Wait until they meet, Itsik decided, and he felt a strange sense of relief. Then he immediately grew sullen again. What if Rabbi Uri is next, after Pimpleface Simeon; if during his long life he had concealed some sin or offense, what kind of punishment would there be? What more could he be punished with, he from whom the Almighty had taken everything except his mind? He tormented his eyes with blindness, He dried up his limbs, He filled his ears with mortuary clay. With death, perhaps. But death would be mercy for Rabbi Uri, not a punishment. And was God the one who took all this away from him? God, and not the sick times? Which of these is more merciless?

Itsik was horrified. How dare he think this way about God, the Master of the Universe! And what's more, by an open window at such a late hour, when only the heavens are listening!

He quickly slammed the window shut and snuffed out the lamp.

To sleep, sleep, sleep, to think about nothing, nothing at all. Tomorrow night is *Shabbes*, the only time he gets a good night's rest. In the morning he'd go to the synagogue, pray, and beg forgiveness for his nighttime thoughts. Maybe he will see *him*—the messenger—at the synagogue. But how will he recognize him if he's never seen him? Before he fell ill, Simeon had described him as short, with a small Jewish beard and little button eyes, and wearing a velvet yarmulke that was fastened to his thinning hair with either a clip or a pin, so that the wind wouldn't blow it off.

A small Jewish beard and eyes like buttons, even if they're like those on a czarist uniform, are not a distinctive mark, but a clip or pin—that's something!

Alone in the corner room he rented from Golda, Osher's widow, Itsik lay down on his bed. He spread his heavy arms and listened to the mice scratching in the cellar, which always made him anxious. Golda poisoned them with all sorts of concoctions and powders from Vilna, but the mice were stronger than any poison.

"Why aren't you sleeping?" rang out from the other side of the wall.

"I *am* sleeping," Itsik answered and huddled up.

"Come over here and bother me," Golda demanded from the other side.

If only she doesn't come in here, if only she leaves me in peace, Itsik thought, and he pulled the blanket over his head. If she presses, I won't let her in. What an insatiable woman! She only has fun on her mind. Such fun was the death of her husband. Not to mention that Golda had beaten him at night! She would beat him while saying, "If I were a man, a muzhik, I'd teach you, Osher!"

When Osher was alive, Itsik had heard just about everything. They started to abuse one another, and he'd have to run out of the house. But where to go? To the forest, perhaps. In summer you can go to the forest. The air is pure, the birds are singing. You can sink down in moss and fall asleep. In the morning, get up—and go off to work. He would take his axe and start cutting. Itsik was the only Jew there felling timber; there were also Lithuanians and two Russian Orthodox brothers, Afinogen and Guri Andronov, who teased him: why, they said, do you sleep in the forest at night? You could climb into some sweet widow's bed. It's warmer there—good for your stomach and she'll feed you for a caress. But look out, Itsik, here in the forest a wolf might bite off your pecker by mistake. Who will want you without a pecker?

The damn pecker, Itsik swore to himself and pulled the blanket over his head again.

Golda came in and sat on the edge of the bed. Her body, barely covered by a torn nightgown, smelled of a warm bed and shamelessness. She threw off the blanket, caressed Itsik's tousled hair, and said quietly,

"You need a haircut. Do you want me to trim it?"

Itsik didn't answer, and Golda kept on caressing his head and neck. Finally her irrepressible, frantic hand fell onto his hairy chest, which was as coarse as bark, felt a nipple, and stopped.

"I'll bring the scissors right now," she whispered. "Snip-snip and it's done."

"Stop," he said, but didn't push away her hand.

"Why?" Golda asked in surprise, bending down, her head hanging above him like an enormous ripe fruit ready to fall at the first puff of wind.

"It's not permitted," Itsik let out.

"Where is that written?"

"In the Torah."

"I haven't read the Torah," Golda said, and the fruit began to sway—in a minute it would fall.

"Move over!"

Itsik didn't move.

"Move," Golda repeated. "I'm cold. I'm always cold when you're beside me but not *with* me." Her voice was quiet and cautious, like that of a nightbird that has lost its nest.

Golda slid under the blanket and their legs became entangled like branches of a tree.

They did not hear the mice scratching, or Rakhmiel, awake now, banging on his clapper, or the squeaks of the partly open door. The world had lost its sounds, and nothing existed but semen and darkness.

"Golda, aren't you afraid?" he asked when he came back to himself.

"What should I be afraid of?" she sighed.

"You know."

"And you . . . are you afraid?"

"Yes," he said.

"For nothing."

"You were never an orphan," he said, freeing himself from her embrace.

"I am an orphan," Golda replied.

"That's not true," he objected. "You have a sister . . . and a brother in Gomel . . . and a mother."

"Older women are always orphans," Golda sighed and licked his nipple.

"Stop," he said angrily. "You have no shame."

"If there's no happiness, why should I care about shame?"

"God will punish us," Itsik said quietly. "You've probably heard that a strange man showed up in town. They say he's a messenger from God."

"You're my messenger," Golda whispered fervently, clinging to him again. "I don't give a damn about others. You are my god."

"Go back to your room, Golda. I want to be alone for a while. Leave."

"All right, all right," she agreed. "But don't be afraid. No one will come for us. I don't want to share you with anyone. Even children. I don't want that as long as you are mine."

Golda stood up, straightened her nightgown, and claimed, "Everyone is dying to have me. I have that kind of body. Sleep!"

She turned around in the doorway to ask, "What does he look like?"

"Who?" Itsik was puzzled.

"You know . . . that man . . ."

"Smallish . . . with a velvet yarmulke that's fastened to his hair with a pin . . . or clip."

"Probably some madman . . . in a velvet yarmulke with a clip. He should be fed and sent away in peace. I don't like crazy people, though I'm crazy myself. When I was a child—we lived in Gomel then—a man like him, but without a yarmulke, walked up to me, looked in my eyes, and said, 'Whore!' I was ten. He chased after me . . . almost as far as the Sozh River, howling 'Whore! Whore! Whore!' Afterward, the only one to call me that was Osher, may he rest in peace!"

"Why did you suddenly remember that?"

"I don't know. Sleep!"

Golda slipped away on tiptoe, as if her husband Osher were sleeping below and might wake up and catch her cheating on him. She always left that way, on tiptoe, which astonished Itsik. So many years had passed since Osher died, and she needed to move like a thief in her own home.

Sleep finally took pity and shut his eyelids. Itsik dreamed that he was standing up to his waist in water, and the water carrier Ezer Bloom was crying out to him from the shore of their forefathers' river Jordan: "You good-for-nothing, why did you drop the bucket! To sink a bucket like that!" Itsik dove to the bottom and searched feverishly, but he found nothing. As he rose back to the surface of the Jordan, he woke up. The sun had just gilded the firmament, and it poured over him with a glaze like the one on holiday bread that made you want to just take it and give everyone a slice.

3

On Shabbes morning, Itsik got up, dressed, and headed off to the synagogue without eating breakfast. How could you pray there on a full stomach? God listens to the well-fed, but he doesn't hear them.

The policeman Nesterovich, stripped to the waist, was washing himself at his own well. Nesterovich was a tall man who tried to be like the czar in all ways—with the same bearing and splendid, dashingly twisted mustache, and even the same hair style. The town barber, Bershtansky, cut his hair, as he put it "in imitation of the emperor," by first looking in the mirror and then at a portrait of the czar which hung for this purpose on the barbershop's dirty wall.

"I am most grateful," the local policeman Nesterovich said.

And Bershtansky answered humbly, "I am happy to try my best, Your Majesty."

"What sort of majesty am I to you, you fool?"

The words "fool," "Your Majesty," and "Your Honor" had become confused in poor Bershtansky's head. He cut Nesterovich's hair with great enthusiasm; if he had a razor in his hand, he held it in front of the policeman's face as if offering a bribe; and he never took any money from him.

Nesterovich was not an unkind man—unlike his predecessor, who thought that for all His good work the Lord God had made a blunder when He created Jews. That was the cause of all earthly suffering, the former official believed.

"Russia's greatest misfortune," he once said to the timber merchant Fradkin, "is you."

"Me?" Fradkin's eyes nearly popped out of his head.

19

"Not *you*, Mr. Fradkin, but your tribe," the former policeman quickly explained. His zeal was noticed, and he was transferred either to Grodno or Molodechno.

As Itsik strode along the sun-washed street, thoughts about Golda and the police official kept running through his mind, but then turned from them to pounce, like sparrows on breadcrumbs, on the stranger in the yarmulke.

For some reason Itsik didn't want the stranger to disappear now. If he had really been sent by God, perhaps Itsik would get an answer from him to the question that had troubled him for many years: who killed his father? Robust men like Gabriel Magid don't just die easily.

One thing Itsik had no doubt about—the stranger would come to the synagogue for certain. God's messenger could not miss morning prayer.

The person Itsik expected was *not* at the synagogue, however. Downstairs, old friends were clustered in the men's section: the barber Bershtansky; the tailor Dov-Ber; Pinkhes, the oldest son of the miller Braverman, who had not married, was sickly, and had a harelip; and the shopkeepers Naftali and Chaim Spivak. Even Rabbi Uri appeared—sitting in a wheelchair, he rolled in. But the fellow in the velvet yarmulke . . . was not there.

As if he were a stranger, Itsik was looking around in all directions, and the synagogue warden, Naftali Spivak, said sarcastically, "If you're looking for the door, my good man, it's straight ahead and to the left."

Zelda Fradkin was also there.

Itsik was ashamed to look her in the eyes. He felt that Zelda knew all his secrets—daytime and nighttime—and although she did not blame him, she felt sorry for him. Sometimes Itsik even racked his brains over what was best about Fradkin's daughter—her beauty or her compassion? Her beauty itself was somehow sad. She had a long, pale, almost translucent face; a tiny nose that seemed uncomfortable under the scrutiny of her pensive, dark eyes; curved brows like the trace of a silkworm on a leaf; and long dark-auburn hair which flowed lightly and freely even from beneath a scarf. It's sinful to admit that Itsik attended the synagogue mainly because of her. Of course, he had other interests—to find out what was happening in the world at large, there was no better place than at prayers. He would relish some local gossip with Pimpleface Simeon, or simply express his devotion to God so that no one would think that he, Itsik, lived like a total savage in the forest. But what drew him here was neither gossip nor the news from around the world. One day the talk was about Chaim, and the next it was about you. He also didn't care about the virtuous nods and glances of the devout, who valued diligence more than the Most High himself. No, it was Zelda. She attracted him like a magnet, and he lacked the strength to resist that disturbing, sweet pull. The widow Golda, his landlady and mistress, always found a seat near Zelda. She would prop up her chin with her sinful hands, and whenever Itsik raised his eyes to the balcony, to the women's section of the synagogue, Golda received a share of his tenderness and adoration.

Today Zelda looked especially lovely. She was all aglow, fluttering like a Shabbes candle, and her radiance and fluttering made Itsik's head spin.

My God, he thought, what joy it is to see her, to breathe the same air, to pray to the same God.

Once, after evening prayer, Pimpleface Simeon had taken him aside and said, "Give me three gold coins and I'll fix you up with her."

"With whom?"

"Don't play the fool. Zelda is worth three chervontsi."

Itsik pulled his arm away.

"Maybe in installments," Simeon proposed.

"Get lost!" Itsik blurted out angrily.

Pimpleface Simeon seemed not to hear. "You don't want to, you don't have to," he said. "Of course, Golda costs less. In fact, it seems she's paying you." He burst out laughing, showing his crooked, stained teeth, which looked a bit like cloves of garlic.

Itsik wanted to grab him by the collar and shake him up. But he controlled himself and only spat, and then wiped the spittle away with his boot—to defile the threshold of God's house would be wrong.

Nevertheless, Pimpleface Simeon's words stuck in his mind. Three chervontsi—almost half a year's work, and not just any kind of work, not with a needle or a razor, but with an axe and a saw, in rain and in snow. But for Zelda he wouldn't be sorry to give half a year, a year, or ten years. If you thought about it, Itsik was already working for her. She was a Fradkin! Zelda Fradkin! The daughter of the timber merchant Markus Fradkin.

Could Itsik have been drawn to her because she was suckled on his mother's milk?

The tavern keeper Yeshua and his wife Chava have just walked in. Usually they arrive ahead of others. When coming to God, or to Officer Nesterovich, it's better to be on time—why anger them? Apparently they are late because of Simeon.

The service is beginning. The young Rabbi Hillel, a righteous man and orator, has stepped up onto the platform, opened the ark, and revealed the scrolls—the windows to Heaven.

But *he* is not here. Itsik turned and looked at the door again. No.

Rabbi Uri rolled up to the platform, and in the descending stillness the wheels on his chair whooshed like an angel's wings.

The old, wooden synagogue had burned down. In 1863, soldiers had set it on fire when they were looking for Antanas Mackevičius, a rebel and state criminal. No one in town knew what his crime involved. From time immemorial the town had never seen a single rebel or criminal, if you didn't count Osher, the husband of the widow Golda, who had tried to hang himself in broad daylight from the town watchtower. Someone had informed Governor Muravyov that Mackevičius was hiding in the *zhid*'s church. Their synagogue went up in smoke, but the rebel was not found. For a long time after, there was no synagogue in town—people prayed in a hastily cleaned-up barn taken on lease. After everything had calmed down, in a burst of generosity, Markus Fradkin donated timber for the construction of a new synagogue. There was more than enough wood for a synagogue, a house for a rabbi, and even for an outhouse. When nature called during services, the devout worshippers no longer had to run a mile! From that time on, God's house bore the name of its benefactor—it was the Markus Fradkin synagogue. If it burned down, his name would also burn, but no matter how precious the honor was to Fradkin, the piece of land was more valuable.

"Master of the Universe!" The young Rabbi Hillel basked in his own voice, and old Rabbi Uri placed his withered hands on the edge of the chair, closed his eyes, and listened to the prayer with his drooping ears—he knew it by heart, like all the prayers that the Jews had ever addressed to God. Rabbi Uri listened and heard something that only he heard in the prayer—the steps of death. Of late, he heard them as clearly and distinctly as he had heard the steps of his beloved when he was young and his ears were like a canyon. Every sound echoed a hundredfold. Death followed him around the town the same way his wife Rokhl once had done, and her steps were exactly the same—irregular and with a skip. Sometimes she would drop in on someone and leave him standing in the middle of the road, but then she came back quickly and they were together again.

At this very moment she is standing behind his back, praying. Until this day Rabbi Uri had not meditated on the question: for whom does death pray? For the living? For the dead? It did not seem proper for death to pray for the living; as for the dead—the living pray for the dead. Death prays for itself, Rabbi Uri decided. Stupid, how stupid. He had never prayed for himself. Always for others. And today he's praying for her, not for himself.

Rabbi Uri opened his eyes a little, but he lacked the strength to turn around, and he closed them again, pressing shut his eyelids like a snuffbox.

Why had he come here, he asked himself. He could have prayed at home. Did he also believe in the vagabond Messiah? He—Rabbi Uri—was the wisest of the wise, the most learned of the learned. He knew better than anyone that although God is great, He does not perform miracles. In any case, not the God of the Jews. He did perform one miracle: He created them; and then He forgot about them. He abandoned them to the mercy of fate, delivered them into the hands of czars and police officials. During the entire existence of the Jews, from our forefathers Abraham and Jacob to the night watchman Rakhmiel, the Almighty did not once show them mercy. Pogroms—is that mercy? Is the Pale of Settlement mercy? It can hardly be claimed that He, the God of the Jews, ignored all of them. He must have chosen someone, though we don't know who or why, and endowed him with His blessings. But if one person is happy (and *is* he happy?), does that mean that all the Jews should rejoice?

Rabbi Uri breathed heavily. It was stifling in the synagogue. No small matter—so many mouths voicing their complaints and expressing their hopes. Death is praying behind his back, and nearby his student Itsik Magid is moving his lips. What had he taught Itsik? To fell trees. Rabbi Uri did not have a logger's hatchet in mind, but rather Itsik's thoughts. They were sharper than a hatchet, and every minute they were cutting down some person. Rabbi Uri knew who Itsik was cutting down to size: the timber merchant Markus Fradkin. But why? Because of Itsik's mother, who had nursed Fradkin's daughter, or for his brother, who did not live long enough to touch his mother's nipples? Or was it because he would never be Zelda's husband?

The world is a repository of evil and vice, Rabbi Uri reflected during the murmur of prayer, and if God has not uprooted them, what can some pretender do?

Nonetheless, curiosity and jealousy consumed Rabbi Uri. Apparently, you can be jealous of God. Just as you can be jealous of a woman.

Rabbi Uri had no doubt that the man Itsik had told him about yesterday was a charlatan and rogue. You didn't have to be a clairvoyant to imagine the vices of the tavern keeper's offspring. All sorts of vices were visible on Simeon's face, like freckles. Just take a look—if you put him in chains and took him to jail, you wouldn't be wrong.

Rabbi Uri was already sorry he had asked Itsik to acquaint him with the newcomer. What might he hear from the stranger? What admonitions? What verdict?

As if he had guessed his teacher's thoughts, Itsik leaned toward him and whispered, "It's strange. He's not in the synagogue."

"For a messenger from God the whole world is a House of Prayer," Rabbi Uri mumbled. His own response astonished him. No sooner had he cursed the stranger, calling him a rogue and charlatan, then suddenly such lofty, such compelling words came out, and the Almighty had not locked his lips as He had always done in the past whenever Rabbi Uri tried His patience with stupidities or sacrilege.

Just now he could have spared Itsik from unnecessary trouble—he could have said in no uncertain terms that Itsik should not bring anyone, but for some reason he didn't do it. Therefore, let him come—all kinds of madmen had passed through his home, and a madman might be a delight in one's old age, for, if you think it over properly, what is old age? Is it not actually a peaceful madness without resistance or glimmers of hope? Solitude and insanity are always related. Let him come. Rabbi Uri's door was open to all.

"I think I saw him last night," Itsik whispered again.

Why is Itsik so obsessed by the stranger? Rabbi Uri wondered. Even a messenger from God won't help him. A woman, not God, makes the bed. Golda or Zelda—to each his own, and there's nothing to be done about it.

"Rabbi Uri, do you know who I thought about at night?" Itsik said suddenly.

"Do you really think at night?" Rabbi Uri muttered.

"Sometimes . . . sometimes I think."

"What did you think last night, my son?" the rabbi asked condescendingly.

The tavern keeper Yeshua looked askance at him: of all people Rabbi Uri should know how to behave during prayer. Those two were crowing back and forth like roosters. If you want to chatter, you're welcome to come to the tavern. Rabbi Uri was not overly fond of the tavern keeper, who reeked of his customers' alcohol, the smell of which emanated from his prayer shawl and yarmulke.

"Maybe he's a fugitive soldier?"

Rabbi Uri did not answer.

"Maybe he's a fugitive soldier," Itsik repeated.

"Fugitive soldiers don't hang around taverns," Rabbi Uri grumbled angrily. "Be quiet. You're disturbing Reb Yeshua's conversation with God."

"The two of them have already made an agreement. Starting tomorrow, vodka is going up by two kopecks," Itsik snapped.

"Freemason," swore Yeshua, who sometimes used bizarre curses.

The Jews ended their prayers and slowly went their separate ways. Itsik followed Zelda with the eye of a hunting dog, and to his great surprise she glanced back and confused him with either a mocking grimace or a smile. Seeing it as a smile, for a moment he felt he'd lost his footing—the earth tossed him high into the air and he dangled from a cloud as if from a tall palisade.

Suddenly Itsik remembered himself and grabbed on to Rabbi Uri's wheelchair, which rattled off down the unpaved street. Rabbi Uri squinted in the sunlight, muttering something under his breath, and the muttering was like a wheeze and an incantation at the same time.

Itsik looked back and, from afar, he saw near the synagogue the figure of a man with a yarmulke who was dressed in a *balakhon*, like wagon drivers and raftsmen wore, and he cried out, "It's him, him!"

He quickly turned around in the wheelchair carriage, but Rabbi Uri stopped him.

"There's no point in chasing after him. If he has indeed been sent by God, he will come on his own. Take me home!"

Itsik, his beloved student, dared not disobey.

The man wearing a velvet yarmulke and *balakhon* carefully opened the synagogue door and went inside.

Except for the gentile caretaker, hired to do the things Jews couldn't do on Shabbes, there was no one was in the synagogue. For a long time, as the caretaker swept the floor, the stranger watched his rounded back, the broom, the tiny pile of dust, the dustpan, and again the rounded back. Suddenly the caretaker turned, saw the outsider, and shuddered.

"Why are you frightened?" the stranger asked. "Can you fear someone in a place of worship? You should only fear your own sins. And you do have one—you're not good at sweeping."

"How do you know? You're not a local . . ."

"I'm from *everywhere*," the stranger said.

What a wonderful word, the caretaker suddenly thought.

"As long as the soul has been swept, the dust on the floor is not a great sin," the man in the velvet yarmulke said.

"The service is over," the caretaker mumbled, rattled by the newcomer's strange remarks.

"Services will end when the world ends."

"True enough. Pray! I'll sweep up later. Pray!"

"Thank you," said the man in the yarmulke fastened to his hair with a pin. And he began to pray quietly and indistinctly.

Holding his breath, the caretaker watched him and put his foot down on the dustpan, scattering the dust he had just gathered onto the creaking plank floor. The stranger's speech did not fit with his shabby appearance—the unbleached linen *balakhon* with its holes and spots either of candlewax or oil; the velvet, rather threadbare yarmulke and the rusted pin that looked like a dragonfly—if you blew on it, you'd think it would fly off his head; his boots, too heavy for summer, which were tied with twine instead of laces; and his Jewish beard, a handful of gray hair. On the other hand, his eyes were just as mysterious and fiery as his speech. They looked like they had been transformed by a potion, especially the whites, tinged with a pale blue, and with restless dark streaks.

After the stranger had finished praying, the caretaker said, "Come this evening! It's better to pray and cry together. So God commands us."

"What do you know about God?"

"Nothing."

"Nothing. But you say: He commands."

"I'm a lowly man . . . ignorant," the caretaker started to defend himself.

"A man is never lowly. Either he is human or not human. God commands us to distinguish the crying of a human being from the tears of a nonhuman. As well as their prayers and laughter and every deed. For instance, you cry tears, but your tavern keeper cries slops."

"How can that happen? Slops!"

The caretaker felt that the outsider was casting a spell on him, ensnaring him with his obscure talk. He did not have the strength either to disagree or to stop listening. He wanted only one thing—for the stranger to leave soon because the young Rabbi Hillel would turn up and bawl him out. The young rabbi was a stickler for neatness—his synagogue had to sparkle like a bald spot!

"Slops," the stranger said. "And I don't want to cry with him. His tears stink."

"I've never seen how Reb Yeshua cries," the dumbfounded caretaker said.

"Nor have I," the stranger answered.

"Then how do you know?"

"There," the stranger raised his finger and pointed to Heaven, "all is known. We will make him cry, and you'll go up close to him, take a whiff, and see for yourself what his tears smell like."

He seemed at first to speak like a normal person, the caretaker noted to himself, but he ended like a madman. My God, so much time wasted on a madman!

"We will make him cry," the stranger promised once more, then took his leave.

4

Pimpleface Simeon shook with fever for two weeks. For two whole weeks—from the first star of July sixth to the first star of July twentieth—he lay languishing on a feather bed which seemed not to be stuffed with goose feathers but with tongues of flames that licked him from morning to night. He tossed and turned, throwing off his blanket, but Morta, who was put in charge of him, freed from all other work in the house—washing the clothes and the floors and the dishes—wrapped her large, weary arms around him and tucked him in like a child and stayed at his bedside day and night. Morta fed him and gave him medicine, but the tavern keeper Yeshua and his wife Chava were afraid to touch their son—if everyone became infected, who would pour the vodka? The German doctor in the pince-nez came from Germany twice, crossing the Neman River. The first time he examined the patient, shook his birdlike head, thrust brand-new marks into his pocket without counting them (at Yeshua's tavern there were not only rubles), and left. On the second trip he almost drowned. A storm blew in during the day and overturned the boat on the channel, and there would have been a funeral banquet had the raftsmen not pulled the doctor out of the river like a fish. Soaked, scared to death, he nonetheless discharged his duty and proceeded to the patient's home. Indignant, he sat for a long time behind a screen until his things dried out and Morta had ironed his underpants, shirt, and checkered jacket. The doctor flatly refused Yeshua's trousers—God save him from a Jew's clothes!

Humiliated by the long wait, the German hurriedly felt around Simeon's elastic, white stomach, slid his fingers down past the navel without inhibition, and asked,

29

"Does it hurt here?"

"No-o-o," Simeon sighed, shaking from the discomfort.

"Here?"

"No-o-o."

"What did you eat before you became sick?"

Pimpleface Simeon could barely keep his head on his shoulders. If he moved just a bit, it would fall and crack open like a clay pot. And now there's this German, this non-kosher fish without scales, tormenting him with his stupid questions.

"I ate fish," the patient strained to say.

"What kind?" the doctor continued.

"River . . ."

"I mean boiled or fried?"

"Morta, tell the doctor what kind of fish I ate," Pimpleface Simeon muttered feebly.

"He didn't eat any fish, doctor. He ate meat with fried potatoes," Morta reported. "He doesn't like fish."

"I see." The German felt his pants—were they dry? He continued, "Meat with fried potatoes, you say. And what kind of fat were they fried in?"

"Same as always. Goose fat."

"Goose, goose," the German repeated, and he began touching Pimpleface Simeon's testicles again.

"What are you staring for, fool?" the tavern keeper's son screamed when he caught Morta's glance. "Turn around. And you, doctor, stop twisting my prick . . . someone looked at me and gave me an evil eye."

"What does that mean, an evil eye?"

"He was given an evil look," explained the tavern keeper Yeshua, who had been standing to one side the whole time, his hooked nose covered with a large handkerchief.

"So what?" the German turned to him.

"That caused the illness," the tavern keeper noted politely.

"That's *unmöglich*—impossible! Our organism has nothing to fear from any kind of looks. Looks aren't fried in bad butter. In any case, I have never come across any. There are germs . . ."

"We don't have lice," the tavern keeper mumbled. "God is my witness!"

The doctor winced. His left eye trembled, and the pince-nez dangled on its silver chain.

"Some looks can be worse than your germs and lice!" Pimpleface Simeon raged, even half-rising from his bed. "I'll tell him off. I'll show that bastard what fever is! I'll find him no matter what!"

The German fidgeted with his pince-nez, as if weighing it, and muttered sympathetically, "I treat illnesses, not superstitions."

Clipping the pince-nez onto his nose, he prescribed some concoction and departed.

Pimpleface Simeon grew worse after the doctor left. He lost consciousness, became delirious, and yelled something or other. As Morta applied a rag that had been dipped in ice water to his forehead, she whispered, "Don't die, Simonas, don't die."

She rushed off to a second cousin said to be a sorcerer and asked her for a potion infused from herbs. Without telling Yeshua and Chava, she forced it down the patient's throat, which was bright red, as if coated with the glow of a sunset. Delirious, Pimpleface Simeon sunk his teeth into Morta's hand and bit down, and the nurse shrieked out of pity and pain.

After giving Simeon the healing concoction, Morta sat down at the foot of the bed and looked at him from a distance. Let him be sick, she thought sweetly, let him be sick for a little longer, but don't let him die. For her, Simonas's illness was both torment and joy. It was so different from the usual daylong washing and rewashing of tavern dishes, and the need to crawl across the floor on her knees to clean every spot of spit and pick up scraps of food and dirt. In this large room with two tall windows, Morta felt, though not for long, like the mistress of the house. She would walk to the window, open the curtain, and look into the courtyard. She watched the peasants' wagons that drove up to the tavern; the light droshky of some tipsy landowner, lighthearted and blissful, like someone in a dream; the policeman Nesterovich, who was hurrying to the tavern—not for a glass of vodka but for his daily bribe (Yeshua did not pay him for nothing!);

and she watched the women and children who stayed by the wagons waiting for their carousing breadwinners. Until now Morta had not known this feeling of beauty and melancholy. Even her gait changed: a lightness appeared in her legs, like that of the carefree landowner; her hips unexpectedly became plump and protruded much less than before; having absorbed so much warmth, her breasts swelled; and her heart pounded from the aches and itches beneath her dress.

When she was a young girl, a thirteen-year-old tomboy, Morta's parents brought her from the country and hired her out as a servant to Yeshua. The tavern keeper paid them with vodka and took care of her—he didn't touch Morta, he fed and dressed her, and he protected her from the drunken stallions who would try to get under her skirt with their trembling hands. After the 1863 uprising, Morta's parents, her three sisters, and her twin brothers were exiled to Siberia, allegedly because they allowed insurgents to milk their cow. The cow survived. When the soldiers arrived, she was grazing in a pasture far from home, and they left her alone. Later Morta brought her cow Burenka to the tavern.

At first the tavern keeper Yeshua would not agree to anything.

"What if they find out?" he scolded Morta.

"Find out what?"

"Find out that she was milked by those . . . ! We'll end up in exile!" Yeshua was ready to explode. "Better to sell her and put the money in your name."

Marta dug in her heels.

"In that case I'll leave with her. It's not the cow's fault."

"Since when is milking a cow a crime?" Chava, a woman as quiet as God Himself, unexpectedly stepped in.

For the first time in his life, the tavern keeper Yeshua listened to his wife.

The cow stayed, along with Morta.

While the cow was alive, Morta felt like more than a servant. Burenka was the only thing in the unfamiliar world of the tavern that belonged to her.

In less than a year the cow died. Morta mourned her for a long time, because there was no one else to mourn.

"Father poisoned her," the seventeen-year-old Simeon once said. "If you don't obey me, he'll poison you, too."

That said, he flung himself down on the straw.

On Sundays and holidays Morta was permitted to go to the Catholic church to pray or make a confession. She sat somewhere in a back pew and never took her eyes off the priest and the gold crucifix where the Savior Jesus hung helplessly. The tavern keeper Yeshua assured her that Jesus was a Jew like him, only a younger one who had never sold vodka. Her Savior, he said, had the face and hair of a landowner's son who had squandered his fortune at some wayside alehouse and then rushed past the small town in which there was nothing worthy of note except cheap hops.

Morta winced before the Savior's fixed expression. She gripped a tiny cross that sparkled like an agile carp in the pure white cleavage between her breasts—taut swells, uneasily ripe—and she whispered a few incoherent, incomprehensible, superstitious words. Biting her swollen lower lip, which showed the same uneasy ripeness, she furtively looked at the backs of the women and men in front of her, who were spellbound and lost in prayer. Although Morta had not sinned against God in any way, she thought of herself as a hopeless sinner.

One day, in the church vestibule, someone hissed at her:

"*Zhidmerge!* Jewish whore!"

People are evil, she thought. Shouldn't someone who is close to God be virtuous? The Almighty knows everything—He knows about those who are pure as a tear and those who are sinful. He, and He alone, would be her judge.

Living *close to sin* does not mean living *in sin*. All day long the tavern swarmed with rakes and drunkards; after a few shots, each one tried to pull and lift up her skirt, especially now that she, Morta, was no longer thirteen and each part of her was swelling with an irrepressible juicy ripeness that burst through her clothes.

What's more, from abstinence and loneliness Simeon was becoming more impudent. If only he could find a Jewish woman and pick from her garden, pluck all her fruit . . .

Why, Morta thought, as she sat at the foot of the master's wide bed, is one person in the world fated to sell vodka and another to trudge to Siberia for no reason at all? By what standard does God in Heaven measure out our fates? If the standard is the same for all, then why is the soldier less guilty than the person who let the insurgents milk the cow? Milk the cow, that was all. Before he fills his mug, is it necessary to ask a person who wants to drink some milk: What are you up to, dear fellow? Are you for or against the czar?

Pimpleface Simeon opened his sick eyes, looked around tipsily, saw Morta, licked his chapped lips and asked,

"Have you been here long?"

"Yes."

"Oh, you," he uttered in amazement, and shook his heavy head which did not feel like his own. "It's like I lapped up all of father's vodka."

"Lie down," Morta said, afraid that he would get up and she would have to return to the hated tavern. "Here, drink up!"

"What is it?"

"Some herbs." Morta cautiously extended the glass to him. "From my aunt."

"Which aunt?"

"Antose . . . Have him drink it, she said. He'll be better in a day. I poured the German's medicine into the slop pail."

"The German?"

"Your father sent to Germany for a doctor."

Pimpleface Simeon stared at Morta, caught sight of the cross, and placed his hand on his burning forehead. He refused the herbs— if you believe this Auntie Antose, he thought, you might as well order your funeral service.

"Go away! Call Father!"

"The Master's in the city. The vodka ran out."

"I'm here croaking and he's riding around to find vodka," Simeon snapped.

"People are demanding it," Morta defended the tavern keeper. "The holidays are coming. The Assumption of Mary. How can they celebrate without vodka?"

"There's time for the Assumption. But you . . . you should sit a bit closer," Simeon muttered, as he rested his foot on her supple and sensitive buttock.

His touch startled her. She froze, then straightened her heavy homespun skirt and moved a little against her will.

"Closer! Still closer!" Simeon pressed and tossed aside his blanket. His legs were long and hairy.

"Don't be afraid!" he urged her on. "I won't eat you up."

He grinned, and with a sick, piercing look, like a fishhook, he caught sight of the carp-shaped cross again, and he grasped for it with his bare feet.

"Well?"

Morta narrowed her eyes, ashamed, and began to breathe heavily. Pimpleface Simeon leaned toward her, clenched the cross until it crunched, squeezed it to the point of nausea, then in a quiet, guttural, doleful voice said,

"Take it off! Go ahead, take it off!"

"Never!" Morta uttered furiously. "Why are you Jews like that?"

"Like what?"

"Don't you fear God?"

"Why should I fear the old man? He's up there, but you . . . you're here. Hold out your hand . . ."

"No, no." She drew back. "There's a reason they say all trouble comes from your people."

"And from yours?" Simeon inquired good-naturedly, aroused by her dismay.

"From us? Milk . . . bread . . . berries . . . land."

"Nonsense!" He smiled and tried to embrace her.

"Don't . . ."

"Fool! Who are you saving yourself for?"

Pimpleface Simeon pushed her away, dropped his heavy head on the pillow, and for a long while he lay there silently, offended, unusually meek and merciful. His face, flushed with fever, suddenly became strangely attractive. Only his bushy eyebrows were a blemish, giving him a look of sullen resolve, while his cracked lips, coated with white, were suffering not so much from the fever as from an irrepressible lust.

"In any case, everyone thinks you're a whore." Simeon spoke freely, as if he were reciting a verse from the Bible.

"No!" Morta screamed.

"Whore! Who'll believe you're not sleeping with me?"

"God! He sees and hears everything!"

"Nonsense!" Pimpleface Simeon jumped up, grabbed Morta by her shoulders, and drew her closer, fixing his eyes on her plump, soft lips. "There is no God . . . We all work for the devil," he said, kissing her like a blind man.

Morta tore herself away from his shameless arms, now weak from illness. She smoothed her ruffled hair and moved toward the door in slow steps, as if mounting a scaffold.

Pimpleface Simeon heard the familiar sound of the bolt clicking as Morta left without saying a word. She always acted like this: leaving without speaking, clenching her teeth as if she were on her way to death. Sometimes he thought that she would go hang herself somewhere in the barn where his father kept empty bottles and the horse crunched oats, or she would drown herself in the river. At such moments Pimpleface Simeon was shaken by feelings that were unbearably repulsive, and he would take note of every sound from outside in order to convince himself that he was wrong and too suspicious; yet when Morta's deep voice from somewhere outside reached his ears again, he felt strangely hollow and even deceived. Not that he really wished for Morta's death—she was the only person in the house for whom Simeon felt something like an effortless and unselfish love. Morta never demanded anything from him, she didn't reproach him with anything, try to reform him or set him on the true path, as did his father, for whom the right path was a tiny corridor between the marriage bed and the bar of the musty tavern, full of smoke and alcohol.

Pimpleface Simeon did not love his father. He put up with his mother, feeling sorry for her, but for his father there was no love, at times to the point of fury and frenzy. Why did his father make drunkards out of these drowsy, taciturn peasants, all day long? They became boisterous under the influence, as if a bottle of vodka was their only, bitter joy. And why didn't his father drink? Why did he become enraged when his son poured himself a glass? Didn't he, Simeon, have good reason to get soused, muddle his brain with liquor, and bring some joy to his shriveled soul, frigid from boredom and comfort? "The God of drunks" is what Simeon called the person who gave him life. A life consisting of a drunken day, drunken evening, and even a drunken night. Even after midnight people would rap on the shutters and call out, "Yeshua, a bottle!"

Then Yeshua, half-asleep in his underwear, his bare feet in slippers, would go to the tavern with a candle in his hand and bring vodka out to the porch.

When Simeon was a small boy he had drunken dreams. One he remembers to this day. The tavern is packed tight, with lots of commotion; his father is sweating, on edge, and his mother is in an apron with a mug in her hand. Amid the hustle and bustle, he suddenly faces everyone and says, "Vodka is pouring from the sky."

Everyone rushes outside to the yard—the peasants, his father, his mother. The peasants crane their necks, open their mouths, and streams of vodka run down their faces, over their beards and over their *sermyagas*, their coarse gabardine coats. His father is half dead from fright. He looks at the sky, at the streams flowing down, then shouts, "Chava! Bring some buckets! Don't just stand there!"

Sometimes it seems to Pimpleface Simeon that he has never woken up.

No, he won't become a tavern keeper. He doesn't intend to hang around the bar his whole life. Vodka is gold rain, of course, but he will seek out something a little better.

"In the whole empire there is nothing more profitable than vodka," his father has preached many times. "What does bread bring? You just stuff your belly. But drink a little vodka and grief turns to joy."

His father is cunning, but Simeon is nobody's fool. Someone else can make a living from vodka, but he will choose another trade. One that is unsullied, inconspicuous, without vomit and drunken hangovers, without peering into people's eyes, and without that rap on the shutters: "Yeshua, a bottle!" Something is already brewing in Simeon's head. His father doesn't suspect anything. No one must guess what it is. Not a single soul in the world. It's too bad that he, Simeon, has taken to his bed at the wrong moment. Otherwise, everything could have turned out perfectly. Officer Nesterovich keeps his word. He may not be much of a sage, but in certain matters he understands more than Rabbi Uri, the man of wisdom.

Once Pimpleface Simeon, like Itsik Magid, was a student of Rabbi Uri. Then they both left their teacher. Simeon scrounged off his father and Magid went off to the forest to fell trees. What could the old man teach them, after all? A lot of brainy stuff. Belief in God? These days belief in God isn't worth a kopeck, and any wisdom that people get is worth less than a glass of vodka in the tavern. Rabbi Uri is right, of course, that the world and its people are imperfect. But Pimpleface Simeon is not the world or its people. He's just one person, and not just a person, but a Jew. For a Jewish person with such a ridiculous nickname as his, it's not even worth thinking about people and the world. It's time for him to think of himself. Why on earth should he be concerned with correcting the mistakes and imperfections of others?

If the rabbi had taught them anything, it was the sober understanding that—sooner or later—all the countless imperfections and vices will be paid for with trials and tribulations and a tormented conscience.

But what if people who are imperfect and guilty of vices had to pay back in cash, Pimpleface Simeon wondered. What about opening a vice shop? The vices of others could be more profitable than vodka.

The policeman Nesterovich once proposed that Simeon open such a business. He, Nesterovich, would be the sole customer. And he would have plenty of money because the Russian Empire, not he, would pay for these vices. Here is my gold rain! Simeon thought. If only I'm able to dunk my head in its abundant streams! Simeon knew well that certain vices would fetch a high price. No vices are more profitable than free-thinking and insubordination. More profitable, needless to say, for the one who sells rather than possesses them.

"You yourself know," Nesterovich told him when they met, "that where there's booze there's blabber."

Although Pimpleface Simeon rarely dropped in at the tavern, he had often heard how the discontent, heated up by home brew, came to a boil there. At the time of their encounter, Simeon did not give Nesterovich a final answer.

"A Jew should never give a final answer," Simeon's father had taught him. "A final answer is like the grave—you dig it yourself and you bury yourself."

"I'll think about it," the officer heard him say,

Lying in bed now and struggling with the disease that had been brought down upon him, Pimpleface Simeon was weighing the pros and cons of Nesterovich's proposal. He remembered how, when he was a child, the gendarmes had seized a peasant from his father's tavern, and as they dragged him to a wagon, he was spitting blood. Simeon's mother sprinkled the spots with sand. Later, when he played in the tavern's yard, Simeon would still look warily at the ground with a vague sorrow.

He weighed this and that, but all the while something didn't tally, and again his shadowy thoughts fell upon the stranger. Who was he? Some day—after Simeon opened the vice shop—he would deal with him, he wouldn't let him get away. If he had to, he would *think up* a vice. Not only existing vices can be peddled—you could also sell invented ones. Invented ones bring just as high a price.

Until I give my answer, Pimpleface Simeon reflected, Officer Nesterovich might not trust me. Besides, it makes sense for me to agree—and it will turn out badly for the stranger with the velvet yarmulke. I'll cook up something about him.

What should he think up? That he was a runaway soldier? A convict? A soldier's better. He doesn't look like a convict. A convict wearing a yarmulke!

Pimpleface Simeon burst out laughing. His laughter echoed ominously and somewhat ridiculously through the empty room, causing the patient to break it off. Where the hell was Morta? Why hadn't she brought him something to eat? He was just now feeling hungry again.

"Morta," he called. The righteous Morta has become unruly, Simeon thought. Her God, if you can believe it, won't let her go to bed with a Jew. Do you really need to ask God who you can sleep with? You do have to ask him who to make children with. Not with an orphaned servant—a girl like that isn't fit to be a mother. Now Zelda Fradkin—she could be a wife. But, just like Morta, you won't be able to lasso her. Markus Fradkin would chop off the lasso and your arms. Still, there might be a way to stop even Markus Fradkin. He shouldn't boast so much about his wealth.

Forty thousand *sazhens* of forest is not real wealth. But forty thousand *sazhens* of vices! I just need to sniff out Markus Fradkin's vices, and then reap the harvest—Zelda.

"Morta!"

There was no answer.

5

It was a day like all others—not cloudy, not bright, but somewhere in between. Since morning, as usual at the end of July, sweltering heat had poured in from the opposite bank of the river, from Germany. The heat mixed with moisture, and there was nowhere to go—it was hell in the yard, and at home there is no heavenly sanctuary, so you sit there and are drenched in sweat. My God, a man can sweat entire rivers!

Rakhmiel, the night watchman, sat at the table bareheaded and shirtless, wearing only his underwear, while working to patch Kazimieras's drab coat. The *sermyaga* was old, the cloth stiff. As Rakhmiel tried to push in the needle with a thimble, time and time again it was stopped by the coarse material, as if it had hit a stone. After a sleepless night Rakhmiel deserved a rest, but how can you sleep in such heavy air? The minute you lie down and close your eyes, you're sopping wet. And where does all this sweat in a man come from? Rakhmiel knew why young people sweat—he was once young himself. But in old age?

Rakhmiel sat at the table, legs crossed, thinking about why old people sweat. He thought about strength and frailty, but his thoughts got stuck in the stiff cortex of his skull, like the needle stuck in the cloth of the coat.

From time to time, Rakhmiel gave his thoughts a rest. He would start to sing some song or other, often mixing up the words, yet he didn't care because the words never had any importance for him. A person has even more words than sweat. Sweat has some use, especially on a shelf in the bathhouse, but words have none, offer no advantage. Rakhmiel had made do without them his whole life. He's not Rabbi Uri, who still believes in words. God had said a lot, and so what? Did anyone listen to Him? It's fine to speak all sorts of words when you're sitting on a cloud looking down from above. But when you fiddle about down here in dirt and shit, then these two words are all you know. And they will suffice until the grave.

Rabbi Uri has spent his whole life sitting on a cloud, on the dusty cloud of Torah, but he, Rakhmiel, has fiddled about down below.

When he was young, he built roads. He also built this one, the one to Kovno. In summer and in winter he slaved away on the Kovno road, and his leg was flattened like a pancake there. For half a year he couldn't move. He fell into bed and screamed his head off. For half a year he couldn't stand, and his brother carried him in his arms to the outhouse and sat him down like a doll. Then God took pity. The carpenter Hanokh Katz made him a crutch, and little by little he slowly began to drag his leg, first around the house, and then around the yard, and when he got stronger, even around town to visit someone who needed a pan to be soldered, someone who needed a hole patched in a *lapserdak*, the long overcoat Jews wore, or someone who needed a handle attached to a pail. Rakhmiel didn't shun any kind of work and took whatever pay they offered. He frightened dogs and girls with his crutch. Sometimes he dragged himself to the highway, sat down on the side of the road, and watched carts rolling along, or a gendarme dashing by in a droshky.

One fine day Rakhmiel disappeared from the small town. He reappeared four years later with a woman. She led by the hand a grubby little boy who wore a funny-looking cap pulled down over his devoted, doglike eyes, and a patched jacket without buttons or a lining. The family settled down on the outskirts of town in an abandoned barn whose walls and moss-covered roof were the only parts that remained intact. Under this same moss-covered roof the woman gave birth to a daughter. After that, siblings kept pouring out every year. No one in town could count how many children Rakhmiel had. Bony, gangling, dirty, they ran around the neighborhood, dragging whatever caught their eyes into the barn. People watching them would shake their heads disdainfully and murmur, "He must be making them with his crutch."

Crutch or not, the barn swarmed with kids, like a pond with baby fish.

Rakhmiel somehow managed to rebuild the wrecked barn by himself. With his golden hands he cut out windows, patched the roof with straw, laid a floor of rough boards, knocked together a table, chairs, and beds. He was more concerned with making a living than caring for his offspring. As before, he soldered, mended, and put in windowpanes, but he earned most of his money by singing in the strong, high voice that had developed during the time he spent in bed with his crushed leg. In the entire district—from Jurbarkas to Memel—there was not a single Jewish celebration, not one wedding, at which Rakhmiel did not sing. The Jews listened and were amazed: what kind of bird is chirping in his hungry throat?

When he headed off to a wedding, Rakhmiel took along the whole gang of kids, and while his marvelous singing entertained the newlyweds and the in-laws, who were beside themselves with joy, the gang cheerfully and freely stuffed themselves with whatever they saw, then made raucous noises to upset the wedding feast or went running into the yard to do their business.

They all went on living this way until misfortune struck and everyone took to bed except Rakhmiel and that young boy in the cap and jacket without buttons and lining, who by now had sprung up almost to his father's shoulders. Within a month all the sick ones had died like flies.

Whether something at a wedding poisoned them or another unknown calamity did them in, Rakhmiel was slow to bury them.

After he buried the last one, the timber merchant Fradkin came to see him together with the policeman, not Nesterovich, the present one, but the earlier one who was later transferred either to Molodechno or to Grodno. They ordered Rakhmiel to get out of town because—"God save us and have mercy upon us"—the infection was spreading around the town. And from the town—"God save us and have mercy upon us"—it would quickly jump to the surrounding area, and from there to other provinces.

"What about my home?" was all Rakhmiel said.

"Who cares about your home?" Fradkin said.

"I do," Rakhmiel said.

He tousled Aaron's hair—the boy's name was Aaron. And as if defending himself, he uttered the words, "We won't sing at strangers' weddings again."

He took a step toward the door.

The timber merchant stopped him. "We'll arrange something for the boy. When it's all over, you'll be able to return."

"But we're better off together," Rakhmiel murmured.

"Leave the boy," the policeman said, backing up the timber merchant. "You can count on Mr. Fradkin."

At the time Rakhmiel didn't understand, fool that he was, what Fradkin was up to. At the time he believed that Aaron would do better with Fradkin. He thought that Fradkin would place him somewhere, help him get set up.

And place him somewhere and set him up he certainly did!

"Rabbi Uri, where is my Aaron? Remember the one who ran around with a funny-looking cap on his head?" Rakhmiel asked when he returned one year later.

"Handed over to the draft," Rabbi Uri answered.

"By Fradkin?"

Rabbi Uri was silent. He sat on his cloud and remained silent.

"Fradkin handed him over in place of his Zelik?"

"Never blame others," Rabbi Uri said, and from his mouth a heavenly frost drifted over Rakhmiel. "Let's rather think about our own guilt."

"What am I guilty of, Rabbi? That I'm Rakhmiel and not Markus Fradkin? That I'm not a policeman?"

Rakhmiel kept on poking the needle into the *sermyaga*, and with every jab something flashed in his head, faded, and then flashed again. There's nothing in the world more stifling than thoughts, he decided. At least shade saves you from sweltering heat. But what shade can save you from thoughts? Why had Rabbi Uri invited him to his home, just to have tea with him? Rakhmiel was never one to schmooze. Rabbi Uri serves tea without sugar, not because he's stingy, but because he's used to people sharing bitterness, not sweetness, with him.

Who is this messenger of God that he was trying to find out about? Then he had switched the conversation to Aaron, who Rakhmiel had always called his son, not his stepson. And the clapper? Why would such a righteous and pious man like Rabbi Uri, in the middle of the night in his own home, begin to bang the clapper? Something was wrong.

Rakhmiel didn't notice that a man had walked in through the open door. He wore a velvet yarmulke that was fastened to his hair with a pin, and he stood for a time, looked around, and slowly, as if sorting out what he saw, headed toward the table.

"Good day," said the man in the yarmulke, and Rakhmiel gave a start. He couldn't remember a time when anyone had greeted him that way. In their small town it wasn't customary to greet others. You could say "Good day," but the day was not good at all—it was backbreaking, you couldn't breathe, and your soul felt like a deserted marketplace full of trash.

"Good day," Rakhmiel answered, examining the man in the yarmulke from head to toe. Was he the one Rabbi Uri was speaking about as they both sipped the warm tea?

"Sew, keep on sewing!" the stranger said quietly without looking at Rakhmiel. "I just dropped in for something to drink. Where is your water?"

"Outside in the bucket," Rakhmiel said, pulling the needle through the coarse fabric.

"Sew, sew," the man in the yarmulke said again, and just as slowly as he'd entered, he headed for the door.

While he was on his way, Rakhmiel pulled up his loose underwear and tightened it with a yellowed string. To be on the safe side, he covered his sweating head with a small hat.

"There's algae in the water. I'll go to the river to bring back some fresh."

The newcomer stood before Rakhmiel with a bucket in his hand, and the old watchman was even more perplexed.

"Why didn't you just go straight to the river?" he mumbled.

"You wouldn't understand," the man in the yarmulke remarked and left the house, clanging the pail.

The clanging caused Rakhmiel to sweat even more. He slipped out into the yard, and for a long while watched the stranger as he disappeared into the distance. Suddenly—who knows why?—he wanted the man to drop the bucket into the river and never come back.

The stranger returned, however, placed the bucket at Rakhmiel's feet, and said, "Drink!"

Rakhmiel waited. Something restrained him—whether it was the tightened underwear, the man in the yarmulke's fixed gaze, full of an indifferent concern, or the memories suddenly surging into his mind of a small boy in a cap and a jacket without buttons or lining.

"Drink!" the stranger repeated.

Rakhmiel bent down and poked his head into the water, and the visions arising in his numbed brain spilled over, washed away, and subsided. Sweat no longer streamed from his old face covered with coarse, white bristles; instead, river water flowed over it, so natural, so much a part of him, that he breathed more easily.

"Good?" the man in the yarmulke asked.

"The best," Rakhmiel murmured. "Thank you."

"Thank the river, not me. Do you ever thank it?"

"No," Rakhmiel said, dumbfounded.

"Why not?"

"No one does that," the watchman mumbled.

"Then go and say it. And you'll be the first one in town."

"They'll make fun of me," Rakhmiel objected, trying to defend himself from the stranger's words. "They'll call me crazy."

"Do you think it's better to be like everyone else than to be crazy?"

"Yes, it's better . . . to be like everyone else."

"Even when *they're* all crazy?"

"I have three chickens and a rooster," Rakhmiel said suddenly. "And last year's potatoes. What if I boil up a pot? I can quickly . . ."

Rakhmiel knew that whether you're eating alone or with others, when you're eating, you don't think about anything. If there's plenty and if it tastes good, food is the best escape from all your thoughts. No matter how smart a head is, it can't compare with the stomach. The stomach always has its way. If truth be told, God slipped up— He gave man two ears and two eyes but only one stomach. You can fill it with whatever you like—potatoes, eggs, radishes. But when your head is hungry, that's worse. There's nothing to stuff it with.

Ever since his wife and children died, and his stepson Aaron was drafted, Rakhmiel's head constantly needed some kind of food. He tried to saturate it with forgetfulness, but all the same it gave him no peace. A meal is good, Rakhmiel thought, because you don't have to talk much. You scoop up a spoonful, slurp, chew—and keep quiet. Silence isn't gold, of course, but it's a kopeck for a Jew—you can't buy or sell someone who keeps silent. Especially when there are others all around, when your words are passed on to the policeman and you have to do what he says, even if you don't understand a thing. Isn't that why he, Rakhmiel, chose to become a watchman? Stillness, silence, you walk around the town, take a look at the shutters, and you are like a shutter yourself with iron hinges.

"Let's have potatoes," the man in the yarmulke agreed, and he carried the bucket into the house.

"What's your name?" Rakhmiel asked when the potatoes were steaming next to the coat on the table.

"What would you like my name to be?"

Taken aback, Rakhmiel dropped a potato. It plopped onto the floor and fell apart.

"You can call me any name you like."

"How's that?" Rakhmiel asked. "Everyone has a name of his own. So, my name is Rakhmiel. And yours?"

"Choose any name at all. Is a name so important to you? It's important that this name reminds you of something."

"Reminds me of what?"

"What do people remember in the twilight of life? Sins!"

The intruder sat across from Rakhmiel and looked steadily into his eyes. Something in the watchman's eyes melted and began to overflow until a large tear fell onto his plump cheek and stuck in the stubble.

"Call me by the name of your sin." The guest broke apart a potato, dipped it in clumps of gray salt, and stared at the host again. "There are no nameless sins," he said, and delivered half a potato to his mouth.

The stranger emitted a sucking energy, like that of a whirlpool, and Rakhmiel obediently surrendered to it, the way a thread follows a needle.

"Aaron," he sighed, and a new stream of sweat washed over his chin.

"Aaron, so it's Aaron," the man in the yarmulke said indifferently. "What do you want to say to me, to Aaron?"

"What's there to say?"

"Everything. No need to hurry. The day is long."

"Listen," Rakhmiel said, with a start. "You don't know me, and I don't know you. Have a bite and go in peace. I need to patch this coat before evening. Kazimieras has already come by twice."

"I'll go, but the sin will stay," the stranger said, as if everything were fine.

"I don't have sins! None!" Rakhmiel shouted. "For sins go to Fradkin! Go to Yeshua in the tavern!"

"Their time will come," the guest replied calmly. "No sins, you say, but you're lying. All right, let's have our meal and go our separate ways."

They ate glancing at one another without speaking, and the more Rakhmiel looked at the intruder, the more strenuous the silence became. Who knows who this man is who crossed your doorstep today? Rakhmiel thought. He began to choke on an ordinary potato, the same as others he'd eaten a thousand times. A homeless tramp, of the sort you meet in every town and village, an overgrown loafer who'd picked up a smattering of scholarly wisdom at some yeshiva? And who, more out of laziness than erudition, had become slightly damaged in the head? Or his own son, driven away many years ago to somewhere at the ends of the earth? What if he had replaced the funny-looking cap with this velvet yarmulke fastened to his hair with a pin? And in place of the jacket without buttons or lining, he now wore a tunic. His *balakhon* gave off a faint smell of manure. Why didn't he drink from the river right away, instead of coming to this wreck of a house? There are nicer and richer houses in town where you can find buckets of honey and milk instead of moldy water. What drew him here? Still, Rakhmiel couldn't throw him out. He had to give him shelter, accept him as he would any orphan or homeless person, and stop wondering whose messenger he is.

Isn't a person who reminds us of our sins a messenger of God?

He appears to be a reasonable man: he went to the river, collected fresh water, brought it back; before starting to eat he said a blessing; and he doesn't eat like a madman at all, but slowly, in a dignified manner, as they do at the home of Fradkin or the Spivak brothers, without frenzy, without grinding his teeth; he peels each potato, dips it into salt, and brushes the crumbs from his small beard onto his palm—not onto the floor. It's clear right away that he's no peasant or glutton. And the fact that what he says is confusing—well, who in town except the police officer expresses himself clearly? They all confuse you; they all throw dust in your eyes and try to put one over on you.

Rakhmiel had not sat down to eat with anyone for a long time—always just by himself. When you're by yourself, the grub doesn't get stuck in your throat.

"But where do you live?" he asked, when they'd had their fill of silence.

"Everywhere," the man in the yarmulke answered.

"That can't be," Rakhmiel said cautiously. "Everyone has his own roof, like his own name."

"The sky is my roof," the guest said, and took off his *balakhon*.

"But in the fall? When your roof leaks?"

"I live there in the fall, too." The man in the yarmulke looked up at the ceiling.

"In an attic?"

"Beyond the clouds," the guest replied. "It's light and spacious there. Do you think I'm telling you fairy tales? You believe that there's an attic, don't you?"

"Believe in an attic? Yes, I do." Rakhmiel cast a sideways glance at the intruder and his *balakhon*, and the smell of manure struck his flared nostrils. When Reb Rakhmiel became agitated, he always flared his nostrils.

"It's stupid to believe only in things that you can feel with your hands. The policeman, the tavern keeper, the timber merchant Fradkin. The potatoes that you and I just wolfed down."

"You . . . you know Fradkin?" Rakhmiel suddenly pricked up his ears.

"Yes."

"He is czar and God here." The watchman spoke quietly, and his lower lip drooped.

"God can only be one who is loved by all, but a czar is someone who people fear. You are afraid of Fradkin, so to you he's a czar. But I'm not afraid of him."

"Fradkin turned in my stepson . . . Aaron . . . to the draft," Reb Rakhmiel said suddenly. "In place of his Zelik. He came here and took him away."

"I remember that," said the man in the yarmulke.

"You do?"

"I do. I, Aaron."

"But you . . . I just called you Aaron. My Aaron has a birthmark on his right shoulder . . . the size of a ripe strawberry."

"They burned off the birthmark, plucked the strawberry," the stranger said.

"Who burned it? Who plucked it?" Rakhmiel mumbled.

"You," the guest said simply. "Now, anyone who comes to you can be Aaron!"

"That can't be," Rakhmiel countered. "That can't be. Show me the birthmark! The scar! A mark!" he said indignantly.

"I'll show you," the stranger said calmly. "How could I forget that you believe only in what you can see or smell? But there are things in the world that the eye can't see and the nose can't smell. Otherwise, the sense of smell would be God. You just said 'Fradkin came and took him away.' But only what is given away can be taken away."

"Fradkin didn't come here by himself. He came with the policeman. Just try not giving . . ." Rakhmiel went limp.

"So what? Even if he'd brought with him all the soldiers in the Russian Empire, you had no right to give him away. You say, 'What could I do? Who am I, compared to all of the soldiers in the Russian Empire? Rakhmiel, a grain of sand, a speck of dust, a bug!' I'll answer you: if everyone in the world keeps saying, 'I'm a speck of dust, a grain of sand,' then everyone we love will be taken away from us. Even God! Now you're probably sorry that you fed me."

"Why should I be sorry? I don't begrudge you the potatoes. The harvest will come soon, and not long ago I planted four more rows. I gave two to Kazimieras, who puts out my candles on Shabbes. Sometimes he brings goat's milk. And so we live . . . Every day his goat rubs against my wooden fence . . . Though goats are stupid creatures, they're better than people. They give us milk and cheese and wool. But man? What does man make? Policemen? Soldiers? Madmen?"

The stranger kept silent and listened, and astonishment softened his irregular, scarecrow-like features.

6

The tavern keeper Yeshua usually went through Veliuona and Jurbarkas to get vodka. In Jurbarkas, if he was traveling without Morta, he would stop at the home of a distant relative, Simkhe Vilner, the owner of an imported goods shop. There Yeshua would unharness the horses, bathe them in the Neman River, and after finding a sandbar, would take a dip himself, though he didn't go far out into the water. There are treacherous spots, the current can grab you, twist and spin, suck you down into the depths, and then—goodbye!

Simkhe Vilner was a hot-tempered, quarrelsome man. You couldn't sit with him for long, because he was always looking for trouble. He didn't talk about raisins and prunes; instead, he went on about persecution and oppression, like something was stuck in his throat: here, did you know, they strangled a Jew, there they cut another one's throat, there a woman was raped. Well, what was he, Yeshua, to do? Was he an old woman, or what? You stop for a quick rest and get back on the road. But the road is long, you hope to God to get there before evening, and if you do, vodka is a lot cheaper at the distiller Vaysfeld's in Kovno. You take some fifty buckets or so, load up a wagon, and, mind you, you've made a good profit. Not a single bottle opened, and money already lines your pocket.

True, there is real fear because the road goes through forest all the way. You must keep your eyes open, look all around so that you don't get waylaid by anyone. These days hunters of other people's goods are as plentiful as fish in the sea.

To this day, Yeshua's hair stands on end when he recalls his trip to Kovno the summer before last, just before Saint John's Day.

The weather was marvelous—not a cloud in the sky, bright sunlight dazzled the horses, the birds were singing so sonorously it seemed they were on holiday. Yeshua drove the horses carefully, at times listening to the songs of the birds, at times to the sound of the bottles in crates lined with fresh hay. He steered around potholes and ruts, and he thought about the fact that in half a year, right on the eve of Hanukkah, he would be fifty-four, and he didn't have a single gray hair in his beard or sidelocks. And Yeshua thought, too, as befits a father, about his son, Pimpleface Simeon, his only heir. His daughter Hannah had lived in this world for only eight years. Ach, Hannah, Hannah! Even dogs live longer.

Yeshua was not pleased with his son. He had inherited no traits from their family, the Mandels, who were known for their energy and hard work. They started with only a kopeck, destitute paupers, and what did they achieve? All the taverns and roadside inns are in their hands—drop in and have a drink if your pockets are jingling! The oldest Mandel, the seventy-year-old Nosn, had received Governor Muravyov himself in his home and clinked glasses with him as an equal, an unprecedented honor for a Jew!

But Simeon? Who would clink glasses with him? If, God forbid, something happened to him, Yeshua, then in no time at all, Simeon would let the tavern go to ruin. He wouldn't drag himself to Kovno to earn extra money, don't expect that from Simeon.

What's to be done? Yeshua reflected to the creak of the wheels. There are children who are profits and children who are losses. Simeon is a loss. A loss can be made up. But can you make it up with Chava? Even though she's five years younger than Yeshua, Chava is as barren as the wasteland behind the tavern. What's the use of planting if the earth bears no fruit? If I, Yeshua, just get myself some black soil, I can plow and seed it.

The timber merchant Markus Fradkin's daughter is pure, fertile soil. The purest, without any admixture. What does it matter that there's an age gap of thirty years? An old horse doesn't spoil a furrow. And he's still not an old horse, he's in fine shape! Yet for as long as Chava is alive, he'll hang around the stable, and if there's anything to plow, it will be loam and not black earth.

It would be good to become related to Fradkin, if only through Simeon. But Simeon plays the fool, and for him even Morta is good. Who does he take after? His mother, Chava. My God, why has she become so hateful, resenting her dear husband chosen by God. No such thing. God didn't choose him. It was her father, the shopkeeper Yehuda Spivak. For Chava's dowry, he gave the tavern, and Yeshua took it.

Once Nosn Mandel, their family head, asked him, "Who did you marry, Yeshua?"

He answered, "The tavern, Reb Nosn!"

"Yeshua, a fellow like you should have married a distillery."

If Chava died, Yeshua thought to the clatter of the horses' hooves, I'll marry a distillery or, even better, some oak grove. These days oak timber brings a good price. I'm sick of hanging around the tavern from morning to evening, looking at all the insatiable, drunken faces! I'm sick of it!

My God, it's good to be on the road! The birds have simply gone mad! How they rejoice! How they trumpet! Hush, hush! Why are you crowing? What are you rejoicing at? I've lived in this world for over fifty years and I've never become tipsy from the open air. If only, little birdies, you would sing in the tavern! Or when I'm in bed with Chava beside me, gray and as cold as ashes.

"Stop!" rang out from the bushes, and the tavern keeper Yeshua froze.

He pulled on the reins, jerking them several times, letting the horses know that he didn't like their pace. But the horses didn't understand him. They were also thinking about something, paying attention to the songs of the birds, and then Yeshua cried out in a voice not his own, "Giddy up!"

For the first time he regretted that he'd been getting by without his whip, which hung somewhere in the barn. The tavern keeper had bought it from some peasant for a tankard of vodka, but he didn't use it because he couldn't bear seeing livestock beaten with a rod. "Only a person should be flogged," he used to say. "It's not the ox's fault, but the driver's."

"Giddy up!"

The horses switched to a light trot, but a shout caught up to them.

"Stop, filthy Jew!"

A peasant tore through thick bushes, breaking deadwood, and ran out on the road.

"Stop, you Jews!"

He was calling out to the horses now, but they, not used to such a threatening shout, continued to run, flicking their large ears.

"Faster, my dears, faster!" Yeshua begged them.

When the danger seemed to have passed, some five meters ahead of the wagon a young pine tree fell on the road with a loud thud.

This is the end, flashed in Yeshua's mind, and he stopped the horses.

Two men with axes stepped out of the woods. They drew close to the wagon and ordered the tavern keeper to climb out.

"Jozef, tie the Jew to a tree," one of them snapped.

The one called Jozef shoved Yeshua to the side of the road.

"Move and don't look back!"

"Why? Why?" the stunned tavern keeper repeated, shaking out his pockets as he went. Out fell a few crumbs, a comb, and an embroidered handkerchief.

"I swear to God, not a kopeck, not a single kopeck . . . as I live and breathe."

"Stand against the tree! Over here!" Jozef said. He bent over and picked up the handkerchief and comb.

"No, no," Yeshua cried out, not understanding a thing. "I don't want to go to the tree . . . I don't want to."

Jozef kicked him once in the stomach, and then again, and Yeshua went limp.

"Have mercy!" he pleaded quietly. "I'll give you drinks a whole year . . . two years, for free. Word of honor. Take everything . . . the

horses, the vodka. Just let me go. I won't say a word to anyone . . .
Not a word."

The one called Jozef set him back on his feet, leaned him against
a pine tree, and began tying him up with leather straps. He first
pulled a strap around his stomach, then secured it with a double
knot.

"Ow! It's hurting me! A lot." Yeshua twisted and gasped, but
Jozef seemed to hear neither his gasp nor his pleas. He dragged over
an armful of sticks, threw them beneath the tavern keeper's feet,
pulled out flint from his pocket and set the wood on fire.

"What are you doing? Aren't we people?" Yeshua shouted, and
he began to cry.

"People," the echo responded. The flames tossed about like a
young fox.

"Jozef!" a voice called out from the road.

"Coming, I'm coming!" Jozef examined the fire, then plodded his
way to the wagon.

Tears poured down the tavern keeper's large, bearded face.

"Weep, Yeshua, weep! You've never cried in your life," he whispered. "Let your tears rush like a river . . . over your beard . . . your
stomach, your legs, down, down onto the fire . . . You won't put it
out only with tears . . . with tears . . . God, give me as many tears as
the vodka I have poured into tankards. My God!"

The sticks beneath him crackled merrily. Flames were already
near his shoes . . . There was a smell like burned meat.

"Aren't we people!" Yeshua shouted.

"People," responded the echo.

"God, oh God, why must I suffer so?"

"So-oo," the echo repeated.

In the branches above him the birds were going crazy.

"Birds, birds," Yeshua moaned. "Can't you see anything? Do you
really not care?"

"Care," the echo taunted him from above.

"Drek. Everything is shit . . . the birds, people. Master of the
Universe, forgive me . . . have mercy upon me." Yeshua tried to untie

the knot with his hands, but he couldn't, it was too tight, too stiff. The way they tie up rafts on the Neman.

He suddenly caught sight of his horse, his bay.

"My dear girl," Yeshua sighed and dissolved in tears.

The bay, who felt his breath, approached the pine tree and stopped dead before the fire.

"My dear girl!" Yeshua managed to free one hand and held it out.

Thinking that the hand was not empty, that it held a crust of bread, the horse took a step toward the tree. She sniffed Yeshua's hand and rubbed her face into his beard. Yeshua grabbed the horse by the neck, drew her close, and kissed her as if to say goodbye and to thank her for her devotion. But the fire had now grown even stronger and hotter, and it scared off the bay. She neighed loudly to the whole forest, and the echo imitated her like a foal. For a long time, the sad, bereaved horse looped around the pine tree, shooing away forest flies and flying sparks with her tail.

Yeshua would have roasted in the robbers' fire had Markus Fradkin's loggers not smelled the smoke and chanced upon him. Itsik Magid was with them. They untied the tavern keeper, tramped down the fire, laid Yeshua on soft moss, took off his burned shoes, examined his dirty, stinking feet, and gave him water from a flask.

When Yeshua came to his senses, Itsik asked him, "Are you hurt, Reb Yeshua?"

"I'm all right . . . all right," the tavern keeper wheezed. He looked toward the top of the pine tree he'd just been tied to, and suddenly he felt pain. He pitied himself to the point of screaming as he lay spread out on the moss, helpless and barefoot, and he felt pity as well for this tall, patient tree and the cloudless sky that hung dispassionately above all—tavern keepers, robbers, loggers, and innocent horses.

"And who decided to roast you like a chicken?" Itsik asked, trying to turn it into a joke.

"Jozef," Yeshua groaned. "My shoes—do they need to be thrown away? Such shoes! As good as new . . ."

With a grunt, Yeshua got up. He looked askance at the charred shoes and walked to the wagon barefoot.

"Kuzya, Kuzya," he called, and the bay obediently followed him.

The loggers looked at each other, poured the rest of the water from the flask onto the embers, and vanished into the thicket.

The wagon had been looted. Vodka from the broken crates was dripping onto the road, and for a few yards around, the air was permeated by its strong, intoxicating smell.

The other horse was nowhere to be found. Evidently the bastards stole her. Or she got lost, the fool. But it wasn't worth it for him to look for her. Before it got too late, he had to clear out of here.

"Let's go," he said to the bay. "To hell with it all! The wagon, the harness, and your fool sister!"

Barefoot and miserable, he led the horse.

Why, Yeshua thought, on that fine cloudless day, why must I suffer so? How have I offended you, God? That I was born a Jew and sell vodka in this damned hole? If you people don't want to, don't drink! Do I force it down your throats? You open up your mouths yourselves . . . And you can't go a day without some drink. Not even a day—an hour! Holiday or not, misfortune or not, I have to put bottles on the table. Fill it up, dirty Jew, get moving! And the Jew won't act offended, no, no—you won't earn a kopeck if you're offended. The Jew bends over backward and runs with a tray to Jozef, and to Petras, and to Afinogen! And these Jozefs, Petrases, Afinogens—did they ever consider why he, a Jew, had opened his tavern here in the midst of thick forests and boggy swamps, and not somewhere on the other bank of the Neman? Because a German doesn't drink himself into a stupor, a German drinks just enough to entertain his spirit. You won't earn anything off a German. Open a tavern and the next day the gendarmes will turn up there and board it up. *Verboten! Der Kaiser erlaubt es nicht*, the emperor forbids it! But here . . . here neither the policeman nor the emperor will lay a finger on you! They will even thank you, for there's no better bondage than vodka. Why sentence people to hard labor when you can send them to him, to Yeshua! "Well done, Mandel, you are serving the fatherland, the throne!" When people hang around the tavern, when there's fog in their eyes, they don't demand *anything* except another bottle. Vodka is their overseer and guard. White, sweet and bitter, vodka will be forever. The whole Russian Empire rests on vodka, and may God let it continue. If you shut down Simkhe Vilner's shop of imported goods, or the Spivak brothers' hardware store, or Perelman's butcher shop, and board them up—nothing will change! The tavern is another matter. It is eternal, like the throne, like the fatherland. Yeshua will die and Simeon will stand behind the bar, Simeon will die and Chava will serve there, Chava will croak and Morta will start pouring, and if Morta is set on fire, the horse will take up the job—this very bay. Let anyone pour, so long as the mugs are filled!

On that fine summer day, the rank smoke of the forest tarred Yeshua's soul. The hair on his head was coated with white, and only his beard remained bluish black as before.

Yeshua didn't tell anyone about how he was almost burned alive, nor did he inform on Jozef. What was the point of telling? Let's say he was caught and convicted. So what? Is he the only one like that? You won't catch them all and lock them up in the cooler. You'll cause rumors to spread and only give people ideas—go out to the road, someone will say, tie him to a tree, and put brushwood underneath.

Even so, every time he entered the tavern Yeshua glanced around the tables searching for the one who had almost sent him, burned to a crisp, to his forefathers. He'd look at the mob of drunks and wince, because all of them, every last one, looked like Jozef!

With the help of the policeman Yeshua bought a rifle, and when he set out for Kovno, he put it under his seat. In truth, he didn't know how to handle it, but Nesterovich reassured him, not without derision, "If they don't kill you, you'll learn!"

Yeshua could send his son to Kovno, of course, but he was ill. And later—if he let him go to the city, he would stay for a week. He wouldn't spend money on business but on all kinds of mischief. He would leave the horses in the yard of the distillery and go to the whores. There on Vilenskaya Street they take fools like him to the cleaners. Once Yeshua had gone after him there. He whipped him and brought him home. Luckily Simeon didn't catch some shameful disease.

Morta was still around. He could trust her with everything—the load, the wagon, and even the tavern. She's a smart, clever, reliable girl; she works on Shabbes and holidays and returns all the proceeds to the last kopeck. She doesn't conceal anything. If Morta were Jewish, she would be completely suitable to be his daughter-in-law and she would bear him, Yeshua, a whole bunch of grandchildren. Merciful God, why did you invent so many different tribes? Wasn't one tribe—*human beings*—enough? On the earth there would be no Germans, no Russians, no Lithuanians, no Jews to praise You—only human beings! Master of the Universe, do you need to be a tavern keeper to understand this?

Yeshua sometimes took Morta with him on the road because he felt safer with her than with the gun. They wouldn't attack a woman, a Christian, especially if she dressed like an old woman. Who would hanker for an old woman? The tavern keeper would bury himself in the hay, fall asleep to the measured creak of the wheels, and wake up back home in their little town. Morta would shake him and say,

"Master! We're here!"

"Thank God! Thank God!" the sleepy Yeshua would mutter.

"Thank God and the horses," Morta said as she unharnessed them and patted their withers.

On the road Morta would talk about her village, about her father who was uncommonly strong, and her twin brothers, Petras and Povilas, named after the apostles. She often asked Yeshua about Siberia.

"Where is it?"

"Far away," the tavern keeper answered.

"How much does it cost to get there?"

"I don't know," the tavern keeper said, evading the question. "You can't get there by foot, and you don't have horses."

"One day, Master, you will give me yours . . . Haven't I earned that after so many years?"

"You have, you have." The tavern keeper fidgeted. "But to get that far you'll need more than a pair—a team of six."

"A pair is enough for me," Morta remained resolute.

"Let's say I give you my nags. Let's say you make your way—what will you do there?"

"I'll help my father and my brothers."

"And what if they have already died? What then?"

"Then I'll help the dead."

"How will you help the dead?"

"I'll die beside them. Otherwise I'll die in the tavern, and they'll bury me somewhere in the wasteland, like a cow . . . Who needs someone like that?"

"Like what?"

"A nobody . . . Not one of mine, not one of yours. So, Siberia is better."

Today Yeshua was returning home by himself. The wagon was packed to the top with vodka, and the horses moved slowly, staring at one another strangely, something they had never done before. A vague but intense anxiety crept into his heart. Yeshua even opened his collar, scratched his hairy chest, and planted the toe of his shoe on the gun. Yet all around lay stillness. The late summer twilight was descending lazily onto the forest, which seemed to be alive, full of mysterious rustlings.

Town was ten or fifteen miles away. Either from anxiety or from the substantial meal at Simkhe Vilner's, Yeshua suddenly writhed in pain. He released the reins, clutched his stomach, and began to knead it in an effort to soothe the colic. The pain didn't lighten, but instead became more intense, and as it spread to somewhere in the groin, the tavern keeper shouted "Whoa!"

He darted into the woods, quickly took off his pants and found a mossy spot beneath a spruce. Could he have caught an infection from Simeon? he wondered, looking beneath his feet at a small insect on the moss, alarmed by the yellow stream.

He remembered that on the profitable Saint John's Day—the summer before last—he had also been tormented in this forest, but the pain was different and more intense then. That time he thought that someone's envy and revenge might kill him, but now . . . now the pain came from the twisting in his own intestines, or else from a sickness he had caught from his son.

Yeshua's legs ached, but he didn't give in.

Above him the spruce stirred serenely. The noise wasn't from the leaves but was rather a calm sleepy hum that rose from the tree's core, from its very center.

Yeshua got up and put two fingers in his mouth, like two cartridges, and tried to vomit.

But his throat was blocked by fear.

Of what?

Of the forest? Of an illness? Maybe of the man in a yarmulke fastened to his hair with a pin? He had stopped by the tavern, and then the misfortunes began—colic, fever.

Why did Simeon throw him out?

Trying hard to overcome the pain, Yeshua made his way to the road, climbed into the wagon, and moved on.

God forbid I get sick. God forbid! On Assumption Day you can't even push your way into the tavern. On Assumption even women drink. What sort of people are these? Even death is a holiday for them! The death of the virgin, the death of Jesus Christ . . . What sort of people?

Yeshua had lived side by side with them for fifty years, but for the life of him, he didn't understand them . . . Not even Morta, he didn't understand her either. Who is she? A fool? A saint? An innocent? A fox?

They would soon be in town. They were passing Mishkine now, and from there it was a stone's throw to home.

The pain seemed to have faded.

As it should, Yeshua thought. The closer to home, the less the pain. Chava would brew horse sorrel and everything would be all right.

Beyond Mishkine, Markus Fradkin's forest had turned black. Yeshua always stopped at a fork in the road or turned into a clearing where the loggers would take two crates of vodka from him.

He didn't turn off today, though, today he would ride straight into town. The loggers in the forest will be patient, and if they feel a great urge, they'll send the Andronov brothers to the tavern—sturdy guys, they'll hoist the crates onto their shoulders and off they'll go to their spot in the woods. Markus Fradkin scowls at him anyway: "Why, Yeshua, do you make my people into drunks? They get plastered and sleep all day." Nothing satisfies Markus Fradkin. Chop and keep on chopping—he has no conscience. He should be happy that they drink. Some spare tree may be saved from chopping, but then, at the same time, they won't chop him either. When the brain sleeps, the axe sleeps. That's how it is, dear Mr. Fradkin. And he passes for a smart fellow!

Yeshua had not managed to pass through Mishkine and get on the Rukla country road before something in a spruce tree rattled and began tossing and turning like a wild boar, giving the tavern keeper the chills. He quickly let go of the reins and pulled the rifle out from under his seat. From lack of habit, and perhaps out of fear, Yeshua couldn't fix it on his shoulder. The gun kept slipping off, his hands were shaking a little, and his mouth was dry. His throat was so constricted it seemed that even a trickle of prayer could not break through, yet it did break through incoherently and feebly. A prayer had saved Yeshua many times; perhaps it would also save him from misfortune now.

The horses moved on quietly. In the twilight their heads swished like treetops.

Yeshua prayed, heeding every sound and every rustle, and when the stirring in the tree had calmed, he put his gun down between his legs and leaned on the barrel like a staff.

Then suddenly the horses shied away, and the tavern keeper felt chills again, stronger than before. He put the gun to his shoulder and said to whoever was there, "Don't come closer. I'll shoot."

"Shoot!" The word rang out in the silence. "You can't kill me anyway."

Yeshua's heart lifted. He recognized the voice of the tramp who had quarreled with Simeon at the tavern two weeks earlier.

"Anybody can be killed," Yeshua muttered calmly, feeling that everything around him—the forest and the Rukla country road and the serene heads of the horses—had regained their original nature and names. "Anybody can be killed," he repeated blithely, breathing lightly like a young man.

"I'm not anybody," the man in the velvet yarmulke said, continuing to move alongside the wagon.

"Every one of us is somebody," Yeshua said, squinting at the stranger. He didn't understand how this strange Jew had happened upon the Rukla road at a late and dangerous hour, staggering through the forest like a runaway convict.

"Will you give me a ride to Rakhmiel's barn?" the man in the yarmulke asked, stroking one of the horses as he went.

"You should ask the owner, not the horses," Yeshua said, pretending to be offended.

"I'll ask when the Master has been harnessed," the tramp answered and laughed.

"I like you," the tavern keeper mumbled. "Climb into the wagon."

The twilight grew thicker. Somewhere the first spark of light flickered, shyly, almost unreal. It blinked like a sore eye, and its blinking disturbed and taunted the darkness enveloping the wagon. The man in the yarmulke climbed into the wagon, found a spot behind the tavern keeper, and stared at his broad back, which was as gray as the country road, though not planted with trees.

Yeshua felt the glance, scratched his back, and kept silent, dismayed by the unexpected company.

"They say some Jew shot at the Governor," Yeshua whispered in a conspiratorial manner, and his own voice surprised him. "Apparently a search was announced."

The stranger was silent.

"I don't feel sorry for governors, but why should we shoot at them?" the tavern keeper continued, sprinkling his contentment with a touch of caution. "Bullets won't bring us happiness."

"Nor will money," the man in the yarmulke interjected, then once again dove into silence.

"Better money than bullets," Yeshua rattled on, delighted with his answer. "With rubles not only can you get to the Governor but to the Emperor himself. It's good for us and good for the authorities."

"Can you really buy your way out of hatred?"

"If only one could buy off pogroms . . . and death. Let them hate us, despise us, but let us live."

"Why live when there is hatred and contempt all around?"

"Why? In order to last until better times."

"Times don't change . . . not for Jews anyway. But why do you scratch yourself all the time?"

"Fleas," Yeshua lied.

"Isn't it fear biting you?" the man in the yarmulke asked frankly.

"Fear? And what, pray tell, should I fear? You?"

"If nothing else," the tramp said simply.

"Why be afraid of you? You're just a Jew like me."

Yeshua stopped scratching his back and fell silent. On both sides of the Rukla country road the forest rose in front of the wagon. The trees looked like a crowd of black-bearded widowers. They didn't move, and the still thick blackness released an eternal peace, emptiness, and either a blessing or a curse. The strange Jew who had perched behind Yeshua's back also resembled a tree—black and funereal. Yeshua remembered a saying of Rabbi Uri's: while we live, we are all like memorial trees. All of us. Sooner or later the Great Logger comes, and that's the end. You can't escape with a gun, a prayer, or with money.

"Why do you have such a strange yarmulke?" the tavern keeper asked, turning around for the first time.

"Strange? A yarmulke's a yarmulke," the fellow traveler said indifferently.

"And the pin?"

"The only thing left of my mother's."

"Did she die long ago?"

"Long ago. Drunks killed her. My mother used this pin to fasten a scrap of cloth with money to her blouse. One silver ruble and one paper one . . . The blood on this pin has not yet dried, and it won't. A mother's blood never dries. Never."

"It's safer in your pocket," Yeshua said, touched by his story.

"Safer, yes, safer. But who carries a memento in a pocket?"

This tramp is no simpleton, Yeshua thought. There's no reason to argue with him. A tamed wolf serves as a faithful dog.

Sensing that their home was near, the horses trotted more briskly as, with a gentle coolness granted by God, twilight washed over their flanks, drawn in behind the protruding bands of their ribs. God created horse and man on one day for good reason. If anyone in his life made Yeshua happy it was only them, his horses, especially the bay. Probably because Yeshua also loved the road. A hare would run across it, a bird would take wing, a roadside aspen would rustle, and his soul would feel lighter and brighter—you won't feel that way in the tavern or even in the synagogue. If only he could ride and ride and never have to harness the horses or cross a threshold—your own or anyone else's. There, on the other side of the threshold, all is vanity and eternal suffering.

"What are you looking for in our parts?" the tavern keeper asked more boldly. "Why did you leave your home?"

"What am I looking for?" The man in the yarmulke chewed over the question, grew thoughtful and, while listening attentively to the clatter of hooves, answered, "I'm looking for my mother's silver ruble. Did you come across it by any chance?"

"Where?"

"In your earnings."

"No," Yeshua said, with unfounded conviction. "I've come across all kinds of coins—silver and sometimes gold . . . but not your mother's."

"How do you know?"

"A ruble like that burns the palm . . ."

"Really?"

"I swear. The next morning there's a blister."

"I'll find it no matter what."

"Let's say you find it. So what? You can't buy a mother with a silver ruble."

"If I can't find it on earth, I'll search in Heaven." The man in the yarmulke lifted his head. "See that star over there?"

"I see it," the tavern keeper said with a feeling of doom.

"It's the silver ruble of someone's mother," the tramp noted. "It rolled up there and it's shining."

"How could it roll up there?" The tavern keeper was confused.

"Very simple," the man in the yarmulke explained. "Everything will go there. Everything."

"Rubles?"

"All our mothers, fathers, children . . . and rubles. But not everything will shine like stars."

"Why not?"

"To flare up like a star you must first bleed." He stopped speaking.

"Keep on talking," the tavern keeper spurred on the man in the yarmulke. "Your words make me feel better, though they also frighten me. Go on!"

"For today, perhaps, it's enough," the tramp said wearily. "Look. There's Rakhmiel's barn."

He's hiding something, and the thought of a secret brought Yeshua closer to this strange, spellbinding man. Everyone has some sort of secret. I have one too, the tavern keeper reflected as he stared intently into the dark and at the horses' drooping tails, which—another incomprehensible secret—seemed only to be given to horses to wave away horseflies.

"Listen," Yeshua said, seized by a twilight tenderness, "is there something you need?"

"I don't need anything," the tramp answered.

"Only the dead don't need anything," the tavern keeper replied, feeling hurt. "Don't be shy . . . ask! If you want, tomorrow we'll go to the bathhouse, wash, have a steam bath, and afterward we'll get our hair cut at Bershtansky's. I'm speaking from my heart. You have no idea . . . I've also had many troubles. I wandered, lived on the road, and walked around in hand-me-downs until I was thirteen. Who knows, maybe someday I'll also bleed, as you said. The summer before last I almost went up in flames. They tied me to a tree and lit a fire. I was terrified. But, to tell the truth, there was no need to be scared. I've been burning for a long time . . . My son is also burning, and my wife Chava, and the servant girl. Even the horses smell a little like smoke. Come to my place. Rakhmiel doesn't have a decent bed. Don't be afraid of my son. He's not bad . . . he's unhappy. I'll try to find some work for you. Are you listening?"

"Yes."

"You're listening but you don't believe me. Why, you say, is the tavern keeper Yeshua, who's nobody's fool, going out of his way to be kind to me. I'll tell you . . . I'll explain it to you now."

The roof of Rakhmiel's barn appeared for a moment in the dusk.

"Stop the wagon," the man in the yarmulke said.

"Wait! I'll explain now . . ."

But his fellow traveler jumped out of the wagon and walked quickly toward the barn.

Yeshua watched him for a long time, and after the man disappeared into a small grove of birches, the tavern keeper, hiding his hurt, spoke quietly to the bay. "No one believes anyone! God, why don't You just harness me to a wagon? I'll trot home from Vaysfeld's distillery and praise You for granting me such mercy, for not making me a human being! Someone always needs a horse. But who needs a man? A horse, a two-legged horse . . . a silver ruble in someone's pile of cash . . . a secret everyone is fed up with! Giddy up! Giddy up!"

7

At the moment when a messenger arrived with a document from the county police chief, sealed with an official stamp, regarding the urgent search for a state criminal who had made an attempt on the life of His Excellency the Vice-Governor, the town policeman Ardalion Ignatich Nesterovich was gathering strawberries in his garden with his nine-year-old son Ivan, whom he affectionately called Grozny, and his seven-year-old daughter Ekaterina, named after the celebrated empress. There were lots of strawberries. The beds were turning crimson beneath the sun, which beat down more intensely than usual at this time of year.

"Ivan, put fewer in your mouth and more in the basket," Nesterovich chided his son. "And you be more careful, Katenka! Berries, like children, want to be treated gently, tenderly."

The officer wore shabby pants with suspenders and a Persian cap, which he had acquired while serving in the Caucasus, before his transfer to Lithuania. Ardalion Nesterovich, with light wicker shoes on his feet, bent over for the berries in an orderly manner, like a soldier, then straightened his broad back, as strong as an oak door. He squinted from the sun, grunted happily, and looked doubtfully at the children.

"Ardasha, there's a messenger for you from the county," the policeman's wife Lukerya announced, wiping her sticky hands on her apron. "My jam will run over. Hurry up, change your clothes."

While Ardalion Nesterovich was changing into his uniform, the messenger—squat, fair-headed, with a nose as flat as a cigarette case—looked over the mansion. The house had two stories and was well built, though not of stone. Its windows were cleaned to a shine, with decorated frames; the porch was tall as a throne; the roof was covered with tin sheets rather than shingles; the outhouse had a neatly cut-out little heart; and the barn doors were flung wide open. Hens marched around the yard in an orderly manner, as if they had been drilled. Like a sentinel, a wide-winged rooster with a bright red crest stood guard on the fence. His comb sparkled like an enormous strawberry. A bit further from the house, apple trees bent under the weight of the fruit.

Nesterovich changed his clothes, unsealed the dispatch, read it from top to bottom and from bottom to top, as if admiring the chief's ornate signature. He then invited the messenger into the garden, where they sat beneath an apple tree.

"They're not leaving Russia in peace!" Nesterovich said.

"No, they're not," the messenger answered, casting a glance at the green apples hanging over his curly head.

Lukerya approached them silently, put a bottle of vodka on the table and some heavy silver glasses, a bowl of pickles, bread, and ham cut into slices, then just as silently left.

Nesterovich filled the glasses, braced himself as if getting ready to jump, and said, "We'll find the son of a bitch and deliver him in one piece to the county police station."

"Even if he's dead," the messenger remarked indifferently, over-turning his glass to show he didn't want any more vodka, and crunch-ing on a cucumber.

"No, my dear fellow! What good is a dead man?"

"What good is a live one?"

"You can hang a live one in full view of the public."

"A live one's no end of trouble," the messenger said, sticking to his guns. "You can hang one of ours and everyone will be quiet, but try to hang one of theirs and immediately the whole world's in an uproar. 'Oy, oy,'" he mimicked someone, "'they're disrespecting us and hounding us to death' . . . From the first day I served in the Pale of Settlement, I've understood them through and through."

"The son of a bitch won't leave us, he won't go," a tipsy Nesterovich threw out, and suddenly he yelled, "Ivan, Katerina! Come on, bring your baskets over here!"

The children brought the strawberries.

"Help yourself," Nesterovich told the messenger. "Straight from the garden. Meet the children. My son Ivan. The younger one—Ekaterina."

"Andrey Andreev."

"My first assistants," Nesterovich bragged. "Children, did you hear?" he turned to his son and daughter. "A Jew fired a shot at His Excellency."

Embarrassed, Ivan and Ekaterina remained silent. They looked at their father, and at the messenger, and then at their wicker shoes.

"So, children, shall we look for the Jew?"

The children became even more uncomfortable.

"Don't be shy, damn it. Shall we?"

"Yes," Ivan said.

"Good boy! And you, Katyushka?"

"I can't," the policeman's daughter said, at a loss. "I promised Mama that I'd help her make jam . . . Go look for him with Vanya."

"We'll make jam, and we'll also catch the Jew," Nesterovich said, almost in a singsong, while gnawing a tough chunk of ham with his yellow teeth.

"Yes," Ekaterina gave in.

The children hung around the table for a while, then took a half-empty basket and returned to the garden downcast and despondent. The rooster on the fence sang lustily, and the hens answered his singing with impatient and appreciative clucks. A stray bumblebee buzzed in the branches of the apple tree, and its buzzing angered the messenger. He gave it dirty looks, but the bee continued to drone with impunity and argue with the apple tree about something.

Nesterovich asked about the health of His Excellency the Vice-Governor, and after learning that there was no cause for concern (the bullet passed through his right shoulder, but didn't harm the lung), he began the farewells.

Nesterovich walked the messenger all the way to the main road, handed him a birch-bark box of strawberries, half-listened to his drunken words of gratitude, and, tipsy himself as well as tired from the heat and bureaucratic fervor, returned to his home.

Couldn't this scoundrel, this Jew, wait until the winter when there are no mushrooms or berries? During the entire short day, all you do is walk around town and look into Jewish faces, asking who's that one, who's this one? Now, when there's a lot of garden work, when the cow will calve any day, when he, Nesterovich, was planning to put a new roof on the barn (Markus Fradkin brought him boards long ago), right now he would have to let everything go to hell just to snoop around, search out, hunt down. His Excellency was alive, thank God, he would lie in bed for two weeks and get better. Was it really necessary, as the dispatch said, to search for this Yankel or Moyshe immediately? Did it matter if they hang him in six months or a year? The throne won't collapse—but meanwhile he, Nesterovich, wouldn't be able to pickle or dry mushrooms for the winter, and the barn roof would keep on leaking . . .

Nesterovich felt embarrassed in front of the children. He had behaved stupidly and should ask for forgiveness. What he did was obviously not enough to make them into hounds, to make them hunt people, for what is a Jew or a Lithuanian to them? It doesn't matter whether they are the ones with beards or others—sometimes you can't even tell them apart. When you have such a low rank you can go too far in expressing your feelings of loyalty to the state. A messenger might come to the county police station and report to the official there, "The policeman Nesterovich even enlisted his children on the search . . . They'll catch the Jew together!" Not on your life! Whatever happens, he won't get his children involved in this business; if he did, he'd have to kick himself later. If that Yankel or Moyshe fired at the vice-governor, he's not afraid of the gallows, and he wouldn't spare cartridges for Vanya and Katyushka. No matter how valuable the official's praise, the children are more precious. Poor things, they don't see the world at large here. After they take a trip to the city on the Feast of the Protection, they're happy—they've seen the priest in the church, played with their own kind in the church vestibule, and heard their native Russian language.

What luck he had! Five years he'd spent on guard in the Caucasus, where it's like pulling teeth just trying to pronounce the name of a Caucasian village and there's gunfire and pursuits every day. You return, stagger into bed, only manage to stretch your legs, and again you hear the cry: "To arms!" Then it's back to the mountains and gorges. When I was transferred here, I thought the country was subdued, quiet, with forests and swamps, and I'd live like a man. I started a family, Lukerya bore Ivan, and two years later, Katyushka. In this small town there are only Jews, and it stinks from their garlic, but at least they aren't mountain folk—garlic's not a bullet, and even if your nose wrinkles from the smell, it won't kill you. The Lithuanians here have entrenched themselves like moles in their farmsteads. They sow and plow, they don't stick their necks out. They tried to rebel in 1863 but didn't have what it takes against Count Muravyov, and they were put down quickly. You'd think you could enjoy life, pickle mushrooms and cabbage, make jam—but no, people always demand something. Some want equality while others want schools, but how can His Majesty the Czar provide these things to everyone? Consider the Germans: all kinds of nationalities also live on their territory, but everything stays German—it's German equality, German schools. No one rebels or shoots at the vice-governor or roams the forests.

Just then Nesterovich remembered the tavern keeper's son. That's who would help him! Pimpleface Simeon knows every single one of the Jews from the latest beggar to Markus Fradkin. Simeon is a slovenly fellow, lazy but bright. Nesterovich had solicited his help earlier, but at the time Simeon avoided an answer, didn't say yes or no.

"To the tavern, Ardalion, to the tavern," the policeman said aloud while walking faster. Denied the opportunity to command a regiment, a company, or at least a squad, Nesterovich—especially when under the influence—gave orders to himself, and during such moments he felt like a field marshal, rather than a county officer of low rank. "To the tavern!"

Pimpleface Simeon was able to walk now, though he was weak. His face had thinned, his nose had become sharp.

"Are you still sick?" Nesterovich asked, clasping the bed's carved headboard.

"Yes, I'm sick," Simeon answered sullenly.

"It's a sin to loll around in bed these days," the policeman said in a deep voice. "If you're just lolling around alone." He grinned.

"Are you going to drink?"

"No. A messenger from the county came, and the two of us shared a bottle."

"You could have waited until I recover," Pimpleface Simeon said under his breath.

"Gladly, Simeon Yeshuevich," the policeman addressed him using his patronymic, "but the matter is urgent. As I just reported, a messenger from the county came and brought a dispatch. An attempt on the vice-governor in Vilna . . . A search has been declared for the whole Northwest territory."

"What does that have to do with me?" Simeon pretended to be unconcerned. "*I* didn't shoot at him."

"One of yours fired the shot."

"So what?"

"So, Simeon Yeshuevich, I thought that one of his own would be more likely to nab him."

"One of his own is more likely to nab him, and also more likely to let him go," the tavern keeper's son said, to provoke the policeman.

"If yours is ours, then he won't let him go," Nesterovich grinned. "Didn't we make some sort of deal?"

"We made a deal," Simeon agreed.

"There's a reward for him," Nesterovich let up a bit. "Five hundred gold . . ."

"Jews have gone up in value," the tavern keeper's son muttered. "In the past they didn't give more than a hundred for them. His Excellency was killed, then?"

"Injured."

"A pity."

"For whom?"

That's my answer, you drunken puss, Pimpleface Simeon thought.

"How should we split it? Half to me, half to you? Yes, or what?"

"A quarter's enough for me," Nesterovich answered seriously, impressed by his own generosity.

"Isn't that a lot to ask?" Simeon mumbled derisively.

"We'll fix things somehow," the policeman said, and winced. "Just help . . . sniff out . . . scout out . . ."

"Sniff out with you! Why did you drag yourself here in broad daylight?"

"Maybe I came for vodka."

"You may be able to catch a Jew, but not cheat him. This town is small, and everything's out in the open."

Pimpleface Simeon played with him like a cat with a mouse, and the game gave him a strange, almost unbearable pleasure. He experienced something unlike anything he'd ever felt before—he seemed to have split completely into two parts. He had grown another skin that was thick and invulnerable, and behind which, as if behind a fortress wall, the real Simeon Mandel was coming into being.

"Stop coming to see me in the daytime."

"Yes, Sir!" The words escaped from Nesterovich abruptly, and he stared at the tavern keeper's son in dismay.

"Have they identified his distinctive features?" Simeon asked impatiently, turning to look at the door—was Morta standing there eavesdropping?

"Yes, they have."

"Tell me and make it fast! Our talk has dragged on too long."

"Right away, Simeon Yeshuevich, right away, just let me remember. It's a pity I didn't bring the dispatch with me. Everything is listed there: average height, weak build, frail, a beard . . ."

"Nothing there about a yarmulke with a pin?"

"Nothing about a yarmulke with a pin."

"According to your list, you might as well go up to anyone and seize him by the collar! You don't remember any special feature?"

"No. But why did you ask about a yarmulke with a pin, Simeon Yeshuevich?" Nesterovich pricked up his ears.

"It doesn't matter."

"Don't lie. You had a reason to ask. Tell me, brother, honestly, like a friend. You know that concealing information can get you hard labor."

"A man like that dropped by the tavern."

"With a beard?"

"With a beard and frail . . . But he doesn't look like a killer."

"How long ago?"

"Before I fell ill. About two weeks ago, and I quarreled with him. He sat in the corner looking at everyone, not drinking. I went over to him and said, 'Can I pour you a glass?' He says, 'I've been served. Can't you see?' I look at the table—there's no mug, no glass. 'What was served?' He answers me, 'Our suffering! A full glass! Sit down, and we'll drink together!'"

"Well," Nesterovich prompted Simeon. "What happened next?"

"Next? Next I threw him out!"

"A mistake, a mistake," the policeman said, distressed. "You should have sat with him for a while, to find out about . . . how did he put it . . . 'our suffering.'"

"It was because of him I fell ill."

"Because of him?" Nesterovich's colorless eyes grew larger.

"He cursed me. 'You'll shake from fever!' he said. For two weeks I was shaking, and I'm still not my old self. My legs are like putty, I take one step and they buckle."

"Where is he now?"

"I don't know. Probably roaming around somewhere nearby. Where can he go?"

"Strange, very strange," Nesterovich said. "You say he doesn't look like a killer. But if I'm without boots and a uniform I also don't look like . . ."

"A killer?"

"You joke, Simeon Yeshuevich, but don't forget. You yourself know that I'm with your people with all my heart . . . I haven't hurt anyone yet, though the esteemed Police Chief Nuikin and even the priest in the church say that you're all a band of thieves. That if you were free to do it, you'd take all of Russia into your hands and lease it out to the Germans at high interest. But I'm sticking to my own opinion. People are people, I say. You just need to issue a decree, baptize all of them, and convert the baptized ones to Russian Orthodoxy. Then there will be more order and peace."

"But don't baptized men also shoot at vice-governors?"

"They do shoot, true, but bullets from one of our own shoot straight, while yours are like shrapnel—they shoot in all directions."

There was a knock on the door.

Pimpleface Simeon said, "Come in, Morta, come in!"

She stuck her head in the door and asked, "Do you want something to eat?"

"I do," Simeon said.

"Should I also serve Mr. Policeman?" Morta asked.

"Thank you kindly," Nesterovich answered and bowed in jest.

Morta didn't leave, though.

"I'll eat alone today," Simeon said, and she disappeared.

"So, Simeon Yeshuevich, is it a deal?"

"We'll talk when I'm better."

"Why drag it out? I'm not proposing anything shameful. Is it shameful to serve the fatherland?"

"I don't have a fatherland," Simeon said quietly.

"How is that possible?"

"I don't, and that's it. The tavern—even that's not my fatherland."

"But everything around, everything but the tavern—the land, the forest, the fields . . ."

"I'd like to pray before dinner," Pimpleface Simeon said. "I haven't prayed for two weeks now."

"Pray." Nesterovich gave in. "Put your trust in God, but don't slip up."

He suddenly scowled, lowered his head, bit his blood-red lips, and headed for the door.

"If I learn anything, I'll let you know. But don't come here again."

"If you help find him . . . the whole five hundred's yours. I swear! You think a policeman has no conscience or honor?"

"When I'm thinking about God, I can't think about the police," Simeon said and looked up. But Nesterovich was no longer in the room.

The tavern keeper's son walked over to the eastern wall and began murmuring his daily prayers. He did not pray because he believed in God, but because he longed for different words, words other than "vice-governor," "money," "bed," or "food." True, the Hebrew words in the prayers were familiar, but there was a different, otherworldly sense about them, both inoffensive and captivating. The only thing that bothered Pimpleface Simeon was a wall—numb, soundless, unresponsive. It loomed before him at home and in the synagogue. For him even the sky, where God dwells, was simply an enormous light-blue or cloud-covered wall tipped over backward, which no single mortal had the strength to break through. Unlike his father, who bombarded the Almighty with petty and needless requests, Simeon instructed God and constantly tried to make Him understand that—if the wall between mortals and the object of their prayers would collapse, if men became clearly convinced of their power and they stopped fearing the cauldrons of boiling tar waiting for sinners—everyone in the world would be allowed to do anything. They would kill, hang, betray, renounce, and denounce. If the Third Department, the empire's political police, was more powerful than God, it was only because the policemen's reward—five hundred or five thousand gold coins—could be touched by human hands, and its effects could be felt on your own skin. As for God? His gold and his gallows, his anointing oil and tar are there, beyond the clouds. Therefore, don't fear and honor God, but fear and honor Ardalion Nesterovich, the county Police Chief Nuikin . . . and if you can, become a policeman yourself. Not necessarily in uniform.

Morta brought in the food while Simeon was standing at the eastern wall, putting on his *lapserdak*.

As he ate, bolts of thunder rolled in from somewhere beyond the forest, and he half-heartedly scooped up spoonfuls of the sorrel soup with sour cream. Outside the window strips of lightning streaked across the sky—flashing, flooding the whole sky, then fading away. Unexpectedly the sad thought came to Simeon that he was like lightning himself, but without thunder and without a sky. If he could set fire to someone, it would only be to himself. He was unhappy, not loving anyone, not loved by anyone. He had lived in the world for more than thirty years, and what had he seen, what had he become? A parasite, a loudmouth, a dumbass, a serf girl's boyfriend, the accomplice of a policeman. Yet not that long before, about ten years earlier, he had dreamed of becoming a great rabbi, like Rabbi Eliyahu, the Vilna Gaon. He had dreamed of devoting himself to ridding Jews of their vices, of their humiliating servility before every policeman, and of leading them out of captivity, as Moses led the Jews out of Egypt.

How often he saw himself at the head of a crowd. He heard his thundering voice say, "Jews! I call you to the land of your forefathers. All who have at least a drop of honor and dignity, follow me! Follow me, sons and daughters of Israel!"

How did it end, though?

It always ended the same way, in indifference and fear. Damned Jewish fear. It turned out that a rundown store, a tavern, barbershop . . . were valued more than the stones of the Temple in Jerusalem.

Even his own father, who had sent him to study with Rabbi Uri and later to the yeshiva in Telšiai, said: "Simeon! Give up this nonsense, better to take up a trade. Your bones will rot before the Jews gather in the Promised Land. Take these two hundred rubles for a start. Open a shop, sell herring, and forget about the stones from the Temple in Jerusalem."

He obeyed. He opened a shop but went bankrupt because the Jews bought their herring from his neighbor, not from him.

When Pimpleface Simeon returned to the town, he no longer wanted anything—not herring and not Jerusalem stones. Herring simply made him sick, and from that time on it wasn't served in the tavern, though the tavern keeper Yeshua suffered losses as a result.

Simeon finished eating. He put his bowl on the table and lay down.

Beyond the forest it continued to thunder, and the lightning, unusually bright and fleeting, flashed in the window like a bad omen.

At last the rain started. Large drops pecked at the glass like chickens at crumbs of bread.

The tavern keeper Yeshua tiptoed into the room.

"Are you awake?" he asked.

"What do you want?" Simeon rudely answered his father.

"Nothing."

"If nothing, why did you come?"

Pimpleface Simeon was looking for a fight, but Yeshua was ready.

"Greetings from Vaysfeld," the tavern keeper said from a distance.

"I'm supposed to believe you?"

"It's God's truth. Vaysfeld asked about your health. You also have greetings from Simkhe Vilner."

"He also asked about my health?" Simeon gave his father an angry look.

"He always asks . . . Even if he's distant, he's still a relative."

"That's all?"

"All what?"

"All the greetings?"

"So it seems."

"I'm touched." Without warning Pimpleface Simeon got out of bed, walked up to his father, took him by the shoulders, turned him toward the door, and commanded in a wheezing voice, "Leave! Or else, God forbid, you'll get infected."

Yeshua bore even this insult.

"Yes," the tavern keeper said thoughtfully. "The whole house is in a fever . . . from the floor to the roof . . . and the flames are spreading from here to the rest of the town."

"What are you talking about?"

"I saw him . . . the one with the velvet yarmulke."

"Where?" Simeon perked up.

"I took him to Rakhmiel's barn."

"You . . . gave him a ride?"

"What of it? A Jew has to get along even with the devil."

"So, what did you learn?"

"He's an orphan. Pogrom thugs killed his mother, and he says that the blood hasn't dried."

"What blood?"

"His mother's. On that pin he wears."

"He's lying, the dog!"

"I drove him from the fork in the road to the edge of town, and I can't get him out of my head. I tossed and turned all night, couldn't sleep."

"He went to Rakhmiel's barn, you said?"

"Yes," the tavern keeper answered. "Leave him alone, Simeon! Maybe he's not to blame for your illness. I even invited him here. We'll feed him, give him some money for the road, and let him go in peace."

Pimpleface Simeon was silent as he thought it over.

"And if he doesn't come?"

"So much the better," Yeshua answered.

"No," the son objected. "He won't get away so easily."

"Why take another sin upon your soul?"

"One or one hundred . . . Whoever is guilty of one is guilty of all."

"So according to you I'm responsible for the policeman's sins?" Yeshua needled his son.

"You *are* responsible!" Simeon exclaimed. "Do you grab his hands when he is flogging someone or when he sticks them into someone else's pocket? We're all sinners. This wretch of yours with the yarmulke, too. His sin just needs to be dug up. And I'll uncover it even if it kills me. So the vile righteous one turned up. God's messenger . . . We're all the devil's messengers, all of us . . . Get out!"

"Oh, my God! We're burning, burning," Yeshua muttered.

"Yes, we're burning," Pimpleface Simeon said. "We burn and we burn, and we put out the flames with vodka."

At the door Yeshua turned around.

"Why did Nesterovich come to see you?"

"He passed on greetings," Simeon grinned. "From the county Police Chief Nuikin, from the Vice-Governor of Vilna, from His Majesty Czar Alexander II. They inquired about my health and asked if the merchant Simeon Mandel is in need of anything."

"Don't have anything to do with him," the tavern keeper advised.

"And who should I have something to do with? Markus Fradkin? The Spivak brothers? To them I'm a tavern keeper's bastard, and they can smell the vodka on me from a mile away."

"You can leave here."

"And go where? Kovno? Vilna?"

"America."

"What, to sell herring? Some policeman or official there will keep an eye on the merchant Simeon Mandel. Why change officers?"

"For a clever Jew, a policeman's not an obstacle."

"But I'm not clever, I'm a fool. For a fool even his own father is an obstacle."

"You're still sick, Simeon."

"I've never been well."

"Even so, I advise you to keep a little distance from Nesterovich. If a Jew can achieve something in life, then it's with his own hands, not with other people's handcuffs."

Three days later Pimpleface Simeon stepped outside for the first time. He loitered around the courtyard and the tavern, took deep breaths, and didn't think about a thing. For a long time he sat beneath a wild pear tree and looked at the small, shriveled fruit, the gnarled trunk, and the crystal-clear sky. A single stray cloud was making its way somewhere, fast and light as a child's dream. Simeon followed it with a sorrowful, envious glance, and the cloud, lit by this foreign pain, seemed to slow its flight.

"Why are you sitting here?" Morta asked him.

"I'm looking." Pimpleface Simeon paused, then added: "Up there, that cloud . . . what do you think it looks like?"

"What?" Morta lifted her head. "A cat . . . There's its face, and there's its tail."

"A cat, you say," Simeon drawled, disappointed by her choice. "I thought that—of course, it's stupid— I thought that it's like my soul . . ." He laughed. "A small white speck in immense emptiness that rushes, flies, and dissolves. No one, not even God or the devil gives a damn about it."

"Let's go water the horses instead of sitting here," Morta suggested unexpectedly. "I'll lead the chestnut and you take the bay."

"Let's go," Simeon agreed just as unexpectedly.

They went through the woods. Morta walked ahead, leading the chestnut horse by the reins, and Simeon and the bay were close behind. Shaking off pine needles from their manes, the horses moved at a slow trot.

Simeon was looking at Morta's tan neck, at her strong legs rustling through the grass, and with every step he felt his own strength returning as well as the cravings of his body, which had been starved but not suppressed by his illness.

"I'm going to bathe," Morta said after the horses had been given water.

"I will, too," Simeon went along.

"You can't . . . Look the other way!"

"All right."

"Don't look!"

"My God! Another Virgin Mary!" He let out a deep breath and looked away.

Morta quickly threw off her skirt and her blouse, then plunged into the water in her chemise.

Her hair swayed like a plant in the water, and from under her chemise her breasts glowed like ripe pears.

"Now you can look!" she cried as she swam farther from the shore.

The chestnut and bay stood in the water, with their large, tired heads touching. Their manes were entangled, their legs entwined, their nostrils widened, and their whiskers rose, the way an ear of grain sprouts from the earth—soundlessly, sensuously, insistently.

When Morta stepped out of the water, she grabbed her clothes, rushed into the bushes, and dressed without wringing out her hair.

"You're beautiful," the tavern keeper's son said.

"It's all in your imagination, Simonas!"

"Beautiful," he mumbled. "And I know what I want . . ."

"I don't know," Morta said warily.

"I want—to be like them . . . like our horses . . . our manes together . . . our legs joined . . . one mouth."

"Stop it, Simonas! For the sake of all the saints!"

Morta rushed to the river, drove the chestnut and the bay from the water, gripped the reins and, without looking back, began walking away. She remembered a day ten years earlier, returning from the watering place, when she and Simeon found themselves on her father's land. The cottage had fallen to pieces and the pond was covered with duckweed. Morta circled the courtyard, looked at a boarded-up window, picked up a rotten wooden shoe from the ground, pulled it onto her bare foot, and mournfully said, "Mama's shoe . . . Mama's."

Pimpleface Simeon, then young and restless, sat on the chestnut and waited for Morta to cry to her heart's content. He simply could not understand why she had dragged him to this wasteland, this ravaged and godforsaken yard where there was nothing for even the wind to do—the shutters had been ripped off, the trees chopped down, and the grass was not growing.

"Sargis's doghouse!" Morta was overjoyed. "And the chain. Can I . . ." she turned to Simeon, "take it?"

"It's yours, rust and all," the tavern keeper's son muttered, astride his horse.

"Can I?"

"As far as I'm concerned, you can take everything—the chain, the shoe, the doghouse."

"Only the chain, Simonas."

Her impulsive questioning and submissiveness grated on him.

"Go on, take it! Take it," he had brushed the matter aside. Without a word, Morta threw the chain over the bay's rump, looked around the vacated land one more time, and tugged at the bridle.

"Sometimes I envy your people," Simeon said when their horses drew level.

"Us?"

"Your father, your brothers, you . . . Lithuanians, in general."

"Why envy us? We have nothing."

"You have a chain that attaches you to this sky, this field, this doghouse. We don't have a chain like that. Do you understand? We don't have one!"

"But you have money. With money you can buy everything."

"You can't buy such a chain with money. People pay for it with blood . . . and a sentence of hard labor."

How strange. Why did she remember that time, that conversation, and the chain? Was there anything left of her father's house? Suddenly Morta felt she was being pulled there, pulled powerfully, irresistibly, as if everything had come alive again—the well and the shutters and the cow. As if once again, after so many years, the boarded-up windows were open wide, and in the farthest one, the one that looked out on the garden, her mother stood in a colorful shawl, shouting in a loud voice, as if to the whole world, "M-o-r-t-a-a-a!"

"Go the rest of the way by yourself," Simeon's hoarse baritone broke into her recollections. At Rakhmiel's barn he gave her his horse and said, "I have some business with the night watchman . . . If my father asks where I am, say that I'm at the river."

"Will you return soon?"

"Yes."

Pimpleface Simeon did not find the night watchman at home. Behind the house, in the garden, Kazimieras was puttering about, the same Kazimieras who on the Sabbath would blow out the candles for all the Jews in town.

"Where is Rakhmiel?"

"He left."

"By himself?"

"By himself."

"People say that some kind of tramp is living with him."

"Aaron," Kazimieras readily explained.

"Aaron?"

"His stepson."

"Are you by chance getting things mixed up?"

"Maybe I'm mixed up," Kazimieras lifted the shovel again. Long talks tired him, and he became tired from words faster than from the pitchfork or sickle. "Wait, Rakhmiel will come back, he'll explain everything to you."

8

When will Father come? When?

Zelda, Markus Fradkin's daughter, is sitting at the piano and playing a Bach fugue. No one is home except Osher's widow Golda, the cook and housemaid. Zelda's father never stays in the backwoods for long. After all, he's a timber merchant; he travels all over the northwest territory, arguing with raftsmen and spending his time in sawmills. Her older brother Zelik, his wife, and his feebleminded mother-in-law live in Vilkija, where he manages a match factory. When he comes here, it's not for long, a week or two at most. They gulp down spoonfuls of linden honey and eat handfuls of wild strawberries or blueberries. Her brother Zelik hunts quails and woodcocks, which he brings home in a game bag, throws on the kitchen table, and proudly says to Golda, "Pluck them!"

Golda plucks them, and at night the plucked birds fly in Zelda's dreams.

Father sometimes brought suitors to her who were quiet and undemanding, like the scarecrows in the garden. He made Zelda play the piano for them and recite Russian poems, and the suitors were overcome by insincere bouts of ecstasy. After they left, a smell of stupidity and pure sweat remained in the house and, at Zelda's request, Golda aired out the rooms for a long time. Zelda might have married one of them, but she didn't want to give birth to Jews. If she did, she'd be sentencing her children to the Pale of Settlement and, as from a sentence of hard labor, they wouldn't be pardoned. But her father will never give her away to a non-Jew. Never. A non-Jew could be absolutely anything—a friend, a customer, a companion—but not a relative, let alone a husband.

Zelda sits at the piano and imagines she is not Fradkin's daughter but some Princess Trubetskoy, who has just followed her Decembrist husband into permanent exile; the role of faithful wife and martyr pleases her deeply, though no one she knows—not her brother Zelik, not the tavern keeper's son Simeon, and not the local policeman, Nesterovich—resembles a disgraced prince, and the only rattle of chains comes from their old hunting dog, Cain.

Zelda lets her fingers sink down onto the keys, and she falls into a sweet and fluid reverie. The faces of her martyrs and heroes appear out of the disparate sounds and thoughts; they take on form, rise, and disappear. Among them is the face of Verochka Karsavina, her best friend at school. Zelda and Verochka once came up with a plan to work as nurses fighting cholera in Saratov province, probably in Rtishchevo, but Zelda's father put up a fight.

"It's their cholera," he said. "Verochka can go to Saratov, but you're going to Petersburg."

Verochka went to Rtishchevo, fell ill, and didn't return. Zelda was not admitted to the Higher Courses for Women in Petersburg.

Zelda remembers how she and Verochka Karsavina played this fugue as a duet, and she remembers Verochka's long and thin fingers, like holiday candy canes.

Zelda also remembers her graduation ball in the large, bright hall of the gymnasium. She's wearing a fancy dress and black patent-leather shoes, standing against a wall with a portrait of His Imperial Majesty Alexander II. His Majesty looks at her in a stern, patriarchal manner, gives her courage, and she smiles at him and at Verochka Karsavina, who whirls past, dancing to a sparkling waltz. Verochka tosses back her elegant, delicate head and laughs, and her laugh is carefree and infectious.

"Why aren't you dancing, Zelda?" Verochka asks, laughing.

Why? Zelda just shrugs her shoulders. She is the only Jew at the ball. Once Noah Berman, a lawyer's son, was also there, but he died a year ago. When Noah was alive, he always asked her to dance and clasped her to his hollow chest, which had been ravaged by tuberculosis. Noah loved her. All the dead ones loved her—mama and grandmother. But what good is the love of the dead to Zelda? What good is that?

She looks enviously at her girlfriend and then at His Imperial Majesty, and she imagines that he steps out of his portrait, clicks his heels in front of her, twists his hussar mustache, and begins to whirl her around the floor. Everyone makes way for them as the czar whirls and whirls her.

"I'm a Jew, Your Majesty," Zelda says.

"Really?" The czar is amazed. "I'd never have believed it."

"A Jew, a Jew, a Jew," she repeats to the beat of the festive music. The czar presses himself against her tightly like the consumptive Noah Berman.

"At a ball all are equal," the sovereign says casually.

And following him, echoing the sovereign of all White Russia and Little Russia, these words are repeated in a singsong fugue by the headmaster, Aristarkh Fyodorovich Bogoyavlensky, by the ferociously anti-Semitic Latin teacher Kozhinov and by Father Georgi in his floor-length silk cassock: "At a ball all are equal . . . at a ball all are equal . . . at a ball all are equal."

When will Father come? When?

Zelda suddenly switches from the Bach fugue to a waltz. My God, how boring this is! Your Majesty, why is it so boring after the ball? Father is probably bargaining with someone right now, counting losses and profits. And what joy do his profits bring? He'll build another house, buy forty more silver spoons and forks, order a new coat from the most fashionable tailor in Kovno and hang it in the wardrobe, where it will be eaten by moths. All of father's trust in money is useless. Did it open the door for her to the Higher Courses for Women in Petersburg?

Verochka Karsavina had tried to talk her into getting baptized.

"But you're Russian," she earnestly tried to persuade her. "What kind of Jew are you? You just have a Jewish name and maybe eyes, but they only look a little Jewish when you're sad. I'll talk to Father Georgi, if you'd like."

She's right, what kind of Jew am I? Apart from her identity papers and sympathy for her people, nothing Jewish is left. Language? She speaks Russian a thousand times better than Yiddish. In any case, no one has ever laughed at her accent; she can even roll her "r"s like a Russian.

"*Karl u Klary ukral korally!* Karl stole Clara's corals," she used to shout the tongue twister triumphantly during breaks at school, without a trace of a Jewish accent.

Father and brother Zelik clung to Judaism, though more for the sake of propriety than from devotion. Russia is a sea, but Judaism is a pond . . . or a little stream overgrown with duckweed . . . a swamp, a quagmire.

Something kept Zelda from taking that step. Would her life really be better as a convert to Russian Orthodoxy, a "convert from the *zhids*"? Someone would dig back to her grandmother Hinda, to her mother Sara, to her father, Markus Fradkin, and to her brother Zelik, and the boundless sea would immediately turn back into the same shallow little stream teeming with leeches and native frogs.

After they returned from Petersburg with nothing to show, father offered her a place in his office in Vilkija, but Zelda turned down the office job. What did she care about how many logs were floated and how many rafted? Poring over papers, checking accounts, catching errors in bills of sale—that's also like changing faith. Zelda Fradkin of the *mercantile* faith. Oh, how merry, how happy she had felt after the ball!

When will he come? When?

Father had promised to bring a piano tuner from Kovno.

When he brings him, Zelda will approach him and say, "Kind sir, first of all, be so good as to tune *me*! Something inside is broken."

Nonsense, nonsense. She won't tell him anything. She won't tell anyone anything. Something is broken inside everyone. Everyone. Probably because happiness is boring, and unhappiness exciting.

Soon it will be the Feast of the Assumption. Zelda will go to the Catholic Church and give to the poor.

"Your daughter's kindness has no limits. But is it right for a Jewish woman to stand in front of a church and give handouts to gentiles?" the young Rabbi Hillel would complain to her father.

Rabbi Hillel need not worry: You can also do good out of boredom. She'll remain a Jew because the Russians are also bored. And the Lithuanians and Kalmyks, and whatever you call them, the Nogais. Oh, how boring it is after the ball, Rabbi Hillel! As the Torah says: "God created a bored man from the dust of the earth, and blew boredom into his nostrils, and man became a bored creature . . . and God planted a boring garden in Eden where he placed the man he had created out of boredom."

Golda enters the room with a rag in hand.

"You're still playing, Miss?" she remarks. "Why don't you take a walk while I wash the floors, before your little pupils arrive?"

"Go ahead and clean," Zelda answers, leaning back against her chair, and for a long time she rubs her hands, which are stiff from playing.

"Don't get angry at me, Miss, but the best music is a man." Golda bursts into laughter, then dips the rag in a bucket.

"And you? Have you had many?" Zelda asks unexpectedly.

"Good God, no!" Osher's widow shakes the rag, and dirty drops splash on the silent piano.

"And when you don't love?" Zelda presses, without turning to her. "What kind of music is there then?"

"What's true is true. When you don't love, there's no music but—and don't be angry, Miss—there's a grinding sound . . . it's like they're sawing wet logs in the yard."

Golda bursts out laughing again and starts wiping the floorboards in a cheerful frenzy.

"And your lodger?" Zelda continues. "Who is he?"

"Itsik." Golda arches her back like a cat. "A logger."

"A Jewish logger?"

"One of your papa's workers. Go on and play, Miss, play. It's nicer to wash floors to music."

Zelda doesn't even touch the keys. She watches Golda, her tousled hair, her tucked-up homemade skirt, her heavy calves.

"In the synagogue your lodger won't take his eyes off me."

"A young bull looks at the whole herd," Osher's widow says, working the rag around the mistress's feet. "Raise your legs, please. My God, they're so thin!"

"A leg's a leg," Zelda says defensively and for some reason draws back. *The best music is a man*, she thinks to herself. Crude, but perhaps true. It's not fresh air that cures melancholy, and not Bach or Chopin—it's love and death. Verochka Karsavina said that "everyone in the world is powerless before one tyrant—and that tyrant is love."

"Your little pogromniks will come and make things dirty," Golda grumbles.

"They're not pogromniks."

"Like father, like children."

"The father's not like that, either. Police officer is a rank and not a vice."

"Don't be angry, Miss, but you don't know people at all. Police officer is a rank *and* a vice."

Maybe Golda is right. Maybe she shouldn't have had anything to do with Nesterovich. But he had pleaded to the point of tears.

"Think about it," he said, "the nearest school's almost fifteen miles away. The kids will run wild."

"But I'm not a teacher," Zelda had objected. "I'm an ordinary person . . . and a Jew besides."

"So, does a Jew always have to teach stupid things?" the policeman said, sweet-talking her.

"If you're not afraid of me, then bring them," Zelda acquiesced.

"What's there to fear? The Fradkins are virtuous and trustworthy people."

As long as trustworthiness is determined by policemen, there won't be any trustworthy people, Zelda thought, but she kept silent.

"Go on, Miss, go outside." Golda says as she works. "The little devils will wait for you. I'll wash the floors and heat up the bathhouse.

God willing, maybe Reb Markus and Zelik will come down to hunt. I haven't plucked game for a long time . . . a very long time."

Zelda goes out to the garden.

She walks over to the doghouse and tousles Cain's hair. Cain sits on his hind legs and whines nobly. His face is tired and intelligent, like a human's. His brown eyes water in the bright sun, but they watch with sympathy and anticipation.

"How about a walk, Cain?"

The dog's eyes shine with happiness. Usually, they leave the house before evening and wander across the fields and through the groves. Cain scares off birds and Zelda thinks about her life which, apart from the ball, has had nothing good in it. Cain has taken the place of her classmates and teachers, and she often addresses him not by his dog name but by some person's name.

"Aristarkh Fyodorovich! Zaretsky put a snake in my desk."

Or: "Trubitsin! Karsavina asked me to tell you she doesn't love you."

Cain answers to all names, even female. Sometimes Zelda takes him down to the Neman River, where she sits on the damp sand and draws things with a stick. With his ears pricked up, the dog watches, his brown eyes twinkling with patient wonder, as she smooths down the lifeless man she had drawn.

Near Rakhmiel's barn Zelda runs into Pimpleface Simeon. "Hello," the tavern keeper's son says cheerfully.

"Hello."

"Doggy, doggy, always with your doggy. Aren't you bored?"

"No," Zelda snaps and tries to walk past him, but Pimpleface Simeon moves closer, forgetting about the tramp in the yarmulke as well as his own horse.

"Can I take his place?" the tavern keeper's son proposes, and a smile brightens his sullen face.

"Whose place?"

"Your dog's."

"No, you can't take his place," Zelda said, brushing him off.

"Why not? I know how to bite, walk on my hind legs, sit with a chain. What more does a dog have to do?"

"Shut up!"

"That's all? I can shut up. Watch me!" Pimpleface Simeon becomes silent.

"See?" he breaks his vow a moment later. "Is that enough? Come to the old pear tree tonight, and I'll show you the kind of stick that draws men."

Zelda blushes and runs away.

"Come back," Pimpleface Simeon hurls after her, as if he were throwing a stone, and he starts barking: "Ruff, ruff!"

Smart aleck! But why does everyone call him "Pimpleface"? He doesn't even have any pimples. When Simeon is quiet, he's even handsome: his face seems strong and masculine, especially the lines around his mouth, which look like they're carved in stone. His sad eyes have a wild look and his lips press together resentfully—only his crooked and greedy teeth fall short.

When they reach the forest, the sun is streaming through the crowns of the trees—a grandmother's spinning wheel spinning golden thread.

"Simeon," Zelda calls out to the dog. The hound rubs against her, and it's hard to tell if these are tears or a ray of sun streaming from his eyes.

"Tell me, Simeon, do you care what kind of legs I have?"

Cain-Simeon wags his tail, and hearing a rustle in the juniper shrubs, he rushes into the dense smoke-colored undergrowth.

Zelda bends down and breaks off a shoot of overripe wild strawberries. She twirls it in her hand, brings it to her lips, and bites off the berries.

In the forest everything is plentiful and fragrant, like a wedding table.

Zelda leans against a pine tree, rests her eyes on a patch of blue sky, and, as if in a trance, she mutters, "My God, am I worse than Golda? I can't . . . I don't want to go on drawing with a stick in the sand . . . my God!"

She sobs and brushes the tears off her cheeks.

"Who are you saving me for, God?"

Silence all around. Not a leaf stirs.

Cain comes running.

He tugs at her skirt, calls her.

"Where do you want me to go, dog? Don't you see I'm speaking to God?"

The dog whines and keeps looking at the juniper.

"What is it, did you see some fool in there?"

Zelda follows Cain, and when she gets near the juniper thicket, she sees a man in a velvet yarmulke sprawled out. She screams and runs away.

"Cain! Cain!" she shouts, pushing her way through the bushes.

The hound catches up to her at the edge of the forest, sticks out a pink tongue and exhales juniper air.

"Who was it?" Zelda asks impulsively. "Who's in there?"

"What's wrong, Miss? You're pale as death." Golda stands in the courtyard, chopping firewood with short, powerful swings, like a man. "Who was chasing you?"

"No one chased me, no one . . . I'm just tired," Zelda answers.

She goes inside, flops down on a plush-covered sofa, buries her face in its velvet and tries to nap, but she can't sleep. She turns onto her back and stares at the intricate design of the chandelier that her father had bought from some ruined Polish nobleman. Then she contemplates the carved ceiling, which looks like a chessboard without any pieces. Suddenly she jumps up, opens the sideboard, takes out a bottle of liqueur that Zelik had put aside to celebrate a successful hunt, fills a silver tumbler, and downs it.

Golda knocks at the door and calls her mistress, but Zelda doesn't answer. She stands with her arms crossed, looking out at the garden, the pregnant trees, a small bird hopping from one branch to another. Why won't it sit still? What does it want, if all branches are alike? She can still hear the rustling in the juniper and the stomp of her thin legs on the country road. She doesn't understand why she ran away. Was it out of shame or fear? Shame, of course, it was shame. What if he . . . the one wearing the velvet yarmulke . . . is alive and tells the whole town: "Good people, you know what? Markus Fradkin's daughter asked God for something sinful. She begged Him to send her a man. You, Pimpleface Simeon, leave your Morta and go help her!"

Zelda pours herself another full glass. The liqueur stirs her blood, then calms her.

"Do you want to wash now, or will you eat first?" Golda drones from behind the door.

"I'll eat."

Golda brings her broth with matzo balls and chicken cutlets.

"Enjoy your meal, Miss. I'm going to wash. My breasts have been itching for two weeks."

"Go on!"

After Golda leaves, Zelda pours herself another glass of liqueur, raises it to her lips, and then puts it down on the table without taking a sip. Her head is already spinning from the first two glasses.

When will father come? When, when?

He had brought her to this house and hired Golda, so now she's supposed to be living in Paradise. Fresh air. Fresh milk. Music. This is Paradise? No, it's enslavement, captivity! Zelda is a prisoner of her father. In Vilkija she might have found some gentile. But here? Riffraff, poor folk, and the only non-Jew is the policeman Ardalion Nesterovich. Zelda certainly has not set her eyes on him. Markus Fradkin is a man with foresight. The best medicine against whimsical ideas are the backwoods and solitude. Likely enough, he satisfies his own flesh and soul with some woman. Zelda knows he visits someone when he has time away from work.

"Papa has a woman in Vilna," Zelik told her. "Silly girl, you probably thought he hurries to come see you every Sunday, but he goes to her. Papa even built her a house. And do you know, dear sister, who the chosen one is? A Pole! Pure-blooded! A former countess! Our God-fearing father sleeps with a Polish countess!"

A countess, a countess. And mama was a fishmonger's daughter. Grandmother's house always smelled like carp. What does the countess's home smell like?

When father comes, Zelda will remember to ask, "Father, what does the countess's home smell like?"

A stream of smoke, thin as a mouse's tail, curls over the bathhouse.

Zelda hides the bottle in the sideboard. Soon the Nesteroviches will come for their lesson.

What will happen to them when she leaves? Who will teach them? Maybe Golda is right. Maybe there's no point in teaching them. They'll still grow up and become pogromniks, just like Kozhinov, her former Latin teacher.

"Why are you always complaining and slandering Russia?" he would tell her. "You should kiss her feet for taking you in."

How far away everything seems now—her Latin teacher Kozhinov, and her father with his house and countess in Vilna.

The thin curl of smoke from the bathhouse swept with a flourish like the signature of Aristarkh Fyodorovich Bogoyavlensky, headmaster of the gymnasium. From the garden the smell of decaying leaves and withered peonies flowed into the room through the open window.

"I'm done washing," Golda returns and says blissfully. "Go lie on the shelf, steam yourself, you'll feel like a newborn babe." She lifts up her drooping breasts with her hands, then begins to gather the dishes, swinging her hips, which struggle against the tight, homespun skirt.

"You've been drinking, Miss!"

"I have."

"Why?"

"They say liqueur fattens up your legs."

"Really?"

"Yes. Several inches per glass."

"You're joking, Miss."

"I'm not joking."

"Don't get angry, Miss, but I'll tell you a woman's secret."

"Tell me."

"What matters most is not a woman's legs."

"What is it then?"

"The sweet cake between them. And how much honey God's put there."

Golda begins to laugh and carries out the dishes. At the door she turns around. "When you're in the bathhouse, don't forget to splash water on the coals. In such dry heat, one spark is a disaster! And lock all the doors."

"Who's going to show up other than the Nesteroviches?"

"You never know who'll get the idea. There are things worth looking for here. Forty silver forks and spoons alone . . . They say a tramp has turned up in town. Says he's a messenger from God. But I know a thing or two—he may be a messenger in word but a thief in deed."

"What does he look like?'

"I haven't seen him myself. Itsik told me."

"Itsik?"

"He says he's stocky, wears a velvet yarmulke pinned to his hair. Be careful, Miss. A fellow like that might rob you and have a taste for honey cake," Golda blurts out quickly. Then, rattling the dishes, she walks away.

Dusk fell. An ornate signature of smoke was still curling over the bathhouse. What can she do? She doesn't have the energy to wash herself or douse the coals.

Zelda locks the door and climbs up to Zelik's room on the second floor. She takes her brother's gun from a rack and goes back down. With nothing else to do, she takes aim at the window, then at the piano, then at the chandelier her father bought for next to nothing from the ruined Polish nobleman, and then at the large photograph of grandfather and grandmother. Zelda imagines that her grandmother turns pale from fright and moves her head very slightly to the left.

"That's what a Russian gymnasium does to a Jewish girl," the old woman in the photo grumbles, and Zelda somehow feels that her voice is permeated with the stench of carp.

Ding, ding, ding, the doorbell sounds.

"Father!"

Zelda runs to the door.

Why didn't he have his key?

"Who's there?"

Ding, ding.

Is it the Nesteroviches?

"Who's there?"

"Open up!"

It's an unfamiliar voice, hoarse, entreating.

Zelda lingers. If misfortune is destined to come, it will break open the door.

She turns the key and lets him in—the man from the juniper thicket, the one in the velvet yarmulke.

"Your floor's been washed," the stranger says, "so I'll take off my shoes. There's dirt stuck on them."

Zelda stands and watches as he unlaces the misshapen shoes, pulls them off his feet, and carefully places them in the corner.

"Forgive me," says the man in the velvet yarmulke. "I saw the steam from the bathhouse and decided to drop by. I haven't bathed for a long time. Don't be afraid of me."

"I'm not afraid."

"Why the gun, then?"

"It's my brother's gun. Zelik's. Go and wash . . . while the coals are still hot. I'll give you a towel and soap."

"Thank you." The stranger looks around the room. "That's me as a child," he says, and points to a photograph on the wall.

"You?" Zelda smiles, bewildered. The photo is of Zelik, looking fat and stupid in a white shirt and suspenders.

"Me. I remember how father and I went to the photographer, how he sat me down on the chair, adjusted my yarmulke. The photographer hid under a black cloth, stuck his head out, and said, 'Sit still, son. A little birdie will fly out now.' It was at the corner of Station and Market Streets. Then father bought me a bun with raisins, and I kept on asking, 'Where's the birdie?'"

"There's no bird," Zelda explains calmly, with the slightest touch of gaiety. "The light falls on your face, then the image is fixed on a glass plate, then the plate is developed in chemicals."

Her fear had subsided. Would a thief or a rapist remove his shoes at the door before committing a crime? They wouldn't even notice that the floor had been washed.

"There is a bird," the man in the velvet yarmulke insists. "Yours apparently has not hatched yet."

"Where?"

"In your memory. Because you probably also want me to leave quickly. No matter who I visit, they all want me to leave quickly."

"Why do they all want that?" Zelda asks, struck by his perceptiveness.

"Why? Because their memory is a mound of fears. Some people think I'm a thief. Others—a madman. And others—a beggar."

"And in fact?"

"In fact, a thief and a madman and a beggar. A thief because I stole away from my family and my loved ones. A madman because I'm not like other real thieves. And a beggar because I gather other people's sins. In the forest I heard you ask God for a sin."

"I didn't ask for anything." Zelda blushes. "What do you want with other people's sins? Don't you have enough?"

The man in the velvet yarmulke pays no attention to her caustic remark and goes on talking.

"Until Yom Kippur I'll make the rounds of all the shtetls and the cemeteries. Last year, before Yom Kippur arrived, I even reached Vitebsk—a sinful province, very sinful. I can't bear it, I thought. The burden's too great for me."

"What couldn't you bear?" Zelda asks, amused.

"The transgressions against God. On Yom Kippur, as soon as the first star comes out, the Almighty lowers a ladder to me, as he did to our forefather Jacob. I climb up and sit with God on a cloud, eating potatoes baked in their skins, while God punishes some and pardons others. Last year God spared no one. I pleaded for a tailor who had killed his wife out of jealousy, but it didn't help."

"Have you gathered a lot of sins in our town?" Zelda asks, smiling.

"I've just begun," the man answers seriously. "But already—a lot. There's one sin in your family."

"In our family?"

"Your father's."

"Was it Mama?"

"No. It was Aaron, the stepson of the night watchman Rakhmiel. Your father sent him to the army in place of his own son."

"Another boy in Zelik's place? I never heard about that."

"The Master of the Universe won't look kindly on such a sin. And what did he do to your mother?"

"Nothing. He just didn't love her."

"That's not a sin. That's a misfortune. I don't love my wife, either."

The man in the velvet yarmulke takes his shoes and slips out barefoot to the back yard.

Zelda watches him walk around the garden, wearing his shoes on his hands. She watches him bow his head, as if the sky is too low for him, sees him look back at the house and disappear into the doorway of the bathhouse.

What a day! At least he didn't rape her, strangle her, or carry off the silver. Zelda shivers. The poor fellow collects sins. Well, let him collect to his heart's content. The poor fellow is searching for a little bird, so let him search. The house has everything—money, mahogany furniture, the Polish nobleman's chandelier, the German piano, but there are no sins and no little birds. Rakhmiel's Aaron wasn't a sin, but some sort of deal, a transaction. The poor fellow is waiting for God to lower a ladder to him on Judgment Day. But he must have forgotten that it's made of Markus Fradkin's pine! Her father is assured of a favorable judgment and God's mercy.

The doorbell rings.

The Nesteroviches, Zelda guesses.

"Greetings, Zelda Markovna," Katyusha Nesterovich says. "We've brought you fresh strawberries."

The girl places a basket at Zelda's feet.

Zelda wants to cry. She also wants to hang up there on the wall, next to the old Jewess who stinks of carp, and look out of her frame at the sins of others. She'd look at Golda's feline spine, at the fresh strawberries, and from time to time, overcome with boredom, she'd croak the tongue-twister: *Klaraukarlaukralaklarnet.* Clara stole Karl's clarinet.

9

The night watchman Rakhmiel knows that misfortune, like a match-maker, never comes alone. Without fail, it will arrange some other disaster for you. In the spring, on the eve of Passover, his lower back tightened up as if his spine were bound by a cooper's hoop. He would take one step and cringe from the pain, which shot out in all directions. Rakhmiel used to think that the lower back, like the buttocks, never hurts. What hurts are the parts that work—the legs, arms, eyes, ears, even the heart, but the back takes it easy.

All day Rakhmiel tossed and turned, moaned and groaned. Following Kazimieras's advice, he applied a white-hot brick wrapped in burlap to his lower back, but when the brick didn't help, he went to Yeshua, bought a bottle of vodka, and called Kazimieras—thank God for him and his goat. He stripped to his waist, lay down on a rough bench, and ordered, "Rub!"

Kazimieras splashed a drop on his palm, sniffed, and rubbed. He rubbed, glancing first at the bottle, then at the patient. He felt sorry for Rakhmiel and for the vodka. Lying with his underwear pulled down, Rakhmiel groaned and gave off a smell like compost. Like a plowed field.

"Let's drink it instead," Kazimieras said in despair. "Maybe that will help."

Rakhmiel drank and—what do you know?—the pain vanished at once.

That was before Passover, however, and after Passover a new illness came to call. His left leg, the crippled one, was seized by cramps.

To tell the truth, it was hardly a leg, more like a dried-up sunflower stalk, a wooden post—if a calf butted it, it would split in half.

With such a leg you can't walk around town. You can't even walk around your own yard. With such a leg you can't be a watchman, and you'll go straight to the grave.

For twenty years Rakhmiel had trudged around town with his clapper, and now they would take it away from him, take it away for sure, and the Almighty Himself couldn't help.

Twenty years earlier he had been lucky to get this position. At the time Markus Fradkin was the man in charge at the synagogue; he took pity on him, stood up for him. You gave me a stepson, he said, so I'll give you a clapper in exchange. And also, one scraggly sheep, with a tuft of wool. In any case, there was no way of getting Aaron back from the draft. They gave Rakhmiel a salary—five rubles in the winter, three rubles in the spring, summer, and fall. Money that's nothing to brag about, but, on the other hand, it was a position for life. A shoemaker sits and waits for someone to bring him a stinking shoe. The same for a tailor or leather worker, who sit and wait from morning to night, watching the door—is it squeaking or not? Being a night watchman is a completely different thing. Whatever happens, night will always come. Always.

And now? His leg was cramping again. There's no Markus Fradkin to help. The new administrative head of the synagogue, Naftali Spivak, won't stand on ceremony; he'll find someone younger and healthier for Rakhmiel's job. If no one else, then Menachem Baum, an old veteran.

Menachem Baum had fought in Crimea, and his ear had been damaged there. But does a night watchman need both ears?

Last night, just as the moon came up, Rakhmiel sat down on the porch of the Spivak brothers' hardware shop. He said to his leg, "What are you doing to me, you shameless thing? Why are you ruining me, you old rat?"

Toward morning he dragged himself home, rolled his pants leg up to the groin, stared at the bone, covered by wrinkled yellow skin, and almost began to howl.

"Listen," he told his left leg, "I didn't look after you, didn't spare you . . . that's true. But since you've trudged with me so long, trudge a little more, that's not asking too much. And then we'll die together. I give you my watchman's word of honor! Have my eyes and ears had it easier? At least you didn't see my children die or hear my wife's screams! What's a grave mound to you, or the floor planks in the latrine? Nothing matters except solid ground."

His leg seemed to heed his request and the pain faded, quieted down like a wasp in honey.

"Who are you talking to there?" Rakhmiel unexpectedly heard the voice of the man who called himself his stepson Aaron.

Where did he come from? Since the time he'd stopped in for a drink of water, he hadn't shown his face here. Rakhmiel even told Pimpleface Simeon, "God knows where he's gone!" Simeon had yelled, cursed, and threatened him: "Fetch him, no matter what!" But now he suddenly appeared as if out of thin air.

The stranger slid off the bed, stretched, yawned loudly, and glanced at the rolled-up pants leg.

"Your leg hurts?"

"It hurts," Rakhmiel admitted. If his guest was really a messenger from Heaven, let him heal his left leg. He won't ask anything for his lazy lower back, but for the leg . . . yes. It's completely stiff, damn it!

The guest removed his yarmulke, walked over, and took a look, like a dog looking at an old, dried-out bone, and turned away.

"It's bad," Rakhmiel mumbled. "You could take an axe and chop it off. They were good legs once. Strong, nimble . . . But it seems they went to the wrong man."

"Why?" With one hand, the one who had said he was his stepson Aaron fanned his head, which was sweating from his thoughts.

"They should have gone to Markus Fradkin or Naftali Spivak—then they would have lasted forever. They would have ridden in droshkies and worn silk stockings and gaiters." Rakhmiel wrinkled his brow, cast a sullen glance at the stranger, and added, "Do you understand anything about legs?"

"No. You need to show that to a doctor."

"Why a doctor? He'll look and take the money, but he won't be able to give me a new leg. Why has God punished me?"

"God punishes the soul," said the one who called himself Aaron.

"My soul is in my legs?"

"Maybe."

"Maybe, or maybe not, but I'll no longer be a night watchman."

"You'll be a tailor, a tinsmith, a potter . . ."

"I only know how to keep watch," Rakhmiel whispered.

"What joy is it to keep watch over what's not yours?"

"It's a joy," Rakhmiel replied with feeling. "Joy. But you'll never understand. What is night for you? Darkness, sleep . . ."

"And for you?"

"For me?" Rakhmiel grew thoughtful. "You walk around town, bang your clapper, and all around everything is yours, no longer others'—the shutters and the sky and even the horse droppings on the road. Who am I during the day? A poor soul. I have nothing but my little house and the cemetery. But at night? At night I'm a rich man. Better off than Markus Fradkin and the Spivak brothers."

Rakhmiel lowered his pants leg, slowly made his way to the table, and picked up his clapper.

"You're listening and probably thinking: he's a fool."

"I'm listening but not thinking," said the man who called himself Aaron.

"In our family everyone was a fool. Everyone back to the ninth generation. Grandfather, great-grandfather, and great-great-grandfather, may they rest in peace. They worked like fools, loved like fools, prayed to God like fools. I used to run home and complain to grandfather, 'Everyone calls me a fool.' 'Be proud, Rakhmiel!' he said. 'The best title on earth is not czar, or general, or merchant, but fool. Be proud! Only the tears and prayers of fools reach the ears of God, because God is the supreme fool, and He doesn't like sophisticated people!'"

"What's true is true," the guest agreed with Rakhmiel. "The smart ones don't believe in anything."

"Faith is the bread of fools," Rakhmiel said, and clasped the clapper to his chest.

"If you want," the guest unexpectedly proposed, "I'll bang the clapper for you until your leg comes to its senses."

"You think it will come to its senses?"

"Of course. It's just tired itself out. It needs peace and quiet."

"Maybe silk stockings and droshkies, too?" Rakhmiel said sarcastically. "There won't be any droshkies. They've passed me by. But as for you, the policeman won't allow it."

"Why not?"

"Who would entrust the clapper to a stranger?"

"Will anyone know for sure who is banging—you or me? The policeman sleeps at night. Should I pretend to be lame and old?"

"The policeman won't allow it," Rakhmiel objected stubbornly.

"Give me the clapper."

"Do you know how toward morning you can start to nod off? If you fall asleep, they'll catch you."

"I won't fall asleep."

"Whenever I feel I'm nodding, I immediately begin to . . ."

"To what?"

"To talk," Rakhmiel said. "Is there someone you can talk to at night?"

"There is."

"It's best to talk to the dead. There are more of them than the living. I have a whole dozen myself. Do you have any dead ones?"

"My mother . . . brothers . . . sisters . . . my son Yisrael."

"Good. Even if dead, a mother won't let you fall sleep. You can also talk with fools. There are more fools than dead ones. Just call and they come running."

"Give me the clapper and lie down," said the one who called himself Aaron.

"Night's a long way off," Rakhmiel noted. "Leave when it's dark, take the hill down to the market square, turn right, and with God's help start near Markus Fradkin's house. But be very quiet . . . Markus Fradkin doesn't like loud bangs. He even complained once to the policeman. The officer came to me and said, 'Why are you rattling beneath the Fradkins' windows, old man?' 'All windows are the same to me, Mr. Officer,' I replied. 'You'd better not rattle again beneath the Fradkins' windows. Understand, old man?' But I didn't obey. I banged, and I go on banging. Let him know that the clapper's the same for everyone. For those who sleep and those who stay awake."

Rakhmiel cleared his throat and continued.

"Rabbi Uri is just the opposite. He likes it when you bang as loud as you can. Sometimes he opens a window and orders, 'Louder, Rakhmiel! Louder! The Master of the Universe should know that such a hole as our town exists in this world, and there are such fools as you and me. Louder! Louder! God should know!' I think I really will lie down."

"Lie down, lie down. I'll cook you some sorrel and potatoes. Kazimieras will bring goat's milk, and you and I will have a feast in honor of all the fools in the world." The one calling himself Aaron began to bustle about. "I'll heat the water. Soak your leg in hot water at night and you'll feel better."

"Avoid Yeshua Mandel's tavern," Rakhmiel advised. "The day before yesterday Simeon came here looking for you. He threatened to kill you. Grabbed me by the throat and started to shout: 'You swine, are you going to tell me who he is?'"

"What did you tell him?"

"I said, 'Simeon, God forbid that your children and grandchildren talk this way to you!'"

"That's all?"

"And I said, 'You ask who he is, and I'm answering you—the son of a fool and father of fools.' Stay out of his sight. Keep away from the tavern. When you get to the Spivak brothers' hardware shop, take a shortcut and go straight past the priest's house. Simeon's not someone to toy with. He's the Spivaks' nephew and he's in cahoots with the policeman. He'll see you with the clapper at night and we'll be done for. Don't tell our policeman that you're the son of a fool and father of fools."

"And you tell him that Aaron has returned from service."

"But you're not Aaron . . . you're not Aaron. There's no birth-mark on your right shoulder. None!"

"There is," the man in the yarmulke said, and he went to the cel-lar for potatoes.

Rats were living in the cellar. Hungry, they were apparently wait-ing for Rakhmiel to breathe his last. The rats rushed to attack the one calling himself Aaron, but he jumped back from them and flat-tened himself against a musty wall encrusted with mold and mildew. Behind a rusty iron railing, in the dark, he searched for a pile of last years' potatoes. He suddenly thought: Is it possible that man comes into this world in order to be food for rats and graveyard worms? What are palaces and droshkies and silk stockings and gaiters com-pared to his breath? The soul's breath flies into the air like fluff from a poplar, the same as everyone's, rich or poor.

The rats scuffled in the dark. Their impatient noises, their hungry, displeased squeaks sickened him as though he had been poisoned.

The one who called himself Aaron quickly crammed the spuds soiled by the rats into a tattered wicker basket, and without look-ing back, he climbed up the rickety ladder. Here is the beginning of the ladder that the Master of the Universe would lower to him on the Day of Judgment! This is it—the longest and hardest beginning, though he is not climbing up with a pile of other people's sins but with sinless potatoes gnawed by rats.

Rakhmiel was asleep. The one who called himself his stepson Aaron walked over to the bed and covered him with a blanket thin as a shroud. He sat on the edge of the bed and began to watch Rakh-miel's tranquil face, and the more closely he looked at him, the more paths he found to the cemetery. For are not wrinkles pathways to the grave?

How much he looks like my father, the man in the yarmulke thought, and memories blinded him, as when a candle is unexpect-edly brought close to the eyes and singes the eyelashes.

"Father," he said softly. "There are more rats than potatoes in the cellar."

Rakhmiel was breathing heavily and unevenly. His nostrils, covered with dirty gray fuzz, blew out fumes, like those at the site of a fire.

The one calling himself Aaron opened his eyes and suddenly passed his hand over Rakhmiel's numb forehead, as if with this gesture he hoped to smooth out one pathway to the grave.

But Rakhmiel didn't feel his touch or hear his words. It didn't matter to him how many rats or how many potatoes there were in the cellar.

Let him sleep, the one who called himself Aaron decided. Let him sleep. The Master of the Universe grants a peaceful death in sleep to the righteous. If Rakhmiel dies in his sleep, it means he is a righteous person. It means that the Almighty has forgiven his only sin, *obedience*—although in times of unjust rulers, in times of depravity and lawlessness, there is no greater sin than obedience.

The one who called himself Aaron imagined for a moment that the rats would crawl out of the cellar, and how they would bite Rakhmiel's dead hand as it dangled from the bed. They would drag him onto the floor and poke their insatiable faces against the silenced clapper.

He passed his hand over Rakhmiel's forehead again and rejoiced when he felt drops of someone else's sweat on his palm. "Man is a garden that God has sown." He remembered his father's words. "All his life he waters it with his own sweat and blood."

Rakhmiel had watered his garden with his own sweat and blood. Only dew drops remained. Only drops. And the crop was rats.

The one calling himself Aaron stood up, washed the potatoes, and began peeling them with a large, dull knife. He carefully removed the skins, then tossed the peeled potatoes into a cast-iron pot. He tossed them in and listened to the splashes of water, to Rakhmiel's heavy and unsteady breathing, and for what no one is able to hear but all are destined to experience.

The rain kept falling outside the window. It fell to the earth thoughtlessly and meekly, as an exhausted, poor worker falls into bed.

Heavy drops hammered the leaky roof and autumn dripped onto the floor from the soot-covered ceiling.

When Kazimieras entered the house, the water in the pot was boiling.

"Is Rakhmiel sleeping?" he asked as he stood on the doorstep, towering and wet.

"He's sleeping."

"I brought him some goat's milk," Kazimieras said, without moving, as if he was afraid he would spill the white milk from an open clay bowl.

He walked into the middle of the room, put the bowl on the table, and bowed.

"Where are you going?" the one calling himself Aaron stopped him. "Wait. The potatoes are just boiling. Sit down and we'll eat."

"Thank you," Kazimieras said. "I already ate potatoes once today."

"Eat more," the man in the yarmulke said. "You can eat potatoes all day long. You can eat potatoes your whole life."

"Soon we'll harvest the new ones," Kazimieras said hesitantly, flattered by the attention. "But why aren't you asking me anything?"

"What should I ask you?"

"Who I am."

"You're Kazimieras," said the man who called himself Aaron.

"Yes."

"You put out the candles for the Jews on Shabbes."

"Yes. For almost fifteen years." Kazimieras assumed an air of importance. "It's good work. Clean. You come, blow them out, that's it."

"And how many have you blown out in fifteen years?"

"How could I remember that?"

"But I remember."

"What, do you also put out candles?"

"Yes."

"But aren't you a Jew?"

"I am."

"It's a sin for Jews to put them out," Kazimieras said.

"It depends on which candles," the one calling himself Aaron said, and poured the water out of the pot.

"All candles are wax . . . they're all the same," Kazimieras said doubtfully.

"Only the ones on the table."

"Where else?"

"Where else? Right here," said the one who called himself Aaron, pointing to his chest.

"In the heart?"

"In the heart," said the man in the velvet yarmulke. "I've been extinguishing one for so many years, and I can't put it out."

"How can you put it out?" Kazimieras asked simplemindedly. "When the heart goes out, then the candle will go out," he added and looked over at the bed where Rakhmiel was snoring.

"Even then it won't go out," the one who called himself Aaron said quietly, stirring the coals with a poker.

"What sort of candle is . . . ?" Kazimieras wondered, blinking skeptically.

"Sit down. The two of us will have a feast now," the man in the yarmulke interrupted.

"What about Rakhmiel?"

"Rakhmiel is ill. Let him rest."

"Only . . . I won't have milk. That's for Rakhmiel," Kazimieras warned. "I won't drink the milk."

They sat at the table and began to scoop potatoes out of the pot. Kazimieras ate slowly. Occasionally he raised his pale eyes, which seemed to consist of the whites alone, looked at the ceiling, shook his large, stump-like head, and wondered what kind of remarkable candle there is that burns in the heart and can't be extinguished.

"Have you known Rakhmiel a long time?" the one who called himself Aaron asked.

"Yes. He brought me to Markus Fradkin and said, 'Mr. Fradkin! He'—that is, me—'has lungs like blacksmith bellows. He can blow out a candle a hundred steps away!' In the early days, Markus Fradkin couldn't refuse Rakhmiel anything."

"Why not?"

"Because of Aaron, it seems."

Kazimieras felt a strong urge to ask the stranger if it was true that he was Aaron, but he hesitated. If he asked, it might harm Rakhmiel. Let them sort it out for themselves—there was no reason for him, Kazimieras, to get mixed up in Jewish affairs. Of course, he would be grateful to Rakhmiel until his dying day; otherwise, he'd be hanging around somewhere in the country or wearing himself out felling trees. But why anger Markus Fradkin or the tavern keeper's son, Simeon. Simeon had a reason to come running here—he was sniffing out something, spying, searching for something. If the stranger *is* Aaron, what good will that do Rakhmiel? You might as well show up at a funeral. Kazimieras will bury the old man himself, and even pray for him, if not in the synagogue, then in the church. You can pray to any God for a good man, and God won't get angry. Aaron arrived too late, much too late.

Kazimieras asked the one who called himself Aaron, "Where did you serve?"

"On the Turkish border."

"Imagine that!" Kazimieras exclaimed, almost enviously. "What do they look like?"

"Who?"

"The Turks. Like Jews or like us?"

"Like Jews."

"Do they put out candles on Shabbes?"

"What, do you want to go to the Turks?"

"Fate might take me there some day. Didn't it take you there?"

"It did, it did," the stranger repeated in a singsong voice. "Where has it not taken me?"

"And I sit in one place all day long," Kazimieras complained.

"What's keeping you here? The candles?"

"The goat," Kazimieras answered.

"You can sell the goat."

"I can sell her, but without me she'll die right away."

"Why? Isn't the grass the same in another place?"

"The grass is the same . . . But they'll only milk the goat . . ."

"What else is there to do with a goat?"

"Love it . . . A person can do without love, but not a goat. My goat wouldn't last a year, she'd die right away." Kazimieras was silent for a while, then asked, "Will you stay with Rakhmiel until the end?"

"What end?"

"You know . . . this . . ."

"I don't know," said the one who called himself Aaron.

"You have things to do?"

"You have a goat, and I have a whole herd."

"A herd? How can you love a whole herd?"

Kazimieras got up from the table, bent his index finger, straightened his mustache, and abruptly, almost angrily, made a dry cough.

"If Rakhmiel doesn't get up before evening," he said, "I'll take his place . . . I always do his watch on Friday night and holidays."

"Today's not Friday, and the holidays are far off," the one who called himself Aaron answered. "The roof needs fixing. It's leaking on my head."

"It needs fixing," Kazimieras muttered. "But Rakhmiel won't do it. He says there's not enough money. Nails are expensive now, as you know. Oh, how the Spivaks soak you for a handful. He says Aaron will return, and he'll fix it. Rakhmiel is saving up money for him."

"Money for Aaron?" The man in the yarmulke perked up.

Kazimieras sensed that he had blurted out too much, and he began to rattle on. "What sort of money's there! Pennies! God grant there's enough for the funeral. Though Rakhmiel doesn't want to lie with the others. Better to lie separately, he says . . . somewhere in the garden . . . But I say it's better together. Being together, even underground, is better. And besides, all the dead are brothers. There aren't timber merchants or goatherds or night watchmen among them—they're all equal. There's one roof for all, and it doesn't leak. But he keeps saying: no and no. If Rakhmiel dies, God forbid, what will I do?"

"Get up earlier, milk the goat, and bring milk," said the one who called himself Aaron. "Bring it here and put it on the table. Everyone who comes to see him will look at the large clay bowl and remember that you can't drink up everything in this world."

Kazimieras looked at the stranger with mistrust, shrugged his shoulders, and walked slowly to the door. The one who called himself Aaron moved closer to the bed, bent over the sleeping Rakhmiel, felt his breath, put a blanket over his bare legs that stuck out like rusted candlesticks, shooed away a fly that was circling above the clay bowl, and left the house.

In the yard the rain was coming down in buckets. Everything around was blotted out by the rain. Only the trees stood steadfastly and mournfully as though at a funeral service, and Kazimieras's goat bleated somewhere under the eaves.

No one was in the Spivak brothers' shop. The man in the velvet yarmulke waited a long time before the obese owner appeared, a pince-nez sitting atop his fleshy nose; he made slow tortoise-like movements and looked like a tortoise himself. Coming to a full stop behind the counter, he stared at the customer with his sleepy eyes, enlarged by the glasses.

"What do you want?"

"I'd like some nails."

"To crucify Christ?" Spivak asked and burst out laughing. His laughter scattered across the counter like change.

"To fix a roof."

"You have a roof?" Spivak laughed loudly again, but this time there was more change.

"I do. But it's full of holes, as usual."

"Isn't that the truth? That's the truth!" The portly man rattled on and stuck his hand into a box of nails. "As usual, full of holes. Well said. Excellent! When, may I ask, will we have a roof without holes?"

"Someday," the man calling himself Aaron answered.

"When there won't be any more Jews?" Spivak snapped, adding "Forty kopecks."

"Put it on the account."

"On what account?"

"On the Almighty's account," the one who called himself Aaron said, beginning to put the nails into his pocket.

"Ha, ha, ha," Spivak roared with laughter. "I'll give credit to any beggar, to any starving man, but to God? Do you hear, Chaim?" He turned to someone out of sight. "God is taking forty kopecks of nails from us on credit. Ha, ha, ha! Do you hear, Chaim? Doesn't God have forty kopecks in His pocket? Oy, I'll die laughing! Oy, stop me! Chaim! Chaim! Do you hear?"

"The Master of the Universe will reward you and your brother Chaim a hundredfold for each nail," said the one who called himself Aaron, and he left the shop in a dignified manner.

Spivak's laughter pursued him all the way to Rakhmiel's barn. It clinked like forty kopecks, like countless nails, and the rain was powerless to muffle it.

All day, until the evening, the one calling himself Aaron went on repairing the roof. His clothes became soaked, but he sat on the top and drove nails into the boards. With every blow of the hammer he kept saying: "The Master of the Universe will reward you a hundredfold for each nail, for every drop of sweat and blood. A hundredfold . . . You laugh?"

He had never felt so close to God as now, sitting on the roof of Rakhmiel's ramshackle house and wielding a short hammer that others' hands had grasped.

It was just a stone's throw to the sky, which had suddenly cleared and acquired a fathomless depth rare for autumn. The man in the yarmulke did not want to come down to earth. What had he not seen there? Forty years, like forty kopecks, like forty nails . . . To whom had he given them? Where were they now?

The one who called himself Aaron put down the hammer—you can't soar to the sky with a hammer—spread his arms open wide and waved them like wings.

"What are you doing? Get down!" Rakhmiel shouted as he came out of the house.

The one who called himself his stepson Aaron did not even think of climbing down, though. He was still waving his arms; the wind winnowed his face, clouds floated above his head, and his head felt light, like a dandelion, as light as in his childhood, in those blessed times when his beautiful and buxom mother washed clothes at the river. He, a small boy, stood beside her looking at his reflection in the water, with the birds flying above him. The willow branches flowed down to the shore, and a big happy fish flapped its fins.

"Climb down," Rakhmiel shouted.

He didn't hear him. He didn't want to wait until Yom Kippur for the Almighty to lower the ladder. He wanted to go now . . . to go this minute into that fathomless depth rare in autumn, beyond the clouds, where in the dark blue water his beautiful, buxom mother was washing underwear, his father's shirt, white from the salt, a gaudy apron, and short pants with patches on the buttocks.

Frightened, Rakhmiel called for help. "Kazimieras! Kazimieras!"

Why is he shouting, the stupid old man? thought the one who called himself Aaron. He should be happy the roof is fixed. It won't leak any more. True, he would not be able to bang the clapper for him at night . . . May he forgive him . . . for at night he will be there, in the Garden of Eden or among angels who don't sell nails or vodka or wood. He will put in a good word for poor Rakhmiel. And for Kazimieras, too.

Rakhmiel and Kazimieras stood below, watching him wave his arms in helpless rage. They looked at each other, and suddenly, as if by some mutual understanding, they spread their arms wide open and began to wave them, saying: climb down, for God's sake!

He was delighted and shouted back to them from the roof. "Take the goat! The goat!"

They lowered their arms—in old age you can't wave them for long. They hung around for a while and then, in low spirits, dragged themselves back into the house.

Apparently, he got tired, too. His movements slowed and the wings at last came to a stop.

The one who called himself Aaron sat down and fixed his gaze on the sky, and the longing in his eyes was as bottomless as the depth that had been revealed to him, and in that longing, in that depth, in that dark blue water, his beautiful, buxom mother was washing the clothes, but he no longer saw anything. Not himself and not the birds flying above him, not the willow branches that flowed down to the shore, and not the big happy fish flapping its fins.

Kazimieras's goat rubbed against Rakhmiel's wooden fence. In the cellar the rats were squeaking.

Rakhmiel and Kazimieras waited for him in the house. The night watchman was scratching the clapper with his fingernail, while Kazimieras sucked at a homemade cigarette, ashes scattering over his thick beard.

"Drink some milk," Rakhmiel said when the one who called himself Aaron came into the house.

"Have some, have some," Kazimieras said in his deep bass voice. "There's nothing in the world sweeter than goat's milk."

"That's true," Rakhmiel agreed. According to the sages, in earlier times only gods and czars drank it. "Have a drink," he said, as he pushed the clay bowl toward the one who called himself his stepson Aaron.

"Thank you," he said, disoriented.

"Drink," Rakhmiel mumbled. "Goat's milk chases away all stupid thoughts."

"I don't have stupid thoughts," said the one who called himself Aaron. He put the hammer in the corner. "It's getting dark. Soon it will be my time to watch."

"Or maybe I'll go," Kazimieras said. "Everyone knows me."

"I'll go," the man in the velvet yarmulke insisted.

The three of them took turns drinking the goat's milk from the clay bowl, and the milk united them like a vow. There was no distinction in years, jobs, or fates—they were all night watchmen, goatherds, and messengers of God, of a single Almighty, a merciful God who was offering human beings a sip of milk in order to cleanse the soul of bitterness, enmity, and mistrust.

He left Rakhmiel's ramshackle house for town, passing through a field of rye flattened by the rain, and every now and then, ahead of him, a frightened quail chick shot into the air, blinded by darkness and fear, a little lump of life, strange and mysterious. Somewhere an orphaned nest, which had been built with grass and hope, was growing cold. Everything is afraid of something else, he reflected while approaching the town—birds fear people, and fear is the only nourishment for all, for the well-fed and for the hungry.

Stars were twinkling in the sky. Their flickering made the path seem endless, like the Milky Way.

The one who called himself Aaron did not hurry. He took in deep breaths of the damp night air, which was infused with the pungent smell of wilting flowers, pine needles, and soil, like an enormous soggy loaf of half-baked bread.

As Rakhmiel had directed him, the man in the velvet yarmulke started out from Markus Fradkin's house. He banged the clapper once or twice, and the strange staccato sound shattered the silence, stopped, and fell silent.

Markus Fradkin's house was sunk in darkness. The wide windows were shielded tightly by shutters—you couldn't have broken them even with the trumpets that brought down the walls of Jericho. The one who called himself Aaron stood at the gate, and not trusting the clapper, quietly and distinctly said, "The Almighty will reward you a hundredfold for each recruit, for each nail."

He stood waiting for the bolt to creak, for Fradkin or his son Zelik to step out onto the porch with a gun and shoot him like a quail.

But the house was dead.

"The Master of the Universe will reward you a hundredfold," he repeated, then moved along.

He walked down the one, long street of the shtetl, banging the clapper. And the more frantically he banged, the more dead it seemed all around.

The tavern was dead.

The Spivak brothers' hardware store was dead.

Rabbi Uri's wooden house was dead.

What do they care about his banging? They're asleep. Asleep in an embrace with sin. The whole world is asleep in an embrace with sin. It sleeps and sniffles sweetly. Sinful hands! Sinful bellies! Sinful heads!

And the night was empty, like an enormous prayer house with thousands of flickering candles, which no Kazimieras could extinguish even with lungs like a blacksmith's bellows.

Why is everyone sleeping and no one praying?

"Wake up, sleepers," the one who called himself Aaron said as quietly and distinctly as before. "How can you sleep when someone's roof is leaking, and there is nothing except for the night and the cemetery?"

Somewhere a dog was heatedly and furiously barking. The man in the yarmulke listened closely to the barking and walked toward the dog. He went up to the fence and in the darkness called out, "Who are you barking at, dog?"

The dog became more furious. He tried to break from the chain, the chain began clinking, and the rusty sound caused the stars in the sky to dim.

"I'm a dog like you," said the one who called himself Aaron. "Like you, you see . . . but I don't bark at passersby, I bark at the whole world . . . because it is bad."

The man in the yarmulke hadn't noticed that the street had come to an end, and he found himself in a tiny cemetery thick with pine trees, among sparse tombstones bathed in starlight and covered with pine needles. Straining his eyes, he read the first inscription he came across: *Khone Brayman.*

"Hello, Khone Brayman." The one who called himself Aaron bent down and touched the stone that was sprinkled with dew.

"Hello," Khone answered.

The man in the yarmulke heard his voice clearly, more clearly than the dog's bark.

"Where is Rakhmiel?" the dead man asked.

"Rakhmiel's not well," the newcomer answered.

"I made that clapper for him. I'm Khone Brayman, the carpenter."

"It's a fine clapper," said the man who called himself Aaron.

"Go ahead, bang," the dead man said. "I want to hear my work. The work never dies, if it's good. Bang it."

The one who called himself Aaron sat down on the grave and quietly banged the clapper. In the stillness the taps echoed joyfully yet alarmingly.

Day was breaking. From here, from Khone Brayman's grave, the man in the yarmulke could see the whole shtetl—the crowded, cheerless houses, the church steeple, the tavern's tin roof that gleamed like vodka in a bottle, and the tall pipe on top of Fradkin's bathhouse.

The one who called himself Aaron was sitting and banging his clapper, while the carpenter Khone Brayman was listening to his work as if he were at a memorial service.

"Why are you banging here?" the synagogue caretaker lashed out at the banger as he carried out trash from the prayer house.

"What of it? Is it forbidden?" asked the man who called himself Aaron.

"This is a cemetery."

"Are you sure?"

"I'm sure," the caretaker muttered.

"The cemetery is there," the one who called himself Aaron said, pointing to the tavern.

"In the tavern?"

"In the town. There are more dead ones there."

He stood up from the grave of the carpenter Khone Brayman. Hunched over, he wandered through the field of rye flattened by the rain to Rakhmiel's barn.

"I haven't slept all night," the old man confessed.

"Were you listening?" The one who called himself his stepson Aaron smiled.

"I asked you not to bang loudly at Fradkin's house."

"Was I so loud?"

"Loud, too loud . . . and then either I dreamed it, or someone was banging at the cemetery."

"At the cemetery the former watchman used to bang . . . What was his name?"

"Shmuel," Rakhmiel recalled, taken aback. "Can you steal something from the dead, too?"

"You can."

"What?"

"Memory," said the one who called himself his stepson.

"Memory?" Rakhmiel mumbled. "To me that's not wealth. Memory—that's misfortune!"

"For some people even misfortune is wealth," the man in the yarmulke responded.

"You probably got hungry during the night, didn't you?"

"No. I want to sleep."

"Sleep," Rakhmiel said. "Sleep."

He fell asleep immediately.

Rakhmiel walked around the house, killing flies with a damp rag. The flies were more than seventy years younger than him, and none of them had a left leg crushed by a log on the Kovno highway. They were flying over the table, over the bed, and landing on the face of the man in the velvet yarmulke, moving from his forehead to his unshaven chin and from the unshaven chin to his uncovered neck.

Why don't I try to . . . ? Why am I worse than a fly? Rakhmiel thought. The old man hobbled over to the bed and touched the stranger's bare neck. His old fingers shook and for a long time Rakhmiel tried to overcome the terrible trembling. At last, when it had settled down, he undid a button on the worn-out shirt, opened it and stared with his nearsighted eyes at the right shoulder of the one who called himself his stepson Aaron. Either because he was hurrying, or because his eyes were unpleasantly watering the whole time, Rakhmiel didn't see anything on the right shoulder—not a speck, not a spot. Limping on his sore leg, he went to a chest with iron hinges, rummaged through it, and pulled out a pair of old spectacles on a piece of string. The glass on one half was missing, and the other half had a crack in the center and barely held together. Rakhmiel put them on his nose, tied the string around his head, and once more bent over the sleeping man.

The one who called himself his stepson Aaron opened his eyes, saw Rakhmiel wearing the ridiculous glasses and, as if in a dream, quietly said, "What are you doing? Are you searching me like a gendarme?"

"No," Rakhmiel answered, dumbstruck. "I . . . I'm swatting flies . . ."

"With glasses?" The one who called himself Aaron smiled.

"With a rag," Rakhmiel said, and held out his empty hands.

"So, you found the birthmark?"

"I did," Rakhmiel answered without hesitating. "I found it . . . on the right shoulder."

He began to cry.

The tears landed like flies on the cracked lens of his glasses and dripped down like honey from the half without glass, and everything was so sweet, sweet, sweet for Rakhmiel that he felt sick, and his head spun in circles.

10

The death of Chava, the tavern keeper Yeshua's wife, roused the entire town. If only she had merely died, but instead—even to say it is horrible!—she hanged herself. Morta went out at the crack of dawn to feed hay to the horses. She had just picked it up with the pitchfork and carried it to the feeding trough when she caught sight of the mistress. The moment she saw her, she dropped the pitchfork, tripped over an armful of hay, fell onto the barn's earthen floor, and lay face down, afraid to move and look up at the place where reins had been thrown across a beam and Chava was dangling from a noose like an extinguished, hanging lantern.

Not used to Chava, the horses were nudging her black shoes with their muzzles, and her corpse swayed from side to side, making it seem that Chava was walking in the air.

Morta jumped up in a panic and ran to the tavern. She didn't know whether first to wake Simeon or Yeshua. Simeon, Morta decided, and she quietly stole into his room, tiptoed over to the bed and, panting from fright, whispered, "Simonas! Simonas! Get up!"

Pimpleface Simeon turned over on his other side, grabbed a pillow in his hands, and half asleep he muttered maliciously and bluntly, "So, what did *you* barge in for?"

Morta bore the insult, leaned over him, and in despair gasped out, "There . . . in the barn . . . your mother . . . and the horses . . ."

"Leave me alone," Pimpleface Simeon grumbled. But Morta didn't leave.

"Your mother . . . in the barn," she repeated, and her teeth were chattering.

Then all of a sudden something lit up in Simeon's drowsy brain and he began to jerk as if he'd been burned. He rolled out of bed and made his way to the door, buttoning his underwear as he went and scratching his hairy chest, warm from his sinful dreams.

"Mama," Simeon called out softly as they entered the barn. "Mama!"

He hadn't called her by that name for a long time, oh so long. For twenty, maybe thirty years. He said "you" or "she," but his mother didn't take offense; a person bereft of God cannot surprise you with anything, neither fleeting affection nor deferential indifference.

"Mama," Simeon called out again, and as he emerged from a fog of sleep and anger, he was coming back to his senses.

Morta was trembling uncontrollably.

"Why are you trembling?" the tavern keeper's son wheezed.

"I . . . I'm not trembling . . . not trembling at all . . . It just seems that way to you, Simonas," she answered, biting her lip.

"Where is she?" he asked.

"There," Morta said. She pointed her finger toward the trough.

"In the trough?"

"No . . . now . . . now you can see her yourself."

He's pretending, Morta thought. He already . . . saw her a long time ago. He's pretending. He's completely terrified. My God, how terrible to see your own mother in the air with a noose around her neck. How good it is that my parents are at the end of the earth, in Siberia. I would die if I saw them . . .

They approached the spot where Chava was hanging like an old dress on a rope.

"Mama!" Simeon moaned. He buried his face in her stiffened legs. "Forgive me. Forgive me."

He was crying, and his tears fell on her black shoes, her black stockings, her black fate. Her entire life—as long as he could remember it—she had worn black.

"Help me!" Pimpleface Simeon said. "I'll hold the ladder. And you . . . you climb up and untie her."

"Maybe you, Simonas," Morta weakly objected.

"I'll stand below and catch her. I'll hold out my arms and catch her. I don't want her to fall on the floor. Let it be into my arms. She carried me in her arms. She carried me, didn't she?"

"She carried you," Morta agreed.

"Now it's my turn. Climb up!"

Morta reluctantly started climbing up the ladder.

"I have no idea how she got up there. She never climbed anywhere her whole life. Nowhere . . . not a step . . . not one little step," he whispered. "Only to the balcony in the synagogue, and then only on holidays . . . Why are you wavering?"

"Oy, Simonas!" Morta cried out.

"Climb up! Climb!"

The first rays of dawn were spilling through the cracks in the roof. Chilly and erratic, they lit up the ladder, the dozing horses, and Pimpleface Simeon, who was barefoot in his white underwear.

"Why are you taking so long?" he set upon Morta.

"I can't do it! The knot is too tight. I can't do it, Simonas!"

"I'll push her up now and you'll untie her."

Pimpleface Simeon clasped his arms around the dead woman's legs and lifted her up over his head of disheveled hair.

"Is it good now?" he asked Morta.

"Yes, it's good!"

Now the restraint and the distance and the estrangement between Pimpleface Simeon and his mother were gone. He held her tightly, as he would have held Zelda had she come in the evening to the old pear tree, or if she had wanted to gather a basket of ripe strawberries on the other side of the river without getting her feet wet.

He carried his mother through the barn as across a torrential river. He carried her to her final shore where no old pear tree or strawberries exist, where there are neither love nor insults, to rough boards and the only white spot in her life—a shroud.

Simeon carried her into his own room, laid her on his bed, covered her with his blanket, and sat down at the head of the bed.

"Get dressed," Morta said.

He didn't move.

"People will come, so get dressed," she repeated sadly.

Pimpleface Simeon sat at the bedside and fixed his unblinking eyes upon his dead mother. Everything inside him rattled and gurgled as in a bog.

"Chava!" he heard his father calling. "Chava!"

Then: "Morta! Morta!"

"He's calling me," Morta told Simeon.

"Let him call!"

"Simeon! Simeon!" Yeshua's voice roared. "Have you seen your mother?"

"I haven't seen her. Haven't seen her. No one has ever seen her," Simeon said quietly.

The tavern keeper Yeshua came to the door. "Why aren't you answering?" he asked, sensing that something was wrong.

"Hush," Pimpleface Simeon silenced him. "Hush, Mama is sleeping."

"Where?"

"Right here," growled the son.

Yeshua stood in the doorway, afraid to approach the bed. One step, and he stopped. Another step.

"Why is she sleeping in your bed?" he asked from a distance.

"Because she feels cold with you, father. Cold . . ."

"Chava!" the tavern keeper cried out. He rushed to the bed and flopped down in his clothes next to the dead woman.

"Chava!"

"Stop that," Simeon said.

"Oh, my God!" Yeshua bit the pillow. "Oh, dear God!"

He abruptly drew his dead wife to him and covered her with hurried, wet kisses.

Pimpleface Simeon turned away.

Morta stood at the head of the bed and crossed herself.

"Go away," the tavern keeper said. "Go away. Leave the two of us together. You hear?"

Pimpleface Simeon stood up and without a word headed for the door.

"Get dressed, Simonas," Morta begged. She grabbed his clothes and ran after him.

"Chavele," Yeshua whispered after his son and Morta had gone. "Yesterday you promised to make pancakes from fresh potatoes. You know how much I love your potato pancakes, Chavele . . ."

He stroked her hair, touched a gold earring.

"My God! How beautiful your hair is! How alive! You shouldn't be embarrassed, you shouldn't close your eyes. Think a moment—what's wrong with what I said? I said that I love your potato pancakes, and just that. Come, Chavele, let's go . . . Thank God we have our own bed. Our bed is softer. Every flea there knows how much I love your potato pancakes and your beautiful hair . . . My God! Merciful God!"

Tears built up but no tears came. In the past, Yeshua had cried for any reason, even the most trivial. Tears brought relief, washed cruelty and sullenness from his face, made him young as in earlier days, returned him to the time when he—a spirited, lighthearted offspring of the Mandel family—had traveled all around Lithuania in search of Jewish fortune, which was uncertain and fleeting, like smoke. But now beside the dead, blue-faced Chava he couldn't squeeze out a single tear. Tears betrayed him, abandoned him, his throat tickled as from linden honey, his head ached from emptiness and weakness, and grasshoppers chirped in his ears. Yeshua suddenly became aware of the sickly-sweet smell of death, and frantically tried to suppress his nausea.

He walked over to the sideboard, took out a carafe, and for the first time in his life poured himself a large silver cup of vodka. He closed his eyes and gulped it down. The vodka burned his kosher gullet and scared away the grasshoppers, and then suddenly everything became painfully easy and clear.

Yeshua returned to the bed, cup in hand, stared at Chava and said, lucidly and despairingly—for the first time in his life—"To you, Chava! To your goodness and faithfulness."

He turned the cup in his hand and, not knowing what to do with it, he impulsively lifted it to his wife's stiff lips and touched them with the silver brim.

"Did you take off the earrings?"

Fully dressed, Simeon stood in the doorway.

"The earrings?" Yeshua winced, and dropped the cup, and the remaining drops of vodka fell like tears onto the dead woman's stomach.

"I can't," he told his son. "You take them off."

"The one who gave them to her must also remove them," Simeon answered.

"The women will come and cleanse her body, perform the ritual, and remove them," the tavern keeper Yeshua said, shielding himself.

"No one will come. Morta will do everything."

"Morta?"

"Or perhaps you want her to be buried in the vacant land outside the cemetery fence?"

"I don't want that." Yeshua gave way, and again his head was like a meadow full of grasshoppers. Everything was twitching, chirping, chattering. What a disgrace, what a disgrace, he tortured himself, struggling in vain against the rising, suffocating nausea. Chava, his wife, the mother of his children, had to be hidden from the living so that not a soul would guess how she had passed away.

Morta heated up water in a cast-iron kettle and poured it into an enormous pot used for cooking jam. She undressed Chava and began washing her cold body. She tried not to look at the dead woman as the washcloth moved over her legs and hips until it reached the pouches of shrunken breasts. Morta whispered something to muster her courage. She did not understand what she said, but the words calmed her, took her away from this bed, these flat, fallen breasts with wrinkled nipples that looked like dried wolfberries.

The hens were clucking their heads off in the yard. The old goose, who had outlived her mistress, hissed. Morta changed the water, turned Chava from her stomach to her back, washed her, turned her over again, threw the washcloth in the pot, sat down for a moment on the edge of the bed, wiped off her sweat, and, without looking at the body, said, "Thank you."

She thanked Chava for not sending her away, for letting her keep the cow, for never yelling, and for pretending, as long as she lived, that there was nothing and would be nothing going on between Morta and her son Simeon.

"Thank you," she said again and burst into tears. She quickly controlled herself, however, carried the pot into the courtyard, and emptied it onto the withered grass. The hens came running over, hoping to get some food. But the old goose cocked her head with dignity, as if she had immediately realized what kind of slops these were.

"Is everything done?" Simeon asked Morta as he dragged two coarse boards from the barn.

"Everything," Morta said.

"The earrings, too?"

"I can't, Simonas."

"They'll go to you," he said.

"I don't want any earrings," Morta said, feeling afraid. "I'd rather cut off my ears."

"Take them off," he ordered, carrying a board under each arm. "They're of no use to the worms."

"No, no." Morta became agitated. "Ask whatever you want from me, but not that."

"They will suit you well. Very well." He did not give up. "Hurry! We must bury her today so there won't be gossip. Tomorrow is Friday, and then Shabbes . . . We don't bury the dead on Shabbes. Go!"

Morta covered her stomach and chest with the pot, as if Pimpleface Simeon had struck there with his terrifying, stark words.

"People will come soon. Father went to get Rabbi Hillel. Everything must be ready before his arrival. Go!" She obeyed him and went into the house, covering her stomach and chest with the pot.

Morta stiffly walked over to the bed. While she was removing the cursed, beautiful earrings, an eternity seemed to have passed.

In her palm they glittered like two gold beetles, two ladybirds; if you blew on them, they would spread their wings and fly, and she, Morta, would open the window and—happy as at her first communion—would say, "Fly! Fly away!"

She herself wanted to fly out the window, rise up beneath the clouds, and float over the tavern, above the small town, high above the earth with its worms inside and outside of graves.

All at once she caught sight of another Morta, just like herself, but only waist-up, without legs and without her homespun skirt. She walked up to the mirror.

It was an old mirror in a heavy oak frame set on a small table with curved, carved legs. Carefully, with two fingers, Morta removed one earring from her palm, held it up to her right ear, with a quick twist of her head tossed back a lock of red hair that the sun had bleached, and looked at herself in the indifferent but fair glass.

"Oy!" She felt ashamed and turned to look at the bed.

The lobes of Chava's ears were turning black like stale pancakes.

Morta pricked herself with an earring and ran out of the room and into the yard as fast as she could.

By the time the synagogue caretaker arrived, Chava was no longer in the bed. She was lying on the floor wrapped in a shroud. For the sake of appearances, Pimpleface Simeon had put some kind of powder on her face and bound a white lace kerchief around her neck—a kerchief that had been in the house since the time of her wedding.

"A great misfortune! What sorrow!" the caretaker droned like a bee, noticing the smell of the powder and casting a sideways glance at the white kerchief around Chava's neck. "Who would have thought? Who would have thought?"

Wearing a black frockcoat, a black velvet yarmulke, and shoes he had never worn before, the tavern keeper Yeshua nodded his head sorrowfully and rocked forward and backward, apparently praying. Pimpleface Simeon pushed the caretaker into a corner and in a hoarse voice asked, "Where is Rabbi Hillel?"

"Rabbi Hillel took to his bed," the caretaker muttered with excessive respect. "His liver. It's his liver. So young and already the liver."

Simeon made a face. "You don't need a liver to conduct a funeral service. You need a voice."

"A great misfortune! What sorrow!" the bee droned again. "What's that smell?"

"Death," the tavern keeper's son rudely silenced him.

The caretaker annoyed him. Small and nimble, he kept his eyes on the deceased and kept sniffing with his hunter's nose all the while.

"Who would have thought? Such a woman! A loving husband . . . a loving son. Esteemed and respected. When that tramp told me, 'We'll make Reb Yeshua cry stinking tears,' I didn't believe him. I thought—he's a madman!"

"What tramp?" Pimpleface Simeon became alert.

"He was sitting in the cemetery yesterday on Khone Brayman's grave and banging on a clapper. 'Why are you banging?' I ask. He says, 'The cemetery is there!' and points to the tavern."

"Was he wearing a yarmulke . . . with a pin?"

"With a pin . . . He's staying with the night watchman Rakhmiel," the caretaker nodded to the tavern keeper's son. "That kerchief! Such a beautiful kerchief on the deceased! Like the veil for a wedding! No one here has ever been buried in a head scarf like that!"

Pimpleface Simeon had stopped listening. His thoughts were no longer on the caretaker or his late mother but on the man with a yarmulke fastened to his hair with a pin. It was he who had brought misfortune upon their home, he who had tied the knot around his mother's neck, he who had laid her on these rough boards!

Naftali and Chaim Spivak—the brothers of the deceased—arrived. Standing by the mirror that was now covered with a flannel cloth, they approached the deathbed in a dignified manner, let a miserly tear fall, shook their gray-haired heads. The brothers asked no questions. With or without questions, it doesn't matter, because you can't bargain with death, you won't get anywhere with that. Even though the kerchief bound around their sister's neck aroused vague and troubling suspicions.

"Say, Chaim," Naftali whispered. "Why is her neck bound?"

"So that it will be hard for her to breathe in the other world," Chaim answered. He took a handkerchief from his pocket and, for the sake of decency, began to wipe his dry eyes.

Naftali followed his example. He imitated everything Chaim did. And so they stood, in unison, wiping their keen, penetrating eyes with small scraps of scented silk.

Morta was harnessing the horses in the yard. They were surprisingly docile for having sensed death. Only the chestnut horse anxiously pounded the ground with a hoof.

"That's enough, enough," Morta scolded him gently.

She was in no hurry to enter the house. There was nothing to bother her at this moment. So now, she thought, I am left alone with two men, and this thought, plain as a horse's hoof, stung her with shame and alarm.

People were walking past the wagon, but Morta didn't notice them. She senselessly tightened the saddle girth, thrust her hand into the chestnut's mane, and held it there for a long while, sweetening her meek and joyless life with warmth. The elder Andronov brother staggered by—Afinogen, a jovial and bawdy fellow. He took the bay by the bridle and in a hoarse voice asked, "Why is the tavern locked?"

"The mistress died," Morta blurted out, sounding as if she had been found guilty of something shameful.

"Will you give me two bottles?"

"I won't," she answered.

"At least one, then?" Afinogen begged. "My head's been throbbing since yesterday—I can't stand it. A pity about Chava."

"A pity," said Morta.

"She was a good woman," Afinogen said, trying to soften up Morta. "Quiet. And she didn't look like a Jew. What didn't she have in life?"

"I don't know," Morta said.

"Everyone on earth lacks something. For some it's money, others—vodka. Come on, give me a bottle."

"All right. Just leave me alone!"

Morta ran into the tavern and brought out a bottle.

"If they die, you'll get it all," Andronov grinned. He took some small change from his pocket, gave Morta the coins, stuck the bottle under his shirt, and walked off.

No sooner did Afinogen leave than Zelda Fradkin arrived.

"Good day," she greeted Morta stiffly.

"Good day, Miss."

Zelda wore a black mourning scarf pulled over her pale forehead, a dress of gray fabric with a pattern resembling sprinkled grains of buckwheat, and knee-high boots with leather buckles. Morta had never seen such boots.

"Go into the house, Miss."

"No, no," Zelda became agitated. "I'm here only for a moment. How did she die?"

"How?" Morta hesitated. "She went to bed and didn't wake up."

"Like Mama," Fradkin's daughter said.

The autumn sun was shining serenely in the sky. The horses shook their heads, making the harnesses jingle, and the jingling made the air quiver. Or perhaps it was quivering from the stillness, from the scant rays of sun, or from sparse words lacking warmth and light.

"I've never buried anyone," Zelda unexpectedly admitted.

"And your mother?"

"Mama died when I was so young. They left me at home with a wet nurse. The nurse took one look at me and cried. I dipped my fingers in her tears, licked them, and asked, 'Why are your eyes salty, but not mine?' 'Yours will be salty, too, they will,' she answered. 'Just wait.'"

"Go, Miss, go into the house. They'll be happy to see you," Morta kept on talking, surprised by her own assertiveness. "They won't carry her out yet."

"I'll wait in the yard," Zelda said.

"As you wish, Miss," Morta gave in. "Are you bored living here with us?"

"People live everywhere," Fradkin's daughter answered evasively.

"Well, I think it's boring to be with people," Morta dared to say.

"Where is it fun, then?"

"Where?" Morta tensed up. "With them." She pointed to the horses. "And with the hens. It's fun to be with ones who understand you . . . Should I call Simeon, Miss?"

"There's no need to call anyone. Will they drive her there?"

"They'll carry her," Morta answered, surprised by Zelda's ignorance.

"Then why the horses?"

"To drive the Master back. And Simeon. And you, if you go to the cemetery."

"I see you've become a real Jew."

"Not really," Morta smiled. "Though I know how to cook and pray your way."

"Even pray?"

"Yes. My God doesn't listen to me. I tell myself maybe yours will hear. But that makes Simonas angry. He says the ears of all gods are blocked. I don't believe that though, Miss. God's ears are never blocked. Especially if you aren't asking for something for yourself. But what do people do? They only ask for themselves and for their dear ones."

"For whom should you ask, then?"

"For everyone," Morta said. "For all. For you, Miss . . . for this horse . . . for that hen over there so that the rooster will cuddle with her. Otherwise, she walks around the yard and clucks so pitifully you'd think she were being cut with a knife."

"She'll be carved up anyway, pray or not," Zelda said, then suddenly added: "Come to my house!"

"What for?" Morta raised her eyebrows. "You have Golda."

"We'll pray together, you and I," Zelda said. A smile brightened her pale face.

"I would be happy to come, Miss, but I don't have time. And now there'll be none at all."

"Come," Zelda repeated her invitation.

"All right," Morta said. "Sometimes when I go to get water or the tavern is empty, I hear you playing. How fortunate you are, Miss!"

"You're the fortunate one," Zelda mumbled uncertainly.

"Me?"

"You have *them*," Zelda patted the chestnut's neck. "And the hens."

"But your father . . . Mr. Fradkin has a whole herd of horses like these. And he can buy a thousand hens!"

"He can, he can," Zelda nodded. "But what good is it if the horses don't understand you and the hens—a thousand hens—are served in gravy."

She was about to leave when she saw that the logger Itsik had come into the yard.

"Here's Itsik," Morta said happily. "That means they'll carry her out soon. Simeon will grab one end of the board, Itsik the other, and the mistress will float as if on a raft."

Itsik had already recognized Zelda from afar. He walked more slowly and erratically, like a drunk.

"Why are you standing out here?" he asked with assumed indifference. "Let's go into the house."

Don't let me lose her, Itsik thought. Don't let her go.

He was ready to grab her in his arms and carry her into the house like a gift from Heaven, even before the funeral, with an unexpected joy not to be shared with anyone. Zelda apparently felt his desire. She lacked the strength to resist, and she strolled behind him as if on water, feeling an unusual burst of energy and not thinking about the shore she had left behind.

"What a joyful day it is," Itsik said, slowing his already unhurried step. "I have wanted to tell you that for a long time."

"What?"

"What a joyful day it is. But the days passed and there was no joy."

"And there is none now, I think."

"My late father used to say that whoever meets his beloved at a funeral will remain happy with her until the grave."

He was in a hurry to astound her with his impatience, to stun her with his sincerity, because he didn't believe that he would ever again be able to confess his extreme, overflowing feelings to her. Let her laugh at him, run away, and never look at him again, but let her know and feel the cloud that was swirling above him.

"My father is never wrong," he tried to joke, surprised by her silence. Hadn't his confession made *any* impression? Could a cloud like this possibly swirl over her head every day?

"My father is never wrong either," Zelda answered.

"Yours is wrong," he almost shouted. "Because he measures everything by height and weight. But I'm not a tree . . . And you're not a tree, Zelda."

"Stop it," she cut him off. Her face had turned red from his words, and her heart was jumping and skipping beats. In between, in those moments when it stood still, she was trying to catch every sound, the way a fish tries to catch a morsel carried by the current.

"My late father used to say, 'Itsik! Don't make a declaration of love in a grove or on a riverbank, but at a deathbed or in a cemetery. If you are heard, you will have a long and happy life because a woman is like death—she can't be outwitted or cheated.'"

"Why are you lying? You don't even remember your father," Zelda said quietly.

"But I . . . I remember his words," Itsik replied, beginning to sweat.

They circled around the tavern, but they couldn't find the door to the room where the dead woman lay on rough floorboards. Her husband, the tavern keeper Yeshua, had never made a declaration of love to her—not in a grove, not on the riverbank, and not in the marriage bed. Perhaps he would now, swallowing tears and seeking sympathy, at the burial pit.

The cemetery was much younger than the dead woman. The first Jew had been buried in the town cemetery before the uprising of 1863. Before that, the dead were driven to Mishkine, since it was too far for pallbearers to carry them to the cemetery, as was customary in other small towns.

While Pimpleface Simeon and Itsik were carrying Chava down the street of the town, onlookers joined the handful of relatives. Funerals were an event, like hail in August or a thunderstorm with lightning in the full sun. Stumbling, people spilled out of their houses and followed them. They sniffed and snuffed, cursed the bumpy cart road, complained about their shortness of breath and their fate, while filling their chests with the fresh air. There is no air like this anywhere else in the world, it seems, whether you travel far and wide, or whether you circle from one end to the other all the way to the Promised Land. The air of the Lithuanian countryside flows from the day of one's birth to the day of burial, from the first breath to that last breath that accompanies every creature. Paying no heed to the Pale of Settlement, to Christians or to Jews, it envelops and permeates every *lapserdak* and *sermyaga*.

Children rushed to the cemetery behind the adults, and behind the children came the dogs. No one chased them away because even a dog has the right to stand at the grave for a moment, shed a tear, and even bark at death.

The tavern keeper Yeshua could hardly put one foot in front of the other. Next to him, the Spivak brothers, Naftali and Chaim, strode along solemnly. Itsik kept on looking back to see if Zelda was coming.

Zelda held on to the edge of the wagon in which Morta sat, running her fingers over the reins as over a rosary.

"Stop!" Yeshua let out suddenly.

"What's happened?" Pimpleface Simeon shouted without turning to see.

"The policeman! The policeman is waving."

"So let him wave," the tavern keeper's son bristled.

"Let's wait a minute. Why get the man angry?"

"Wait if you want to wait," Simeon said, without slowing down.

The policeman stood at the gate of his house, waving his cap in a friendly and sympathetic way. In the air the cap gleamed like an enormous mushroom.

The tavern keeper Yeshua raised his arm and waved weakly in response: "Thank you, Ardalion Ignatich," he said, "I won't forget." Lowering his arm, he caught the unfriendly glance of his brother-in-law Naftali Spivak and cringed as if he'd been hit. God, what's happening to me, Yeshua thought. Who am I waving to? At least there's one good thing—Nesterovich didn't want vodka. And if he had wanted it? Would I have left Chava and gone back to the tavern? Probably.

Then suddenly Yeshua's attention was drawn to someone's dog, a piebald with a crooked, oblong face and ears that drooped like potato tops. A stray that was running along the cart road, wagging the stump of its tail as if saying goodbye to someone.

"Whose dog is that?" the tavern keeper asked into his brother-in-law Naftali's back.

"Come to your senses, Yeshua! What are you thinking about?" Spivak put him to shame.

"About the dog," the tavern keeper admitted.

"You should be thinking about Chava," Naftali scowled.

The tavern keeper slowed down, and when the wagon caught up to him, he told Morta, "After the funeral bring it home."

"Bring what?" Morta asked, taken aback.

"That dog over there."

"Why?" Morta stopped fingering the reins and stared at the master.

"Because," Yeshua snapped.

He himself didn't understand why he needed this mangy dog, but he didn't take his eyes off it until they reached the cemetery, and the longer he looked, the stranger his impulsive desire became.

What's happening to me, he thought. Why can't I think about Chava, who I lived with for almost thirty-five years? Why am I thinking about this homeless, scraggly dog instead? Yeshua suddenly lashed out at the Spivaks. The brothers are pretending to be grief-stricken. They're pretending. They'd gotten rid of their sister, passed her off to him like stale goods . . . Everyone pretends. They lie when they conceive and lie when they bury. The entire life of a human being is one long lie, sometimes profitable and sometimes not. Truth is like this dog—scraggly and homeless. If the world were a place of truth, not a single person would survive in it for even a day. People would cut each other's throats, strangle one another, murder. Everything depends on lying. Everything. And it makes you sick, like a hangover. But can you throw it all up? Can you throw it all up?

When they lowered Chava into the grave, Yeshua cried at last.

The synagogue caretaker hovered nearby, sniffing with his hunter's nose the whole time.

"Why are you sniffing?" the tavern keeper couldn't contain himself.

The caretaker said nothing. He was ready to swear that an odor was coming from Yeshua's tears—slops, a rotten egg, or a child's filth. As the caretaker remembered the tramp with the yarmulke fastened to his hair with a pin, and his incomprehensible words about the tavern keeper's stinking tears, he himself began to sob loudly from confusion and alarm.

Everyone—Pimpleface Simeon, Zelda, Itsik, Morta, the onlookers, the children, the dogs—looked askance at the caretaker and were unable to make any sense out of why he was disturbing the heavens with his sobs.

Pimpleface Simeon went up to him, took out a three-kopeck coin, and said, "You're good at crying. Keep it up!"

"Thank you," the caretaker mumbled. "Thank you. Do *you* smell anything, Simeon?"

"Something stinks." Simeon said, taking some cemetery air into his nostrils.

"What did I tell you?" the caretaker said quickly.

"Are you the one who shit in his pants?"

"No. It's the tears that smell that way. Reb Yeshua's tears. The man . . . in the yarmulke with a pin . . . told me."

"I'll kill him," Pimpleface Simeon whispered, and the stench of hatred enveloped the caretaker's face, the sorrowful figure of the tavern keeper Yeshua, the fresh grave, and the dogs sniffing one another.

11

"How much can you sleep, Uri? Get up! The peas on the table are getting cold!"

Rebeyne shel eylem, I'm delirious. How terrible—I need to plug my ears. On hearing his wife Rokhl's tremulous voice, Rabbi Uri looks around suspiciously. No one was in the house, and no one could be. A week before they celebrated the giving of the Torah on *Shavues*, two years earlier, she had died—expired, smelling of decay, in this bed where Rabbi Uri is now lying and hearing her say, "Get up!"

Rabbi Uri is old and unwell, but so far he has kept his wits. He hears the voice of his Rokhl just as clearly as in the days when they both arrived here. He was young, well-built, with jet-black sidelocks winding down like charred clusters of grapes; she was thin, tiny, and easily startled, like a bird.

"Enough sleeping!"

With his wrinkled index fingers Rabbi Uri plugs his hairy ears and his wife's voice fades, but fear keeps flashing in the old man's eyes, which are red from sleeplessness. His finger plugs tremble, and unexpectedly he begins to shiver, as if peas were rattling throughout his body.

"I'm sick of peas, Rokhl," Rabbi Uri says in an unnaturally loud voice, looking around once again.

Why on earth is he looking around, the numbskull? Rokhl is dead. Rokhl is buried in the cemetery, and no dead person has ever returned from there.

In the house, apart from Rabbi Uri, there are only a spider and an autumn fly. Rabbi Uri noticed the fly a long time before. In the last month, all the other flies had hidden from the frost in cracks or had died, but she keeps on flying and flying.

Rabbi Uri used to shoo her out the window, close the doors tightly, and sweep the crumbs from the table, but the fly flew back in. She was small, clever, and devoted, like Rokhl. What did she want from him? She should have crawled into a crack somewhere and waited there until the spring; instead, she circles around buzzing and follows him everywhere. Rabbi Uri had never in his life seen such a fly. Although he couldn't stand flies, he surrendered to the will of the Almighty, who created them as He created man. He became used to her and even protected her from the spider, who was persistently weaving her lethal web and who hated everything that flew.

The spider had lived in the house for ages. Sometimes she crawled down the wall to the master of the house, and Rabbi Uri watched her with deferential fear as she stepped with intricate little legs that resembled Hebrew letters.

After the cat died, the spider remained the only other living creature in the house, not counting the cunning bedbugs that crawled out of their hiding places at night and sucked Rabbi Uri's blood, which had cooled like cold beet soup. But the prudent and enigmatic spider was nothing compared to the fly.

As soon as Rabbi Uri went to bed, the fly would land on the pillow and root herself there awaiting words of affection. Whether or not he threatened her, she sat there and watched the old man and his frozen soul. When her closeness warmed him, his soul turned white, like a stork in the darkness.

Yesterday, when Rabbi Uri was sipping the beet soup, cold as his blood, the fly landed on the table where Rokhl had set her tireless, strong hands when she was alive. The fly stared at his toothless mouth and his bleeding gums, and for no apparent reason her tiny wings began to rustle. From this plaintive rustling, full of some secret significance, Rabbi Uri suddenly suffered an attack of hiccups, and no matter how much he tried, he couldn't overcome it until morning.

In agony from insomnia, Rabbi Uri picked at the pillow with his hand from time to time, and then the fly would take off, crackling in the nighttime silence, sounding like a log in the stove.

"Who are you?" the old man asked her, but she just hummed sleepily, bumping either into his beard or the wall. "I am Rabbi Uri," he said quietly, swallowing the stagnant air and fighting the hiccups in vain. "I had a wife. Her name was Rokhl. She also hovered over me and watched me at night from the pillow beside me.

"Rokhl! Rokhl!"

He listened closely to the sound of that familiar name, and it blended strangely and peacefully with the buzzing of the tiny fly wings.

"Surely someone should listen to us," Rabbi Uri whispered. "A dog or a fly—it doesn't matter."

He fell into a short, agonizing dream, woke up, heard the silence, once again picked at the pillow with his hand, and felt something close to joy when—in the bedbug-filled darkness—he heard the faint hum of the one who voluntarily shared the lonely bed with him.

He did not understand why he had not chosen the Almighty for his confession but rather a simple fly, thousands of which fly over every stinking garbage dump or swarm in summer around the butcher's shop, sticking to skinned and gutted carcasses. Perhaps because she was alive, palpable, and accessible, and God was far from him, as far as sixty years earlier when he, Rabbi Uri, had first set foot on this threshold made of logs, on these creaking floorboards. Perhaps because he had repeatedly made confessions to the Almighty who, all-powerful and merciful, knew everything about him down to the smallest details, to the stain on his yarmulke, to a pimple on his body. Or perhaps because both the Almighty and the fly were similarly silent and unfathomable. When all is said and done, though, is it so important why?

Rabbi Uri remembered how as a child he had confided his secrets to a nameless green tree in the vacant land behind his grandfather's house. He would run to it every evening, in spring and in summer, in fall and in winter, and lightly touch its rough bark with his lips. He touched it and incoherently whispered things he never would have disclosed to anyone on earth, even his father and mother. He believed that his impassioned and confused words, like tree sap, would flow up to the very crown, and from the crown would soar into the sky, and God would hear them and would send joy and good fortune down to him and all his loved ones. To this day the aftertaste of the bark has remained on his withered, nearly lifeless, lips. The aftertaste of faith.

Lightning later struck his childhood tree and fire consumed it, along with all his secrets and hopes.

Master of the Universe, how many such trees had burned down during his many years! A whole forest! But he didn't give up, he didn't lose hope, he didn't surrender to the lightning. He searched for a new green tree in vacant land and touched its rough trunk with his lips.

For almost sixty years he had touched Rokhl, and then lightning struck her, too.

Rokhl! Rokhl!

"You love God more than me," she would reproach him. "You get up and you lie down with His name on your lips. But no one has ever begotten children with it."

What could he say to her?

"All the Jews in our town are our children."

"No, Uri, no. When we die, there will be no one to close our eyes."

He wouldn't budge. One's love for God should not be shared with anyone, even one's children, even one's wife. What are children, what is a wife, if not gain? And where there is profit, there is no faith.

Had he come here to bring forth a bunch of children and busy himself with them? He had a higher and more important goal. In the yeshiva, God had already put his own word into Uri's mouth and appealed for the salvation of all the lost souls who were mired in a search for profit, mired in indifference and humiliating servility. Every year saw an increase in the number of Jews who betrayed the language and law of their fathers and forefathers by converting to Russian Orthodoxy or Catholicism and, in exchange for their new faith, they received the good graces of policemen and other authorities. Rabbi Uri had made his way to the backwoods, to this hole, only in order to save them from this pernicious temptation. A people, no matter how small, how weak and defenseless, should stand up for its sons. People and birds don't drink from the sea, but from rivers and streams. What would happen if one of these days people suddenly decided to drain the streams?

Rabbi Uri could have stayed in Vilna. Had he stayed there, in his native city, before you knew it, he could have become chief rabbi of Vilna, *Yerushalayim de-Lite*—the Jerusalem of Lithuania. He was not thinking about fame or honors, however, but about the good of his congregation. Before he arrived, there was no synagogue or cemetery in the shtetl. The deceased were driven to Mishkine—what a disgrace!—and everyone prayed anywhere, or else they completely forgot about prayer. It was he, Rabbi Uri, who established a synagogue in the town and who founded the cemetery.

"You should think about offspring," Rokhl scolded him. "When there are as many of us as stars in the sky, nothing will scare us. Look how many Russians and Chinese there are in the world. We need to have children, Uri, we need children."

He made excuses.

"If we don't have a child, we'll go to Vilna."

When she was forty, she became pregnant, but the baby was stillborn, and the uncircumcised boy was not buried in Mishkine but in that place in town where, within five years, the cemetery would spread out. Rabbi Uri's son was fated to be the first one buried there.

"Do you see?" was all he said to his wife when they returned from the field, and she simply could not understand whether he was grieving or glad.

For a long time, Rabbi Uri was tormented by the fact that the first person buried in the new cemetery had not been circumcised. He expected revenge from God, but God took revenge on Rokhl instead. She nearly went mad at the time; for almost a year she didn't talk to anyone, walked around the house like a ghost, bought a wooden cradle from a Lithuanian man, hung it in the middle of the house,

and rocked it all day long while he, Rabbi Uri, sailed on the sea of
Torah with his students.

"Rokhl," he implored her.

But she didn't answer and would not move away from the cradle. Sometimes Rokhl jumped out of bed in the middle of the night,
rushed to the cradle in only her nightgown, and like a madwoman
repeated, "We're wet again . . . we're wet again."

Or else she sang a lullaby that she had composed herself:
Sleep, go to sleep, my beauty,
Close your dark eyes.

Then, in that distant and terrible year, Rabbi Uri became angry
with God for the first time. He was more hurt than angry. Anger,
he consoled himself, estranges you from the Almighty, but a broken
heart brings you closer, and so he did not consider his feeling rebel-
lious or sinful.

The people in town felt sorry for him and waited for him to send
Rokhl to a madhouse, yet he just prayed more zealously and lingered
more frequently in the study house with his students.

"Rabbi, you should borrow a baby from someone. If from no
one else, then from Feybush, the stove-maker. His wife recently had
twins." That's what Ben-Tzion Guralnik, the government rabbi at the
time, advised. Eight years later he renounced his Jewish faith.

For a long while Rabbi Uri hesitated, but finally he heeded the
advice and went to Feybush's house to talk it over. He explained his
request, stammering and suffering the whole time from inarticulate-
ness and awkwardness, and when he stopped talking, he felt a terrible weakness that paralyzed his will, as if he were wholly composed
of soft candlewax rather than sinew.

"We can't refuse you anything, Rabbi," babbled Dvora, the freckled mother of the twins. "Take either one. They're both nice ones."

She praised her twins the way a peasant woman at the market
brags about her wares, and her cheerful voice and abject servility
made him almost feel sick.

"What about milk?" Dvora continued.

"What milk?" Rabbi Uri was taken aback.

"Breast milk," freckled Dvora blurted out. "Rokhl's has dried up, you see, but I have more than enough of it, Rabbi."

Dvora moved toward him, proudly bearing her full breasts. Rabbi Uri shrank back from her, his eyes filled with shame and despair, and he started to choke. Reaching into his pocket for a handkerchief, his hand could only find his prayer shawl, which dangled helplessly beneath his frockcoat.

"I'll come to see him," Dvora blabbered on. "Like a wet nurse. That's how it's always done in rich homes."

"How?" Rabbi Uri was confused.

"Some give birth, others nurse. Let my Iser grow up in a rich man's house."

Rabbi Uri chose not to contradict her.

At dusk, freckled Dvora carried Iser, swaddled in rags, to Rabbi Uri's. For a long time she couldn't bring herself to go inside. She waited on the porch with the child, stood on her tiptoes and kept peeping into the curtained windows. She was suddenly seized by an instinctive fear, and she pressed Iser to her breast, full of maternal love and milk. She bent over him, guiltily whispered something, and took a step back, as if she had stumbled. At just that moment Rabbi Uri appeared in the doorway.

"Come in," he said.

Rokhl was sleeping.

Dvora took a look at the cradle, kissed the baby, and put him down gently. Her colorless eyelashes started to blink.

"We'll pay you," Rabbi Uri said quietly.

"For what?" Dvora was startled.

"For Iser."

"What are you saying, Rabbi, what are you saying . . . Let at least *one* of ours grow up to be a learned person. Not a stove-maker."

She bowed to the cradle and left.

In a dream Rokhl heard a child's cry, and she woke up. She went to the cradle and was shocked.

"That's not our son, Uri," she said and began to sob loudly. "What have you done?"

Rokhl stood there watching the unfamiliar child, his face, creased like an old tobacco pouch, and his half-closed puppy eyes, and her tears dropped into the cradle. Her madness slowly receded before a sudden wave of goodness and feminine compassion.

Suddenly, Rokhl leaned over the cradle and chanted, like a prayer, "We're wet . . . wet . . ."

Nimbly, as if she had long been accustomed to this, she changed Iser's diaper, laid him down, grabbed the rawhide strap, and began to swing the cradle.

Rabbi Uri fixed his gaze on her, and everything swayed before his eyes—the cradle, the house, the trees, the starry sky outside the windows, and his wife Rokhl—and this motion intoxicated him, like wine, and gave him strength and solace.

"Rokhl," he said. "I never . . . you know yourself . . . I never spoke those words to you."

"And you didn't have to," she answered.

"But today . . . today I think I love you more than Him."

He did not dare speak God's name aloud.

"That's blasphemy," Rokhl said.

"Love can't be blasphemy. Who are we without love? A bunch of insatiable guts full of tomorrow's filth."

"Hush, Uri, hush," she pleaded.

"Forgive me. Ever since childhood I wanted everyone to be happy. Everyone but me."

"Why?"

"When you're happy, you don't really live. You're afraid . . . afraid of losing your happiness. Long ago I made a vow to the Almighty."

"That you'd never be happy?"

"Yes. I told Him: 'Oh, God, forget about me, remember the others. They're more worthy of Your mercy!' You, Rokhl, and the stove-maker's wife Dvora and this innocent child wrapped in need."

Rabbi Uri stopped short unexpectedly. He walked over to the cradle, and stood beside Rokhl, and her breath spread toward him like a wind; it entered his nostrils and from there flowed deeply into his body, bringing warmth, filling his heart and stirring his blood, and he, like never before, comprehended the secret of the fetus growing in the womb and fruit growing on branches—he was amazed by it and felt himself to be a pathetic eunuch.

Rabbi Uri carefully pulls his finger plugs out from his hairy ears, and once again he hears Rokhl's impatient, irritated voice.

"I won't call you again. Get up!" Her voice was commanding and sounded unfriendly.

Rabbi Uri waits and looks around. The cold autumn sun streams through the window.

How can this be, he thinks, trying to reconcile reality with his memories—Rokhl and I were just standing here together, looking at Iser, breathing together, and all at once, in an instant, everything is gone, everything has vanished, and I'm in my cold bed, the autumn sun is streaming through the window, the pillow case on the pillow is dirty, the sheet and blanket are tattered, my feet are sticking out, my hair is tangled and hasn't been washed for so long, and my chest is like the side of a pig, with clumps of coarse white bristles. God, is this disgusting old man with abscesses and scabs, like Job in the Bible, really me—Rabbi Uri, the founder of the town's synagogue and cemetery, a sower of goodness and harmony, a fortress of faith? Are these my eyes that see not Mount Sinai but only a spider and a fly? Are these my ears that hear, not the sound of timbrels, but the tinkling voice of my wife? Are these my hands that don't part clouds but only poke around a dirty pillow? Where are my neighbors, who were once so abundant? Where are my faithful students who followed me in droves and caught my every word, even if it made them shudder? Where are my enemies who thought about one thing only— to hound me to death, shut my mouth, and deprive me of my faith? Faith! Are you just a moment, just a wooden cradle without a baby, which people sing lullabies to in vain until they die?

There's nothing here, Master of the Universe, nothing. Just a spider weaving her web, just a fly pursuing me and speaking in the voice of my Rokhl.

Rokhl is the fly!

Why didn't I think of that before!

Thank You, God, for this miracle. Thank You. Truth be told, I deserve it. I have served You my whole long life and never asked for any reward for myself, not even a sniff of tobacco. Is faith alone not a reward?

I'll get up from bed now. I'll sit at the table and start eating the peas.

Never mind that there are no peas on the table or in the kitchen cabinet. What does it matter if something is *absent* in the wide world—we can still *taste it*, merciful God. *Taste it*, and *rejoice*, and *sing Your praises*. Sometimes it even seems sweeter to us than what we *have*.

I'm getting up now, God. Don't pay any attention to my grunts and groans, don't be angry with me, merciful God—it's always hard for me to get up in the morning. In the morning only the sun rises easily. And it sets more easily than people do.

If my groans are unpleasant, plug Your ears with Your wrinkled index fingers. It's a sure remedy, believe me. Available to both a poor wretch and to the Almighty.

Now I'm standing at the washstand. There's no water but I am washing my hands.

Now I'm praying, blessing my daily bread.

Now I have a spoon in my hand.

Now I'm eating, God.

"Don't chomp," says fly-Rokhl.

She circles above the bowl, buzzing.

"I'm not chomping," I reply.

"You've aged a lot," fly-Rokhl says. "If you had chomped like that in your youth, I would never have married you."

As a matter of fact, it was not worth it for her to marry me. In Vilna there were better suitors. She could have married some shopkeeper or barber. Barbers are good husbands. They don't chomp and they always have a nice smell.

"Should I set aside more?" fly-Rokhl asks.

"Leave it for Iser."

"Iser's not here," fly-Rokhl says. "While you were lolling about in bed, Iser left, and he will never return to us again."

In the yard it is autumn—a time of harvest, a time of bareness. Outside the window leaves are falling from the maple tree.

Thoughts fall exactly the same way, Rabbi Uri thinks. Righteous God, who will count how many of them have fallen on the wooden floor of my house, on the study house's rough planks, on the town's only street, on the cemetery's peaceful grass? If you were to gather them into a pile and start a fire, what an enormous flame would soar above the world!

Rabbi Uri is sitting at the table where there are no peas and no spoon. His bare feet dangle, and occasionally he glances at the door.

What is a door, one might ask? A dozen boards that a carpenter has put together, and nothing more. But there are times when a person expects more from it than from the Almighty.

And Rabbi Uri is waiting for something.

In the past the door was always open. To Jews, Lithuanians, and Russians, and even the district bosses. Some came for advice, some for confession, some with their dreams. Not only was Rabbi Uri a rabbi, he also interpreted dreams, and he was famous throughout the district for that.

Once the policeman Ardalion Nesterovich came to see him. Agitated and sweating, he yelled from the doorway, "I had the damnedest dream. What nonsense! It was nasty!"

"Tell me," Rabbi Uri said calmly.

"Well, in my dream," Nesterovich began, "I am not a policeman, and not even Ardalion, but I'm Chaim. I'm wearing a yarmulke instead of a cap, I have sidelocks instead of side-whiskers, there's no sword at my side, but—what do you call them?—those things that hang down from under your waistcoat."

"The tassels. We call them tzitzis," Rabbi Uri suggested.

"Exactly. The tzitzis."

"So?"

"What so?"

"I'm asking what happened next."

"Nothing happened next. I woke up in a cold sweat."

"Well, then," Rabbi Uri uttered with satisfaction. "If it feels terrible for you to be a Jew in a dream, then what is it like for us in reality?"

"Is that all you can tell me?" the policeman mumbled, disappointed.

"The tzitzis," Rabbi Uri explained, "means joy."

"What joy can a policeman have?" Nesterovich had his doubts.

"Many kinds. A higher rank, for example."

"And why the yarmulke?" Ardalion Ignatich asked next after accepting a new rank.

"The yarmulke stands for a long life."

"How about that! Also not bad. And the sidelocks?"

"Well, the sidelocks are not so good."

"Tell me, tell me. I want to know the truth."

"Sidelocks mean lice," Rabbi Uri smiled.

"I don't know about the promotion or a long life, but you can count on lice. We live in that sort of hole!"

Rabbi Uri dangles his feet and takes a sidelong look at the door. If only the policeman would come. Does no one dream anything anymore?

Where did fly-Rokhl go?

Apparently, she's washing dishes in the entrance hall.

Rabbi Uri strains his ears, as if trying to hear the clinking of dishes, and all at once he changes completely.

What's that? Is the door creaking?

It *is* creaking. Definitely creaking.

Rebeyne shel eylem, who can it be?

Into the house comes Golda, lively, a force of nature, bursting with health, with a kerchief pulled over her forehead, her skirt puffing up, the hem rumpled, with leaves stuck to her boots—she's not afraid of the wind or of autumn.

"Greetings, Rabbi Uri."

Golda's voice is deep and devilish. Her teeth are white, like Passover candles, and she cracks her words the way a squirrel cracks nuts: the kernel goes into the mouth, the shell to the ground.

"Good day."

"I see, Rabbi, that without me things here have become a mess. Your house—please don't be upset with me, Rabbi—stinks, the table is bare. What's wrong, have they all forgotten you?"

"Everyone forgets old people." Rabbi Uri laughs it off.

"You're not an old man! You're in fine shape. If I weren't so flighty, I'd . . ."

"I'm glad to see you," Rabbi Uri interrupts. "You haven't come here for a long time."

"There's lots of work," Osher's widow excuses herself. "Cleaning, washing. I'll clean everything for you, too."

"Thank you."

"And make buckwheat kasha. I brought some grain with me. You love buckwheat kasha, Rabbi, don't you?"

"I love it, love it," Rabbi Uri mumbles, and his eyes open wide, as they did in the best days of his life, when he was young and healthy and a favorite of women. They distracted him with their glances in the synagogue, where his soul languished and his flesh grew weak.

"You're still doing well, Rabbi," Golda laughs.

"Why?"

"I love it, love it."

"You're a sinner," Rabbi Uri happily scolds her.

"Sinners are merciful, the righteous are heartless," Osher's widow says. "Where are all your darlings? They abandoned you, left you without a piece of bread, and ran away like rabbits."

"They didn't run away, they went their own ways," Rabbi Uri says, trying to dampen her ardor. If Golda starts ranting and raving, God forbid, she won't stop before evening. Her tongue is as sharp as a knife.

"Let's say that not everyone went their separate ways. Forgive me, Rabbi, but I'm telling you straight—it's easy to be righteous in words, but when shit needs to be wiped off your neighbor or his wounds need cleaning, you won't find a single righteous one around."

"The righteous are also people."

"People?" Golda becomes angry. "Of all the people I know, only one is righteous. And even he—please don't be upset with me,

Rabbi—is a fool. You've lived almost one hundred years in this world and you're still poor."

Rabbi Uri winces, as if in pain. He finds Golda's words unpleasant. But Osher's widow doesn't stop.

"What kind of righteous ones, Rabbi, are those others who think of their own good?"

Golda suddenly pulls herself together, becomes silent, unbuttons her jacket, puts the bag of buckwheat grain on the table, and rolls up her sleeves, uncovering elbows that are white and plump like risen dough. She casts a sympathetic and disdainful glance around the house, walks over to the wall on which hangs an antiquated clock that practically shows Napoleonic time, opens the old wooden clock door, looks inside, and pulls on the weights.

"You can't do anything with them," Rabbi Uri says.

"Why not?"

"They haven't worked in forty years. They stopped working the day Rokhl's child was stillborn. I brought watchmakers here, and I poked around myself, but the clock won't budge."

Golda looks at him skeptically.

"They stopped by themselves," Rabbi Uri says. "And they'll start by themselves."

He senses that Golda has come here with a definite purpose. She's sure to ask him for something, but what can she ask from him? To be honest, he owes her a lot. After Rokhl died, Osher's widow washed and cooked everything, and cleaned the house, and went to the store and the market for him. Last summer Rabbi Uri wanted to give her two silver goblets as a present, but Golda flatly refused them.

"One day you will marry me, Rabbi," she said. "It's a sin to live with a man outside of marriage."

Rabbi Uri understood she was speaking about Itsik.

Is Itsik really her partner?

"Get dressed, Rabbi," Golda suggests. "I'll open the windows to air out the house. It's a beau-ti-ful day today!"

Rabbi Uri puts on an old shirt and linen pants, pulls socks over his clumsy feet, fumbles with his shoes for a long time, laces them up with shaky fingers. When he smooths out his gray beard, which is as thick as it was in his youth, for a moment he becomes younger.

Golda flings open the windows and into the house burst the smells of milk from the milk pail, musty leaves, and scorched cloth. The tailor neighbor must be ironing someone's trousers.

"Master of the Universe, how good it is!" Rabbi Uri says. "So good!"

"Good," Golda repeats.

"And how much there is!"

"Of what?"

"Air! For a hundred lives! And for everyone! For every cow, for every bug, for every leaf."

"Yes," Golda says. "Nothing in the world is more righteous than air."

All at once Rabbi Uri notices the fly sitting on the windowsill—fly-Rokhl. The sun gilds her tiny wings as she basks beneath its rays. It feels good to her, as good as it feels to him and Golda. Maybe even better than to them. How distinctive she is, how beautiful and carefree!

Fixed to his spot, Rabbi Uri keeps an eye on her, but suddenly he's afraid: what if fly-Rokhl opens her wings and flies away right now and doesn't come back to him, just like Iser, like his students, like his best years.

"Close the window!" Rabbi Uri yells.

"Let the room air out," Golda answers calmly. "Don't be afraid, Rabbi, you won't catch a cold."

"Close it!"

"But I just opened it. What's wrong with you, Rabbi?"

"She . . . she'll fly away."

"Who?"

"Her," Rabbi Uri says, pointing his finger at the windowsill.

"The fly?" Osher's widow can't believe her ears.

"Yes."

"So, let her go. What's so special about a fly? One flies away, another one will come."

"I don't need another," Rabbi Uri persists.

"As you wish." Osher's widow shrugs her shoulders and heads toward the window.

Rabbi Uri stares hard at the windowsill. He whispers something.

"She's flying away!" he sighs.

Fly-Rokhl takes off and seems to be going toward the sun.

Rabbi Uri watches her flutter in the air—so small, courageous, all alone in the universe.

Golda looks at the disheartened old man. Trying to comfort him, says, "She'll return, Rabbi. She'll circle over the marketplace or over the counter in the butcher's shop, and then come back. Though, just think, what can she do in your house?"

Rabbi Uri remains silent, and his silence frightens Golda. The old man has lost his marbles, for sure. He's fallen apart because of a fly, because of a simple insect. If only I had his worries. Osher's widow becomes angry. Now is not the time to come to an understanding with him. But her matter is serious, not simply talk about some fly.

"Rabbi, I have a request for you. Are you listening to me?"

"Yes, yes," the old man says. He looks out the window. The sun blinds his old eyes in which—what misfortune, what a delusion!—tiny golden flies are swirling around and around.

"Have a talk with Itsik," Golda presses him.

"About what?"

"Explain to him . . ."

"What?"

"There's no way things will work out well for him with her."

"With whom?"

Not words so much as pitiful, tiny crumbs fall from his lips, and yet Golda eagerly pecks at them.

"With Zelda. Markus Fradkin will never agree to it. Have a talk with Itsik . . . For some reason, everyone thinks I'm a whore, Rabbi, that I'm ready to sleep around with anyone and everyone . . . It's a lie! I am not a saint, of course. But where, Rabbi, have you seen saints who are happy?"

Golda is trying to coax Rabbi Uri out of his silence, like a mouse from a mousehole.

"Everyone thought my late Osher was someone kind with a good build. But—please don't be upset with me, Rabbi—he wasn't a man. As a child he fell off a tree and broke his leg. That's what he said, and that's what his mother said. But it wasn't a leg he broke, Rabbi . . . I suffered, I put up with him, I felt sorry for him, but at night he knocked me about, beat me as if it was all my fault. Is a woman to blame if she has the candlestick and the man has the candle? And my Osher had no candle, just a stub. I want children so much, Rabbi . . . I want them so much. I'm dying to have children. Are you listening?"

"I'm listening," Rabbi Uri mumbles. "But how can *I* help you? As you know, during the last forty years I haven't been making babies," he says, turning it into a joke.

"Am I asking *you* for children?" Golda is annoyed.

"Itsik's not a son to me. What good will it do if I talk to him?"

"Maybe he'll listen to you anyway. If he marries Zelda, we'll both die."

"Both?"

"Me . . . and him . . ." Golda gently strokes her stomach. "He's already four months, Rabbi."

Rabbi Uri looks at her stomach, at her large, calloused hands and her homespun skirt, and bitterness, together with contempt and pity, parches his bloodless lips.

Which of his learned books—and he has three chests filled with them—can provide him with an answer and solution? What is all his wisdom worth, all his faith, his entire life, if he cannot help even one simple woman? One simple woman! What had he taken upon himself? He had wanted to help an entire people laden with misfortune.

"Have you told Itsik?"

"No. Not only do I need a father for the child, I need a man—please don't be upset with me, Rabbi."

"What are you saying! Fear God!" Rabbi Uri becomes angry. "All right, I'll talk to him."

"But don't say a word about my stomach!"

The windows are wide open, the sky is as clear as it is in spring. Somewhere on a branch a crow stirs and the neighbor's cat carnivorously arches its back.

"I will repay your kindness, Rabbi."

"How?"

"I will catch the fly."

Golda bursts out laughing. Rabbi Uri has never heard such loud and resounding laughter from a Jewish woman. It's the laughter of a happy whore, happy even in her misfortune; someone free, not making a fool of herself with otherworldly concerns, but embracing earthly concerns as a burden that is joyous even if difficult.

He has always envied her, and he forgave her for things he never forgave anyone else—neither himself nor another. Golda could dissolve in laughter during the service in the synagogue, disrupting a prayer's harmonious flow; she could laugh outright at a newly dug grave and he wouldn't take offense at her because he knew that Golda laughed scornfully at everything—death, slander, adversity. She fired back like a wounded soldier, with laughter, refusing to be captured by the enemy.

"I'll feed you, Rabbi, and then be off," Golda says, wiping a thick layer of dust from a chest of drawers with a piece of an old, moth-eaten prayer shawl that had turned into an ordinary rag.

"Where will you go?"

"Anywhere. A house is like a pen, the world like a pasture."

"It's too late for me to graze there, too late," Rabbi Uri answers. "My grass has been trampled, my calf slaughtered."

"Nonsense," Osher's widow shoots back. "There's enough grass for someone your age, too. And enough heifers. Just wait, one will stray and bury her head in your frockcoat. Go outside! Or don't you trust me, Rabbi?"

"I trust you, I trust you," Rabbi Uri whispers, deeply moved. "You're an honest woman."

"Thank you." Golda blushes.

"If you like any of my belongings, take them. There are dresses hanging in the wardrobe. Nice ones, almost never worn. Rokhl only put them on for holidays. Take them! Before the moths get to them . . . And take the porcelain tea set. Who do I drink tea with? Strangers will come and take them."

"Have you no shame, Rabbi?"

"You think they won't take them?"

"I mean—aren't you ashamed to think about death all the time?"

"Don't be afraid. No one will call you a thief. I'll make a will."

"For me? A will?"

"For everyone. Just say what you want."

"Itsik," Golda laughs. "Leave Itsik to me, Rabbi. I don't need anything else."

A smile floats in her eyes like a slice of lemon in tea, but the edges shine like gold.

"I have two wedding rings," Rabbi Uri calmly continues. "One is mine, the other Rokhl's. If God wills and you get married, they'll be good for you and Itsik."

"No, no," Golda waves them away with the torn prayer shawl, though her eyes are sparkling like a cat's.

"My father-in-law gave them to us. My parents were poor. Their only riches were ten sons."

"Oh, my!"

"They all died long ago, and I'm still alive."

"Long life to you, Rabbi. Live!"

"To tell the truth, I've had enough days . . . Both rings are in the porcelain teapot in the sideboard. They didn't bring us happiness. Perhaps they'll bring it to you."

"For me, Rabbi, for the wedding a silver coin would be enough. Pennies . . . If only Itsik will agree."

Golda sits the old man in his wheelchair and pushes it into the yard. In parting, she says, "Come back for dinner."

"Don't overwork yourself. It's hard for the two of you, I'd say."

"What do you mean, Rabbi—it's easier for two."

"I mean maybe you shouldn't teach her how to wash floors at four months."

"And what makes you think, Rabbi, that I'll have a daughter? I'll have a boy."

"May God grant it!"

"I will have a righteous man."

Golda laughs again, and her laughter seems to push the wheelchair.

The tailor leans out the window next door, with an iron in hand. He spits on the red-hot iron and greets the old man.

The iron hisses, and the tailor, like a woman in labor, lets out a sigh and follows Rabbi Uri with his eyes.

It will be faster to bypass the street and take the high road, thought Rabbi Uri. By the high road it's no more than two miles to the cemetery. I could go on the cart road, of course, that's closer, but there are potholes and bumps all along the way. If you stand there and stare, you'll plop into a hole and won't get out without outside help—you'll have to wait until someone passes by. Better to take the high road. Although it's longer, it's safe and you don't need to ask anything from anyone or bother them—you can roll yourself all the way to the cemetery.

Rabbi Uri had not visited Rokhl for a very long time. Either rain stood in the way, or illness, or a wheel on the wheelchair fell off on the way to the cemetery, but that time the cart driver Efraim Vinokur fixed it. Efraim also fixed the wheelchair itself; he got hold of springs, lined the seat with flax tow, and even covered it with calfskin.

Rabbi Uri felt indebted to Rokhl, both alive and dead. She didn't live for herself, she had grown old in this hole for him; then she withered and lost her health. He dedicated his life to God, but Rokhl—to him. Whatever you say, it's easier to serve God than a man. God doesn't stink from sweat, God doesn't shout at you, doesn't swear at you, you don't cook three times a day for God, don't wash his socks and underwear, you don't suffer insults and abuse from Him. But Rokhl had suffered plenty from Rabbi Uri!

She had thought about leaving him many times, but where could she go, whom could she leave him for? No God forgives as much as a woman, and not a single living soul in the world—neither a husband nor a son—is capable of paying off the debt to her.

Rabbi Uri will go to the cemetery and say, "Rokhl, do you want me to lie next to you, as on the first night of our marriage? I don't want to lie with others, Rokhl. Only with you, as on the first night of our marriage. To lie down and say 'Forever! Be with me forever—in the days to come, and till the end of time!'"

All day long carts move along the high road, especially toward evening. But now it's not evening, thank God, and if anyone passes me this morning, it will just be someone on horseback. The rider will come alongside the wheelchair, raise his cap, wet with sweat, shake his light-brown hair, utter two or three words in Lithuanian, dig his heels into the bay's side, and take off, never to return, galloping, tearing past, vanishing into the morning haze.

The cemetery is already in sight.

Rabbi Uri likes it more than the synagogue. You can go to the synagogue in rags or a fur coat with a squirrel collar, or you don't have to go at all. You can pray in your little house or in a mansion. The cemetery is the only place where nothing is required except your soul laid bare, and it's the place where the Almighty divides everything equally: He gives a stone, a tear, and a crow to everyone.

You can refuse a set of porcelain, or a gold wedding ring; you can reject your own father and son, your faith, and your people, but you cannot say no to the cemetery. The cemetery is the dowry and inheritance of all, and Rabbi Uri will leave it to the righteous and the sinful, their grandsons and great-grandsons, and every coming generation of Jews will pray in this place for the man who fenced in these pine trees and this green scrap of earth, and who mourned here for his own uncircumcised offspring, for his wife Rokhl, and for himself.

His descendants will call him Rabbi Uri the Builder.

The wheelchair glides along the high road. Rabbi Uri squints in the sunlight, the swish of the wheels relaxes him, his eyelids grow heavy and, dozing off, he falls off the side of the road into a deep ditch, overgrown with weeds and filled with moldy water. First a sharp pain penetrates his shoulder. Then it moves to his sunken chest, and in his head, spattered with mud, his thoughts scatter like scared tadpoles, and among them not a single one is coherent or consoling, no matter how hard he searches.

Rokhl doesn't want me to lie next to her, it occurs to him. She wants me to lie here, in this nasty ditch, this damned trench, in thorns and mud. This is her answer to my words. Here is my punishment for having ruined her life and not rewarded her with either children or love.

"Hey, you!" Rabbi Uri hears a man's voice.

He raises his head and sees a man on the edge of the ditch wearing a velvet yarmulke, the same man Itsik had told him all kinds of tall tales about and who he'd met on the way from the synagogue. *Rebeyne shel eylem*, he looks more like a beggar than a messenger from Heaven!

"Help me, Sir," Rabbi Uri says, addressing him politely.

The man in the yarmulke doesn't move, as if he is teasing him or reveling in Rabbi Uri's powerlessness.

"God Himself sent you," the old man continues. "I dozed off and, lo and behold, rolled into the ditch."

"It's the holy truth . . . God sent me," the stranger agrees, standing still. "Go, He told me, and pull Uri out of the mud. But before you pull him out, ask him three questions."

"Only three?" Rabbi Uri giggles inappropriately, forgetting about his pain.

"Three," the man in the yarmulke says seriously. "Let's begin with the first. Rabbi Uri, have you even once doubted My power?"

The stranger must be joking. But Rabbi Uri is used to answering all of God's questions, whoever asks them—wise man or madman.

"No," he answers at once.

The man in the yarmulke doesn't hurry with the next question, and Rabbi Uri becomes angry at himself. Why did he get mixed up in this foolish game? Wouldn't it be better to wait until some peasant passes by and helps him?

"With my heart, never," Rabbi Uri adds, after thinking a bit.

"And with your mind?" the stranger asks imperturbably.

"With my mind?" Rabbi Uri thinks it over and sighs. "With my mind—yes. 'Master of the Universe,' I said to Him, 'when You gave me faith, why did You not deprive me of reason? Reason eats away at faith like a bug in a chest of drawers.'" The old man suddenly catches himself.

What is happening to him? Is he so frightened that he's ready to open his soul to the first tramp who comes his way?

"Question two," the man in the yarmulke announces. His expression upsets Rabbi Uri more than the pain and humiliation. "Is it permitted to spill the blood of other people for your faith?"

Rabbi Uri rubs his injured shoulder and wipes sweat from his forehead. The stranger's examination confuses and disturbs him more than the pain, and the old man lacks the strength to cut him short.

"There is no faith on the earth for whose sake even a drop of others' blood can be spilled," he answers, as if to himself. "Faith defended with blood is worse than no faith."

"How does one defend it, then?"

"Is that the third question?"

"No. Only a step toward it."

"Faith cannot be defended by the axe or the scaffold. Unlike everything in the world, faith has no materiality."

These words cast a spell on Rabbi Uri, and for a moment he forgets about the ditch, his pain, and the stranger. Is it forbidden, after all, to talk to God from a stinking ditch? Did not Job speak to Him from an ash heap?

"Have you climbed the steps yet?" he asks the man in the yarmulke.

"Yes. Last question. Rabbi Uri, which is better—slavery or madness?"

"Madness, of course," Rabbi Uri mutters. "Madness is freedom."

"Then why did you choose slavery?"

"It seems that is already the fifth question, but I will answer you. There are two things that a person is not given to choose—the time in which he lives and the madness into which God plunges him."

"You have answered all the questions," the man in the yarmulke says, oddly triumphant. "Now I can lend you a hand. Your place is in Heaven, not this dirty ditch."

The stranger climbs down the slope, splashes his shoes in the dirty water, helps the rabbi out of the wheelchair. Grabbing him under the arms, he carries the light, almost weightless, body out of the ditch.

The man in the velvet yarmulke says quietly, "On the anniversary of my mother's death I always set out for the cemetery to visit her grave."

"But your mother's not in our cemetery. I know all the living and dead in this district."

"She is."

"Mothers usually lie in the place where they were buried."

"All except mine," the stranger explains. "My mother reposes wherever there is at least one fresh grave."

"The newest grave in our cemetery is Chava's, the wife of the tavern keeper Mandel. She was a beautiful woman."

"Then she was like my mother. She was a real beauty. Young men came to bloody blows because of her."

"If you'd like, I will say the Mourner's Kaddish for your mother."

"All right," the stranger agrees.

He plods along behind the wheelchair silently, as if behind the chariot of the prophet Elijah. Rabbi Uri is also silent as he thinks about this strange meeting, and the more he thinks about it the more acutely he feels that it was predestined.

"Listen," he says suddenly, and emotion constrains his breath. "I have seen your face somewhere before. Though forty years ago. You were a baby then, rocking in a cradle, two women were standing over you—one looked haggard and sad, and the other was plump with full, generous breasts, and a man was there, too."

"I never swung in a cradle."

"You just don't remember it."

"I remember everything," the man in the yarmulke says. "Everything. They laid me next to my brother on a trestle bed, and when I screamed, he gagged me with a chewed-up crust of bread. Ever since then I've hated bread."

"How can you do without bread?"

"What's the use of bread if you have to pay for it with your breath?"

Springs creaking, the wheelchair rolls into the empty cemetery and turns right, heading toward the fresh grave of the tavern keeper's wife Chava.

The man in the yarmulke bends down and scoops up a handful of loose yellow clay. He sifts it between his fingers and whispers something. Rabbi Uri sits in the wheelchair and says Kaddish.

Needles are dropping onto the grave from a pine tree, and every needle is like a hair fallen from the head of a Jewish mother—from Chava and Rokhl and the stranger's mother, on account of whose beauty young men came to blows.

12

Itsik Magid, Rabbi Uri's favorite student, seemed like other yeshiva boys until he abandoned his Torah studies and turned to logging. By the time he was seventeen, the Almighty had endowed him with unusual strength, which aroused envy and admiration from every weak Jew in town. Itsik had broad shoulders and was taller than the rest. He had red hair and blue eyes like a Christian; and he was able to hoist a one-year-old calf on his back without any trouble. He would grab him by the forelegs and then, in front of everyone on the market square, spin it around ten times without stepping out of an outlined circle. Or he would make some strange bet with one of the locals that attracted everyone's attention.

"I'll lift two hundred pounds of potatoes on my back, and you take one hundred," he said one day to Moyshe-Ber Khasman, the gawky and envious son of the miller, who stared at him wide-eyed.

"I can lift two hundred pounds of potatoes," Moyshe-Ber said.

"Wait a minute," Itsik dampened his enthusiasm. "Whoever's the first to haul his sack to the edge of town and back to the market is the winner. The loser pays for both sacks."

"Agreed," the miller's son said, accepting the challenge.

They walked over to a cart and made a deal with a peasant. Itsik looked at Moyshe-Ber out of the corner of his eye as they waited for the barber Bershtansky, a *makher* and a go-getter who'd been languishing without work, to give the signal "Go!"

The barber Bershtansky had felt the sacks to be sure that they were not stuffed with sawdust, placed them on a scale, weighed them, and at his command Itsik and Moyshe-Ber set out on their way.

At first, they ran side by side, remaining close to each other. Moyshe-Ber even pulled ahead a little. Bershtansky trotted behind them, like a foal, proud of his responsibility as referee, and sweating more than the two rivals. Bershtansky was followed by a gang of local rascals who were yelling as hard as they could, "Come on, Itsik! Go!"

Somewhere near the Spivak brothers' shop, Itsik overtook Moyshe-Ber and breathed the contempt of the victor upon him. But the miller's son did not give up. Crimson-faced, he clumsily rushed ahead, fixing his eyes on Itsik's back and hating it to the point of a scream.

Finally, Moyshe-Ber had to stop. Acknowledging defeat before they reached the edge of town, he threw the sack off his back, untied it, and furiously began flinging potatoes at the gang.

"Not tough enough?" the rascals jeered at him, picking up the potatoes and stuffing them under their shirts. "You can't beat Itsik!"

Itsik turned around at the end of the long shtetl street. He went back to the market, leaned the sack against the peasant's cart and said, "You'll get your money now."

"Samson! Samson from the Torah," the barber Bershtansky cooed like a dove, shaking Itsik's hand as if he were the czar. He looked into his eyes and, letting a breath of air into his smoke-filled mouth, exclaimed to everyone in the marketplace, "Jews! We are protected from now on! Follow Itsik's example, as I told you long ago—it's strength we need, not the Torah!"

The defeated Moyshe-Ber paid the peasant for both bags and went home to the mill empty-handed. The whole town exulted and rejoiced at Itsik's victory. Except for Rabbi Uri, his teacher, who was like a dark storm cloud.

"It's not proper for someone like you, who studies the Torah and is preparing to become a rabbi, to act frivolously in the eyes of the congregation," Rabbi Uri said, when Itsik brought his sack into the house. "Wouldn't it be better to earn your potatoes through prayer?"

"Did I earn them dishonestly, then?" Itsik recoiled at the rabbi's words.

At this point, something in their relations started to go wrong. Itsik harbored an unconscious grievance against Rabbi Uri. It stood between them like the wall by Itsik's bed, and he couldn't find even a tiny crack or chink in it. He continued to sit with Rabbi Uri until late at night, discussing a line of Torah or carrying on endless arguments about the future of the Jews, but their talks lacked the passion that had once engrossed him, lacked the fervor and confidence in his teacher's correctness that once inflamed his being. Yet neither this grievance nor his amazing strength pushed Itsik into Fradkin's forest.

What pushed him away was the seclusion of a life limited to such old-fashioned concerns, and the depressing, isolated circle around Rabbi Uri. Wasn't there anything more in the world besides Torah study, the prayer book, fasts, and holidays? Sometimes Itsik heard rumors about a different, attractive world that was hard to envisage. That world was far away, like some Nineveh or Babylon. But its very existence filled his soul with a vague and perplexing anxiety.

"We'll die here," Khonen Zaydburg whispered to him. He was one of Rabbi Uri's other students. "It's time to understand one simple fact, that you and I live in Russia. Not somewhere among the Cedars of Lebanon. And nothing will turn this place into the Land of Israel. Let's run away from here before it's too late."

"And go where?"

"To Vilna! To Moscow! To Petersburg! To the ends of the earth!"

"What about a residence permit?"

"Residents permits aren't epaulettes. We'll get them somehow—we're not fools," Khonen tried to persuade him.

"I want to remain a Jew," Itsik answered Zaydburg innocently.

"Is anyone dragging you by the ears into a different religion? If you want to remain a Jew, remain one as long as you like. But a roof . . . you can change a roof so that it doesn't leak, so that the wind doesn't blow in."

"What roof?"

"Some people pretend to accept Russian Orthodoxy and . . ."

"And what?"

"And remain Jews until they die."

"I'm not willing to live under such a roof. I'm not willing," Itsik said firmly. "Better to live in the cold. Better to suffer in the wind."

"Don't think that I'm inciting you to do anything wrong. I'm speaking to you as a friend. Do you intend to sleep behind a screen at Rabbi Uri's house for the rest of your life?"

"No, I don't."

"You feel sorry for the old man, of course. But we all have our own fate. It's easier for you, because you're an orphan. But I have parents . . . They sleep and dream that their son is a rabbi."

"Why wake them up?"

"You think I should crawl under a blanket and have the same dreams . . . Dreams, dreams, dreams! The eternal Jewish companions!"

Khonen Zaydburg's speeches frightened Itsik but also strangely fascinated him. He admired his quick mind, his grasp of the world, and his persistence that bordered on fanaticism. Yet there was something slippery about him, something elusive, like a ripple on a lake. He never spoke loudly, always in a whisper; he never walked with an upright back, but always stooped, as if he had just been lashed with a birch rod; he never looked anyone in the eye, but always looked at the mouth of the person he was talking to.

More than anything, Itsik was bothered by Khonen's constant readiness for betrayal, which he justified with thousands of cases that he found in the past and present. He would refer to Moses, who led the Jewish people out of Egyptian captivity. He also talked about a justice of the peace he knew, a former Jew, and the heretic Baruch Spinoza.

"A man always betrays someone," Zaydburg assured him. "Himself or others. He has no choice in the matter. The only thing you can trust, without deceiving yourself and those close to you, is death."

After Zaydburg left town—and he was the first to leave—Itsik felt both relief and regret. On the one hand, he was spared from temptation, as it were, and he was free from the web that had enveloped his whole being and blinded him. On the other hand, he had lost the one person with whom—though in secret, sporadically, and lapsing into a terrible transgression—he could dream of a different, forbidden, and cherished world. Pimpleface Simeon remained Rabbi

Uri's student, but he was not capable of filling the void, of making up for the unavoidable loss that pained Itsik. Despite all his friendliness and foolhardiness, Simeon had different standards. They were most often not determined by God or evil spirits but by the four walls of the tavern. Even if Simeon's ideas were not as petty as his father Yeshua's, they were not much higher than the tavern bar.

After Khonen Zaydburg ran off and Simeon Mandel stopped studying, Itsik's stay in Rabbi Uri's home became more burdensome and uncertain with each day. Sometimes Itsik caught himself thinking that Rabbi Uri had not really given him shelter in order to make a rabbi out of him, but rather to turn him into his serf or Rokhl's servant. Itsik carried water and chopped wood, washed the floors, and—if the rabbi's wife was sick—removed the chamber pot from beneath her and carried it out to the yard, gagging with disgust.

After Rabbi Uri's other students left town, Itsik felt the awakened spirit of his father Gabriel Magid. Born in Zhitomir, his father was an unruly, wild man who, in his hometown, had finished off a policeman. My God, Itsik thought, what would have happened if my father had caught me crawling around someone else's house licking up every speck of dirt and spit? Probably he would have choked me with his bare hands and finished me off with an axe, like the policeman. He wouldn't consider the fact that for twelve years Rabbi Uri and his wife Rokhl had fed me, an orphan, and clothed me, and prepared me to become a rabbi. My father would not take any such reasonable arguments into account, because he didn't father a son so that Itsik would become a slave and crawl on the ground on all fours. I spit on your clothes, on all your food and faith, Gabriel Magid would have said. My son should not be a slave for bread, clothes of brocade or gold, or even faith. Better an axe and the forest than well-nourished slavery—that's what his father Gabriel Magid would have said.

After twelve years, how can you just leave a home where they have done so much for you? Itsik could not betray Rabbi Uri, like Khonen, or leave, like Simeon Mandel, who supposedly had headed for a yeshiva in Vilna but ended up in a brothel on Safyanka Street, where he tickled the heels of whores until Yeshua brought him home.

Itsik was seeking a reason, and a reason turned up.

His name was Guri Andronov. People in town teased Itsik, saying he had replaced Rabbi Uri with Rabbi Guri.

"Say, my friend, are you by chance a relative of that Gabriel?"

"What Gabriel?" Itsik couldn't believe his ears.

"The one they found in the forest."

"A relative."

"Well, I'll be damned. I can see—you're the spitting image! His son, then."

"Yes, his son. Did you know him?"

"A little, as a kid. What a man he was! I'd never seen anyone like that, especially not a Jew! What shoulders! What hands! A throat like a church bell! He couldn't say the first thing in Russian, he just swore a blue streak and guzzled vodka—my God, what a sight to behold! And you . . . What's your name?"

"My name is Itsik."

"Are you a drinker, Itsik?"

"No."

"You're not like your father, then. I remember when he was trying to learn our language, Gabriel used to say, 'Guri, words are like vegetables, you need to water them so they don't dry up.' I say how about we drop by Yeshua's for a glass?"

Itsik never touched a drop of alcohol. He would sip a honey liqueur on Passover and make a face.

"Yeshua will give it to us on credit," Andronov assured Itsik. "We'll work and pay it back."

"You drink, and I'll sit with you," Itsik said.

"Do you know why people don't like you and your kind?"

"I don't."

"Because you're all sober. I remember—when we lived near Borisov—the Buneyev brothers, the bastards. They up and started a pogrom. They let everyone have it, and only one Jew was spared. Meyer, the shoemaker . . . He'd been dead drunk since the morning. A drunk is always a brother. Him you leave alone. In Russia a bottle makes brothers of everyone."

Why am I standing here listening to this nonsense? Itsik became angry at himself, but he dragged along behind him into the tavern on the chance he would say more about his father. In the forest you can hear plenty, even when you're a kid.

They settled down in a corner of the tavern. Andronov signaled to Yeshua and asked for a bottle of vodka. He poured two large cut-glass glasses, one for himself, the other for Itsik, put them down on the oak table with his rough hands, and said, "If you want to find out who killed your father, go to the loggers. Of course, I'm not against prayer. I myself go to church on the Feast of the Annunciation or the Feast of the Protection. At one time, before I became hoarse, I even sang in the choir. Your father Gabriel . . . well, he didn't go to the Jewish church, but he always prayed three times a day. He would step aside and whisper something in your language. One night after his evening prayer he was found dead."

"And you . . . didn't hear anything?"

"People blabbed all sorts of things. Some said that Fradkin got angry at him."

"For what?"

"The devil knows. If you come to the forest—ask the old men. Though they keep their mouths shut."

Guri drank, cheered up, moved the second glass closer to Itsik, and shrugged his shoulders when Itsik refused, but he didn't touch that glass.

Itsik didn't learn anything more from Andronov that day. The mystery of his father's death didn't come even a sparrow's hop closer to him, but the thought of the forest settled into his heart. More than once, Itsik had heard about Markus Fradkin's involvement in the murder, but just try to prove it, to catch him red-handed. He doubted that Fradkin himself had killed his father. Fradkin doesn't even cut down a single tree himself.

When Itsik informed Rabbi Uri of his decision to become a logger, the old man almost had a stroke. He controlled himself, though, and said quietly, but firmly, "You're sick, Itsik."

After a moment of silence he added, "Who exchanges prayer for an axe? Come to your senses! In any case, you won't find out anything."

"I will find out, Rabbi."

"Suppose you find out, my son. What would that change? Will you kill whoever killed your father? Send him off to hard labor? Won't you pay too dearly for the truth? Ignorance is better than truth acquired through an evil act."

"You have a ready answer for everything, Rabbi. But I want to think for myself. For myself, do you understand! I have lived so many years with you, hearing: pray and justice will prevail. But for that, for justice to prevail, sometimes evil must be committed."

"Evil?"

"Yes, evil . . . Because evil is the tool—the teeth of justice, Rabbi. Without it you won't crack anything."

"I won't hold you back, Itsik. I will pray for you."

And so they parted, without a quarrel. Itsik rented a corner in the house of the peddler Osher, who was still alive at that time. He dragged his belongings over there and took a job as a logger in Fradkin's forest.

Like his father, he worked fast, with cheerful hatred. From morning to night he felled trees, chopped branches, loaded them into carts. He drank in moderation, had a bite to eat with the old loggers without delight or excess, but he didn't ask them anything, so as not to scare them away. He was waiting for them, on their own, to lift the veil of mystery that hung over the death of his father Gabriel Magid. The veil clung tightly, however, and one had only to brush against it for it to move away like the horizon. With time, the desire to get to the bottom of the mystery that had tormented him gradually lost its edge, subsided, and was replaced by different feelings, which tortured his body more than his soul.

Itsik was twenty-five when he first dreamed of a woman. She was washing her legs in the river, and her calves showed white like sugar-head cones. The sugar dissolved in the water and Itsik bent down, touched the water with his lips and drank it. He drank and became more intoxicated than if it had been vodka. The entire river was sweet, the entire world was sweet, so sweet.

Then Itsik matched a face to the woman in his dream.

The face was Zelda's, the daughter of the timber merchant Fradkin, the same Fradkin who was allegedly involved in the murder of his father Gabriel.

Once, before Christmas, they all turned up at the woodcutting area—Fradkin, his son Zelik, and she, Zelda.

They unloaded presents from a sled, and they distributed gifts to everyone.

Fradkin, together with his son and daughter, moved from one cutting area in the forest to another, handing out holiday gifts to the loggers with a springtime smile on his face.

Each of the Andronov brothers—Guri and Afinogen—received a new fleece undercoat.

Old man Morkunas received an old-fashioned lacquered pipe.

Verzila Ryaba got boots.

"Happy holiday!" the beaming Fradkin roared. "Brothers, thank you for your work!"

On a path in the clearing the horse harnessed to the sled neighed.

The merchant and his two children got ready for their return trip, but all at once Zelda saw Itsik leaning against a birch tree.

"Papa," she exclaimed. "You forgot someone!"

"He's a Jew," Fradkin explained.

"So what?" Zelda was surprised. Itsik heard her ringing, almost childish voice.

"Jews don't have Christmas," the timber merchant noted.

"All the same," Zelda went on, "we must give him something, too."

"Another time, my child," Fradkin silenced her. "We need to leave. They're waiting for us in Vilkija."

"But Papa!"

The head of the family finally relented. "Zelik, scrape together a handful of coins and give them to our fellow Jew."

Zelik strode over to the birch tree, stuck his hand in his pocket, but, after catching Itsik's look, did not pull it out.

Fradkin and Zelda started walking to the sled.

When Zelik caught up to them, his sister asked, "What did he say?"

Zelik hesitated.

"What did he say?" Fradkin gave him an angry look.

He said, "I don't need handouts. I need . . ." Zelik paused.

"Finish," Fradkin ordered.

"He needs Zelda."

"What impudence!" She was outraged.

"Just like his father," Fradkin muttered. "No wonder I didn't want to hire him. But we needed more help."

"'Your sister Zelda is the best present for me,' he said. So, my dear, you won't be an old maid."

The men began to laugh loudly.

Zelda did not show up in the town again until four years later. She languished in her father's home and almost never left it. She would come to the synagogue, pray, and go right back. Occasionally she would walk the dog while Itsik was sweating in the forest.

If not for the funeral of the tavern keeper's wife Chava, Itsik would not have seen her for a long time. You couldn't just show up at her place and knock on the door.

During Chava's burial Itsik stood behind Zelda and breathed into the back of her head. For a moment it seemed to him that his breath was making her hair flutter and curl, grow ears like rye, and if he blew one more time the grain would sprout.

Zelda shivered from his closeness; she tried not to look at him, digging the toe of her boot into the clay soil, and from time to time looking up. And then their glances met like two bolts of lightning intersecting, and something rumbled in her chest like distant thunder. Itsik hovered above her, very tall, well-built, and impatient.

"Don't look at me like that," she pleaded. "For God's sake, don't look. Don't forget where you . . ."

But the cemetery could not stop him.

Itsik followed her like a shadow back to the town. Sometimes he rushed toward her, took her by the arm and whispered, "Be careful! There's a hole ahead!"

There was no hole ahead. He himself was like a hole that had to be avoided so as not to sink into it.

Pimpleface Simeon and Morta looked askance at them, and Zelda was already sorry that she had thoughtlessly agreed to go to the cemetery. Boredom had driven her from her home, and even funerals seemed like amusement.

"You and I nursed from the same breast," Itsik said as the high road came to an end and the town's houses loomed ahead, tinged with the gold leaf of autumn.

Zelda shuddered, but kept it in.

"My mother worked in your house as a nanny at first, and then as a wet nurse." Itsik gave her no breathing space.

So she was the one. Zelda was the one who had dipped her finger in her tears. That time she had asked: When will my eyes become salty? Is this just a coincidence, or fate? His mother—her wet nurse—seemed to have risen from the dead in order to throw them together, bring them together in this small town, in this cemetery, on this high road, to be joined and united. My God, how ridiculous! She and Itsik . . . what could they have in common? No kind of milk, even it was thickened into the strongest glue, could bind them together.

Yet precisely what seemed unimaginable, ridiculous, and impossible did not push her away from Itsik but attracted her to him. Even earlier, before suspecting or knowing anything, she had always looked for him in the synagogue, and when he appeared, she sincerely thanked God. In Vilna or in Vilkija nothing could get her to go to the synagogue. Like Verochka Karsavina, Zelda was an atheist, and she considered all believers, including her father, hypocrites. God, if He is real, doesn't require prayers or worship, but rather self-sacrifice. It's much easier, of course, to sacrifice words. Once in her childhood she dreamed that in the world lived only the deaf and dumb. Zelda imagined her birthplace inhabited by deaf-mutes from whom you would never hear a single malicious, false word. You could walk around such a city and never feel yourself to be an outsider, someone unwanted. Antek, the little boy neighbor, wouldn't start yelling at you and call you a *zhid*.

The policeman wouldn't bark, "Filthy Jew!"

Papa wouldn't curse at them, saying, "Pogromniks! Pigs! Beasts!"

In Zelda's world, a deaf-mute God should have had deaf-and-dumb subjects. Wasn't she living like a deaf-mute in this town? She would exchange a few words with Golda or Cain and then turn silent. For weeks on end, for months on end.

She had nothing to talk about with Itsik either. She didn't know about types of wood, and he didn't have the foggiest idea about what she had learned at the gymnasium in Vilkija.

The simplest thing would be to brush him off, be insolent, rebuff and ridicule him, put him in his place, not let him strut in front of her like a blackcock. No black grouse would make mating calls around her, so she didn't show a bit of interest. Enough of him, the young bull, and Golda, too. A young bull—that's what Golda had called him.

They didn't even notice that now they were alone on the town's street.

"Do you remember that you came with your father and brother to the cutting area?" Itsik said, hoping to keep her from leaving. "It was before New Year's Day. You were wearing such a light squirrel fur coat."

Itsik was nervous. He wanted to interest her in something, but the poor fellow didn't know how. He only sensed with his back, through the back of his head, that something would be decided now. That's how it is in the spring when the ice on the Neman begins to break up, at first from the edge, from the shore, slowly, resistantly, hopelessly, then further and further toward the middle, and at last an unfrozen patch of water in the midst of the ice shows through and one ice sheet moves with a roar, and then another, and the river, now freed and delivered from its burden, flows far away to the sea.

"I remember," Zelda answered.

May the first ice sheet freed be blessed!

"You looked just like a squirrel," Itsik continued, brightening. "For the first time in my life I was sorry . . . don't laugh at me . . . sorry that I was born two-legged."

"What did you want . . . to be born a wolf?"

"No. I thought if I'd been born a squirrel, we could chase each other in the snow, jump from one tree to another, live in the same hollow."

She looked like she was laughing at him, Itsik thought, and he fell silent. What nonsense I'm blabbing—it's sickening. What sort of squirrel? What hollow? In front of me stands a rich woman, the daughter of the boss, the timber merchant Fradkin. Be quiet! Be quiet! You can only win over a woman through silence. Silence is a chain; words are like threads—stretch them too much and they'll break.

"What else?" Zelda suddenly urged him on.

"We would live in a hollow," Itsik said happily.

"You already said that."

"We'd chase after each other in the snow."

"You said that too."

"We would jump from one tree to another."

"Old story." Zelda's mouth lifted into a smile, and Itsik completely lost his mind. "What else?"

A strange excitement took hold of her. Itsik's answers amused her like a children's game, and Zelda was caught up in its current, forgetting about all danger and trouble. All of a sudden, she felt amazingly light, as if her lungs were full of fresh meadow air, and the dark clouds vanished from her head—under everyone's sky. The small town suddenly slid open and extended its borders, the wretched little houses floated away somewhere, and a light blue expanse, never seen before, arose before her eyes.

"What else?" Itsik mumbled. "We could eat nuts."

"I don't like nuts," Zelda said, beaming.

"They're good," Itsik assured her.

"But they rot your teeth."

Zelda showed Itsik her teeth.

"Your teeth are like a flock of sheep, just shorn, coming up from the washing. Each one bears twins, and there is not a barren one among them," Itsik whispered.

"It's all animals and cattle with you," Zelda interjected.

"It's the *Song of Songs*," he said, taking offense.

"What?"

"The *Song of Songs* of King Solomon. I know it all by heart," Itsik bragged.

"I only know Pushkin," Zelda sighed. "Now prophetic Oleg prepares to take revenge on the foolish Khazars. For their violent raid he has condemned their villages and fields to swords and fire."

"Nice," Itsik admitted. "But King Solomon's is better. If you'd like, I can recite it all."

"Some other time." Zelda thanked him with a nod.

"I can also recite the Five Books of Moses—*Bereishis*, *Shemos*, *Va-yikra* . . ." He rattled on like a spring rook.

"Thanks, thanks," she said, feeling a certain reproachable awkwardness. "Why take the trouble?"

"It's no trouble at all for me."

"All the same, it's too late now for me. For appearance's sake, my father tried to acculturate me, but he gave up."

"Acculturate to what?"

"Everything not Jewish."

"Does a bird need to be acculturated to the forest?"

"A black sheep is not a bird." Zelda became sad.

"You gave me that . . . Pushkin, and I'm giving you King Solomon. You won't be a black sheep," Itsik responded.

"It's time to go home," Zelda said.

"May I take you there?"

"No need."

But Itsik tagged along behind her.

Passersby looked them over with curiosity as they walked around the town. The barber Bershtansky clung to the window and even waved a cloth at them.

"I thought you were only strong, but it seems you're that kind," Zelda said when they came to the Fradkins' house.

"What kind?" he asked, anticipating something flattering and unusual.

"That kind," Zelda blurted.

"When will we see each other again?" he asked, assuming a business-like tone.

"Never."

"Why?"

"I'm going away to Vilkija . . . Then, perhaps, to Vilna."

"Don't leave," Itsik said sincerely. "Come to the cutting area."

"To knock down pine trees?"

"To gather mushrooms. There haven't been so many saffron milk caps for a long time. The whole forest is covered with them like honey cakes."

"Are you tired of gathering honey cakes with Golda?" Zelda suddenly asked, pulling back.

"With Golda?"

"I know everything about you," she added maliciously, ecstatic at his dismay.

"Golda," Itsik mumbled, "is my landlady. I live at her place."

"I'm not asking you about anything. Goodbye."

"Wait," Itsik grabbed her arm.

"Let go! You're hurting me . . ."

"Don't hurry off. Listen to me, I want you to know. Maybe what I'm saying is stupid, but I'm going to say it." He let go of her arm, stood up straight, and narrowed his eyes as if he were about to jump into the river. "Wherever you go, to Vilkija, or to Vilna, or to the end of the earth, I'll wait . . . I'll live and pray that God will dig out a hollow for us. There's nothing else I need from Him. Nothing. He took everything away from us except love. And neither Golda nor your father . . ."

A terrible word was on the tip of his tongue, but Itsik checked himself.

"My father is your boss, but not mine," Zelda said. "And the scores we have to settle with him are different. Goodbye!"

She went through the gate.

"Zelda!"

"What else do you want?" She turned around, almost pitying him, but she didn't stop.

The blood rushed to Itsik's face, the heat of insult and powerlessness, and his brain seemed to be dribbling away drop by drop; only one drop remained, in its perniciousness a means of escape, and yielding to temptation, he shed it because he believed that a common sin and a common secret might still unite him with Zelda.

"They say that your father, Markus Fradkin, my boss . . . is a murderer," he forced out.

Zelda stopped and looked around again, not so much at Itsik as at his words. But the words were no longer in the air. An autumn cobweb fluttered, and withered leaves swirled around, invigorated by a slight breeze.

"What?"

"They say that your father, when he was young, killed mine . . . Gabriel Magid."

Zelda examined him closely as if he were a strange plant with alluring though poisonous fruits that had unexpectedly taken root in her yard. Now she felt compassion for him, even more than before, and there was no hint of reproach in her pity. It seemed that what was such a secret for him did not surprise her at all. Just think about it—what else is new?

"So?" Zelda asked. "Make the father answer for his sins."

"My teacher Rabbi Uri used to say, 'Atone for the sins of your father with love, my children.'"

"May God grant," Zelda said, "that she will be capable."

"Who will be capable?"

"Love."

She disappeared into her house.

Itsik stood at the gate for a long time. He senselessly toyed with the gate door, making the hinges creak. He looked into the windows but couldn't see Zelda. Cain barked at him, standing up on his hind legs and pulling on the chain as if to shame Itsik or warn him.

His head was empty.

Zelda seemed to have cleaned everything out of it except for shame and regret. That's it, Itsik thought. Nothing had helped—not the secret, the sin, or his pleading and urging. In a day or two the Fradkin carriage would come and take Zelda away to Vilkija, and then, perhaps, to Vilna or to the end of the earth, to the very end where there are no saffron milk caps or forests, and far from Itsik. That's how it should be, because everyone has his own path, pre-ordained from above. If there's anything left to hope for, it's only a miracle. But is he the only one on earth awaiting a miracle? Everyone is waiting for one, even those it won't help.

Where should he go? Who could give him advice? Rabbi Uri? You can talk to him about whatever you like—but not about love.

Almighty God, how few people there are in the world who can love! Who would answer if you went to the market square and shouted with the full strength of your lungs, "Hey, whoever loves, speak now!"

Except Mandel's serving girl Morta.

Or Fradkin's housemaid Golda.

He had completely forgotten about her, as if she didn't exist. Golda loves him, but what good is her love for him? Anyway, *is* it love when they crawl into your bed?

It's strange, but he had never imagined himself in bed with Zelda. Why? Was he afraid to hurt her? Even in his thoughts he didn't dare remove her chemise and lay his head on her white, supple belly. Itsik himself couldn't explain why.

Everything with Golda was simpler. A den—if not a hollow. Itsik was not the one who first dug it.

He felt like he was in a den whenever Golda lavished her seemingly studied caresses upon him.

The first time Golda enjoyed him in her bed, Itsik couldn't stand it.

"I can't . . . in your bed. I can't," he complained.

"But why not? Why? A bed is a bed." She was surprised and attributed it to his lack of experience.

"You don't hear anything?"

"No, nothing," she said, wrapping her arms around his neck, aroused by his closeness.

"Osher is breathing," Itsik said.

"You little fool! Osher went to his grave long ago . . . How can he breathe?"

"He's breathing," he repeated. "Just listen."

Golda listened carefully to the silence, leaned back her head, sniffed and, satisfied, quietly giggled. "You're just imagining it, Itsik!"

"I can't . . . Understand, I can't!"

"If you're such a baby, let's move to the bed upstairs." She indulged all his whims.

But even upstairs, in his bachelor's bed where the peddler Osher had never slept, the dead man's breath haunted Itsik.

When Golda left him toward morning, he opened the windows wide and aired out the tiny room for a long time. But the wind carried in Osher's breath.

"I'll come to see you in the forest in the summer, if you'd like," Golda squealed. "Why are you and I worse than deer and elks?"

"You're no deer, Golda. You're . . . a dirty boar."

She put up with everything.

He did not want to go back to her, to the dirty boar. Not back to bed again. To bed, to bed, morning and evening, day and night, to bed, to hell with it! Damn that hour when Satan had linked arms with him and led him down the stairs and threw him beside Golda in the place where for so many years the peddler Osher had tossed and turned, suffering from impotence!

It's time to call it quits, he thought, squeaking the Fradkins' gate, listening to Cain's barks, and keeping a lookout for his deer. There was no point in looking—her hooves had already flashed away; she ran into a thicket so dense that no axe could cut it down. Time to call it quits.

He must move right away from Golda's house to some other place. Rabbi Uri holds no grudge. Rabbi Uri would take him in with open arms. He was even ready to bequeath him the house—the old man had no other heirs. Or maybe he could go to the night watchman Rakhmiel. His place was spacious and close to the forest, but apparently that fellow . . . with the pin . . . was living with him. At worst, the barber Bershtansky would let him have a corner—Itsik didn't need much, just somewhere to lay his head in severe frost.

And if Golda doesn't let him alone, then farewell to the town! He could always find work. Just cross the Neman and you're in Germany. Some Hans in a warehouse will hire you, you'll haul sacks and hear *"Schneller! Schneller!"* If you don't want to shave off your beard in Germany, go farther, go on to America, where they have beards, like Jews. If you don't like America, move on, like the water carrier Ezer Bloom, to the land of your forefathers, to the Holy Land. Of course, it's a pity to leave the land of your birth . . . But it's time to call it quits.

Itsik looked in Zelda's window for the last time, then dragged himself home.

"Itsik," Golda greeted him joyfully. "Where have you been whiling away the time? The funeral ended long ago."

With a woman's infallible intuition, she had noticed the change in him, and she tried to conceal her uneasiness with deliberate rudeness.

"Do you want to eat something?" Golda let up.

"No."

"I'll fry some eggs for you. The hens are in a hurry, as if the world will end tomorrow. Two eggs a day."

"Golda," Itsik said, and by his tone she could feel that something was wrong. She placed her hands on her stomach and threw back her head as though her face were in danger. "I'm leaving you."

"Where are you going?"

"I don't know yet. Maybe to Rabbi Uri . . . Maybe to Bershtansky."

"Thank God," she breathed a sigh of relief. "I thought—to a woman! Sit down, I'll bring the eggs right away."

Golda disappeared.

Itsik could hear her break the eggs on the kitchen table, hear them crackle in the frying pan.

It's taking so long, he thought, how long! Why is she fussing so much? A lump started to rise in his throat. It's always this way with Golda—you don't ask her for anything and suddenly she's rushing about frying or cooking or baking something, and her zeal and desperate eagerness will temper the wounded feelings and discontent.

"Eat," she said, putting the fried eggs on the table.

Itsik didn't touch his food.

"Eat," she repeated. "Eat and . . . go. No one has ever left me while hungry."

The fried eggs turned yellow like enormous water lilies.

"It's my mistake," Itsik muttered. "Mine. Mine."

"Have some salt," Golda whispered.

"The Almighty did not create a man in order that he yield to a woman."

"Take some salt," Golda said, moving the bowl toward him.

"I should have left you on the day you made up the bed, puffed up the pillows . . ."

"Let me salt them for you." Golda took a pinch of salt with two fingers and sprinkled it on the eggs. The large crystals sparkled on the yolks like hoarfrost.

"After that time, your bed became a grave for me."

"Do you want butter on your bread?" she asked, and without waiting for an answer, she started spreading it on a chunk. The knife in her masculine hand trembled slightly, but Itsik didn't notice.

"A bed without love is a grave," he went on, hoping to get everything off his chest, from beginning to end, without sparing her. "The next day, even after a wedding night, worms appear in it. They crawl out in the dark and devour our souls."

"Can I bring you a salted cucumber? I'll be right back," Golda said, and she rushed to the hall.

Itsik didn't even have time to object.

"I salted an entire barrel for the winter," she boasted irrelevantly. "Cucumbers are cheap now. A bucket for a kopeck."

What is she talking about? Itsik thought. Who cares about how much cucumbers cost at the market or how many she salted for winter. For us there won't be another winter.

"Are you listening to me?" he scowled, lowering his head.

"I'm listening," Golda answered. "Eat, eat!"

"I'm leaving you . . . forever," he repeated emphatically.

"All right, all right. But first you'll eat."

"Eat, eat," he mimicked her. "I'm fed up!" he cried, his voice breaking. He caught himself, grabbed a spoon and quickly shoved the eggs into his mouth.

"Is there enough salt?"

"Enough!" His pent-up anger was gagging him.

"That's how you men love," Golda said quietly.

"How?"

"Take whatever you can get and then yell that you've been fed worms."

She cut a slice of cucumber and licked it with the top of her tongue, adding, "I've had a craving for sour things lately."

Itsik was silent, sullen, offended. He had expected anything from Golda—swearing, curses, shouts—while she was so calm, subdued, even cold, as if she were someone else. He wanted dry birch logs to be tossed into his fiery determination, not damp blocks of wood, but Golda, contrary to all his expectations, sprinkled the fire with sand.

"All right . . . now that you've eaten, you can leave."

Itsik listened intently, trying to catch a lie in her words, but either because he was too occupied with his own thoughts or because the lie didn't suit him, he felt neither tension nor bitterness.

"I'm grateful to you, Itsik," she said.

"Grateful? For what?"

"Thank you so . . . so much," Golda said, searching for the right words. "You were with me, a dirty boar. A dirty boar also has a soul, even if it's small and even if it has a wet snout. Not everyone on earth can be happy . . . Some people are destined to be unhappy. When God brought me into the world, He said, 'Golda, you will be very unhappy. But know this: God is there for the unhappy; the happy do not need God. I will always be with you.'"

She bit her tongue to keep herself from crying.

"After Osher died and you came downstairs and lay beside me for the first time, I thought that God had kept his word . . . He had climbed into my bed and embraced me with His almighty arms, soothed me with His endless caresses," Golda said, holding back her trembling and her tears. "You say that worms were devouring our souls. Maybe yours, Itsik, but not mine . . . Mine grew like a tree during the nights, and its branches rustled. You mistook its rustling, Itsik, for Osher's breath."

Itsik listened, stupefied by her unexpected words, ready to burst into tears, annoyed by his own openness and sensitivity. But he couldn't just leave like a thief, without explaining anything.

"What can you do," Golda sighed. "A man is always a logger even if he's a barber. He chops down a tree and no rustling remains—no sound, only roots . . . Roots beyond anyone's control."

She drew close to him, looked into his eyes, wrapped her arms around his neck, and said, "Kiss me, Itsik."

"Don't . . . Don't," he mumbled, backing away, but Golda's arms were as strong as fetters.

"Kiss me."

He gave her a quick hug and just as quickly pecked at her numb lips.

"You came to me in the morning the first time and you'll leave me forever in the morning," she said.

"No, Golda."

"Yes."

"No . . . no . . ."

"Yes, yes, yes . . . In the morning, the morning."

Her words rustled above him like branches, but no worms crawled on them, only chrysalises, which were getting cold. In the morning they would unfold their wings and fly.

13

Ardalion Ignatich Nesterovich's passion was mushrooms. All year he waited impatiently for the autumn and its warm sun showers, the time when he and his wife, Lukerya Panteleimonovna, and their children wove baskets and headed for the forest. Everyone in the district knew the "Nesterovich places," and not a soul dared to hunt there. Ardalion Ignatich, a kind and tolerant man, could forgive any offense—theft, arson, brawls—but not that.

Nesterovich's mushroom zone stretched all the way to Vilkija, and no farther. Not because he was afraid he'd get lost or meet a competitor—because a policeman is a policeman everywhere—but because out of the blue he might be needed for some important state business. As we know, for the authorities it's all the same whether it's winter or autumn, mushrooms or apples. When you're needed, don't argue.

Ardalion Ignatich and his family would scour the forest for days. Sometimes they spent the night somewhere, nestled in a chicken coop at the edge of the forest, and they never returned home empty-handed, God forbid. Sometimes they even hunted in the moonlight. They would put Katyusha and Ivan to bed, and then—off to a grove of fir trees.

Praise for Lukerya Panteleimonovna's pickled and marinated mushrooms spread over the whole county, and not just the county, but over the whole northwest territory.

Ardalion Ignatich was honest in his mushroom dealings. He never accepted mushrooms as a bribe, although conniving Jews, who knew his weakness, tried more than once to foist a basket on him.

They don't eat wild mushrooms themselves, the scoundrels—God forbids it, you know—and so they try to palm them off on him.

One day everyone became excited by the rumor that Alexander II, the Czar of all Great and Little and White Russia, together with his imperial retinue, would soon be traveling along the Kovno highway to Tilsit, on a visit to the kaiser. The district chief immediately sent the county police chief Nuikin to Nesterovich in order to secure a tub of Ardalion Ignatich's mushrooms, because a bucket might not suffice for such an occasion.

Nesterovich was, of course, sorry to part with the tub, but what wouldn't you do for His Imperial Majesty? If need be, you'd give up your life for him.

"His Majesty the Czar will taste our mushrooms," Ardalion Ignatich rejoiced.

Lukerya Panteleimonovna also rejoiced. She imagined His Imperial Majesty raising a porcini or an orange-aspen bolete on his golden fork, bringing it to his mouth, and breaking into a smile, asking "Whose extraordinary mushrooms are these?"

"The policeman Ardalion Ignatich Nesterovich's," everyone in the county would answer him in one voice.

"Award that Nesterovich with a decoration," His Imperial Majesty would say, drinking wheat vodka with the mushroom appetizers.

Ardalion Ignatich and Lukerya Panteleimonovna rejoiced in vain, however. The policeman not only failed to get the decoration, he also lost the tub. The tub was seized, and, well, it simply makes your heart bleed.

His Imperial Majesty unexpectedly took a side route. Or perhaps he didn't grant the kaiser a visit at all. Who can figure out those people? Today they exchange hugs, tomorrow they quarrel and go to war against each other.

"Maybe he'll still pass by?" Lukerya Panteleimonovna comforted her husband.

"Maybe," Nesterovich muttered doubtfully.

And so every year they made up a tub for the czar. They ate it all and then set out another.

This year was no exception for Ardalion Ignatich. The autumn was splendid. The old-timers didn't remember anything like it—fine, bright days, and only rarely was the dome of the sky stained with clouds pouring out the blessed, warm sun showers. There was no end of mushrooms in Nesterovich's territory: saffron milk caps poked their small orange faces out of the moss, boastful porcini and peppery milk caps asked to be put in the basket, and there were so many orange-aspen and brown mushrooms that all you needed to do was bend over and cut them off.

Yet Nesterovich knew that in a week or two the north wind would blow, the frost would set in, and—if they were not collected on time—the mushrooms would be eaten by worms, shrivel, or be trampled by the hooves of wild boars. Then even the tub for the czar could not be pickled. Without pickled mushrooms life is not life, and you must wait until the next autumn. And anything can happen: an illness could send you to bed, or the authorities might transfer you to another place, to the Kalmyks somewhere in the steppe. Russia is enormous. But nothing can be done about it, for such is the fate of people who serve. They rush about from one end of the land to another; you just get settled, put down roots and they tell you, "Get ready, friend, hurry up!"

Until now, knock on wood, things could not have gone better. There were no incidents in the district, no unrest; you could live and enjoy yourself, breathe, rejoice, pursue your dreams. Count Muravyov had pacified everyone and showed the rebels who was boss, and they had remained submissive and didn't make any more trouble.

When everything was going quietly and smoothly, Ardalion Ignatich was able to leave the house without any misgivings. But at the height of mushroom season, when every hour was precious, trouble landed on his doorstep. He couldn't go anywhere, had to be on the lookout, make a report. What if there was nothing to report?

Whether there is something or nothing, you can't get by without a report. The county police chief Nuikin will work you to death, and you can't buy him off with a tub for the czar. If you say, "I didn't find anyone, Your Honor," that's bad: he'll turn pale, attack you, stamp his feet, and start yelling, "Find him, you scoundrel!" If you say, "I found him!" that's even worse: he'll demand a criminal, dead or alive. And where will you get this criminal? A criminal is not a mushroom, you can't just make a trip to the forest and cut him down with a knife. Better wriggle out of it as best you can, use your brains, don't slip up. And, God forbid, don't blurt out, "There isn't any criminal in our district, Your High Honor!" Then the police officer will fly into a complete rage, and say, "Remember this, scoundrel, and don't forget it: there is a criminal in every district! Maybe not the one we're looking for, maybe it's some other outlaw, but there is one. You understand?"

How will you answer him? "I understand, Your High Honor!"

Just try not to understand.

Chief Nuikin can't live a day without criminals. He sits in his office waiting for some suspect to be hauled in. For Nuikin, the whole country is full of criminals.

Once the police chief said to him, "You scoundrel, are you not by chance a criminal? Why don't you look me straight in the eye?"

"Your High Honor!" Nesterovich was horrified.

"Chummy with the Jews. On friendly terms with Lithuanians. Well?"

"I swear to Christ . . ."

"Don't swear, scoundrel. I see right through you."

Ardalion Ignatich returned from the county office black as charred wood; he locked himself in his room, drank vodka for three days running, and didn't let anyone in, not even Lukerya Panteleimonovna.

"I'm a criminal . . . You're a criminal's wife. And Ivan and Katka are children of a criminal. Our place is Siberia!"

"Ardasha! Ardasha!" Lukerya Panteleimonovna froze in fear.

"Chummy with the Jews. On friendly terms with Lithuanians. Well?"

"Who?"

"Me . . . Who else? Go summon the slaughterer, Lukerya!"

"Which slaughterer?"

"The one . . . what's his . . . Ben-Zion . . . Let him chop off my foreskin . . ."

"Our Lady in Heaven! Holy Mother of God!"

"And Ivan's at the same time."

"Ardasha!"

"After Ben-Zion chops them off, go to the priest Anicetas."

"Why the priest?"

"I'm changing my faith, Lukerya!"

How much fear he aroused in everyone at the time. Lukerya Pan-teleimonovna flopped down on her knees in front of the holy icon and prayed for Ardalion Ignatich to be delivered from the Jews, the priest Anicetas, and Siberia.

For the rest of his life Nesterovich remembered his conversation with Police Chief Nuikin. He became more cunning and wary; he tried not to quarrel with Jews but also didn't strike up friendships; he told off Lithuanians, especially when in the presence of strang-ers or passersby; and every year he sent Chief Nuikin apples from his garden (Nuikin adored Reinettes!), fresh strawberries, and al-ways a bucket of blackberries because the police officer suffered from indigestion.

Since that time, Ardalion Ignatich feared a summons to the county office more than pestilence, plague, or fire, and every dis-patch from there plunged him into a glacial gloom. If Nesterovich received one in autumn during the height of mushroom picking, he simply fell into a rage and spared no one, not even the members of his household.

"Papa, Papa, are we going to the forest soon?" Katyusha pestered him.

"Soon, soon," Ardalion Ignatich assured her, becoming even gloomier.

Can you really explain to a daughter what sort of catastrophe had occurred? You can't get rid of a dispatch without a reason; you can't throw it away, hang it on a nail in the outhouse, or burn it up. Such papers don't burn, even if you put them in a bonfire. What kind of power lies behind them? Satanic, and that's it. When you get a notice like that, your whole life turns upside down and you don't dare whine. They aren't paying you for mushrooms, after all, but for keeping watch. The most important thing is duty, and this paper is your duty. Look it over and memorize it like a prayer. If he, Ardalion, son of Ignat, Nesterovich, lives to see the day when he himself can issue such dispatches, he would, of course, be able to do whatever he wants. But he'll never see that day, he's too old, and smarter mushroom hunters will turn up there. What a pity, a pity . . . A document with an official stamp is like a key these days: it can lock and unlock whatever you like. A document rules over everything.

Alas, he should have received a document from His Imperial Majesty in which these words were inscribed in black and white: "The bearer of this document, Ardalion, son of Ignat, Nesterovich, of low rank, is permitted to collect, pickle, and marinate mushrooms during working hours for the glory of the Russian Empire. All persons, including the county police chief Gavriil Nikolaevich Nuikin, shall not place any obstacles in the way of the above-mentioned and shall provide every kind of useful and beneficial assistance."

There's no way in hell he'll ever get a paper like that! Let Lukerya Panteleimonovna set out for the grove with the children, while he, at least for appearance's sake, will take some action.

But what?

Look into the Catholic Church as a precaution, hang around the market square, drop by the tavern.

Since the man who made an attempt on the life of His Excellency the Vice-Governor is a Jew, what would he be doing in the church? No one would give him shelter or hide him in the church, Nesterovich reasoned. In 1863 the local priest not only hid the insurgents, but was himself a rebel, unlike the present priest who is now a loyal subject—Anicetas Ivanovich.

Go to the market square? Market day is so packed with Jews, Lithuanians, Russians, and even gypsies, that there's not even room for an apple to fall. The gypsies are horse thieves, but they don't shoot vice-governors. Their sovereign is a good horse.

The tavern is closed. Pimpleface Simeon and Yeshua are mourning Chava, sitting shiva at home, as is their custom.

She died at the wrong time, the wrong time.

Ardalion Ignatich had already come to an agreement with Simeon, when suddenly—of all things—Chava died!

Nesterovich's thoughts turned to the deceased.

Chava was the one who delivered Ivan and Katyusha from Lukerya Panteleimonovna. There was no better midwife in the district.

If it hadn't been for Police Chief Nuikin and those terrifying words of his, Ardalion Ignatich would have gone to Chava's funeral without fail, and accompanied her on her final journey, but he lost courage and just waved his hand from afar.

For shame! A big, healthy man, and he's afraid of Nuikin even from a distance.

Once Nesterovich had heard that either the Germans or the French had invented some sort of spyglass. If you raised it to your eyes, you could see forty miles away. From Nuikin to the town it's less than forty miles. What if he has a spyglass like that?

Ardalion Ignatich sorted through in his mind the places where he might go to fulfill his challenging duty, but he couldn't come up with anything worthwhile.

Better not to question the Jews, he thought. Except for Pimpleface Simeon and the night watchman Rakhmiel, no one would tell him anything. A strange people, damn them! Friendly but inscrutable, like foxes in the forest: everyone seems to be on their own and at the same time all together. It's easier with other people. Others are more comprehensible, more open. They might become enraged and act recklessly, some with cudgels, others with pitchforks, but these Jews tug at their sidelocks, sit and pray—*ssshh, ssshh, ssshh* and *ssshh, ssshh, ssshh,* so the devil himself won't understand what's in their heads. They keep a secret like the grave.

Take Fradkin: a rich man who speaks Russian in a rush, like some kind of priest, as if in words he is devoted to the czar and the throne, but just try to wheedle something out of him. You'll break out in a sweat, your eyes will pop out of your head, and you won't coax out anything.

Or Rabbi Uri, a scholar, you might say a sage, a man of God. Should you talk with him, because he has an answer to any question?

He'll tell you about Christ and about Moses, but if something happens, he's like a mole underground—you can't dig out a thing. The same goes for Yeshua. He'll pour you a glass and take some ham out from beneath the bar, and he'll court you like a suitor, but ask him, "Yeshua, do you know who fired at the Vice-Governor?" and he'll answer, "Not me, Your Honor, not me."

All of them have some trick up their sleeves, the hell with them, and those tricks are worse than cudgels and pitchforks. A gun or a rifle will do against cudgels and pitchforks, but there is no weapon against a trick—you can't examine it through a French spyglass.

To tell the truth, you can't rely on either Pimpleface Simeon or the night watchman Rakhmiel, but at least you can entice the old man with something, whereas the other one can only be intimidated.

Where did they come from anyway?

That rabbi of theirs says, "From Spain."

If you ask him, "Why didn't they stay in Spain?" right away he'll answer you, you know-nothing, "They expelled us. The king issued a decree."

They were expelled from Spain, if you please, yet we can't do that here? Don't we have a king? Is there no one to write decrees? If only there were a document, we'd make short work of it. Instead, we took them in, treated them kindly, gave them a roof over their heads, and now we're chasing them like hounds, searching for the one who shot at His Excellency the Vice-Governor, God grant him a speedy recovery!

He, Ardalion Ignatich Nesterovich, has nothing against them—let them live, breed, whisper, trade, sew, shave, by all means. But he's not simply Ardalion Ignatich Nesterovich. He is also the policeman. And a policeman, like every official, is not indifferent to what they are whispering about and who they shave, what they trade, and what they sew.

For the policeman Ardalion Ignatich Nesterovich, everyone is equal and everyone is good, as long as they don't stir up the people, if they obey His Majesty the Emperor and fulfill his imperial will.

He will never let anyone harm them, and no Nuikin will make him. Whoever has heard of harming honest and innocent people—it would be better if he, Ardalion Nesterovich, lost his rank. But here's the trouble: he is not the only one who determines their honesty and innocence; there are sharper minds and more vigilant eyes. As the saying goes, two heads are better than one.

In a fir grove, right behind the market, a fat mushroom cap gleamed like a pierog. Ardalion Ignatich tore off the boletus and headed in the direction of Rakhmiel's barn.

Maybe the watchman noticed someone during the night.

Nesterovich found Rakhmiel in the yard. The old man was dozing directly in the sun, resting against the moss-covered frame of his ramshackle home. A tuft of gray hair sticks out of his yarmulke, dry and coarse like heather.

Ardalion Ignatich walked past the sleeping man, took a look into the house, didn't find anyone there, and still holding the mushroom in his hand while eagerly, almost sensually inhaling its damp smell, he moved closer to Rakhmiel.

What could he find out from him? Even when he's keeping watch at night, he falls asleep.

For a long time Nesterovich had planned to suggest to Naftali Spivak, the synagogue warden, that he find another person to replace Rakhmiel, but he kept on putting it off. The policeman had a strange feeling for the old man. The old Jew looked like his grandfather—Porfiry Svyatoslavovich Nesterovich, a descendant of a Belorussian peasant who transported potatoes on the Sozh River to the marketplace in Gomel. Damn it, there is a real resemblance. Except that Porfiry Svyatoslavovich was not lame and didn't wear a yarmulke, of course. But otherwise, if you put them next to each other, you wouldn't see any difference.

Maybe that's why Ardalion Ignatich felt sorry for Rakhmiel and even tried to help him. He gave him his old leather coat—an unheard-of act of generosity for a policeman.

"Wear it," he said. "It's for your faithful service."

All winter the Jews gossiped about this at their study house. And Rakhmiel wore his coat while walking in the icy cold, touching it all the time. Ardalion Ignatich never called him anything other than Grandpa.

"Grandpa," he said this time, too, tapping Rakhmiel on the shoulder.

The night watchman gave a start, opened his eyes, and narrowed his eyes again.

"Wake up, Grandpa. We need to talk."

Rakhmiel raised his festering eyelids and, not fully awake, stared at the policeman. "Have mercy," he said quietly.

Nesterovich stood there, turning the mushroom in his hand.

"I'm guilty," Rakhmiel blurted out. "I'll never again, not for one night, hand over the clapper. Never."

"What are you babbling about, Grandpa?" Ardalion Ignatich said, feigning indifference.

Rakhmiel awoke from his sleepiness and fear, and he suddenly understood—the policeman didn't know a thing.

Nesterovich was a wise old bird, however. He immediately sensed something in Rakhmiel's incoherent words, and he shrewdly set off on the trail.

"I was dreaming," Rakhmiel mumbled.

"Don't be cagey, Grandpa!"

Ardalion Ignatich did not even consider letting the catch get away.

"I was dreaming," the watchman tried to save himself by lying. But no matter how hard he tried, he not only couldn't think of a dream, he couldn't even come up with a pathetic piece of one. He had dreamed so many dreams during his life, but right now when he urgently needed something, even the most trifling, the most absurd thing, everything flew out of his head. Rakhmiel prayed to the Almighty: tell me at least one dream. But the Almighty did not come to his aid. So then Rakhmiel said, "I dreamed of God."

"You gave the clapper to God?"

"Yes," Rakhmiel said in despair. "You're ill, He said, let me bang for you . . . and I gave it to Him. You can't deny anything to God."

"Nice lie. And now, Grandpa, tell the honest truth. I don't have time to chit-chat with you. Who did you give the clapper to?"

Rakhmiel was silent, and for the first time, silence did not save him, but hurt him even more.

"Who?" the policeman repeated. "Don't test my patience. No one will punish you for the truth, I promise. But for a lie . . . for a lie, Grandpa, you'll pay and how you'll pay . . . I'll wring a confession out of you without mercy."

"I gave it to Aaron," Rakhmiel muttered. "Or rather not to Aaron . . . He just called himself Aaron."

"Just called himself? Who is he really, Grandpa?"

"I don't know. He came here and asked for a drink. I don't begrudge anyone water, so I said, drink. Then I got a pain in my leg . . . a cramp."

"Hold it with the leg," the policeman stopped him. "Let's go in order. He asked for a drink . . . What next?"

"He had something to eat and disappeared. He won't return, I thought. But in the evening he showed up again . . . Not at night, but toward evening, during the downpour. He went to the Spivaks' shop, got nails on credit, and then climbed onto my roof . . ."

"What was he doing on the roof?"

"First he hammered in the nails. Then he started waving his arms."

"Why?"

"He wanted to fly."

"Where to?"

"Where do people fly? To God, it seems. When things are bad, everyone wants to take flight. And right now, Mr. Policeman, I want . . . I really want to . . ."

"If you answer my questions, you can take off," Ardalion Ignatich grinned.

"I seem to have answered them."

"And the clapper—why did he need it?"

"I already told you. I got a cramp in my leg, so he offered to bang for me. At first I refused, I wouldn't agree. Then I gave in. What's wrong with that? Was something stolen?"

"Nothing was stolen."

"Thank God."

"The Vice-Governor was almost killed," Nesterovich said.

"Here? The Vice-Governor?"

"Not here, in Vilna. They've announced a search throughout the entire region . . . looking for the criminal."

"I'm guilty, Mr. Policeman. I'm guilty, but not him. The one in the yarmulke with a pin. He's not the criminal."

"A yarmulke with a pin?"

"Yes."

Nesterovich remembered Pimpleface Simeon's story.

"He looks more like a madman."

"What normal man would start shooting at the Vice-Governor? Only a madman," Ardalion Ignatich remarked. "Where is he now?"

"How would I know? Wandering around the district somewhere."

"He didn't tell you anything?"

"About what?"

"Where he was going, who he was meeting?"

"I don't remember."

"Better remember, Grandpa!"

"He was going to the forest, he said."

"Why?"

"To the loggers. God is angry at them, he said. Soon not a single tree will be left, he said. The earth will turn into a desert and people will stoke their stoves with people . . . He wants to leave here before it's too late."

Ardalion Ignatich had a different take on the matter.

"Listen to me, Grandpa," he said. "If he—the one with the pin—shows up, don't say a word to him about my visit. If you do, I'll beat the hell out of you. Understand?"

"I understand, Your Honor."

Nesterovich left the yard.

He didn't go straight to the cutting area in the forest, however, even though he terribly wanted to go to the grove where Lukerya Panteleimonovna was hunting for mushrooms with their daughter and son. The policeman decided to pay a visit to the hardware shop and ask Spivak some questions.

"Good afternoon, Mr. Policeman," Naftali fawned over him. "What can I do for you?"

"I just dropped by . . . to express my condolences," Ardalion Ignatich began from a distance. "For me and Lukerya, Chava was like family."

"Chava is no more," Naftali said sadly. "No more."

"When he found out about how my wife gave birth, Father Nikodim reproached me: 'Ardalion Ignatich, why did you ask a Jewess to be a midwife? Have the Russian Orthodox disappeared, or something?' And I said to him, 'Father Nikodim! I won't say anything about the soul, but Chava's hands are blessed!' What did she die from?"

"From death," Naftali said. "Everyone dies from death."

The appearance of the policeman genuinely alarmed Spivak. His pince-nez kept slipping down onto the tip of his nose. Naftali nervously pushed it back up, betraying his agitation.

"From death, you say?"

"From death, from death," Spivak repeated, apparently shaken, and having no idea what Ardalion Ignatich wanted from him. He surely didn't come in order to express his sympathy. And if he came to buy something, why this story about Father Nikodim?

Maybe he, Nesterovich, had the same suspicion that we, her brothers, have. Naftali could not forget the image of the white lace kerchief around Chava's neck. His sister never complained about her health. She didn't usually complain about anything, though there were some things, oy, there were—her son was a lecher, and her husband, a boor and skinflint. But he, Naftali, won't tell the policeman anything, not about the kerchief around her neck, the powder on her face, or the hurry with which they buried her. No reason to wash your dirty linen in public. That's what the grave is for. A place to bury everything—dirty linen and doubts. There's no reason to re-open everything and hobble the living.

"How is business?" Ardalion inquired, fishing for what was most important.

"What kind of business is there in our town? You can hardly make ends meet."

"Don't pretend to be poor. All the peasants in the village are in debt to you and Chaim. And the town as well."

"The whole world around us is in debt, Mr. Policeman."

"Oh, come on! That's going too far!"

"I'm not only thinking of Jews . . . but of everyone," Naftali explained, while fiddling with his pince-nez. "Isn't your world in debt, for instance? God has shortchanged each of us in some way."

They're always this way, Ardalion Ignatich swore to himself. You ask about some trifle and they'll say all kinds of strange things, talk your ears off, criticize God Himself, and fog up your brain. He restrained himself, however, and, looking into Spivak's sharp, evasive eyes, he asked, "Do you give credit to newcomers and strangers?"

"No, I don't." Naftali didn't understand what the policeman was leading up to.

"Not even for a handful of nails?"

"Not even for a handful of nails," Spivak confirmed.

By nature, Ardalion Ignatich was a simple-hearted, trusting man. He had no talent for detective work—long investigations tired him, but he was not a simpleton. His innate peasant sharp-wittedness never abandoned him; it raised him in his own eyes and increased his persistence, if not his strength.

"Listen, Naftali," he said, coming to the point. "Did any stranger drop by to see you recently?"

"No," Spivak replied.

"So, really no one?"

"No one, Your Honor."

Nesterovich detected a ruse in Naftali's answer. If Spivak had honestly admitted it—saying yes, yes, someone did come, in a yarmulke fastened to his hair with a pin, then Ardalion Ignatich would not have suspected anything bad. But now he was consumed with doubts. What if there was some secret connection between the man in the yarmulke and the fat, pompous Spivak? Maybe Police Chief Nuikin is right, and Jews are all working together.

"You'd better think about it, Naftali." Despite his suspicion Nesterovich displayed good will.

Spivak wrinkled his forehead as if the wrinkles, like balalaika strings, could emit a sound of farewell or perhaps one of reconciliation.

"A stranger did drop by, wearing a yarmulke with a pin. He asked for nails on credit and said, 'The Master of the Universe will reward you and your brother Chaim a hundredfold for each nail!'"

"Of course," Ardalion Ignatich sighed. "A password!"

"What?"

"A secret word. They always do that."

"Who?"

"Assassins and rebels who shoot at vice-governors. Do you really think that he just dropped by for some nails?"

"Chaim! Chaim!" Naftali yelled. And after his brother entered the shop from the side door, he exclaimed, "Congratulations, Chaim!"

"What for?"

"You and I are assassins or rebels. Oy, stop me, or I'll die laughing. Oy, stop me!"

"Let's hope you won't have to cry," Nesterovich said calmly and took his leave.

Naftali's laughter mixed up and confused Ardalion Ignatich's thoughts; it blew them away with the wind, thoughts that had just a moment ago in the shop seemed so calm and incontrovertible. But why did this man, the stranger in a velvet yarmulke with a pin, raise such a commotion? Was anyone blaming Spivak? Why would he shoot at a vice-governor? He lives well, doesn't have any troubles, and sets aside money. My job is to question, verify, and report to Nuikin . . . I was placed here for that purpose and invested with authority as well.

Ardalion Ignatich walked past the tavern and regretted once more that it was locked. It would be good to wet his whistle. When you toss down a glass, everything in the world becomes clearer. It's torture to look at the world while sober, torture.

If only Morta would look outside for a moment.

No one.

And I don't feel like showing up there by myself and knocking on the window during the period of mourning.

Lukerya Panteleimonovna, Ivan, and Katyusha have probably already collected full baskets. Three more trips to the forest and the tub for the czar will be ready.

Maybe His Majesty will visit this autumn. He hasn't been in these parts, not even once!

There are provincial holes where there is neither God nor czar—only Nuikin, only cunning Jews and Lithuanians living in silence.

Ardalion Ignatich suddenly recalled how Lukerya Panteleimonovna tried to persuade him to move to the region of the Don River or, if worse came to worst, to somewhere near Ryazan or Vologda; there, people say, everyone is one of our own, there's not a single alien, but he kept on refusing. It's easy to say "move." But what about the house? The garden? The orchard? Livestock? And, moreover, is he, Nesterovich, his own man? He belongs to Nuikin. If Nuikin orders him to the Don, he'll go to the Don; if he orders him to Vologda, he'll learn to pronounce "o" and "a" like the locals.

The clearing area in the forest was far away, and as Ardalion Ignatich walked there, his whole hard and chaotic life passed before his eyes: his childhood on the banks of the Sozh, his military service, the Caucasus. Without anger, patiently, he thought about his life, and no matter how hard he tried, he could not extract even one fiery piece of coal from it, as from under a pile of ashes.

The only time he could remember with joy was nocturnal—the night into which his grandfather Porfiry Svyatoslavovich took him. When he was a small boy, trembling, his grandfather sat him on a horse and the horse carried him away into the night; the horse circled the meadow and the meadow seemed boundless, like his happiness. He would have recognized that horse out of a thousand others; it had a long mane, a shiny velvet crop, and slender, limber legs which were shod not with horseshoes but with his thoughts sparkling in the darkness—just give an order and those legs would take you wherever you wanted.

For a long time the horse's neighs and the clatter of hooves filled his soul with the freshness of meadows and a feeling of union with the person who remained there forever on the banks of the Sozh, in his native Belarus.

Ardalion Ignatich heard the disjointed whacks of axes from the forest and quickened his step.

Looking around the clearing area, Nesterovich immediately noticed two yarmulkes. Since Itsik was the only Jew he recognized among the loggers, Ardalion Ignatich realized who the other one had to be.

The first sensation the policeman felt was surprising disappointment. The stranger in the yarmulke with a pin did not look at all like a state criminal. He seemed rather fragile, small, and decrepit for his age. His torn, short-hemmed *balakhon*, apparently someone else's castoff, buckled on him, making the outsider look hunchbacked, and perhaps he really was a hunchback; the strings he tied his shoes with dragged along the ground; and his straggly beard was streaked with silver and had not been cleaned for a long time. Even here, in the forest, misfortune and anguish wafted from him. The stranger was talking loudly to Itsik about something, and strange words came flying like wood chips to Ardalion Ignatich's ears. Nesterovich was struck most of all by the stranger's hands. They were long, like oars, and he seemed to be rowing the air with them or trying to stay afloat.

"May God bless you," Nesterovich spoke up when Afinogen Andronov—the elder brother—noticed him.

"Thank you, Ardalion Ignatich," Afinogen said soberly. "You're here for mushrooms or on some other business?"

"What other business is there in the forest?" the policeman dissembled.

"There's no telling," Afinogen replied, plunging his axe into a tree. "Let's have a smoke, brothers!" he shouted to the whole forest. "You're welcome to join us, Ardalion Ignatich!"

This way is even better, Nesterovich thought, walking over to Andronov.

Afinogen sat on a stump, opened his pouch, took out some cheap tobacco, and gave some to Ardalion Ignatich. They each rolled up a "goat's leg" and started to smoke.

Guri sat down with them.

The Lithuanians—the old man Riauba and the lanky Anzelmas—kept their distance. The farther away from the authorities, the better. Have a casual smoke with them and you'll regret it later. You might end up spitting blood.

Itsik and the man in the yarmulke were arguing, as is usual among Jews, to the point of forgetting what the issue was. What is he, Ardalion Ignatich, to them? They must be up in the heavens now, talking with their Lord God of Hosts, or wandering through the Sinai desert after fleeing Egyptian captivity, waving their arms back and forth to cool each other from the heat.

Ardalion Ignatich puffed at the cigarette while keeping an eye on them. He had spent the day in vain. In vain. Chief Nuikin doesn't need this guy in the yarmulke with a pin; he needs someone else entirely. But where could he, Nesterovich, dig up another one for him? He's unlucky even at this. During his whole long government service he has never caught a single big fish . . . just insignificant little fish and other small fry. Don't expect an award for a tiny one. What profit is there from a miniscule catch? Only once in his life, and that was in a dream, did he lasso a villain—a bandit in the Caucasus. He lay in wait at night, knocked the sucker down, tied him up tightly and headed straight for the governor general's palace, where there was no end of rooms. For two days he dragged the bandit over his back, sweating like a horse and almost getting a hernia, until finally he dragged him through the last hall and into the office of His Excellency. His Excellency opened a gold chest, took out a Saint George's cross, and hung it over his chest, saying, "Well done, Nesterovich! You came here as a common soldier; you'll leave as a captain!"

"At your command, Your Excellency!"

The governor general got up from the table and led Nesterovich into some room where there were uniforms. They flashed before Ardalion Ignatich's eyes: for generals, colonels, captains, all kinds.

He picked out a uniform in his size, walked up to the palace mirror and . . . woke up.

Dear Lord, Ardalion Ignatich thought while blowing out gray smoke rings, if You can't lure the czar here to taste my mushrooms, at least let me have that one . . . the real one who shot at the vice-governor.

"I see there's a new man here," Ardalion Ignatich said, spitting out some tobacco.

"Aaah," Afinogen yawned, "he's not a logger . . . He's some kind of wanderer." The older Andronov then made circles around his gray temple with a finger turned yellow from smoking. "A tiny bit . . ."

"What?"

"He's not all there."

"He's not by chance pretending?" The policeman showed his suspicions.

"No . . . judge for yourself. He comes here and asks us to make him a ladder."

"What kind of ladder?" Nesterovich asked.

"To reach the sky," Guri said, breaking his silence.

"Oh, come on!" Ardalion put out his cigarette on his boot.

"And, I say to him, do you know how much forest it would take for a ladder like that?" Afinogen continued.

Guri interrupted his brother: "So he says: 'I do know. Just one tree.'"

"You're not a chorus! One at a time," policeman said, intrigued.

"You tell it," Afinogen gave way to his brother. "You seem to have promised him."

"One tree, I say, is not enough. From one, I say, you can only get to the roof."

"And then?" Ardalion Ignatich encouraged the storyteller.

"He says, 'I'll show you such a tree.' And what do you think? He leads me to a stump, points his hand at it, and says 'this one.' But it's a stump, I say, an ordinary stump . . . And he goes, 'This one! This one!' I didn't know whether to laugh or cry."

"But what does he want the ladder for?" Ardalion Ignatich was interested to know, meanwhile keeping a distrustful eye on the stranger.

"He says: 'I will climb to God on it.'" Guri chuckled. "'On the Day of Judgment, I will make my report.' And what, I say, will you tell Him about us? 'About you,' he says, 'nothing . . . I will tell Him only about Jews,' he says. 'You must wait for your own messenger,' he says. 'Well,' I say, 'since you won't ask God for anything good for us, ask for your own, for Itsik.' Looks like he's trying to talk him into something right now. It's amusing. You listen, and it feels like you have one foot over there."

"Where?"

"In the Other World, in Heaven. It's boring to swing axes all the time. It's just a pity there's no tavern up there." Guri chuckled again. "To some, Ardalion Ignatich, a tavern is a tavern, but it's also our heaven."

"You've said enough, Guri," Afinogen silenced him.

They stood up and took up their axes again.

Nesterovich got up, too. For a moment, he reflected on what to do: turn back or approach the man in the yarmulke with a pin; he decided the day's shot to hell anyway, he would have a talk with the stranger.

"Good afternoon," he greeted Itsik stiffly.

"Hello," Itsik answered.

"What are you good people talking about?"

"Different things," Itsik said reluctantly.

The stranger looked at Ardalion Ignatich apathetically, without any interest or fear, as if before him stood not a living person, but a moss-covered tree not suitable for any ladders.

"Do you understand Russian?" the policeman turned to the stranger, speaking simply and without prejudice.

"Yes," the man in the yarmulke said. "I speak all languages."

"Really, all?" Ardalion Ignatich said in amazement.

"All . . . How else can you negotiate with people?"

"That's true," Nesterovich muttered, flabbergasted. "With human beings you need to speak in a human way . . . I can also speak a little Jewish now . . . Did you travel from afar?"

"Depends on how you measure it."

"By miles," the policeman said.

"I have never measured my journeys by miles."

"By what, then?"

"By distances from God and to God."

"This is Ardalion Ignatich, our policeman," Itsik introduced Nesterovich.

"I thought so," the man in the yarmulke said. "All policemen ask the very same questions."

"And who are you?" Ardalion Ignatich inquired, acting as though he had not noticed the spiteful remark.

"Does it matter to the police who we are?"

Ardalion Ignatich was dumbfounded.

"What do you think matters to them?" he managed to say.

"Where are we? Who are we with? What are we for?" the man in the yarmulke explained politely.

"Where you are, let's assume, is clear . . . in Fradkin's cutting area. Who you are with also . . . with Itsik right now. What's left to find out is what you are for."

"What I am for? You want me to tell you who I am."

"Precisely," Ardalion Ignatich seized at his answer.

"But I myself don't know who I am."

"How can that be?" Nesterovich frowned.

"While we're alive, no one knows who they are . . . Only a worm knows until its dying day that it's a worm. Only a cow knows what a cow is."

"And a person?"

"People don't know. For half of his life a man's a man, then he turns into a worm, and in the end he becomes a man again. Whoever doubts this will never enter the Kingdom of Heaven," the stranger concluded.

No, he's not at all like someone insane, Ardalion thought, but he's not rational either. So who is he?

"Who are you?" Nesterovich's patience had reached its limit.

"Who?" The stranger thought for a moment, looked at Itsik, then at the loggers swinging their heavy, sharp axes, as if he were searching for an answer among them, and suddenly he said: "I put on righteousness, and it clothed me; my judgment was like a robe and a turban. I was eyes to the blind and feet to the lame, a father to the poor, and I searched out the cause of him whom I knew not. I broke the jaws of the unrighteous and plucked the prey from his teeth."

"What sort of nonsense is he talking?" Ardalion Ignatich asked Itsik. "Translate. I don't understand Tmutarakan."

"He's talking about himself in the words of Job."

"Who's this Job?" the policeman asked, becoming angry at his own helplessness.

"The one the Almighty struck with leprosy from the soles of his feet to the crown of his head."

"Don't play games with me! Let him answer in a simple way, in our way."

The man in the yarmulke remained silent.

"Do you have identity papers?" Ardalion Ignatich addressed the stranger.

"No," the stranger said.

"You'll need to be taken into custody . . . until your identity is cleared up. Understand?"

"Understood," the man in the yarmulke nodded. "But there are no fetters or prisons that I cannot get out of."

"We'll see about that," Ardalion replied and gave the order "Go!"

"Let him go," Itsik interceded for the man in the yarmulke. "The fetters with which the Almighty has bound him are enough."

"The Almighty may be Almighty, but there must be order," Nesterovich snapped back, and gave the stranger a push in the back.

The stranger lazily trudged along through the forest, stepping every now and then on the untied shoestrings that dragged on the ground; he kept stumbling and looked up at the dark blue sky extended above him, moving his lips silently like a fish thrown onto the shore. Ardalion Ignatich tripped along after him, irritated by the shoelaces that dragged along the ground and snaked in and out of the moss as if to spite him, teasing and catching his eye, as moss-wheels and chanterelles jutted out and even porcini basked in the sun with impunity. It dawned on Nesterovich that if he had a basket right now, he could collect so many along the way! And suddenly it struck Ardalion Ignatich—the *balakhon*, in the *balakhon*! Tie up the sleeves with the string and pour in as many as you can.

"Stop!" he shouted at the stranger. "Take off your coat!"

The stranger shuddered, stared at his escort in bewilderment, and removed his garment slowly, as if he were tearing off his skin.

"Give me the laces, too!"

The man in the yarmulke bent down and pulled the unraveling strings from his shoes.

Ardalion Ignatich used them to tie up the sleeves of the *balakhon*, made something like a sack out of it, and, bending over constantly, began to throw in his prey.

"And what are you doing?" he turned to the stranger, breathing calmly and happily.

The man in the yarmulke looked at the policeman, and in his sad eyes, lit with an unearthly light, there flashed the elusive sparks of sardonic but delighted consent.

"Start gathering!"

The stranger looked around anxiously, trying to find a mushroom. He took a step toward one, hacked it down, and, holding it like a goblet filled to the brim, carried it over to Ardalion Ignatich.

"That's a fly agaric—a bad mushroom, poisonous," the policeman said with good will. "Gather those chanterelles over there . . . My grandfather Porfiry called them Jewish, because they never get eaten by worms . . . Just don't pull out the roots!"

The man in the yarmulke, unused to such work, soon got tired, knelt down and began crawling from one cluster of mushrooms to another. When the *balakhon* was packed full, Ardalion Ignatich said, "Lukerya Panteleimonovna will cook mushroom soup. She'll treat you. And then . . . then," Nesterovich didn't know what to do with the stranger then. "Oh my," the policeman sighed, "you should pick another county, my friend!"

"I hear the very same thing from every policeman: 'You should pick another county, my friend!' But where on earth is it, this other county? Where? The whole land, from region to region, is one county . . . one and indivisible, where they would even demand identity papers from God, with an official seal. And that seal is the stamp of Satan."

Rattled, Nesterovich brought the stranger to town and, exhausted by bad premonitions, locked him up in the barn with the cow and the pigs.

14

Even his mother's death did not reconcile Pimpleface Simeon with his father. They should have sat together during the traditional shiva, for all seven days of mourning, but they grieved separately, each in his own room. Morta rushed back and forth between them, not knowing who needed her more.

She cooked for both, hastily bringing food to them separately, without lingering, trying to busy herself and avoid unwanted questions.

Behind his dark, tangled beard, Simeon remained gloomily silent all week. He wasn't interested in anything; he ate in a hurry and without his former, greedy appetite; he stirred his soup with a spoon for a long time, as if intending to fish something out of the bowl. The uneasiness of his right hand, which resembled a crab's claws, scared her.

For the first time in many years he avoided Morta's glances, as if she might sear a mark of shame on his forehead or expose something, even privately, that he didn't want to show. He was undergoing something larger than his mother's death, but what it was exactly Morta could not understand.

He had unexpectedly developed a strange habit of rubbing his neck, feeling his Adam's apple, and squeezing it with two fingers until he became short of breath. Whenever Morta came into his room, Pimpleface Simeon would quietly pull back his hand and hide it in his pocket or under his shirt.

He slept sitting up with his head thrown back against the eastern wall, where he had sometimes mumbled his prayers when Chava was alive.

Morta didn't try to talk to him, not fearing his anger so much as wanting to preserve the unsullied memory of her mistress. Pimple-face Simeon broke the silence only once, which was enough to make her recoil and freeze.

"Do you know where Father keeps the gun?" he asked without raising his head.

"I don't know, Simonas."

"Don't lie. You know everything in this house."

"But . . . why do you need it?"

"I need it."

He did not utter another word.

After that evening, whenever she entered his room, Morta feared his questions, shuddering—but he did not ask her again, as if she had dreamed it all and there had never been a gun.

Unlike his son, the tavern keeper Yeshua chatted with her and was even affectionate. Whenever she entered the room, he brightened up, smoothed out his black beard, adjusted his yarmulke like a gentleman, and leaned his whole body toward her, his servant.

"Morta, Morta," he muttered as he handed her his empty bowl. "What would I do without you? Why did the Lord send such an angel to us sinners?"

"I'm not an angel, Sir."

"An angel, an angel," Yeshua repeated, while pulling out crumbs that had stuck in his beard. "My son is a stranger, and you, Morta, are like my own."

"Your son is always your own . . . And I am not one of yours, Sir."

"My own, my own."

Conversations like these scared Morta. But Yeshua's sharp, tenacious eyes scared her even more. When he looked at her, shivers ran up and down her spine.

He had looked at her that way once before, five years earlier. They had traveled together to a city, probably Kovno. It was already getting dark when the hub of their wagon broke, and Yeshua, leading the horse by the reins, headed to the nearest village with Morta to have the wheel fixed.

They walked through the forest, guessing their way, and became lost in the dark.

It was senseless and dangerous to go further. At any moment a hungry wolf could tear you to pieces, so Yeshua decided to spend the night in a thicket. They found a place side by side on moss beneath a spruce, tied up the bay, and waited for the morning.

"Sleep," Yeshua said. "Sleep."

"You sleep too, Sir."

"I'm sleeping, I'm sleeping."

But neither of them closed their eyes. Only the forest slept. Not a branch moved, and the stillness engulfed them like deep waters.

"Aren't you afraid, Morta?" Yeshua asked.

"No," she lied. "Are you?"

"I'm not afraid either. I'm not afraid of anything." His whisper fell onto the stillness like rain, and the tavern keeper was moist all over.

He moved closer to Morta, his legs began to twist and turn, and suddenly he jumped up and threw himself into a raspberry bush, frightening the bay. With a scratched and bleeding face he began to pray, to groan and cry in a state of frenzy.

He prayed until dawn broke. When it grew light, Morta saw his exhausted face with its patches of dried blood.

"You have blood on your cheeks, Sir," Morta said.

"It's nothing, nothing," he answered. "God took mercy on me. I stained my cheeks, but not my soul."

Ordinary days flew by quickly, crazily, but these days of mourning crawled like snails: before evening came you might be covered with moss. The single joy was that the tavern remained closed. For the owner, of course, it was a loss, but for Morta it was a break.

True, the dog had been added to all her troubles . . . the dog they had picked up on the way to the cemetery, with ears that drooped like potato tops.

Morta washed him in the Neman, combed him with a scraper, and put him on a chain.

The dog was strange, though; voiceless, he didn't bark at all but just wagged his stump of a tail and caught fleas by licking them off his belly with his long tongue, which looked like it had been scalded.

"One who lives by begging doesn't bark," Yeshua told Morta. "He will live with us and learn. What's new in town?"

"Nothing."

"How is Simeon?" the tavern keeper kept asking.

"He's silent."

Yeshua didn't believe her.

"He keeps silent and thinks," Morta said.

"Let him think. He has something to think about."

"Everyone has something to think about," Morta mumbled, wanting to narrow the distance between the master and his son.

"It's time for you, Sir, to make peace."

"It's impossible to make peace with him."

"Why?"

"Because he doesn't love anyone, that's why."

"He does love," Morta assured the tavern keeper.

"You, perhaps?" Yeshua couldn't resist.

"You," Morta swallowed the hurt. "And he loved Chava, his deceased mother."

"Ha! Because of him, she . . ."

"No, no," Morta protested.

Yeshua was not only accusing Simeon, she understood, but also her. If Simeon had married, Chava would never have stuck her head into the noose. She would have looked after her grandchildren and grown old in warmth and comfort. But perhaps she would not have had any grandchildren even from a Jewish woman. Some sons are more affectionate and faithful, of course, but it was not only because of Simeon that Chava stamped into the barn at the crack of dawn and took her own life. Not only. The tavern keeper Yeshua knows this better than anyone. Morta has lived in the house for a very long time, but if you ask her if she remembers even one time when Yeshua spoke with Chava warmly, she won't recall such an occasion. Still, it's true that the tavern keeper never swore at his wife, didn't yell at her, and didn't abuse her even though he was not a timid creature.

"Mortele," he often said in front of his wife. "Take a look, is there enough vodka left in the storeroom?"

He pronounced the diminutive "Mortele" with an unconcealed tenderness that was not muted by decency.

"Mortele, come with me to the fair in Vilkija."

"Did I catch a little cold, Mortele? Will you put cups on me for the night?"

Chava's eyes darkened from those "Morteles," while the servant Morta's head spun as if she were intoxicated.

"Will you stop calling the maid 'Mortele' in public?" Pimpleface Simeon asked him jealously.

"Why?" Yeshua swaggered.

"Because," his son raged.

"Someone should address her the way a father would."

Despite Pimpleface Simeon, and perhaps Chava also, from morning to evening he poured out "Mortele, Mortele, Mortele," as if he were feeding a turtledove millet from his hand.

Unlike Simeon, who didn't even raise his eyes to look at her, Yeshua did not let Morta leave him for long periods of time, even though, according to custom, excessive chatter and contacts with gentiles was forbidden.

The tavern keeper babbled like someone's grandmother, and Morta couldn't stand his chatter, which was at odds with the misfortune that had befallen them.

She thought: from his side of the wall Simeon hears every word they say, and when the days of mourning are over, he will take out all his anger on her, pour out all his bile, call her God knows what, and maybe even hit her. But she did not dare disobey the tavern keeper Yeshua, her master and benefactor. After all, it was he, not Simeon, who took her in after her home was destroyed and her parents were sent off to Siberia. As God is her witness, she does a lot for Yeshua— she washes dishes, washes clothes, cooks, buys and sells, and watches over him. But a person needs something completely different . . .

especially if that person feels bad. And now Yeshua feels bad, very bad. Even if he didn't love Chava, still they lived together for thirty-five years. During thirty-five years even a stone blossoms once, and if you take a closer look, you'll see that some tiny blade of grass has grown there and sprouted. No matter how hard Yeshua's heart was, even after so many years, a blade of grass has apparently appeared on it, taken root, and now someone must shield it from the wind. What kind of shield is there against Simeon? For Simeon is the wind itself. And she, Morta? She can shield a blade of grass from the wind, but he will blow up a storm, freeze you, and there will be no way for you to get warm.

"Why are you always looking back as if someone is watching you?" the tavern keeper Yeshua asked, as if he had guessed her thoughts.

"I don't look back," she mumbled.

"You shouldn't feel sorry for him."

"Who?"

"My son," Yeshua said. "He's not worth your little finger."

"How can you say that?"

"It doesn't matter to him who he . . . with you or . . ."

"Stop," Morta begged.

"Listen to me and don't interrupt. I don't wish you ill, I don't wish anyone ill. Not even him, that good-for-nothing."

Why does he torment me? Yeshua was thinking: Had I kept my thoughts with Chava until the shiva was over, I could have asked for her forgiveness. Maybe she would even have forgiven him.

Yet the tavern keeper Yeshua apparently did not want his thoughts to stay with Chava. He did not need her forgiveness.

"Sit down and listen," he repeated, and with a sense of doom Morta sat down on a chair.

"Oy!" she cried and quickly got up. "I sat in Chava's place . . . Chava never let anyone sit there."

"Sit, sit," the tavern keeper said, trying to calm her. "Chava never sat in this chair."

"What do you mean, she didn't?" Morta's eyes opened wide.

"That's how it is. You're young . . . You still don't know everything."

"What don't I know?"

"You don't know, for instance, that Chava never sat in this chair."

"But I saw it with my own eyes . . . and Simeon saw it . . . and Naftali . . . and Chaim. Chava sat here." Morta pointed to the chair. "And you . . . you, Sir, sat across from her."

"Chava did not sit across from me."

"Then who did?"

"Can they all be named?" Yeshua paused, then added, "Who seats misfortune opposite him, Mortele? You always sit facing those you would be happy with . . . And that happens not only at the table, Mortele, but also in bed."

Her ears turned red from his words, and her heart was pounding more strongly than from household tasks.

"Are you sleeping with Simeon?" the tavern keeper asked. "I can't believe it. Never. You might sleep with Antanas or with Jouzas . . . or with Jonas . . . not with my son. But they, your people . . . were either exiled to Siberia, or they sleep with others, the fools. Why are you standing? Sit down, sit, relax."

"I will stand, Sir."

"Stand . . . But for God's sake, stop calling me sir."

"All right, Master."

"And don't call me master."

"All right."

She would agree to anything in order to leave as soon as she could. The previously affectionate "Mortele, Mortele" lashed her like a whip, and the mention of Simeon's bed resounded in her head without stopping. She felt as if she'd been smeared with tar from head to toe, and the tar was dripping onto the floor from the hem of her skirt, trickling down her legs and binding them tightly to the floorboards.

"I'm leaving," Morta said.

"Where are you hurrying to?" Yeshua stopped her.

No matter what reason I think up, he still won't let me go, Morta decided. The livestock will wait, there's not a soul in the tavern, and it's best not to bring up Simeon.

Then suddenly it occurred to her.

Overcoming her embarrassment, she blurted out, "I have . . . an urgent need."

"All right," Yeshua gave in. "Go."

Morta ran out of the room.

The tavern keeper Yeshua got up from the table, walked over to the window and stared into the yard.

Beside the doghouse, the dog was playing with the chain.

The old goose was cleaning her feathers with her beak.

A tattered old rooster mounted a hen, then jumped to the ground and, spreading his wings, began to crow triumphantly.

Morta was nowhere in sight. The outhouse was shut from the outside with a piece of wood, and Yeshua walked away from the window.

While Yeshua and Simeon sat around at home mourning Chava, Morta ran off to the priest for confession. She needed to relieve her wounded soul.

The priest Anicetas listened absentmindedly as she spoke. In the confessional his cassock crinkled; when he put his large pink ear to the small window Morta's words seemed to bounce back from there as if from the aperture of a seashell, returning to her and stinging more painfully than before. The largest ear in the world, and even that would probably not have contained her pain and disarray, her rambling and artless confession with its involuntary sighs and inevitable silences. Should she really confess all her sins, the mortal and the venial, to the holy father?

"Bear it, my daughter," the priest told her. "For our sake Christ took even greater torment upon himself."

Christ, Christ! Morta understood why he bore his torment—for the whole human race, the rich and the poor, the healthy and the crippled, the good and the bad. And to him they all looked the same, none of them had the tavern keeper Yeshua's eyes or Pimpleface

Simeon's nose. Christ did not ask anyone's name or rank. He accepted his suffering for all and for no one. But her, Morta's, pain had a face and a name.

Why is it that some people don't drive themselves crazy with tormenting thoughts, while others suffer from the day they are born until they die? Why can't this suffering be divided equally among all?

Did the tavern keeper Yeshua send his wife Chava off on her last journey? Did he shake with horror, washing the breasts that had nourished his son and daughter? He handed off this torment to her, Morta.

And what did she get for it? A bowl of soup? A broken trestle-bed in the pantry? A gold coin on a saint's feast day?

What other torments will they demand from her?

What gun?

What caresses?

In recent days Morta had an unremitting premonition of trouble that would make even Chava's suicide seem less terrible. And Morta was powerless to ward it off, push it aside, scare it away.

She could have said to hell with everything—these two tiresome Jews, this tavern stinking of alcohol, and this damn small town—and set out for anywhere, to the Germans, or to Siberia, whatever she liked.

Wouldn't her conscience trouble her if something happened in her absence? But maybe everything would turn out well, settle down, and they could all heal together, as the Lord commands.

No, she must bear her cross and stop thinking about fleeing. Maybe the priest is right. Maybe God had brought her here, to this tavern, so that she, Morta, would take on all these torments for them, for nonbelievers. By showing them supreme grace through her suffering and her patience, she would set them on the true path and nurture their souls.

What would happen to them if she abandoned them?

The Lord had provided patience and the Lord will also provide strength, she thought, and she believed that her sacrifice would not be in vain. It would be answered somewhere at the other end of the earth, in Siberia, for her parents and twin brothers, Petras and Povilas. They were lost amid endless snowstorms. Her sacrifice would be rewarded, and her patience would bestow grace and good fortune upon them. It would melt the snow, bring them closer together, and perhaps it would even reunite them, exhausted from suffering but happy.

The first thing she had to do was to hide the gun from Simeon. But she didn't know where Yeshua kept it.

The tavern keeper used to return from Kovno or some other city and immediately put it out of sight. You can't search the whole house.

Still, it was unlikely that the gun was in the house. Yeshua had a hiding place. And where—you won't guess.

Once Simeon tried to discover it, but the tavern keeper grabbed him by the shirt and said, looking straight into his eyes, "You louse, how come you're following your own father?"

"And what are you hiding from your son?"

"A rifle," Yeshua said calmly. "I'm not hiding it from my son, but from myself."

"From yourself?"

"If you only knew how many times a day I want to shoot!"

"You think you're the only one who wants to shoot? Everyone does, Father. Me, and Mama, and even her." Simeon nodded toward Morta.

"I don't want to, Simonas."

"That's because you're a saint."

So Simeon did not find out anything.

But Morta remembered the master's words: "how many times a day I want to shoot."

Who did he want to shoot? A drunk who didn't pay for vodka? The lanky Anzelmas who blamed Jews for all the troubles? The policeman Nesterovich, who always bought vodka on credit until Monday and never—not on any Monday—repaid the debt? Who, then, she wondered.

Before his mother died, Simeon had forgotten about the gun, but all of a sudden he needed it.

Why?

Had that homeless stranger in the yarmulke fastened to his hair with a pin really enraged him so? That stupid caretaker at the synagogue started a quarrel, lied, made up some nonsense about Yeshua's stinking tears, all in order to ingratiate himself and get a ruble. And Simeon believed him. Who was it he believed?

The one in the yarmulke was a harmless tramp. How many of them pass through town in a year! Morta never chases them out of the yard, she always treats them with something, gives them old clothes, and hands them a hunk of bread for the road—may they chew and be happy.

Simeon couldn't be searching for the gun because of the tramp. Even if the stranger had blurted out something in the heat of the moment, had lost control—he had a reason for that. He was hungry, lonely, unsettled, without a penny to his name. People don't become evil from a good life. And his kind are not evil at all. They always have amusing things to say; rarely do you hear them talk about money or profit, but more about wonders of all kinds. And this one, in the yarmulke with a pin, is like that. Zelda said that he was waiting for a ladder from the Lord, and as soon as he finally gets it, he will climb up to Heaven.

If only the Lord would really lower a ladder like that! She, Morta, would climb up there, take off her shoes, and head across the clouds to Siberia, to her parents and her brothers, Petras and Povilas. When she got tired, she would lie down on some small cloud, and this cloud, swept along by the wind, would carry her to them at the other end of the world, beyond the seven seas, across cities and towns, across forests and mountains. But then, how would she come down to earth from the heavens? What if Morta was left hanging over Siberia, over the same village where her dear ones live? Then she would spread open the cloud and lean out through a gap, as through a window, and shout, "Father! Mama! Petras! Povilas!"

They would see her, wave their hands, and shout, "Morta, Morta!"

If only I could see them from the sky . . . for a moment . . . Just to say a quick word . . .

Morta's premonition of trouble grew stronger when, arriving home from the church, she didn't find Simeon in his room. He wasn't in the yard or the barn or the storeroom. And the outhouse was shut from the outside with a piece of wood.

Morta was alarmed. He's looking for the gun, she thought.

In order to quiet her anxiety, against her will Morta quietly entered Yeshua's room, but stopped in the doorway, not knowing what to say to him or what to do.

The tavern keeper was dozing. His head drooped, his yarmulke had slid off the top of his head and fallen to the floor like a maple leaf.

A bald patch shone in the midst of his black hair, which was tinged with streaks of gray.

Yeshua's legs were spread wide, circling back together only near his toes, which made them resemble a horse collar, and his knees were shaking slightly.

Morta walked over to the chair, bent down, and picked up the yarmulke from the floor. She held it in her hand and carefully, so as not to wake the master, placed it back on this head.

Yeshua gave a start and opened his eyes.

"Your yarmulke fell off," Morta said.

"Yes, I see," he muttered unclearly, adjusted the yarmulke, and asked, "What do you need, Morta?"

"Nothing," she whispered.

"You never come in here without a reason."

"I thought perhaps you needed something."

Yeshua noted her confusion, but he didn't press her. He waited for her to say on her own why she had come. Not in order to pick up his yarmulke from the floor or to ask if he needed anything. Morta understood him intuitively. Sometimes just a look, a gesture, a sigh, or a slight cough was enough, and she would rush to fulfill his wish. But she never intruded on her own, didn't try to please or flatter. What had happened?

"Mortele, I need you to tell the truth," Yeshua mumbled.

The truth? Morta didn't know it herself. She had not found Simonas where he was supposed to be—well, what of it? If you said that to the master, he would respond by interpreting everything the wrong way. He'd think that she can't go for even an hour without his son, and she'd only end up poisoning Yeshua's soul. Morta never told the tavern keeper, Chava, or Simonas anything, even though they often bothered her with questions. She didn't take any gossip out the door. She didn't consider it her business. It was their quarrel, as they said, and they would make it up themselves. There was no reason to act like either a judge or a mediator. Stay on your own side of the fence. They valued her above all not for her diligence and modesty but for her steadfast impartiality, although at times it enraged them.

And she didn't want to abandon her principles now. The more so because this concerned the person closest to her—Simonas.

The fear of losing him was upsetting old habits. He would kill someone; the gendarmes would appear, seize him, take him off to hard labor; and she would be left alone in this world. This fear both tied and loosened her tongue, motivating her to be careful and to keep a strict silence that would always give her support.

"So? Will we play silent forever?" the tavern keeper Yeshua nudged her.

Morta made a decision.

"Master," she said.

"Call me Yeshua!"

"No, no."

"If you don't want Yeshua, call me father."

"I have a father, and the priest is a father . . . no, no."

The beginning did not bode well. Apparently sensing her dismay, the tavern keeper confused Morta with hints and short, unhurried phrases. She didn't know how to hedge—cunning was hard, stressful. It would be easier to chop wood all day or serve annoying drunks in the tavern.

"A fox has taken to visiting us," she said, trying to catch the elusive thread of her thoughts. "It's killing the chickens."

"Killing the chickens, you say?" Yeshua asked with a straight face but laughing inside.

"Only the rooster is left. And so I thought, what if . . . with your gun . . . the fox . . ."

After she said that, Morta felt relief or perhaps confidence. She glanced sideways at Yeshua to see what impression her words had made on him, but the master showed neither surprise nor understanding. She went on:

"We should stitch together a hat for you for the winter. A fox fur hat would suit you well."

Morta was going with the current, and she had not thought much about where it would carry her.

"You say it will suit me?"

"Yes, yes."

"All right, then," Yeshua muttered. "I'll go to Vilkija and buy one from the furrier."

"Why waste money?" Morta was almost indignant. "When your hat is running around the yard?"

Yeshua raised his brows and from under the thick, black bristles his cold eyes flashed with distrust.

"What, don't you believe me?"

"I believe you . . . For my whole life you're the only one I've believed. Everyone else cheated me, but never you. Why have you suddenly started worrying about a hat?"

"Winter is coming," Morta blurted out. "And you don't have a single decent one . . . The Spivaks have them, and Fradkin . . ." Morta showered him with names.

"You say one rooster remains. From the window I saw him with a chicken . . ."

"The neighbor's chicken . . . came into the yard, and he . . . well, you saw it yourself."

"I saw it," Yeshua growled in frustration. "All right. The funeral's over, I'll finish off your fox myself."

That's that, flashed through Morta's mind. The old geezer has duped me, twisted me around his little finger.

"I want to give you something," she said, not moving a muscle in her face.

"Mortele!" the tavern keeper brightened up.

She didn't care—if only to save Simeon from hard labor. If only to get hold of the gun, and then she would not slip up, she would go to the Neman at midnight and sink it. Let the tavern keeper throw her out later.

"You won't miss?" Yeshua's eyes narrowed.

"I won't miss."

No, she wouldn't miss. She would sink the gun forever and light a candle for God in the church.

The tavern keeper Yeshua always made decisions carefully and, so as not to make a mistake, he never hurried to reach them. Once he did, he acted decisively and assuredly. Now something in Morta's words disturbed him and put him on guard; Yeshua was forced to hesitate and weigh what she had said. Why the hell did he need a fox hat? Where could he show it off in winter? A simple, warm, reliable hat would do. Whatever frost sets in, whatever wind blows, his head would not catch cold. Morta's request touched a chord in his heart that had fallen silent. His body had yearned for female affection, and now an invigorating, sinful warmth poured out on this day of mourning. He fidgeted in his chair and felt a slight itching that confused his brain.

If Simeon needed a gun, Yeshua reflected, Morta would never ask for it, so he calmed down and considered his decision. You can't even let Simeon get his hands on a club, because he'd make trouble and smash someone's skull. Then he'd take the rap, wriggle out of it, and butter up Nesterovich. Where did his son get so much cruelty, so much seething anger seeking an outlet? He hadn't been nursed by a she-wolf, but by the quiet, uncomplaining Chava.

"The gun's in the barn, under the eaves, where the swallows have their nests. It's wrapped up in an old horse blanket."

Morta didn't believe it, but she nodded gratefully.

Yeshua looked at her intently, and his stare, weighed down by his thick black brows, was searing and enigmatic.

"I'm going," she said after a long pause.

"You won't take a measurement?"

"Measurement for what?"

"You can't sew a hat without measuring."

"In the winter," she said nervously. "When the pelt is dry."

"Winter is far away," Yeshua muttered. "There's a tape measure in Chava's chest of drawers. Why put it off?"

To dispel his doubts once and for all and to make her request for the gun convincing, Morta moved toward the chest of drawers, opened a drawer, poked around in it, took out a grimy tape measure and came back.

"Go ahead," Yeshua said, bending his head, and something in this movement made Morta shudder. Simonas! Thirty years older! With a bald head and legs spread lewdly. He'd throw a yoke on her right now . . .

She quickly measured his head and exhaled.

"Fifty-three centimeters."

"Impossible."

"Fifty-three, she repeated."

"It's always been fifty-five," the tavern keeper whispered. "Did my head shrink? Measure again!"

Once more she raised the tape measure and encircled his head, which was covered by curly, thick locks, like Simeon's.

"Fifty-five," she said, without looking at the numbers. "Fifty-five."

"I told you so," the tavern keeper beamed.

Morta imagined that she was holding the tape measure just as Chava had held the reins in the barn. Her hand trembled and her teeth chattered.

"Be careful," Yeshua said as she was leaving. "You shouldn't fool around with a gun."

"I'll be careful."

"See that you don't make trouble."

"I won't," Morta said and hurried out of the room.

She was holding the tape measure in her hand and didn't know where to put it. Finally, she stuck it beneath the neckline of her dress, thrusting it against her taut, agitated breasts, and then rushed like mad to the barn.

She searched every crevice, but nothing was there except frightened swallows, which flew out from under the eaves.

There was no gun hidden inside a blanket.

Had he deceived her? Or was she already too late?

The swallows clipped the air with their wings, flying about over
her head, and it seemed to Morta that their uneasy circling was an
evil omen.

She was too late, too late! Simonas had reached the barn first and
found the gun.

Oh, Yeshua, Yeshua! What a place you found to hide it!

Now I'll never get it from Simonas. He'll hide it somewhere where
the Lord himself couldn't find it.

Morta left the barn and, crestfallen, wandered back to the tavern.

She felt a strange urge to burst into Simonas's room, fall on her
knees before him as before Christ the Savior, and appeal to his conscience and sense, but she restrained herself and started making dinner.

Cooking calmed her. She grew languid next to the fire as her face
flushed. The smell of potato and meat stew pleasantly tickled her
nose, and little by little hunger replaced fear.

Perhaps she had made a needless commotion to no purpose,
Morta consoled herself while tasting the meat. Simeon has a temper,
but he soon gets over it. He seethes and seethes and then cools down.

Is it conceivable that someone can kill a man just for the hell of
it? You can always find someone to blame for your own misfortunes.
You find him—and things seem clearer. You seize a convenient moment and settle scores with him, smash his mug, punch him till he
bleeds, pin him to the wall. But did God give us our minds so that we
could take bloody revenge?

At every Mass the priest repeats: brothers and sisters, love your
enemies, bless those who curse you, pray for those who offend and
hurt you! The priest raises his arms to Heaven and asks everyone,
including Morta, "If you love only those who love you, what is your
reward?"

It's a pity that Simonas doesn't go to church. He would hear the
priest say: "Love your enemies!" And the homeless tramp is not his

enemy at all! He wandered here like that stray dog. He came, and he'll go! Why get involved with him? That's what Morta would say to Simonas—why get involved?

You can't defeat evil with evil, she would say. Good will not grow from a bad seed. Morta has burned so many bad seeds inside herself, and yet they seem to have sprouted through the skin. You, Simonas, she will say, must burn the bad seeds inside you. How can you unleash your own unhappiness from its chains and attack innocent people? How can you put a gun into the hands of your unhappiness?

If all miserable people rushed to get guns, Simonas, who would plow, bear children, and cook dinner?

Unhappy people exist on earth, Simonas, in order to do real work and not to increase their own misfortune. If you think about it carefully, it's the unhappy who hold the world together. Let the happy ones shoot each other, Simonas!

"Where did you go, Simonas?" she asked as she carried a tray with food into Simeon's room.

"To the outhouse," he answered.

"You weren't in the outhouse, you weren't there," Morta said, putting the tray down on the table.

"What were *you* doing there? Running to undo my belt?" he needled her while stuffing large chunks of food into the sinkhole of his mouth.

Morta stood facing him, stunned by his hostility. She lost all her words—about loving your enemies, blessing those who curse you, and bad seeds—and she didn't know how to persuade him and save him from a fatal step.

"Simonas, give back the gun," she said matter-of-factly, without any cunning.

Pimpleface Simeon ate silently and uncouthly. Morta observed the bulges in his cheeks, his jawbones heavy as millstones, and his mouth beneath wisps of reddish hair, and against her will her eyes filled up with tears.

"If you, just a little . . . ," Morta stammered, but Pimpleface Simeon interrupted her.

"Go away, Morta, go away! We'll discuss love later. Who talks about it over dinner?"

He laughed like a fool.

"If anything happens to you, Simonas, then I . . . You're the only one I have left, the only one. In the name of the Lord Jesus, I beg you to give back the gun."

"Listen," he said, stabbing his fork into a potato, "why are you pestering me? Leave!"

His words were not what hurt her the most, but rather the aloofness that was not in his nature. Pimpleface Simeon was looking somewhere over her head, over her pleading, which seemed so pointless and impossible to him.

"Let's leave here," she whispered in despair.

"You're out of your mind," he said. "Leave? With you? Who needs you . . . you fool?"

Morta gritted her teeth to keep from screaming. Enough! Enough! Right now she seemed not to consist of bones and sinews but of this disparaging, brittle yet powerful word that works wonders with men: Enough.

"You're acting like the Mother of God, the Holy Virgin Mary," Simeon said in a hoarse voice. "Maybe you are the Virgin, maybe Mary, but I'm not Christ . . . I am Simeon Mandel—sinner, sponger, beggar."

"What are you saying?" Morta gave a start, glad to hear his unexpected fit of candor. "You . . . are the best . . . kindest . . ."

"The very best," Pimpleface Simeon mocked her.

"Yes, yes," she whispered. "You are the very best, and I am the only one who knows it. But everyone will find out, Simonas. They'll find out for sure!"

"Fool," he said quietly. "You're clutching at me like a straw . . . And I'm not a straw. I'm a stone."

"A stone that is dear to me."

"I don't have the gun," Pimpleface Simeon said.

"Swear to it!"

"I have nothing to swear by. Nothing in my life is dear—not a mother, not a father, not . . ." and he choked on his abuse.

"I promised the master . . . your father . . . to sew a fox hat for him . . . What should I do?"

"Sew it," Pimpleface Simeon answered.

"How can I sew it without a gun, without a fox . . . when only trouble prowls around the yard looking in the windows?"

Morta gathered the dishes and headed toward the door.

"Morta," Pimpleface Simeon called out to her.

"What?"

"Come here . . . when it gets dark."

"No," she said.

"Come."

"No, Simonas, no."

"Why do keep saying the same thing, like a parrot? You say yourself that I'm the only one left to you."

"The only one in Lithuania."

"And to go to Siberia is as far as to God."

"Siberia is far, but God is near at hand."

"Come!"

"No," Morta snapped back.

"But why?"

"He must leave alive and well."

"Who?"

"You know."

"Do you believe that God sent this tramp?"

"Does it matter who sent him?"

"What does matter?"

"It matters that he returns. Everyone should return home, whether from here . . . or from Siberia. He's an honest man. He can't bring trouble."

"There's no greater misfortune than an honest man," Pimpleface Simeon said, and then added, "Come, we'll cluck during the night, we'll flap our wings until the fox arrives . . . Come!"

15

"Oink-oink!"

"Moo-oo!"

"Nei-eigh!"

Oinking, mooing, neighing! Through a crack in the barn wall the Neman is visible, flowing slowly, plentifully, like grain through opened fingers. If you sail upstream on the Neman, the prisoner thinks, then perhaps toward morning you will reach his shtetl. Every year he sets out on his pious wanderings before Rosh Hashana and Yom Kippur, leaving behind his wife, Zipporah, and their children Gershon, Khatskl, and Mordechai, who remain in the shtetl.

Everything began with his son Yisrael. If not for Yisrael, the man in the yarmulke fastened to his hair with a pin would not have wandered through the world. He would have sat at home behind a workbench—mouth full of nails, twisting his shoemaker's waxed thread, not thinking about God or the devil. For him the only staircase to Heaven would have been the shtetl synagogue's low, crumbling porch. But after the death of his firstborn, something inside him split into pieces, and no matter how hard he tried to join both ends of the thread, the gap between them only increased. A mysterious wind blew the unfortunate father off his humble bench, tore the awl from his hands, and immersed him in a debilitating idleness, bottomless as despair.

At first, he would slip away to the river from morning till night. He would remove his clothes, climb into the water stark naked, and grope around wildly with his hands. With hands outstretched, he'd say, "*Rebeyne shel eylem!* Return my son to me! Blind, crippled, or foaming at the mouth . . . just bring him back."

He would blink, dive, and swim, choking beneath the water with open eyes—searching. Once he brought up a linen rag from the bottom of the Neman, dried it, beckoned Zipporah, and said, "It's your fault."

"What's my fault? What?"

"Yisrael always wore a dirty shirt. Look, now the Neman has washed it!"

"You're crazy!" Zipporah said and began to cry.

At that time he had not exactly gone mad, but he had migrated from dry land to the water. Suddenly the entire shtetl was submerged there with all its little houses, its shabby shops, and the synagogue. People traded goods in the water, prayed there, and swam like fish, together with his son Yisrael, alive and unharmed.

"Why aren't you working?" Zipporah reproached him.

"Who works under water?" he defended himself. "In the water people don't need shoes."

"You're crazy!" Zipporah scorched him with loving scorn. "Even so, you won't bring back Yisrael."

"I will!"

"You're crazy!"

Following her example, everyone began to call him that. He was not offended. Relations among people in the water were simple and friendly.

A year later the town—which his delirious imagination had immersed in water—returned to dry land. As before, dry shopkeepers stood behind their counters, a dried-out rabbi declaimed in the synagogue, and at home a dry Zipporah bustled about.

He, the man in the velvet yarmulke fastened to his hair with a pin, was the only one who did not dry completely.

God did not take pity on him. He didn't return his son, either dead or alive.

"You have to earn God's mercy," the town rabbi explained when the man in the yarmulke asked him for advice.

"How?"

During the time the town rabbi was searching for the answer, Zipporah gave birth to three more sons, but that didn't keep their father at home.

"You're crazy," she would shout, bursting into tears, each time he prepared to set out on the road. "Aren't three enough for you?"

Three were not enough for him.

"Maybe you've found yourself another?"

No, he did not have another woman.

Since he could not bring Yisrael back from the water or from the land, his father decided to look for him in the sky.

A bad husband, an unhappy father, a former shoemaker. Drowning in sorrow, he intended to ascend to meet the Master of the Universe, talk to Him in private, and ask Him to return his son Yisrael. And at the same time, if the Almighty would agree, also return his mother Miriam, his sisters, and his brothers, who had perished in a pogrom. To pray for this from the earth made no sense. If every voice reached His ears, the Almighty would also lose His mind.

But how to get there?

He puzzled over this for a long time, until he remembered the story of the patriarch Jacob. As He did for Jacob, the Almighty would lower a ladder and he would climb it. But the Master of the Universe would not lower a ladder to the ground for some small thing. What could he offer the Almighty to prevent Him from refusing his request? Maybe he should make the rounds of all the Jews in the district and collect their virtues? But who can you win over with other people's virtues? Wouldn't it be better to collect other people's sins? There are more sins than virtues. The Almighty would value his zeal and give him and the sinners their just rewards. He would summon an angel and say, "He helped me destroy evil. Call his son Yisrael and his mother Miriam."

"Which Miriam?" the angel would ask. "The Miriam from Bobrino," God would answer. And the angel would bring his son Yisrael, the rascal who drowned in the Neman, and his mother from Bobrino, and if the Almighty would oblige, his sisters and brothers too, and he would throw his arms around each of their necks, kiss his mother, pat his child on the forehead, hold his brothers and sisters tight, and they would all, in turn, climb down the ladder to the ground where, as before, pogroms rage, the Neman swirls, and they will be separated only by the next death.

"Oink-oink!"

"Moo-oo!"

"Nei-eigh!"

Why are they startled, the poor creatures, why did they sound the alarm? Did they smell a stranger? After a chilly night, do they want to go out to the yard and regain their liberty, beneath the rays of the autumn sun?

The man in the velvet yarmulke lay in the barn on hay soft as clouds, looking through a crack at a smooth patch of the Neman, which had once taken his son from him, and he listened to the impatient cries of the animals. He felt like an animal himself, though one without a voice—an animal that had not been granted the ability to make sounds like "nei-eigh" and "moo-oo."

What is our speech, he thought, compared to the neighing of a horse at dawn or the mooing of a cow rubbing its horns against a wooden fence? Why did God put words in our mouths instead of roars or grunts or cackles? Have our words brought us closer to God? Have we learned to understand each other better? Have words increased love in the world?

Words. Words! Like selfish guests at a roadside inn! Whores in the beds of the powerful. Beggars at the temple of wisdom, asking for alms! How many words have been sown, and what has grown, what has been created?

"Oink-oink!"

"Moo-oo!"

"Nei-eigh!"

"Be quiet, creatures! The mistress will come feed you. She'll pet some and scratch the manes of others."

Captivity seemed not to burden him. He happily inhaled the heady smell of hay, and from its marvelous aroma or else from the company of cattle, warm and soothing like a psalm, his head suddenly cleared and before him an unfamiliar space arose. His thoughts flew about like swallows, and each of them united what had been torn asunder: the past and future, earth and heaven, life and death.

It was pleasant in the barn. He felt as if he was in a pasture from the Torah; his eyes didn't hang onto the posts or supports of the stall but glided over the olive groves of the Galilee, and through the crack in the wall a patch of the Jordan, not the Neman, sparkled.

He had a striking ability to transform everything around him, to populate every small corner with exotic people and animals, to be carried off to faraway lands and from there bring back olives and dates.

In the wink of an eye, some shabby fire wall became the Wailing Wall, and he prayed beside it, choking from asthma, as if from happiness. He could easily turn reality into dream and dream into reality, and these transformations nourished him. Only Zipporah did not yield to any transformations. She always remained Zipporah.

A strange woman she was. When her husband was there, sitting at his workbench until midnight drilling a hole in someone's shoe with an awl, she hardly seemed to notice him. But he had only to fasten the velvet yarmulke to his hair with a pin and Zipporah would leave her children with anyone and head out to search for him, cursing the ladder to Heaven. People in the district knew her better than they knew him, because she hunted for him everywhere, even in places where he never appeared.

"Have you seen my husband?" she would pester respectable people.

"Who is your husband?" they asked, puzzled.

"The crazy man," she answered in earnest.

How she exulted when she brought him home—ragged, beaten, bruised, and scratched—and put him to bed beside her, like an unruly child.

While he rested, weakly groaning or reading the prophets, Zipporah sat down at the workbench, picked up a hammer, and repaired shoes, spitting out curses like nails. Jews in the town felt sorry for her, and they brought more shoes for her to repair than to the other shoemakers. Sometimes their oldest son, Gershon, helped, a small redhead with a face covered with freckles like a cinnamon roll.

"Why do you hide your ladder from your wife and children?" Zipporah harassed him time and again. "Maybe I want to visit God too?"

"And what will you tell Him? That your husband is crazy? That Zekharya the shopkeeper shortchanges you? That green apples gave your Mordechai the runs? What?" he would ask, interrupting his reading or turning onto his other side.

"And you, wise one, what will you tell Him?" Zipporah defended herself.

"Not a single soul in the world knows what I will tell Him," he answered evasively, cowering from her questions.

While lying in the hard, messy, stained bed and listening to the tapping of the hammer in Zipporah's hand, he rehearsed his conversations with the Master of the Universe.

"*Rebeyne shel eylem*, how long will lawlessness go on? How can You bear our abasement? Why does the world belong to everyone but us? Your sons and daughters have only a small pasture, only the Pale of Settlement. Why is there more slavery in the world than freedom and more hatred than love? Why?

"Who are You, Master of the Universe? The question or the answer? The Path of Judgment or the Path of Mercy? If Judgment, when will You quench Your thirst for it? If Mercy, when will it come?"

Zipporah went on tapping with the hammer, Gershon chopped wood in the yard, and he, pulling a filthy blanket over his head, over his bruises and scratches, over his sick soul, was whispering to God. Sometimes he waved his arms, argued, shouted, and contended with God. Then Zipporah would soften, place a wet rag on her husband's burning forehead, and try to cool his madness.

One day, unable to bear his feverish trances, she gathered his books and shoved them into the stove.

Of the prophets only ashes remained.

"What have you done, Zipporah?" he cried. "Do you know what you've burned?"

"Your sickness," Zipporah answered, keeping calm.

He adjusted the yarmulke on his thinning hair, stuck his hand into the stove, and drew out a handful of ashes. Raising it up before his wife's eyes, he quietly but furiously said, "Sprinkle my head, Zipporah!"

"I am still in my right mind, thank God."

"Sprinkle my head, Zipporah," he repeated with the same fury, gritting his teeth.

"You're crazy! A do-nothing! A laughingstock! You made a lot of children and act like a clown!"

He looked sadly at his wife, astonished, then sprinkled his head with the ashes. When Zipporah laughed aloud, he slapped her with the back of his hand.

"Does it hurt?" he asked.

"It hurts! May your hands shrivel up!" Zipporah screamed.

"Don't you think it hurts *me*? And *them*? Abraham, Isaac, and Jacob . . . Ruth and Esther . . . And the servant girl Hagar."

"Oh God! Why must I suffer with a fool my whole life?"

What's true is true: she did suffer. And she was probably suffering right now, looking for him, the ill-fated one, looking and suffering.

How unfortunate is he, though? He's lying in the hay, breathing easily, and the sun is rising in his head as it is in the sky.

And he had suffered no bruises or scratches.

The beatings and the rods didn't scare him.

More than anything, the slowness of God depressed him. How many years had he climbed the ladder to Him, bringing the sins of others, and how many years had he sat with Him on a cloud, as on this hay, discussing the Pale of Settlement, the pogroms, residence permits, equality and freedom. The Almighty was in no hurry to stretch out His hand and intervene . . . Where was the God of Mercy? When would the Master of the Universe send an angel to bring back Miriam of Bobrino along with her grandson, Yisrael, the rascal who drowned in the Neman?

Someone else would have taken offense at God's silence and would want nothing more to do with Him; another would sit at the workbench, take up hammer and awl, and stitch boots like mad or nail on heels. Another, but not he. You can betray your trade, but you can't betray God. A trade feeds, but God uplifts.

When the Almighty shows mercy and the angel brings Yisrael, he, his father, will likely not recognize him. It's no small matter—he drowned as a boy and now he's surely become a man. Or perhaps people there, up above, don't grow and don't become old, just as angels don't age. Angels are always young. Maybe Yisrael is also a boy forever?

Perhaps his mother Miriam is not a doddering old woman, but an eternally young girl with black braids as heavy as two bunches of onions? He, a forty-year-old tramp, a gray ragamuffin, will approach her and say, "Mama!"

She will stare at him with her brown eyes and ask, like a stranger, "Who are you?"

"Who am I? I'm your son, Mama!"

"Zvi-Hersh?" she'll ask in surprise, raising her thick eyebrows.

"Zvi-Hersh," he will answer.

"How are you, Hershl, my little deer?"

"I'm well, Mama . . . All the deer in our parts are living well."

"Then why are you so gray and unhappy?"

"Because all the deer in our parts have turned gray, and even those who live well are unhappy . . ."

Mama will take a pin and place it on her palm like a flash of lightning, and it will become light all around. Not as bright as on the Day of Judgment, but as bright as in the early spring when so much blueness and light even becomes a little frightening.

"Oink-oink!"

"Moo-oo!"

"Nei-eigh!"

"Nei-eigh!" He was being asked for something, but what exactly he didn't understand.

"Nei-eigh!" Chiming in, the man in the yarmulke suddenly whinnied at the top of his lungs.

He broke into neighs like a real horse, and the neighing that tore at his larynx was not so much a sound as a sign, a message containing a greater meaning than a call or a greeting.

The policeman's horse drew in the glowing, damp air through its nostrils, began to weave in the stall, turned its head, and replied with a grateful "Nei-eigh!"

"Ardasha! Ardasha!" Frightened, Lukerya Panteleimonovna tugged at the sleeping Nesterovich.

"What?" the policeman asked, half-asleep, as if hungover.

"Don't you hear anything?"

"No," Ardalion Ignatich exclaimed and listened closely.

"Nei-eigh!"

"Nei-eigh!"

An exultant neigh shook the barn.

"Kuzya is neighing," the policeman determined. "She's calling for a stallion."

"Is that just Kuzya?" Lukerya Panteleimonovna muttered doubtfully, and with the edge of a kerchief she covered her mouth, which resembled a crescent moon.

Ardalion Ignatich froze, and in order to become more convinced, with his rough palm he bent back his ear, which was confused by drowsiness.

"Sweet Jesus!" he sang out. "Where did a second one come from?"

"I don't know," Lukerya Panteleimonovna answered. Like crushed strawberries, fright colored her gray face, which remained as still as the face on a church icon. "And the cow is mooing . . . she hasn't been milked yet . . . I'm afraid, Ardasha, I'm afraid," she confessed.

"What's wrong—are you scared of a horse?"

"There are *two* of them," Lukerya Panteleimonovna said. "Let's both of us go, Ardasha . . . I'm afraid."

Nesterovich reluctantly got up, and slowly, with sluggish solemnity, put on his pants, fluffed up his wheat-colored mustache twisted in the style of His Imperial Majesty, pulled a sword out of its scabbard, slashed the air in the bedroom several times, looked condescendingly at his wife, and moved toward the door.

"You should have released him, Ardasha," Lukerya Panteleimonovna said as they went into the yard.

"Nuikin will accuse me again—of feeling sorry for a *zhid* . . . a criminal . . ."

"What sort of criminal can he be, Ardasha? Can't you see that yourself?"

"It doesn't matter what I see, mother," Ardalion Ignatich snapped. "For your own good, sometimes you have to cover your eyes."

Ardalion Ignatich was now almost sorry that he had taken the tramp into custody and locked him in the barn. Two considerations held him back, however. First, he didn't want to discredit his official standing in the eyes of his wife, and second, he was not accustomed to letting someone go free. Let's say his standing would not decrease, yet at the same time his income would not increase. The tramp did not have a kopeck to his name. And no one in town would pay to have him released. No matter how friendly the Jews are, money is money.

Giving in to Lukerya Panteleimonovna's pressure and resigning himself to the loss that awaited him, Nesterovich decided to question the tramp one more time and, if nothing new came to light, he would let him go in peace, for there was no point in feeding the sponger three times a day.

Rays of sun were trickling through a crack in the barn, and the dust swirling in the air looked like a swarm of gnats.

Ardalion Ignatich adjusted the sword at his side and, trying too hard to breathe sincerity into his voice, he said, "Good morning, esteemed ones."

Don't greet only the prisoner. Then he'd put on airs and think God knows what. Greet him together with the cattle, which is polite and will inspire trust.

"Moo-oo!" the cow responded.

"Oink-oink!" the pigs fussed.

"Nei-eigh!" the prisoner drawled.

"Why are you playing the fool up there?" the policeman said. "That's enough, now, come down."

Reluctantly the man in the yarmulke slid off the stack. He was covered all over with hay. Stalks stuck out of his ears, and his eyebrows were prickly. Lukerya Panteleimonovna set the milk pail down, rubbed her hands, and began to pull at the cow's plump teats, which dripped like icicles in March.

As the icicles melted, the man in the yarmulke heard the spurts ringing against the bottom of the pail.

"Did you sleep well?" Ardalion Ignatich inquired, glancing at the tramp as if at a vacant lot overgrown with weeds.

"Nei-eigh," the stranger let out, opening his mouth wide.

"Do you want me to send you to Nuikin?" the policeman threatened. "He won't see that you're . . ." Nesterovich made a vague circular movement with his hand. "For him all crackpots are enemies of the fatherland. He'll declare you an enemy and you'll go to Siberia like a good boy. Then you'll really nei-eigh. Let's go!" he ordered, not hiding his irritation.

The stranger nodded his head respectfully.

"Let's have a smoke," Ardalion Ignatich said as they left the barn.

Nesterovich dug his hand into a deep pocket that stretched down to his kneecap, pulled out a pouch, took a pinch of tobacco from it and offered it to the prisoner, who refused.

"I have no time to fuss with you, brother. Too much work. Show me your identity papers! According to the rules . . . it's your duty! As plain as day."

Ardalion Ignatich rolled up a "goat's leg," lit it, drew on it, choked on the smoke, shed a few tears from the coughing, wiped his eyes with his sleeve, and growled, "Come clean! Without Job or turbans. First name, last name, rank?"

The man looked at the burning tip of the cigarette and remained silent.

"Don't make me angry," Ardalion Ignatich warned him. "I'll tell Nuikin, he'll finish you off."

"Do you ask a horse for its name? Or a cow? Or a pig?" the tramp said in a faint voice.

"But you're not a horse! You're not a pig. A man!"

"And what does the name of one person mean . . . mine . . . yours . . . when the name of an entire people is an empty sound?"

"You're trying to wriggle out of it again!"

"Now is no time for names . . . My nickname is Crazy. That's what my wife calls me, and that's what my children call me. That's what everyone calls me, even the rabbi. And everyone is satisfied, everything is simple and easy, because you don't have to listen to a madman. So what if he's a prophet? So what if he alone is crying when everyone else feasts during a plague? You could accuse a crazy person of being an enemy of the fatherland, even if he were its only friend. In some cases, you can declare a crazy person sane, if you need to string him up in order to satisfy the crowd."

"Listen," the policeman almost begged, "you're talking so strangely it's painful. Try to make it simpler, like 'I am Sidorov, Petrov, Kogan, or Feinstein.'"

"Yes, it can be simpler," the man in the yarmulke unexpectedly agreed. "My name is Zvi-Hersh."

"What's that? Last name or first name?"

"First. It means deer."

"Right."

"Last name—Ashkenazi . . . Zvi-Hersh Ashkenazi."

"Nice! Not like Nesterovich! Zvi-Hersh Ashkenazi!" Ardalion Ignatich rolled the strange name around in his mouth, sucking it like a fruit drop, tasting it.

The man in the yarmulke looked at him and thought how little it took to satisfy the curiosity of the police. Call yourself anything you like but just give them a name. Anonymity arouses suspicion, it's dangerous. Everything must be named, counted, registered, filed, and placed in a box—to the left, a box for the homeless; to the right, one for those who are settled; above, for Jews; below, for Russians and Lithuanians. From a barn to the Imperial residence there must be order in the empire. Order, order! A thousand times order!

"Tradesman?" the policeman inquired of the prisoner.

"Tradesman."

"Year of birth?"

"By your calendar, 1841."

"Place?"

"The town of Bobrino."

"Why were you hiding this before?"

"What difference would that have made? To lock a man in a barn or send him to hard labor you don't need a name, birth date, or papers."

"So what do you need?" Ardalion Ignatich was taken aback.

"Power and desire," the man in the yarmulke answered.

"And guilt," Nesterovich muttered.

"Power can always convert desire into someone's guilt."

Ardalion Ignatich threw down his "goat's leg," stamped it out with the toe of his boot, unfastened his shirt collar, scratched his Adam's apple with his knuckles, and asked with respectful disdain, "Where, Zvi-Hersh Ashkenazi, did you pick up all this stuff?"

"At the workbench," the man in the yarmulke said matter-of-factly. "While you poke a sole with the awl you think. During a quarter of a century you can think up anything. And sometimes it takes only a day . . . In the morning you sit down as a shoemaker and in the evening you get up from your chair as a messenger from God."

"So you happen to be a shoemaker?" Nesterovich was delighted. "A cobbler? That's good. Very good. A messenger from God is not a craft. And being a policeman is not a craft," Nesterovich said thoughtfully. "A craft is not like any old job—a craftsman can't be demoted to the rank-and-file."

A thought suddenly pecked its way into Ardalion Ignatich's head, and like a ruffled chick crawled out of its shell. Nesterovich had no doubt now that he would let this Ashkenazi go—he was not any kind of criminal, just a blabbermouth, a self-made sage gone mad, but before releasing him he would seat the tramp down somewhere in the garden under an apple tree and bring him a sack full of shoes—his, Lukerya's, the children's—and let him repair and patch them all, free of charge. And after he finishes repairing everything, let him go off to the devil's mother and say thank you as well: you don't seat someone under an apple tree just for talk like his. Nuikin won't bother with him. Nuikin's shoes are in good shape, from the best shops in Vilna. He doesn't splash through the mud in them.

Lukerya Panteleimonovna silently came into sight.

"Mother, meet Zvi-Hersh Ashkenazi," Ardalion Ignatich said. "A shoemaker. Lukerya Panteleimonovna, my spouse."

"We already met. You forgot that, Ardasha?"

The man in the yarmulke made a slight bow.

"Zvi-Hersh will repair your shoes . . . and my boots . . . The ones, remember, we bought for Shrovetide . . . Vanyusha's shoe lost a heel . . . he didn't wear it for half a year and it came off. I found it in the garden among the cucumbers . . . completely new. And Katyusha is complaining that her shoe scratches her foot—the insole fell out."

"Very glad, very glad," Lukerya Panteleimonovna babbled like a brook. "Welcome to our house. Have a taste of fresh milk."

More than anything, she seemed delighted about his release.

"Thank you," the stranger said. "But I don't have anything."

"Anything of what?" the policeman frowned.

"Any lasts, any waxed thread, any leather."

"We'll find a last . . . and leather . . . Will we find them, mother?"

"We'll find them, Ardasha. We will find everything."

"Vanyusha will run to town for nails and thread. He's the fast one among us."

"And a knife? And wax?" The prisoner was about to protest, but the look on the policeman's face put an end to his resistance.

"You'll have a knife and wax," Nesterovich bristled. What if this tramp had cheated him, fooled him like a little kid? Maybe he wasn't a Zvi-Hersh or Ashkenazi at all? Where can a Jew get a surname like that? He swindled me, got the better of me, the scoundrel! And he, Nesterovich, an old fool, a bonehead, a birdbrain, had believed him!

Ardalion Ignatich was ready to forgive everything—subversive talk, feigned madness, fraud, the vice-governor's murder, escape from hard labor or military service, every possible and impossible sin—but he did not want to accept the idea that the tramp was not a shoemaker. He had to be a shoemaker. He was obliged to be one. No argument about it.

"So?" Nesterovich pressed him. "Nuikin, or . . . ?"

"*Or*," the man in the yarmulke said compliantly and walked toward the house. A sad smile lit his path all the way to the porch.

"Oink-oink!"

"Moo-oo!"

"Nei-eigh!" drifted after him.

Lukerya Panteleimonovna gave him fresh milk, took out from somewhere her old chintz apron with large dots (can there be a shoemaker without an apron?), and handed him a blunt hammer, an awl, a sharp knife with a blackened handle for shredding cabbage, and warm beeswax (five light-blue hives stood beneath the windows). The man in the yarmulke set himself up in the garden under a bare, crooked apple tree on which worm-eaten fruit hung like orphaned birds. The gray branches on the tree, which looked like charred flashes of lightning, did not move, and sadness permeated their stillness and barrenness.

Sitting on a low stool with sawed-down legs, wearing a woman's apron with large dots, a blunt hammer in his hand, and with a worn yarmulke fastened to his hair by a pin, the stranger looked like an enormous doll, like those the wandering minstrels, buffoons, and revelers use to amuse the good folk on Purim—the merriest of Jewish holidays.

Ardalion Ignatich was not in the garden. Apparently, he was collecting shoes.

The pigs were squealing.

The cow mooed.

The horse neighed.

Yet now the man in the yarmulke no longer heard a greedy appeal in their friendly, sorrowful chorus but rather something like a sign from above, and this omen, which offered no help but was a warning, uncovered the truth of his soul.

While he waited for Ardalion Ignatich, squinting from the un-usually bright September sun, the man in the yarmulke unexpectedly remembered an old Jewish beggar, a wanderer like him, and what he had said the year before last in a corner of the synagogue in Mish-kine where they both, tired and beaten, settled down for the night. He said that animals—chickens, geese, cows, horses, and especially cats—are the first to sense our death. Before his mother died, the cat was said to have meowed for two days in a row, and nothing could quiet her—not milk, caresses, or prayers. And a week before the death of his brother, who was a cart driver, his bay horse beat its hoof frantically the whole night and whinnied as if on the first day of creation.

The man in the yarmulke did not want to think about death, but no matter how hard he tried to distract himself, to occupy his mind with something else, death lurked nearby, and there was nowhere to hide from it.

The stranger was looking around, now at the house, then at the barn, as though he expected someone other than Ardalion Ignatich would appear in the garden. And not only did his life depend on the appearance of some unknown, faceless being, but also the fate of this apple tree, this sky washed in azure and prayers, this autumn, cool-ing from the passion of earth's buds and blossoms.

Never before during any of his wanderings had this anxiety, which was creeping into his heart, been so boundless, and yet seem-ingly so groundless. This was also an unmistakable warning. For the first time in many years he had been domesticated, made to pick up a hammer, put on a foolish apron, and repair someone's stinking shoes instead of the world.

And who was doing this to him? Not someone righteous, respect-able, and wise, but an ordinary policeman!

The end of the world, for certain.

Had he abandoned his wife Zipporah and his children for this—hammering nails into a disintegrating sole?

Had he left home to collect mushrooms instead of the sins of others?

Had he endured hardships every year and taken beatings in order to drink fresh milk in a policeman's house and bow to his wife?

Would the Master of the Universe lower a ladder to someone like him?

Absolutely not.

What could he, if he cowered before the county police chief Nuikin, carry to the Almighty in hand and heart?

What? Chanterelles? A chunk of rye bread? A rotten apple? A policeman's blessing?

That was why the livestock were bellowing in the barn! They sensed his decline, if not his death.

He had not died. He had just fallen off the ladder . . . from the lowest rung.

But he would get up. He'd climb up right now!

"Where are you going?" Nesterovich asked him, lowering a heavy sack stuffed with shoes to the ground. The man in the yarmulke shuddered. He hadn't even felt Ardalion Ignatich come up behind his back.

"To the barn," he said.

"Where?"

"To the barn," the man in the yarmulke repeated. "Back to the barn."

He took off Lukerya Panteleimonovna's chintz apron and hung it on a branch of the apple tree.

Ardalion Ignatich looked at the tree, looked at the stranger again, went up to him, grabbed the front of his shirt, and peered into his large eyes which were awash with obsessive suffering, and he, Nesterovich, suffering from his own subjection, muttered, "Not yet."

"I will repair all your shoes . . . after Yom Kippur, when I return from there . . ."

"From the barn?" Ardalion Ignatich grumbled.

"As God is my witness," the man in the yarmulke raised his eyes, "I'll repair all the shoes for you, and if you manage to get leather, I will sew new shoes for you . . . for Lukerya Panteleimonovna . . . and for your children."

His sincerity confused and rattled Ardalion Ignatich. The policeman was especially struck by how sonorously and respectfully the tramp pronounced his wife's name and patronymic. Nesterovich released his grip without antipathy and even with a kind of crude compassion and understanding. Not a trace remained of Ardalion Ignatich's earlier resolution, in the event that the prisoner refused him, to hand him over to Nuikin. If he handed him over, he would disgrace himself.

"Why did I make Vanyusha go into town?"

"After Yom Kippur everything will be of use, the thread and the nails . . ."

"You can't do it before Yom Kippur?"

"I can't."

"Why not?"

"Before then, God won't lower the ladder."

"And on Yom Kippur?"

"He'll lower it," the man in the yarmulke said firmly.

"How is it, does He lower it to everyone or only to people like you?" the policeman asked sarcastically, amusing himself.

"To someone who destroys evil."

"But everyone sees evil in different ways. Nuikin, for instance, sees it in you, in Jews, and you—in Nuikin. And there's only one ladder?"

"One," the stranger agreed.

"And what if up there, in Heaven, it's all the same as on earth—the Pale of Settlement, and Nuikin, and taverns and a barn?"

"It's all different there," the stranger replied.

"Different, you say?"

"Different."

"But not for the living. The living cannot do without evil. When you think about it, who is your God who uses others to destroy evil? A Nuikin! Except that He's not only in charge of the county or the province, but the whole world. One evil destroys, another creates . . . It seems that if I let you go, I'll be sending you to another Nuikin, all the same."

Ardalion Ignatich laughed. He was pleased by his own wit. But his words summoned the cold breath of death, which blew once more on the stranger.

"Go," Nesterovich said. "Nekhamkin will repair the shoes. He works all year round, pokes an awl into a sole without thinking about anything. It's good work for someone who doesn't think, or thinks like everyone else. Go! If the Lord lowers the ladder to you and you climb up it while alive, tell Him this: In the Russian Empire there lives one Ardalion Ignatich Nesterovich and his wife, Lukerya Panteleimonovna, and their children, Ivan and Katerina. In their house I drank fresh milk with rye bread and ate mushroom soup with potatoes . . . I sat in the garden under an apple tree without any identity papers. This Ardalion Nesterovich could have refused to let me go, but he did let me go because sometimes, in order to atone for his sins and simply to clear his conscience, when not a soul is in sight, he doesn't think or act like a policeman. Will you tell Him?"

"I'll tell Him," the man in the yarmulke answered.

"All right, then," Ardalion Ignatich mumbled. He tugged up his pants, grunted and added, "I have another request. Not to your God, though, but to ours . . . They probably meet up there, don't they?"

"They meet," the stranger confirmed.

"When they meet, let Him quietly ask ours to make His Imperial Majesty finally visit the Kaiser and stop at our house on the way, honor Lukerya Panteleimonovna, and taste mushrooms from the tub for the czar . . . Otherwise we'll pickle and pickle and he still won't come and eat our mushrooms."

Ardalion Ignatich became embarrassed, burst out laughing, covered his mouth with his hand and said, "It seems I'm crazy too . . . One should be wary of the company one keeps. Farewell, Zvi-Hersh Ashkenazi!"

Nesterovich watched him walk out to the country road. Then he lumbered back to the house, lonely and bent over, the Caucasian sword at his side.

16

After the period of mourning for Chava had ended, the tavern doors reopened and life inside began to stir and hum and whoop once more.

The tavern keeper Yeshua stood behind the bar, beaming and looking fit in a new silk shirt and new waistcoat made of expensive English cloth that had been bought earlier at Rosenzweig and Sons' haberdashery in Kovno. Bershtansky the barber had neatly trimmed his unruly beard, had worked magic on it, as if Yeshua was not about to go to the tavern but rather down the aisle. His high calfskin boots, polished to a shine, creaked with every step, and their creaking, like the crunch of matzo on Passover, pleased Yeshua's ear and filled his soul with an indescribable feeling for the strength and stability of everything earthly—a feeling that had not been shaken even by Chava's suicide. What did Chava matter? She was, and she is no more. You can't mourn and shed tears over a grave forever. Torah says "Bury and forget!" for good reason. And what is written in the Torah stands forever. "Bury and forget!" In fact, memory should not be allowed to break your back with an unbearable burden. The day will come when you throw off the burden, if you don't want to be buried beneath it. Such are the cycles of life. Such is the eternal order. Praise to the dead, a toast to the living.

"Yeshua! A mug of beer!"

"A bottle of vodka . . . two herrings . . . cabbage soup!"

"Fish and a carafe!"

Dear God, long live the living who drink, chomp, whoop, stink, belch, and puke!

251

Long live the living, Yeshua thought. During moments like these his spirits lifted. His soul seemed to separate from his flesh and then rise above the bar, and above the tavern, and above the earth.

At moments like these, Yeshua feels like the captain of an old and reliable ship. All around a strange and mysterious sea is roaring and storming, and the hold contains drunken sailors who are just as strange and mysterious as the sea. From morning to night they guzzle vodka, belt out songs, and swear at God; but he, Yeshua, looking fit in his expensive new waistcoat, stands on the bridge and watches the raging waves and the rising waters fling the small ship from crest to crest, and he holds the helm confidently. He does not release it from his strong, pitiless hands even when, out of the depths, the bodies of the dead surface before him like enormous fish and then sink again—his wife Chava and his daughter Hannah, who died before she was nine.

"Bury and forget," he muttered and held the wheel even more firmly.

He had no one or nothing except the helm. No one. His son—Simeon—hates his father's ship. And the sea. And the sailors.

The tiny ship rides over the waves. Yeshua stands on the bridge, gazing into the distance, and it doesn't matter where it carries him, to which port, to what destiny.

The most important thing is to sail and collect tribute from this strange and stormy sea.

"Tribute, tribute, tribute . . . honor . . . praise . . . homage" ring in his head like the ship's bell.

Why does he want so much? Yeshua doesn't know himself.

He does know something, but for now prefers not to name it.

Yet everything has a name, known or secret. Everything.

Morta!

As he thought of Morta, the tavern keeper grinned, braced his legs, straightened, adjusted his waistcoat, took out a watch chain from his pocket, placed his watch to his bad ear, and listened to its tick. Amid the tavern's hum and noise and hubbub her name was ticking.

"Mor-ta! Mor-tele!"

"Hey!" All at once Yeshua heard another voice.

In the far corner of the tavern a traveler sat at a wooden table. He wore a faded coat with a lapel lined with velvet, the kind commonly worn by tax officials or student dropouts. A pince-nez was stuck to his blueish-gray nose like a moth, and a shabby, gray summer hat sat next to a bowl like an overturned paper boat.

"What can I do for you?" Yeshua politely inquired as he approached.

"Smell it," the gentleman said, pointing at the bowl with a short finger that was bent like a trigger. "What are you feeding the good folk? Do you want to go to jail? To hard labor?"

"The fish, Sir, is fresh . . . yesterday's . . . from the river."

"Smell it, Jew! For this hanging's not enough!" the stranger fumed.

Yeshua bent over, sniffed the bowl, raised his head carefully as if to protect it from a blow, then said, "Please don't worry. The fish is fresh! As sure as I'm standing here. If you don't believe me, let's call someone. Morkunas! Guri!"

The newcomer did not need an arbitration court, however. He quickly rose, grabbed his dirty hat from the table, glared from beneath his pince-nez at Yeshua and then at the good folk, as if he cared about them, and headed for the door with a broad stride.

"What happened, Yeshua?" Guri Andronov wanted to know.

"Do I know?" the tavern keeper shrugged his shoulders. "I only know one thing—this is how pogroms start."

"How?"

"A stranger visits your home, eats matzo, washes it down with Passover wine, licks his fingers, and then goes out on the street and says, 'Matzo is made with Christian blood.'"

"Just think—he ate for free, he didn't pay, and you let it go," Guri chided the tavern keeper with tipsy high-mindedness. "How much did he owe you?"

"Is it about money?" Yeshua asked in a hoarse voice.

"About what then?"

"About the fact that we are guilty of everything beforehand . . . Even before we're born, we're already guilty. If a cat is the mistress, the mice are to blame. If mice are the masters, the cat is guilty. And we . . . we're always cats or mice in someone else's house . . ."

Yeshua went back to the bar, but without his earlier glow.

A wave had swelled and broken and almost swept him off the bridge.

The tavern was filled with the smell of cheap tobacco and acrid homegrown weeds. The smoke flew off the tables in layers, mixed with the fumes of alcohol and rose to the ceiling, to smoky beams.

Out of the smoke, the noisy confusion among the tables, and slamming doors, Pimpleface Simeon suddenly appeared. Unlike his father, he was carelessly dressed. His shirt fell out of his pants and his pants were wrinkled as if he had just gotten out of bed; his black beard was in tatters, like rags, and it crept up to his eyes and nose; a crumpled yarmulke barely stayed on his head; and from his feet dangled wooden clogs brought one day from a fair, shoes that no Jews ever wore. But Simeon had insisted: I'll buy them. He wasn't frugal with his father's money, he would waste it on any whim.

"Pour me half a glass," the son requested.

"Jews don't drink on workdays," Yeshua said. "Only on holidays."

"Today's a holiday for me."

"Which one?"

"Today I feel worse than ever."

"Is feeling bad a holiday?"

"Pour it."

Yeshua said: "The patriarch of our family, Nosn Mandel, may he rest in peace, who had poured out oceans of vodka, used to say, 'A Jewish drunk is like a Jewish governor.'"

"We'll have drunks and governors, but never happiness."

"What's wrong with you, Simeon?" Yeshua eased off. "I haven't seen you like this for a long time."

"When you look at people, do you ever see anything but their purses?"

Yeshua swallowed the insult in silence. How many times had he wanted to spit in Simeon's face and kick him out, but then his mother would stick up for him. At other times Yeshua would cool himself off and forgive the shameless son for his rudeness. After each clash, his eyes drowning in unwarranted despair, or in futile regret over an unsuccessful life, Yeshua tried to discover the source of his son's raging, constant hatred. Of all people, it seemed that Simeon had no reason to complain about his fate. In the meantime the tavern keeper didn't deny him anything: if you want to go to Vilna, go to Vilna; if you want to go to Kovno, here's something for the road—study, trade, make your way. Yeshua kept hoping, patiently waited, and kept paying for his hopes with cash. But children are like a field, and their parents are the plow. While the field bears fruit, the plow digs into the soil; after it stops, you look and see that the plow has rusted. Yeshua has rusted, rusted for sure.

Is it his fault that Simeon did not turn out to be anything of worth—not a merchant, not a tavern keeper, not a rabbi? Is it his fault that he's only the tavern keeper Yeshua and not a Count Muravyov, or even just a Markus Fradkin? People don't get to choose their father or mother—they end up wherever God sends them.

"Why do you hate me, Simeon?" the tavern keeper asked uneasily, pouring vodka into a glass.

"Because you're not Moses. Top it up a bit. Up to here!"

"That's enough," Yeshua said. "Which Moses?"

"The one who wandered in the desert for forty years so that all the slaves would die out before he led his people to the land of Canaan."

Slowly, with some secret, almost fatal, significance, Pimpleface Simeon raised the glass to his mouth, warmed it with his lips, rubbed his beard against it, stared into his father's eyes, and tossed down the vodka. Yeshua was cut to the heart, as if a deadly poison had been poured into the drink.

"But you're wandering longer," Pimpleface Simeon said. "And your slaves don't die out, they hang themselves!"

"What are you jabbering about? Best for you to find something to do," Yeshua advised, becoming even more anxious.

"Do what?"

"You could take my place . . . and stand behind the bar," the tavern keeper said.

"And you'll be sewing a hat with Morta?"

"Stop it! People will hear."

"So let them hear. Pour me some more! I'll drink and leave . . . I don't feel like wandering around in the desert with you . . . My legs ache. Here it is, our land of Canaan!" Simeon snorted as he glanced around the tavern with a dazed look. "Here are our Gilead mountains, and Guri Andronov sits on top of them chewing herring. Over there is our Wailing Wall, and the logger Anzelmas stands beside it belching your pea soup for three kopecks . . . But for God's sake, just don't say that I'm sick. I'm healthy, I'm young, I'm happy. I'm the happiest slave in the world!"

"Yeshua!"

"A carafe of vodka!"

"Some sliced sausage!"

"Vodka! Vodka! Vodka!"

"Yeshua! When will you clean the outhouse?" one of the regulars shouted.

"Here are our angels," Simeon said, sobering up a bit. "Our divine retinue!"

He went behind the bar, took a bottle, poured a glass, and said, "To our angels, Father!"

"Don't," Yeshua made a face. One more minute, one more drop, and it seemed he would cry. "I'll call Morta."

"Why Morta? Is she Mother?" He knocked over the glass, put the bottle on the counter and added, glaring at his father with a hostile, envious expression, "Morta is a whore!"

"How dare you! She . . . she . . ." the tavern keeper stammered, struggling to breathe.

"What? Maybe she's already made you that fur hat."

"God of Mercy!" Yeshua said helplessly, grabbing the bottle.

"How is she in bed—like she is in the tavern? Not lazy?"

"Shut up!" Yeshua said, and momentarily lost his voice. "Shut up!" He brandished the bottle.

"But you know you won't hit me, you won't . . . Not because you're afraid, but because you don't waste vodka."

"Get out!"

"You don't like me! Ay-ay-ay! I'm not Zelik Fradkin, of course, but you're not Moses, either . . . You're a slave. And a slave gives birth to a slave."

Pimpleface Simeon drooped, stooped over, touched his Adam's apple and left, his clogs tapping on the uneven, worn-out floor on his way out.

Through an open window Yeshua watched his son walk to the well, grab a withered pole with an attached hook, sink the bucket, scoop up water and douse himself, just like in the sauna, then load the bucket again, pull it up and pour it over his head once more. Yeshua heard how Simeon snorted angrily and obscenely, while shaking his head as if he wanted to quench his disgust, as if fighting with the temptation that consumed him; and from watching this repeated cleansing, this artless and senseless struggle with himself, the father suddenly became terrified, more afraid than from Simeon's feverish, rude speeches or his disgraceful and destructive cravings for vodka.

Yeshua's fear was intensified by the fact that, without any regrets, his son had apathetically ceded Morta to him—like some whore on Safyanka Street, with almost disdainful generosity.

"Yeshua! Why are you just standing around?"

"How long do we have to wait?"

They'll wait, they're not going anywhere.

He ignored the merrymakers with their impatient requests and drunken cries.

He was wholly there, at the well, with his son.

He didn't know how to help Simeon. You can't put out a fire that's been blazing all night with well water or a glass of vodka in the morning.

What is burning inside him?

Advise me, God of Mercy! My son should not also die . . . My Hannah and my wife Chava are not enough?

Why have You punished them . . . for my sins?

Is this my punishment? To watch them suffer and not know how to help? We who witness are more unfortunate than those who perish!

Don't take anyone else from me! Have mercy on me and don't serve me another bitter cup so soon. I'm already drunk with grief. How can I heal myself? You, from whom nothing is hidden, know that we can't take our secrets to the grave . . . Only virtues die; our sins are immortal. But is a marriage of convenience really a sin? Is it a sin when love is not required of you, as it's not required from a bull when a cow is brought to him for mating?

Yehuda Spivak brought me to his home, showed me a sickly sapling and said, "Plant it, Yeshua, and water it . . ." He gave me money for land and water. And I planted it and watered it, and twice it brought forth fruit—Hannah, may God rest her soul, and Simeon. Keep him with me in this world of lies, and have mercy on him! The sapling did not grow into a flowering tree. It remained as sickly as it was, for everything in the world grows from love, not from the soil. The earth is small, but love is boundless. I lived, I suffered, I watered the sickly sapling, and what was my reward? A tavern? When all is said and done, what is our life if not a roadside tavern that you can't shut down even for one night? Where anyone can bang their fists on the door and burst inside. A tavern, open to all and where all are strangers . . . till the day they die?

"Yeshua, are you deaf?"

"I'm drinking and drinking and not drunk at all! Did you pour water into the vodka, you old fart?"

"Ha-ha-ha!"

"Listen, Yeshua! Is it true what they say about you and your son?"

"What do they say?" a coarse little man asked.

"They say they take turns with Morta—the son on Monday, Wednesday, Friday, and Shabbes, and Yeshua . . . only on Sunday, Tuesday, Thursday!"

"Ha-ha-ha!"

"Pigs!" the tavern keeper blurted out. "Damn drunks! Dog shit!"

"Easy, old man, easy!"

"Filthy bastards!" Yeshua thundered, venting his anger and bitterness on the tavern crowd.

"But he can't do it, men," the coarse little man squealed.

"Ha-ha-ha!"

"He can, but only on even days when Simeon is sleeping with Morta!"

"Ha-ha-ha!"

"Get out! Out! You won't get another drop from me!"

Yeshua ran to the tables and, choking with anger, began to pick up the mugs, bowls, and glasses.

"No reason to get mad, Yeshua," Guri Andronov said, trying to save the situation. "People are joking . . ."

"Go to hell!"

"We'll finish our drinks and clear out," Guri said reasonably.

"I'm closing the tavern," Yeshua insisted. "You don't have to pay."

"Don't blow your top, Yeshua. A man blabbed some nonsense . . . Will you punish everyone for that? Hey, you," the younger Andronov said to the man who had gossiped about Yeshua and his son taking turns with Morta, "Ask the boss to forgive you."

"Who are you to give orders?" the instigator asked, lowering his head like a bull. "Should I ask a Jew for forgiveness for taking my money?" he grumbled.

He got up and walked toward the door, wrapping a sheepskin around him as he left.

The others streamed out after him.

Only Guri remained, as if rooted there.

"Why are you still here?" Yeshua asked, and the younger Andronov felt a deadly weariness in his voice.

"Habit . . ."

"What habit?" The tavern keeper was confused.

"Drinking to the last, bitter drop."

Guri pushed aside his glass, ate a slice of pickled cucumber, wiped his fat lips that had hardened, like a cocoon, and sniffed meaningfully with his gristly nose. He said, "No point in starting an uproar, old man. For me, if an insult gets laughs, let them insult me . . . I won't say a word. But you say, 'Get out! Go to hell!'"

The younger Andronov got up, casually tossed some coins toward the table, which landed in a bowl, grunted an apology, and left.

With a spoon Yeshua pulled out the copper coins that Guri had thrown into the bowl, wiped them off in disgust with a short rag that always hung over the bar, and stuck them in the drawer for proceeds. Small and dark as a den, it opened with a scraping noise. Then the tavern keeper's thoughts returned to Simeon, to the dark words that concealed an unclear threat, and to his strange, reckless actions, which somehow confirmed its inevitability. Yeshua was not as hurt by the allusions to his relationship with Morta—which even flattered him!—as he was by his son's sullen determination to carry out something that he, Yeshua, couldn't comprehend with his stubborn, workaday mind. Everything that happens in the world, he supposed, must have an explanation. Everything must be comprehensible, even the most terrible things. Chava's suicide shattered him, but if you take a deeper look, you'll see that she was gone long before, while she was still alive. And Simeon? Simeon? Is he a jealous or vindictive person? Despite his affection for Morta, it's not for her that he would swill vodka in the morning or pour cold water over his head. He won't avenge his mother's death either, because her death was also his fault. Guilt is not a herring—you can't weigh it on a scale and say whose is greater.

My God, hadn't Morta asked for the gun for Simeon? And hadn't he, old fool, so willing to please the girl, swallowed the bait?

"Morta! Morta!" Yeshua shouted, cringing from his guess. His voice echoed in the tavern, as in an empty barrel—muffled and lonely. "Morta!"

He began rushing about, flinging open the doors.

"I'm here . . . here," she said. "I went down to the cellar. We're out of cucumbers."

Morta stood in front of Yeshua, hugging a clay pot of pickles to her chest, like a child.

Yeshua decided to confront her before she could gather her wits. "Why did you need the gun?"

"I told you."

"Don't lie."

"To kill the fox," Morta mumbled, but her mumbling only fanned the flames. Yeshua no longer had any doubts—they were in cahoots!

"Did he tell you to get the gun from me?"

"No."

The tavern keeper went up to her and squeezed her wrist—so hard that Morta screamed and dropped the pot in fear. It fell to the floor with a crash and broke into pieces, while the brine poured out in a stream and flowed toward Yeshua's feet.

"How does he know about the hat?"

"Why not? Is the hat a secret?" Morta bent over and began picking up the shards.

Yeshua looked at her neck, at the ringlet of hair that stuck out like a hook to catch trout, at her flexible back with its sharply defined hollow, and he tried to curb his anger. But neither passion nor lust could reduce his anxiety. It swelled like a bruise, and Yeshua became fearful again.

"Listen, Morta. Don't make me mad," the tavern keeper growled, keeping his eyes on the curve of her back.

Morta didn't respond.

"You protect him, but he . . . do you know what he says about you?"

"I know."

She did not want to straighten up.

"You don't know a damn thing!" Yeshua attacked her. "He says you're a whore!"

"He's right. I am a whore to those who don't know me," she hissed.

Oh, if only the tavern went on forever and there were enough pickles for a lifetime, she thought. Then I wouldn't have to stand up and look into my master's angry eyes.

"Your gun wasn't under the eaves," Morta said, picking up broken pieces.

Yeshua was stunned.

"And there wasn't any horse blanket . . . There wasn't anything," she sang out, as if mocking him. "If there had been, I would have sunk it in the pond."

"You would have sunk it? Stop, I'll pick up the pieces! I'll pick them up," Yeshua yelled. "I'll lick the floor, crawl on my knees . . . just tell the truth!"

Yeshua stood in the pickle juice and looked at her with a crazed expression. Suddenly he pulled her toward himself, brushed her with his beard, thrust his mouth up to her plump, sensual lips and whispered, "Don't deceive me, don't deceive me!"

Then he buried his face in hers.

"Fear God, Master," she said, pushing him away.

Bewildered, he drew back, still standing in the brine, but said with conviction, "You want to go bang-bang? Take my money . . . take over the tavern? Is that it?"

Morta was silent.

"Is that it? Why don't you answer?"

"Can a dead man be killed?" Morta said unexpectedly.

"What are you talking about?"

Morta licked her lips, as if trying to lick away an alien lust, and she felt both disgust and pity for Yeshua.

Blessed Virgin Mary, how lustfully he panted, how indecently he moved, poking his heavy head, filled with shamelessness, into her face until she pushed him away, confused and helplessly shocked. Oh stubborn unbridled tribe! Inscrutable and alluring like its language and prayers!

"Nothing," she said.

"Are you offended?" Yeshua pulled back.

"No," Morta said. "Who is offended by the dead?"

She was trying to hurt him to the core, to humiliate him so that he would no longer dare, would not even think of touching her. I can decide, can't I, flashed in her mind, but she could in no way imagine herself bleeding and in shackles.

"Morta! Mortele!" Yeshua sputtered.

"Don't, Master . . . Thank you for the bread and the shelter . . . but Siberia is better than your . . ."

She broke off, and her silence struck Yeshua hard.

"I won't let you go anywhere . . . Anywhere," he said in a downcast voice.

"Whores are free, Master . . ."

"No, no," the tavern keeper said quickly. "You'll see. We'll get over this!"

"We?"

"Me . . . you . . . Simeon . . . At times it seems that everything falls to pieces, like the pot . . . and there's no hope . . . no opening. And then . . . then an angel appears."

"An angel in a tavern?"

Pity had replaced disgust, and Yeshua's sensitive ear picked up on the change.

"Then an angel appears," the tavern keeper repeated, becoming more animated, "and sits on your shoulder, your left or right shoulder . . . and whispers in your ear."

"The angel would say 'Yeshua! A bottle of vodka! Pickled cucumbers!'" she said mocking him. "And he gets drunk as a skunk and swears and throws up on the floor, and Yeshua and Morta pick him up under his arms, carry him out of the tavern, and throw him into a patch of burdocks."

"No! The angel will whisper, 'Don't despair, Yeshua, I flew into the tavern not to drink but to tell you that you will find love . . . God punishes and rewards. Your life of punishment is over, your life of reward is beginning.' Do you know whose voice that angel has?"

Morta drew back. "Chava's?" She forced out the word, suppressing her trepidation.

"You'll never guess!" the tavern keeper encouraged her, flashing his gypsy eyes. "That angel has *your* voice," he said, reveling in her embarrassment as in his victory.

"Mine?"

"Yours!"

The air became dense, words took on flesh and touched, like lips searching for one another.

"Then the angel has a whore's voice," Morta said.

"Forgive me," Yeshua apologized. "Forgive me . . . And I forgive you . . . It's a sin to call the living dead. A sin . . . I have strength enough for two lives . . . If I pray to the Almighty for anything, it's for one thing only—for Him not to mix up the order."

"What order?"

"He granted me a life of reward now, and a life of punishment only later."

"He'll mix them up all the same," Morta said, astounded by the passion and frenzy of Yeshua's words.

"Don't talk that way! Don't!" Yeshua grumbled. "We'll bide our time . . ."

She was struck again by this short, this indefinite, this endless "we."

"I want to live more than ever. Not for the tavern . . . not for an extra kopeck. You'll never earn enough anyway . . . the hell with it, with money, I'll leave it all to Simeon, just let him take any kind of work. A Jew without work is like a cart without wheels."

"And you?"

"Me? I'll be like a whore—here today, there tomorrow . . . I'll be free, and perhaps someone will not pull away from my beard . . . And we'll put an egg in it and raise a fledgling that will love us until our last breath."

Yeshua's eyelashes began to tremble.

He got the better of himself, though, and smiled, glancing at Morta, but then caved in as if his guts had been removed.

The life of reward cast off from the pier, the angel turned away from his shoulder, and once again in the tavern, as in the whole world, the life of punishment took charge, inconspicuous, cloudy, like pickle juice. His life lay all in pieces like the pot.

"Where did it go?" The gun emerged from the gloom of his consciousness, enveloping Yeshua in alarm. "Was it Simeon?"

"I'm leaving, Master," Morta said. "I'll wash the cucumbers." She pointed to the pile lying on the table.

"Did he ask you for the gun?" the tavern keeper pressed. "If you're not shooting me, then who?"

"No one."

"And I believed you."

"No one!" Morta shouted, and she ran out of the tavern, leaving the pile of cucumbers on the table.

Yeshua remained alone.

For a moment he stood still, as if at a funeral where every movement causes pain. He stood and stuck his hands in the pockets of his waistcoat, and they felt heavy, as if they'd been shod by the town blacksmith. Was he hiding them from sin? An immeasurable sadness furrowed his brow and crushed his soul. Why had he thrown everyone out of the tavern? For his whole life he had never rebelled, and then all of a sudden he started to rage. Against whom? Against some pitiable, shabby little peasant! What good is it to rebel against the weak? Yeshua now lacked the strength to calm his soul in the face of their dirty jokes and obscene roars, their off-key, inarticulate, rousing songs that evoked some rowan tree or Father Neman or the road and a coachman.

God created everyone sober, but we have to live beside drunks, not the sober. And everyone is drunk on something—some on vodka, some on greed, and some on hatred and arrogance.

As you look around, you see no end to people drunk on meekness. There are thousands and thousands and millions of them . . . Yeshua is one of them, but he's not sorry. He even rejoices. Drunk on meekness, he won't be exiled, he won't be sent to hard labor. He will always get his piece of bread, by the sweat of his brow, with aches and pains in his back. You can drink meekness from morning till night, pour it for your children and grandchildren; from cradle to grave, you will suckle the milk of meekness.

If Yeshua's life had not become one of reward until now, it is only because he occasionally added hatred and rebellion to his meekness.

Had he not poured out meekness for Simeon?

He had poured it! Poured full cups! Three times a day, like medicine.

But Simeon had secretly spilled it out under the cradle, under the bed, under the table, and then filled the cup with arrogance!

You shouldn't get drunk on arrogance, just as you shouldn't get drunk on hatred. Arrogance and hatred are sisters and they share the same groom—evil.

Simeon is drunk on arrogance! He's ashamed to stand behind the tavern bar. For him it's shameful to wait on and please others, it's sickening to bow and say thanks for a few coins.

Isn't it also sickening for him, Yeshua?

It is sickening, sickening. Everyone who drinks feels sick . . . The only difference is what makes a person sick.

Still, it's better to be sick from meekness than from hatred and arrogance.

Who will he strike with his arrogance? Who will he shoot?

It's no use to question Simeon. He won't say anything, but only become more incensed. And if you mention the gun, he'll fly into a rage. But it's also stupid to sound the alarm all over town or call someone for help. Everything will be resolved when Simeon shoots a crow or fires off shots in the market square to scatter the crowd. It's impossible to guess what he might do. Best not to disturb him. In the end, what will be will be. I can't treat him like a child his whole life. He has his own head on his shoulders . . . If he wants to risk his life, let him do it. If Simeon gets caught, he, Yeshua, will not stand up for him. If he's guilty, he'll get what he deserves . . . His father didn't teach him, but the Siberian snows will . . . And he, Yeshua, will remain with Morta . . . the two together! Almighty God, it's all up to you!

His face twitched, and a satisfied grin stuck in his beard like a piece of straw.

Yeshua decided to close the tavern and go to the synagogue. If you pray, you're always under God's care. He would stand at the Eastern wall and pray all day, all evening, all night. He would pray for . . . Chava and Hannah, and for his father and mother, cut down by Cossacks . . . In the morning he will call Rabbi Hillel and donate one paper ruble and one silver ruble to the synagogue . . . He'll pray, then go outside to look at the sky, and there, in the sky, the paper ruble will turn into a feathery cloud, light and serene, and the silver ruble will gleam like a new moon.

"Hello!" Hearing a woman's voice, Yeshua turned around.

A woman stood at the tavern door. She was wrapped in a shawl full of holes, porous like a net. Her shabby velvet cape, a hand-me-down from only God knows whom, puckered and glistened with a jaundice-like yellow. Somehow, she seemed ageless—maybe forty, or if you looked more closely, all things considered, forty-five. Her long skirt also made her look older, it fell to her heels, to her worn-out shoes, which were splattered with the autumn mud. In one hand the woman held a small oak chest with rounded sides, well-crafted and apparently packed with something.

"Hello," the tavern keeper answered, not bothering to hide his surprise. Jewish women, of all people, don't drop in at a tavern. Oy! Suddenly, wouldn't you know it, the worst you can imagine—a real Jewish woman, or beggar, or pilgrim. Now she'll start to beg, plead, sob, describe for Yeshua terrible pictures of hunger and injustice, and he will have to listen to her—if you turn the wretched woman out, she'll shower you with curses, and you'll remember her for a long time.

"As I live and breathe, you look so much like my husband," she said in a deep voice.

"Your husband?"

"As I live and breathe, just like you . . . tall . . . a large forehead . . . without the yarmulke, the very image, I'm telling you. Only—and let it not be said about us—without a top in his head."

"With what?"

"A top. How it spins, always spins before the Day of Judgment!"

The woman put the oak chest down on a bench, straightened the shawl, which had slipped off her shoulders, and sighed, "And what a shoemaker! Golden hands!"

"He's a shoemaker?" Yeshua asked to be polite, hoping to get rid of her faster through kindness than hostility.

"A shoemaker! We're all shoemakers . . . My husband, the children and me." The woman tapped her knuckles on the chest.

"While I'm chasing him around the world, I repair soles for some, and heels for others. I can do it for you."

"Thank you," the tavern keeper answered coldly. "We have a shoemaker. Nekhamkin."

"Nekhamkin," the guest repeated. "I've heard something about him. There's a gravedigger Nekhamkin. But the gravedigger—let it not be said about you and me—only patches up the earth . . . He lays down a patch of clay and, as we say in our town, it's over, so put the spoon aside!"

Yeshua had no idea what she wanted from him, but he also didn't know how to get rid of her.

"Everyone knows my husband," the woman sighed. "I suppose he's stopped by at the tavern?"

"Does he drink?"

"Only on Yom Kippur."

"On Yom Kippur? But Jews don't . . ." Yeshua dug deep into his memory and looked at the woman intently.

"When he comes down from his ladder . . . Last year he came down in Mishkine. I'm looking, he's barely able to stand on his feet, and he reeks of something, like he's dying . . . 'Zvi-Hersh,' I ask, 'who was your drinking buddy?' 'Me,' he says. 'Zipporah, God treated me to moonshine . . . He poured a full glass and said: *l'chaim!* To life!' May my enemies drink *l'chaim!* I used to get mad at him, called him all sorts of names. But I'm not angry now. Every man, if he's a man, wants to go crazy once a year . . . What about you? Don't you?"

"Does your husband wear a velvet yarmulke with a pin?" Yeshua hissed, and he walked away without answering, as if to escape.

"Yes," the woman said. "Where is he?"

17

The night watchman Rakhmiel's house seemed full of fresh wind and sunlight. At long last the floor was washed, and now the sloping floorboards sparkled as if it were Passover and on two clean windows curtains fluttered, curtains that Rakhmiel had put away for the time when he would bring a third wife into his wreck of a house. But since the Almighty did not send a third wife—two are enough, Rakhmiel, He said—the curtains gathered dust in a chest along with other stuff their owner did not need: his first wife's long nightgown; a large map, yellowed with age, of the Russian Empire with all its holdings, though without the Kovno highway (Rakhmiel had no idea himself how he came in possession of it); the cloth covering for a wedding canopy, which was painted with whimsical designs and decorated with bizarre animals—either lions keeping silent or growling fish (he's had no time to examine it!); and a small tin horn which people blew into with all their might on the holiday of *Simkhes Torah*. Sometimes, out of boredom and loneliness Rakhmiel pulled out the horn, put it to his parched lips, and trumpeted inside his house. As he blew, unclearly and monotonously, he thought of his children who had died from an unknown illness, remembered a shower of fruit drops in the prayer house when he himself was a boy, and saw the young Rabbi Uri holding a scroll in his hands like a cloud.

At long last the floor in the house was washed, and at long last a woman was bustling about in it! A strange woman (for whoever heard of a woman shoemaker!), but nonetheless a woman.

Something dampened Rakhmiel's joy.

The cleanliness and order that transformed the house merged in Rakhmiel's troubled brain with something inevitable and relentless. Life clutters and death tidies up, he thought, while watching the woman's strong hands, the top of a shoe sitting on her enormous knees, and the intent look on her face that was disfigured by warts. Death had washed the floor so that he, Rakhmiel, would not lie in filth or stench or mold; death had curtained the windows to keep onlookers from looking into the house. But the night watchman did not understand why death was repairing his shoes.

"Why isn't he coming?" Zipporah asked in her deep voice as she nailed down the sole on Rakhmiel's left shoe. Why does he even need this left shoe? What for? His leg still hasn't come to its senses, it hurts and has no strength left.

"He'll come," he answered vacantly.

"Someday they'll finish him off," Zipporah said.

She held the other shoe, the right one, between her enormous knees and began to nail on a heel.

"He . . . your husband . . . what's his name?" Rakhmiel asked cautiously, paying close attention to the taps of the hammer and gradually calming down.

"Zvi-Hersh," Zipporah said.

"Zvi-Hersh?" Rakhmiel sighed in disappointment.

"Did he give himself another name?"

"He said 'Aaron'!"

"Imagine that!" Zipporah brushed it aside.

"Maybe he's Aaron after all?"

"What else did this Aaron say?"

"He served in the army," the night watchman mumbled, and his heart, worn out like his shoe, began to pound unduly loud.

"Zvi was never drafted," Zipporah replied, spitting out a nail from time to time. "And he was telling you he was?"

"Yes."

"And you believed him?"

"Yes."

She's wrong to smirk. If only she knew how much he wants the name to be Aaron—not Zvi-Hersh—and wishes that he had served in the army! That he had served, and had returned, had forgiven him, and would accompany him on his last journey to the place where all of Rakhmiel's brood lies—two ducks and five drakes . . . While Rakhmiel listened to the woman shoemaker, something inside him soundlessly collapsed, and he grieved for what had never been, yet had entered his soul like the sound of a horn on *Simkhes Torah* and the shower of fruit drops falling on his curly light-brown hair, long ago.

"Only fools believe him," Zipporah said, then suddenly caught herself. "I don't mean you."

"Why not? It's true of me. What's to be done if nothing else is left for fools to believe?"

"What's not left?"

"Nothing."

How can he explain it to her?

"It's terrifying," Rakhmiel said, "when everything is taken from you. First what you have and then what you don't have but you believe in."

Zipporah stared at him and, bird-like, leaned her head on her shoulder. Oh, these Jews, may they live and be well, these muddle-heads, worthless sages, tiresome windbags! Don't bother feeding them with bread; just let them gossip, argue, and confuse matters. What does she care about their fantasies, their whims, their non-sense? Soon he will stir, bluster, and rage, and if she doesn't get him home on time, her prophet, her woe, the father of her children will land somewhere, in a wreck of a place like this, or a roadside tavern, the nook of a prayer house, or an open field. Or they'll kill him for all his prophecies. Then he'll get his ladder, and his Day of Judgment!

"I'll wait until evening, and if he doesn't show up, I'll move on," she announced, in a voice that expressed more despair than determination.

Rakhmiel didn't have the strength to console her. And he wouldn't tell her about the policeman who turned up to interrogate him. What would be the point of telling tales? If Ardalion Ignatich grabbed him and locked him in the barn, no Zipporah would get him out. Pimpleface Simeon, who knows the way of the world, calls the policeman's barn "our Imperial Fortress." Fortress or not, best not to land up there. In 1863, when Nesterovich was not yet in these parts, the Lithuanian rebels were kept there—brought in, locked in the barn, placed under guard. Soldiers walked around with rifles at the ready, and the Lithuanians in the barn were singing their songs, apparently bidding farewell to their homeland. They sang and he, Rakhmiel, banged the clapper until dawn, as if to cheer up the miserable people. How many of them passed through this barn at the time! More than you could count.

Apparently, this Zvi-Hersh (or not Zvi-Hersh) in the yarmulke fastened to his hair with a pin was also fated to pass through this barn and sing his farewell song there. He would sing and vanish without a trace and exchange his velvet yarmulke for a convict's hood.

God knows that he, Rakhmiel, hadn't wronged him. He gave him shelter, shared his potatoes and milk, didn't betray him to Pimpleface Simeon, and softened up the policeman, saying, "He's not a criminal, Ardalion Ignatich!" It doesn't matter that they call him crazy. Let him be crazy, as long as he isn't sentenced to hard labor, as long as he returns to his wife Zipporah and his little ones.

Although the newcomer had earlier alluded to his betrayal, Rakhmiel had not betrayed anyone—neither his stepson Aaron nor any son, brother, or stranger. Why should a weak person blame him for weakness? If weakness in the face of evil is a betrayal, then how many traitors are there in the world? Point at every second person and you won't be wrong. For a weak person the whole world is an Imperial Fortress, even if that person is free. And doesn't the strength of the Almighty lie in weakness? That's why He is like every second person, and that is why every second person prays to Him and does not get angry at Him, for what can He do? But when a powerful person yields to evil, he is truly a traitor. Weakness is not a fault but a force that drives people into a barn, or into paradise.

Almighty God, how many years has Rakhmiel lived without thinking, and now at sunset, at the onset of the inevitable winter, thoughts were crashing down on him like an illness.

Kazimieras entered the house silently and signaled to Rakhmiel with his hand. When Rakhmiel drew near, he said, "There's trouble."

"What's happened?" Rakhmiel asked, becoming alarmed.

"Yeshua's son has disappeared."

"Simeon? What do you mean, disappeared?"

"He took a gun and left."

"What are you whispering about there?" Zipporah exclaimed rudely, as if she were the boss of the house.

"Kazimieras is asking . . . he's asking . . . can he bring his boots?" Rakhmiel lied, and sticky sweat began to spread across his pock-marked forehead—a forewarning of strained coughing and agitation.

"He can," Zipporah said. "Has he seen my dear husband? Are you whispering about him?"

"I haven't seen him, haven't seen him," Kazimieras said, nodding his head affirmatively for some reason.

"You haven't seen him, but you're nodding?" Zipporah had caught him. The Lithuanian's unexpected arrival had sowed anxiety in her soul.

"No, I haven't seen him," Kazimieras said, stretching his head out like a goose. Lowering his voice to a mousy squeak, he addressed Rakhmiel. "Has she been here?"

"Who?"

"Morta."

"What's Morta got to do with it?" Rakhmiel was completely confused.

"She's running around searching."

"For Simeon?"

"For both. For Simeon and the man in the yarmulke. That one's husband. But so far she's found neither."

"Listen," Zipporah said, becoming angry. "I can't bear to hear men whisper. God thought up whispering so that women could be lured into bed. Do you know something?"

"We don't know anything," Rakhmiel said with unnatural cheer.

"I'm used to everything," Zipporah let drop. "Like a field."

"Like what?" Rakhmiel spluttered.

"Like a field. Here are your shoes," Zipporah said. She got up from a small bench like one used when sitting shiva, went to the window, and parted the curtains. "I can't wait for evening," she sighed. "I can't wait for night."

"Evening will come, and night will come," Rakhmiel said to himself or to Zipporah, and no one understood what he meant by these words.

Zipporah stood at the window and closed the curtains as if wiping away something from memory or from the sky, and then she slipped out into the hall.

"And Yeshua?" Rakhmiel brushed away the sweat with his palm.

"What about Yeshua?"

"What's he doing?"

"Praying."

"Praying?"

"He chased everyone out of the tavern and went to the synagogue."

"There'll be trouble," Rakhmiel grumbled. "There'll be trouble if Yeshua chases everyone out of the tavern." With no connection to what he'd just said, he added, "We always act that way."

"How?"

"We pray when someone's about to be killed. My God, may he survive and come back alive! Heal poor Simeon's mind!" Rakhmiel scratched his head and turned to Kazimieras.

"You know that I'm not much of a walker. But I'll go to the fork or to the Neman River. And you, go to the cutting area and then to the mill. Morta will make the rounds of the houses. Maybe he stayed up late at someone's place? And I'll talk to Itsik. So many fools should be able to save one fool from a bullet. Eh?"

"Eh?" hung in the air like an autumn spiderweb.

"She's crying," Kazimieras whispered.

"Who?"

"The woman shoemaker . . . Don't you hear?"

Rakhmiel put on the shoes Zipporah had repaired, pulled on a *sermyaga* lined with frayed felt, and took his clapper. Limping on his left, crippled foot, he dragged himself to the door.

Kazimieras followed him in silence, puzzled by his plan. It's not a good idea to roam around aimlessly, looking for a lunatic.

"Where are you going?" Zipporah asked in the hallway, hiding her eyes.

She's crazy too, Kazimieras thought. Who's ever heard of a woman leaving her house and children and setting off after her husband like a hunting dog. He, Kazimieras, would have kicked her out in no time.

"To get the boots," Rakhmiel explained.

"Two of you for boots? Doesn't he," Zipporah said, and pointed at Kazimieras, "know the way by himself?"

"We'll be back soon," the night watchman promised.

"Why the clapper?"

"What do you mean why? To bang!"

"In broad daylight?"

"So what? A white day is sometimes blacker than night."

"That's for sure," Zipporah backed him up.

"Wait for us here," Rakhmiel said.

They left the house.

Again and again, Rakhmiel stopped to gasp for air; he would cough harshly for a long time and pound his chest with the clapper. Kazimieras looked askance at him but didn't hurry him—hawk and pound, it happens to everyone.

"Rabbi Uri said that the clapper is for summoning death," Rakhmiel recalled. "Nonsense! The clapper is the sound of warning, not of death."

"A bell is better when there's trouble," Kazimieras said, "and also when it's a holiday."

"Everyone has their own bell," Rakhmiel replied. "I have a clapper, you have wind in your lungs, Rabbi Uri has a head . . ."

Rakhmiel was catching his breath again and through his snorts, grunts, and sniffs, Kazimieras heard him say, "You—to the cutting area. I—to the fork . . ."

"And the boots?"

"She'll repair your boots if he returns alive. They will both sit down and fix them in an instant. He'll do the left one, she, the right . . . But if Simeon . . . ," Rakhmiel swallowed, "then you and I, Kazimieras, will walk with holes and no shoemaker will be able to patch them."

"With holes?"

"When all of mine died after that cursed wedding, and I was left alone . . . wait, let me catch my breath for a minute . . . I came to the house . . . made my way to the mirror to cover it with a blanket and saw it myself. I looked and was shocked. Everything was like a sieve . . . No life, just hole after hole and the wind whistling through each one. And through each one my children . . . the two ducks and the five drakes . . . were quacking . . . quack . . . quack . . ."

They were ready to go off in different directions—Kazimieras to the cutting area, Rakhmiel to the fork—when suddenly an enormous pillar of smoke soared above the town and into the sky. It swirled around and spread like a monstrous mushroom, rising steadily and heavily, and a flame swept over someone's roof like the crimson tail of a witch.

"Something's burning," Kazimieras said. "Iron . . . it smells like burned iron."

"The Spivaks?"

"Looks like the Spivaks," Kazimieras sighed, and the flame blazed more than before.

"What if the whole town burns down!" Rakhmiel became distressed. "What a wind! The fire will spread to the tavern . . . and then to the Fradkins' house, and then to the church . . ."

He stared into the smoky distance, but his gaze could not penetrate the dark gray clouds of smoke.

Kazimieras crossed himself anxiously, as if he wanted to protect not himself but the wooden church.

"The flames won't touch the church."

"Why not?"

"Your spells don't work on us," Kazimieras said.

"What spells? What kind of nonsense is that, Kazimieras?"

"I'm saying that, maybe, the man in the yarmulke with the pin, who calls himself Aaron, is a sorcerer. And maybe this woman is a witch. Whoever heard of a woman shoemaker?"

Rakhmiel stared at Kazimieras the same way he stared at the fire.

"That time when he was sitting on the roof, with my own ears I heard him say, 'God will reward us for every nail.'"

"I heard it, too," Rakhmiel said. "But what does it matter? Nothing in the world has ever burst into flames or burned up because of words."

"From ordinary words, maybe not," Kazimieras said. "But from a sorcerer's words, even rivers can burn. Maybe you shouldn't take up with an evil spirit for the sake of a pair of shoes."

"But what if, despite everything, he's Aaron?"

"Wouldn't you recognize your own stepson?"

"So many years have gone by!"

"What about the birthmark on his right shoulder?"

"He didn't have any birthmark. That's the truth. I made it up."

"You made it up? Why?"

"Just in order to have something to remember."

"Can you remember something that wasn't?"

"You can . . . But in order to do it you need to forget everything else."

"Why forget?"

"To keep memory from strangling you. So I threw that noose away. And without a noose, it turns out, a man can neither tighten nor loosen it."

"Everything's on fire now," Kazimieras said. "Instead of hunting in the forest, it's better to search for him in town."

"Everything will burn down before we get there," Rakhmiel replied, taking off his shoes.

"The fire won't bring down a house like the Spivaks' so quickly," Kazimieras reasoned. "Even if you're putting it out, it will burn for an hour or so."

"I'll walk barefoot. It's easier," Rakhmiel said, after tying his shoes together with a string and throwing them over his shoulder.

Taking refuge behind Kazimieras's back from his pain and memory-noose, he walked to town along the country road.

The smoke above the Spivaks' roof had subsided, the pillar had thinned, turning from a dark gray to a bluish-gray and becoming translucent. Flashes of fire, like summer lightning, still crossed the sky.

Rakhmiel walked slowly, the shoes tapping on his back, and this tapping calmed and pacified him like his mother's long-forgotten pats.

We are all victims of fire, he thought—those with a roof and those without. Every day something burns in us and above us and all around, but does this make the world warmer? Does this bring light?

"What kind of a candle doesn't burn out?" Kazimieras asked, looking back at Rakhmiel. "I've put out candles for many years and I've never heard of a candle like that."

The night watchman shrugged his shoulders.

"It's supposed to be here." With two fingers Kazimieras felt for his heart, as if fumbling for a pinch of tobacco. "That's what he said . . . the one with the yarmulke." He didn't know what to call him—sorcerer, Aaron, or tramp—that wouldn't offend Rakhmiel. "It burns even after death . . . What kind of candle is it?" the Lithuanian asked him.

Apparently Kazimieras was not interested in anything but this candle—not the lightning-like flashes over the Spivaks' roof, nor the stranger lost without a trace, nor Rakhmiel.

"It's the candle of hope," the night watchman said. "And you can't blow it out."

"Why?"

"Because even when you're completely full of holes, when the wind whistles through you, someone will touch you with a smoldering piece of wood, and it will flare up and burn again."

"And if there's no smoldering wood?" Kazimieras asked earnestly. "What then?"

"Then from the sun . . . from the feather of a titmouse . . . from a kind look . . . or from a scroll in the prayer house. Jews can light a candle of hope from just about anything."

"Can *we*?"

"You and the Russians, and our neighbors, the Germans, and the Turks . . ."

Now they could hear cries from the fire.

"Where are you taking that empty bucket?"

"Come around from the left! From the left!"

"It's going to collapse right now!"

"Get moving! You're standing there like a groom at a wedding . . ."

"Shovels! Get the shovels! Dig a ditch!"

"Chaim! Chaim! I'll laugh myself to death! We're on fire!"

"Take him to the tavern!"

"No, Yeshua . . . Anywhere but the tavern!"

"Dig deeper! Deeper!"

"Naftali Spivak's honest word. I'll reward everyone, everyone!"

"With ashes?"

"Shut up!"

"Help has come!"

"What kind of help is Rakhmiel?"

"And Kazimieras? He can blow it out, like candles on Shabbes."

"But today's not Shabbes!"

All the new buckets and shovels from the Spivak brothers' hardware shop were now clanking. The pitchforks that had been meant for customers, intended for stacking bales of hay or spreading manure, were now raking from the fire the scorched remains of goods accumulated over long and troubled years.

Splashes of water mixed with the muffled sound of collapsing beams, the crackle and goose hisses of smoldering wood, the meows of a cat searching for her kittens, and the funereal rustle of clay soil in the yard. Maybe the ditch would be able to sop the unrelenting, curious flames that were spreading across the ground.

In a dug-up yard opposite the shop, there was a tall pile of rakes and harnesses for horses, drag harrows, and tar that hadn't sold over the summer. Chaim Spivak's luxurious sable coat with its bright silk lining was there, alongside a crimson down comforter.

Naftali Spivak was walking around this pile like a soldier around an armory, and from time to time he filled the yard with a loud cry: "Oy, I'll die laughing!"

"A fire's not death, Naftali," the tavern keeper Yeshua comforted him, after rushing here from the synagogue in his holiday yarmulke and prayer shawl. "You'll rebuild!"

"We'll rebuild, Yeshua, we'll rebuild! But this is what you'd better tell me—why did my sister Chava hang herself?"

"My God, Naftali! You've gone completely mad from grief!"

"Why?"

"Don't try to settle scores during a fire," Yeshua said in a hoarse voice, "or to look for the guilty. Among the living, Naftali, no one is innocent. If you're alive, it means you're guilty."

People kept coming to the pile of junk and goods saved from the fire. They threw down whatever they'd retrieved from the shop and house, looked distrustfully at the pacing Naftali and the tavern keeper, dressed in his best, and then hurried back to the spot where buckets were clanking and ashes mixed with thick steam floated above the site of the fire.

Chaim, who was soiled with soot, was giving orders to the volunteer fire fighters. His yarmulke had been charred and his black frock coat was torn, its flaps were thrown open exposing his paunch and his thin, sickle-shaped legs. Every now and then Chaim would shout loudly and plaintively, "Careful! Careful! Take it easy! You won't find a mirror like that anywhere."

It was clear that the mirror reflected not only the site of the fire and not only a face soiled with soot, but something else, something that made Chaim shudder. He gazed into it as into his serene childhood, or his carefree youth, a time when everything in the world was in harmony—an object and its image, a thought and its reflection, today and tomorrow.

The line from the well to the shop had started to thin, and the volunteers who had been passing water to each other in the Spivaks' brand-new buckets began to go off in all directions. Their joyless joint effort was coming to an end.

"Thank you," Chaim said in a muffled tone, swallowing lumps like fish bones stuck in the gullet, and irritating his throat with dour gratitude. "Thank you! These buckets . . . these pitchforks . . . these shovels are yours! The Spivak brothers' hardware business is finished."

The volunteers lingered, hesitated, and looked at one another to see who would be the first to take home a free gift. What if Chaim came to his senses and fleeced them for triple the value?

"Take it," Kazimieras told Rakhmiel, handing him a bucket with a shiny handle. "Don't be afraid. He won't take it back! I carried away half a well in it!"

"No," Rakhmiel was obstinate. "Whoever demands pay for doing good is not doing good but making a trade. Look!" He began speaking faster. "My God, it's Aaron! But why isn't he wearing his yarmulke?"

The one who called himself Aaron skittered toward the smoldering Spivak brothers' hardware shop, carrying a yarmulke in his open palms like a bowl.

"What's that he's carrying?" Kazimieras wanted to know, forgetting about the pitchfork and shovel.

"I have no idea."

Naftali Spivak also noticed the newcomer.

"Chaim! Just look at who's coming to us! Oy, I'll die laughing! He's the one who borrowed forty kopecks worth of nails from me . . . What's that in his hands? God's hundredfold?"

"What hundredfold?"

"He said that God would reward you a hundredfold," Naftali raged.

"Is he the one who set the shop on fire?"

"Maybe he did." Naftali sowed a diabolical seed.

"Get him!"

"Hand him over to the policeman!"

"Scoundrel!"

The stranger was approaching. He was about a hundred steps from the ruins of the shop, which gaped with fractured windows and charred doors, like ugly eye sockets.

"Get out of here!"

"Kick his ass!"

"Sic the dogs on him!"

The crowd seethed with hatred, hooted, and made a racket. Then suddenly it lost its sight and turned into one thick beard, one wide-open mouth spewing curses. A festival of revenge and impunity swept over it like a flood, and violence became an indulgence as desirable as pierogi with raisins and cinnamon.

Praised be the Lord! Hosanna to the long-awaited judgment and revenge! Hosanna to the pogrom! No matter whether it is inflicted on a sorcerer or a tramp, a messenger from God or from Satan, a Christian or a Jew. Kicks! Blood! Groans! Humiliated, trembling for a whole year, a whole lifetime, before some county Nuikin, or bowing its head from morning to evening before some local policeman or timber merchant, finally the crowd has been given a sweet, extraordinary opportunity to lift itself above its own trembling, its own shit, its own cowardly humiliations. Now each one in the crowd, even the most miserable, will show what he can do. He'll kick the scoundrel, set dogs on him, beat, stomp, tear him to shreds, and blame the sorcerer for all mortal sins—for fires and suicides, for poverty and stupidity, for accidents and unrealized dreams. The crowd no longer needs pitchforks or shovels, bread or salt, lies or truth. It needs a culprit. Praised be the Lord for the guilty one, Hosanna!

"Break his ribs!"

"Throw him out of town!"

With buckets clanking merrily, with the brand-new pitchforks and shovels they were given by the tender-hearted victims of the fire, the crowd moved toward the stranger who was carrying a yarmulke like a bowl in his outstretched palms.

"Stab him with pitchforks!"

"Tar him!"

"Into the Neman!"

He was no more than twenty-five steps from the site of the fire.

"Stop!" Rakhmiel cried out suddenly. "Stand back! Jews, what are you doing? That's my son . . . Aaron! He's returned from duty.

Reb Yeshua," he addressed the tavern keeper, "tell them before it's too late. Reb Chaim! You must remember my boy! In that cap . . . with a peak! Stop them! Reb Naftali!"

Naftali Spivak turned his head toward the cries and began walking around his pile. Hup one, hup two—no military service in the world was harder than this.

"Kazimieras," Rakhmiel pleaded, looking first at the stranger coming closer, then at the crowd moving toward him. "Why aren't you saying anything?"

"It's his son," the Lithuanian whispered.

"Why whisper? Why in a whisper? How long must we speak the truth in a whisper?"

"But it's not true," Kazimieras objected.

"It *is* true," Rakhmiel snapped back. "Whatever saves a person is true, whatever destroys is a lie."

"Ha-ha-ha!"

"Hee-hee-hee!"

"Oy!" the crowd unexpectedly groaned with laughter. "Oy, it's too funny!"

The crowd surrounded the newcomer like a jester on Purim. They banged on the bottoms of their buckets, like drumheads, swung their pitchforks like a conductor's baton, and after raising their shovels like muskets, they walked back toward the charred shop.

"Ha-ha-ha!"

"God in Heaven! He's the biggest numbskull on earth!"

"Time for fun!"

The stranger didn't seem to notice the crowd. He was preoccupied with one thing—no matter what, to carry the thing everyone was laughing at to the charred shop. He seemed to have no interest in his own life, but if he did, then it was only insofar as it was connected with what he was carrying.

"Reb Chaim!"

"Reb Naftali!"

"Reb Yeshua!"

"Come here! Here! Take a look! You'll have plenty of laughs!"

"Why are you hee-hawing like horses?" Chaim was angry.

"What's in his yarmulke?" Yeshua asked warily.

"Water!"

"Ordinary water!"

"From the Neman!"

"Hell, no! From a puddle!"

"It stinks of frogs from a mile away!"

"And he, the fool, keeps saying, 'It's miraculous . . . from the Jordan.'"

"Blasphemer!"

"He's a lunatic!"

"Kick him out, and that'll be that!"

"He got here when the show was over!"

"Who needs his stinking drops?"

The bearded men vied with each other, shouting.

"Quiet! Quiet!" Chaim barked. "If a man has come only with one drop, it's a sin to drive him away from the fire."

"But he's the one who set the shop on fire!"

"That's what Reb Naftali said!"

"The scoundrel's pretending to be a fool!"

"It's Aaron!"

"What Aaron?"

"The one Fradkin handed over in place of his Zelik."

"They found a stand-in."

"Quiet! Quiet!" Chaim barked again. "Let him come. Make way!"

The crowd parted as the stranger, bearing a velvet yarmulke in his palms, walked toward the burned-out shop.

Pacing around the pile, Naftali Spivak didn't take his eyes off him, and mindlessly and mechanically he kept repeating, "Oy, I'll die laughing."

From God knows where, apparently from a neighboring yard, a goat with her kid wandered across the ditch into the ashes. Shaking her beard, the nanny goat was turning her wise head and crying *meh-eh-eh*. At her heels, bounding in delight, the kid was staring at the world with innocent, happy eyes—looking at the people, the smoldering ashes, the sky, and his mother with the gray beard.

He also liked the sound of cracking like broken twigs, but the kid did not see a small cloud of gun powder smoke that was floating through the air like a goose feather.

When the newcomer lifted him in his arms, the kid was dead.

But his eyes were just as innocent and happy as before.

"Almighty God," the tavern keeper Yeshua exclaimed and rushed home.

The mother goat understood nothing. She poked her wise head into the ashes, nibbled the grass, and from time to time she glanced at her kid, which seemed to hover in the air in a stranger's arms. For goats, the sky begins at the human hip.

There was a short, mournful pause between the first and second sound. The stranger jumped and seemed to rise into the air and then, as he crumpled and pressed the kid to his wounded stomach, without letting the fleecy white pelt drop from his arms, he crashed to the ground beside the fallen yarmulke.

"He's dead!"

"That can't be!"

"Who fired?"

"Where?"

The crowd surged toward him, and along with them ran the night watchman Rakhmiel, abandoning the shoes thrown over his shoulder, fifty years of joyless, hopeless life, the Kovno road, the weddings of strangers, and the graves of his family. In the whole world, no legs were as healthy, as strong, or as fast as his, not even a deer's or a jackal's.

"Aaron! Aaron!"

Pushing Rakhmiel aside, someone bent over the stranger, put his ear to the traveler's *balakhon*, and choking up with an unwarranted, redeeming joy, whispered, "He's alive! Alive, it seems!"

"Alive!" the crowd burst out.

"Alive!"

The blood that stained the stranger's *balakhon* and spotted the kid's white hair was not the blood that just half an hour earlier, two shots ago, the crowd had craved, crazed by their own baseness.

No one had the courage to separate them—the newcomer and the baby goat.

"To the tavern," someone said. "It's the closest place . . . Take him to the tavern before he bleeds to death."

"Put on his yarmulke," said Chaim Spivak.

Rakhmiel picked up the yarmulke from the ground. It was wet from river or spring water. The stranger opened his eyes, and then, in this first or last moment, from somewhere out of emptiness, from his boundless longing and love, a stream flowed forth from his old yarmulke, worn around its edges, a stream in whose water his beautiful buxom mother was washing linen and a happy fish was flapping its fins, and everything was reflected as in the mirror that had survived the fire. But without flames or blood, without ashes and soot, and with clouds and baby goats, with a cradle and a ladder to the heavens. This stream flowed over his face and over the goat's hair, washing away the spots of blood, and from his face and the hair it poured down like a waterfall, onto the ruined courtyard of the once powerful Spivak brothers, onto the ashes and onto the only street of the cursed shtetl, and from the street it flowed further and further—throughout the whole county, the whole Northwest territory, the whole Pale of Settlement, all the towns and capitals, and the whole earth, carrying away all troubles and discord, returning to every person all that had been taken from them and all that they had lost . . .

Over there, suffocating, floats his son Yisrael, the little rascal; over there his sisters and brothers, who perished in a pogrom, are waving their hands; over there on a boat is Rakhmiel's stepson, the soldier Aaron, making his way home; over there the tavern keeper Yeshua's wife Chava is emerging from the water, as from a noose; and Rabbi Uri's wife Rokhl is on a ferry boat, crossing to the opposite, happy shore; and over there . . .

The water suddenly changed color—from green to orange, and from orange to a crimson red. It was as though his eyes had been spattered with tomato juice. But the river kept on flowing, not green, but crimson, and in this crimson the profile of his beautiful, buxom mother became less clear and harder to distinguish, and the fish no longer flapped its fins, but just moved its crimson gills.

Onlookers began to pour into the tavern.

Only two creatures remained in the courtyard: Naftali Spivak and the goat.

Naftali was making hawk-like circles around his pile and explaining something to the goat. But the goat didn't listen. She was looking around, searching for her kid and bleating angrily.

"You're still very young," Naftali consoled her. "You will have another kid . . . But my brother and I . . . won't give birth to another shop . . . the only thing left for us is to laugh ourselves to death."

Morta completely wore herself out. She did everything she could to help the newcomer revive. She applied plantain leaves to the wound, she tore up a sheet, clean and crisp like sugar, she wasn't shy about removing his stiff pants in front of others (God knows when they were last washed) and bandaging his bleeding stomach.

"His wife is waiting for him," Rakhmiel said, and his voice, like the whine of a mosquito, punctured the unbearable silence.

"Soon, soon," Yeshua muttered. No matter how much he wanted to get rid of the stranger, he pretended to be anxious, like a father, even offering to take the wounded man from the tavern into the house until they were able to stop the heavy bleeding, which was like a woman's period.

"How is he?" the tavern keeper asked Morta.

Morta sat down on the edge of the bench where the stranger lay, took his hand and held it in hers for a long time, began to blow on it with her lips and, as if she were pulling out one of her own teeth, said, "It's ice cold!"

"May he rest in peace," Yeshua said softly. "As God is my witness, we did everything we could."

Despondent, everyone remained silent.

"Rest in peace," the tavern keeper proclaimed again, then turned to Rakhmiel. "Where will we bury him?"

"His wife will decide," Rakhmiel answered, pressing the clapper to his stomach as if blood were about to gush out of him, too.

Pimpleface Simeon walked in, cast a glance at everyone, and caught sight of the twisted and pitiful corpse and the white sheet covered with large spots of blood. He glanced into the dead man's eyes, bent over, and like a widow said clearly and inconsolably, "Poor man! He fell off the ladder and got smashed to death . . . Poor man! There are no ladders above the roof . . . neither for a righteous man, nor for a sinner. Never!"

In his words there was no malicious pleasure, no hidden taunt, no remorse, but only an uncharacteristic sadness—inescapable, excessive, and unintentional—like blood from a wound, and it could not be stopped with any kind of plantain or yarrow.

"Father!" Pimpleface Simeon said. "Can I remove the pin?"

"What pin?"

"From the yarmulke."

"Why do you need someone else's pin? Don't we have pins here? Ask Morta—she'll find you a dozen!"

"Please!"

They were trying not to look at one another.

"Take it off! He won't need it anymore."

"Thank you, Father. Thank you . . ."

He went up to the dead man, removed the pin, put it on his own yarmulke, and tears ran down his beard.

"Thank you," he repeated, and everyone was astonished by his gentleness and obedience. "And don't forget to pay Osher's widow . . . Golda . . ."

"For what?" Yeshua was dumbfounded.

"For the kid . . . I'm sorry about the kid," Pimpleface Simeon whispered. He bent down, raised the dead goat from the floor, and began to rock it like a baby.

Bayu, bayushki, bayu.

I'll sing the kid a lullaby!

"Go home! Leave!" Yeshua pushed the onlookers out of the tavern. "We'll manage . . . without you! Morta, harness the bay!

Simeon . . . son! Put down the kid and help Uncle Chaim carry their belongings here from the pile by the fire . . ."

"It's terrible . . . terrible . . . to be by myself, without the kid," Pimpleface Simeon said and shuffled toward the door, muttering to himself a song or a spell. In the doorway he turned around and stared at Morta with sad, almost mad eyes, saying, "You were looking for the gun . . . It's in the barn . . . under the eaves . . . wrapped in a horse blanket."

"Simonas!"

"Sew the hat . . . Sew!"

And Pimpleface Simeon left. Morta covered her face with her hands and then ran after him.

But madness, like death, cannot be overtaken.

The stranger, covered by a sackcloth, was lying in a cart. Morta drove the horse, while the shoemaker Zipporah, the night watchman Rakhmiel, and Kazimieras the candle extinguisher trudged behind on the country road. It was faster than the way Yeshua's bay took to Mishkine, where the distant, dense forest was turning black across the whole horizon.

"Now he won't leave us anymore," Zipporah lamented. "Now he'll stay with us. In the morning we'll all sit down at the workbench; in the evening we'll have some cabbage soup and go to bed . . . When he sleeps, he's quite normal . . . like you . . . like me . . . like this horse."

"Son!" Rakhmiel whispered. "Aaron!"

"He's not Aaron, he's Zvi-Hersh," Zipporah corrected the old man. "A deer! And I am . . . his doe . . . Gershon, Khatskl, and Mordechai are his fawns . . . My Hershl, my deer!" she said with tears in her eyes.

Morta gripped the reins so hard it hurt. Kazimieras sighed, and the sun clouded over from his sighs, and the windows of Heaven opened.

There had not been rain like this, it seemed, since the time of Noah.

"Hey, You, don't cry!" Zipporah exclaimed, throwing back her head. "You are all-powerful! Why are You crying, Almighty God? And for whom?"

Zelda Fradkin was packing her suitcases.

Lukerya Panteleimonovna and Ardalion Ignatich were making a tub of mushrooms for the czar.

Osher's widow Golda sewed diapers out of cheap cloth for her innocent child.

The logger Itsik was clearing the forest to open the horizon.

Rabbi Uri looked out the window, waiting for fly-Rokhl to return home from the market or butcher's shop.

At the scene of the fire Naftali Spivak paced like a soldier around his pile.

Simeon, wearing a yarmulke fastened to his hair with the pin, sat on his bed, rocking the dead kid.

Only fools carried water to a fire in their yarmulkes, trudged to hard labor under guard, clambered up ladders to Heaven, and died for the sake of others. And wagons with dead fools, earth dwellers, and celestial beings rattled along over country roads, over highways, over all the earth, from sea to sea, from one end to the other, and the creak of cart wheels echoed in the universe like a moan and an omen.

18

The rain beat down, and the wise ones stayed home.

"Oink-oink!"

"Moo-oo!"

"Nei-eigh!"

Glossary

List of Characters

Glossary

balakhon (**Russian**): tunic or cloak, described in the novel as "the loose outer garment that wagon drivers and raftsmen wore."

chervontsi: Russian term for gold coins.

clapper (**Yiddish**): A wooden hammer or other noisemaker made of wood. When struck by a person who served as the synagogue clapper (*shul-klaper*), the sound served various purposes: sometimes it called congregants to prayers; sometimes it announced a death in the shtetl; and sometimes it would alert the townspeople to dangers like a fire or suspicious strangers.

Day of Judgment (*yom ha-din*): Refers to Rosh Hashana, the beginning of the ten days of repentance till Yom Kippur, the Day of Atonement. The Day of Judgment can also refer to the End of Days, a time when the Messiah comes and all souls will be judged.

Government Rabbi (or Crown Rabbi): Official position of rabbi created by the czarist regime, intending to influence Jewish practices. Government rabbis were not necessarily rabbis, nor did they receive the respect of the local Jews.

drek (**Yiddish**): Muck, filth, shit.

khapers (**Yiddish**): Kidnappers for the czarist army.

lapserdak (**Yiddish**): The long black kaftan-like coat worn by religious Jews.

makher (**Yiddish**): An important or influential person, a "big shot."

muzhik (**Russian**): a peasant

pogromniks: A Yiddish word to refer to the participants of a pogrom, a violent mob attack on Jews.

Reb: In Yiddish, a rough equivalent of "Mister." To be distinguished from "Rabbi" and "Rebbe".

rebbe (**Yiddish**): Hasidic rabbi; can also mean, simply, "teacher."

Rebeyne shel eylem: (Hebrew term for God, literally "Master of the Universe." (Transliteration reflects pronunciation of Lithuanian Yiddish; Ashkenazic pronunciation of Hebrew is *Ribono shel ʿolam*.)

sazhens (**Russian**): A unit of length formerly used in Russia, equal to seven feet.

sermyaga (**Russian**): A thick woolen overcoat.

Shavues (**Yiddish pronunciation of the Hebrew *Shavuʿot*)**: Seven weeks after Passover, the holiday that celebrates the giving of the Torah on Mount Sinai.

shiva (**Hebrew**): A mourning period in Judaism; literally "seven," referring to the seven days that traditional Jews mourn ("sit shiva") at home when a family member dies.

shtetl (**Yiddish**): A small market town in the Pale of Settlement populated by Jews (50–90%) and non-Jews. The word is the diminutive of *shtot* (city); while the plural in Yiddish is *shtetlekh*, the customary spelling in English is shtetls.

Simkhes Torah (**Yiddish pronunciation of the Hebrew *Simchat Torah*)**: Jewish religious observance held on the last day of Sukkot when the yearly cycle of Torah reading is completed and the next cycle is begun.

Torah: From Hebrew, literally "teaching." Usually refers to the Five Books of Moses or to the twenty-four books of the Hebrew Bible, but it can also refer to the Talmud and other traditional books of Jewish learning. Commonly pronounced *Toyre* in Yiddish (or *Teyre* in the Lithuanian pronunciation).

tzitzis (**Hebrew**): Tassels as worn by traditional Jews, with knots that allude to the 613 commandments.

unmöglich (**German and Yiddish**): Impossible.

Vilna: Yiddish name for the Lithuanian city now known as Vilnius.

Vilna Gaon: Rabbi Eliyahu ben Shlomo Zalman (1720–1797), famed Talmud scholar in Vilna. "Gaon" (Hebrew "excellency"), a title that was used primarily in reference to medieval Talmudic scholars, was also bestowed on Rabbi Eliyahu.

Yerushalayim de-Lite (**Hebrew/Aramaic**): "Jerusalem of Lithuania," a phrase that was associated with Vilna because of its famed synagogues and Jewish life.

zhid (**Russian**): Pejorative way of referring to a Jew (male or female), which has a rough equivalent in the slang words "yid" or "kike."

List of Characters

Rabbi Uri is the elderly rabbi who founded the town's synagogue and cemetery. His wife **Rokhl** is deceased.

Rakhmiel is the town's night watchman. Living alone, he longs for the return of his long-lost stepson **Aaron,** who was conscripted into the czarist army at sixteen.

Itsik Magid is Rabbi Uri's student. **Rabbi Uri** took him under his care as an orphaned boy and saved him from the draft by bribing officials. Itsik earns his living as a woodcutter and rents a room from the young widow, **Golda.**

Golda is a widow who supports herself cleaning houses for **Rabbi Uri** and the **Fradkin** family.

Yeshua Mandel is a tavern keeper. He lives with his wife **Chava,** his grown son **Simeon** (sometimes called **Pimpleface Simeon**), and their servant girl, **Morta.**

Morta became a servant to the Mandel family when her parents, three sisters, and twin brothers were deported to Siberia for allegedly helping an insurrectionist. She is deeply religious and attends church every Sunday.

Markus Fradkin, a wealthy timber merchant, is the richest man in town. He is the father of the beautiful **Zelda,** and a son, **Zelik,** who is mentioned but we do not meet.

Afinogen and Guri Andronov, two Russian Orthodox brothers, are woodcutters who work in **Markus Fradkin's** forest.

Ardalion Nesterovich is the policeman assigned to this town. He has a wife, **Lukerya**, and two young children, a son **Ivan** (called **Grozny**) and a daughter **Ekaterina** (called **Katenka**)

Naftali and Chaim Spivak are brothers who own the local hardware store. **Naftali** is also the synagogue warden who organizes the Sabbath services. Their sister **Chava** is married to the tavern keeper, **Yeshua Mandel**.

Rabbi Hillel is the young rabbi of the synagogue.

The **synagogue caretaker** is a gentile hired to do tasks that Jews can't do on the Sabbath and to take care of the cemetery. He has an argument with the mysterious stranger and holds grudges.

Zvi-Hersh Ashkenazi (called Hershl by his loved ones) is a man with a mission. Consumed with grief over the drowning death of his son **Yisrael**, he leaves his home and wife **Zipporah** and takes to the road to fulfill his quest.

Photograph by Evgenia Levin

Grigory Kanovich, one of Lithuania's most prominent writers, was born in Jonava, a town on the outskirts of Kaunas, on June 18, 1929. During World War II, he fled with his parents to the Soviet Union one day before the Nazis entered his town. The family survived the war years in a kolkhoz in Kazakhstan. Returning to Lithuania after the war, Kanovich studied at Vilnius University and began his literary career in 1955.

Depicting the culture and history of Eastern European Jews, he called his novels "a kind of Litvak saga, a written monument to the extinguished Lithuanian Jews." Written in Russian, his first novels were published in Lithuania and were eagerly sought out by Jewish readers throughout the Soviet Union. Eventually his novels gained a worldwide following in translation. Two of his works published in English translation are *Shtetl Love Song* and *Devilspel*.

The author of ten novels published in fourteen languages, Kanovich was the recipient of numerous awards, including the Lithuanian National Prize in Art and Culture in 2014 and the EBRD Literature Prize (European Bank for Reconstruction and Development) in 2020. His works include *I Gaze at the Stars; Candles in the Wind; There Is No Paradise for Slaves; A Kid for Two Pennies; Smile upon Us, Lord*; and numerous film scripts and plays.

Kanovich was elected in 1989 as a deputy to the Supreme Soviet from the Lithuanian Independence movement and served as chairman of the Jewish Community of Lithuania from 1989 to 1993. He settled in Israel in

1993 with his wife Olga. He died in Tel Aviv on January 20, 2023, at the age of ninety-three.

Mary Ann Szporluk is an editor and translator whose published translations include *Escape Hatch: Two Novellas* by Vladimir Makanin and *The Death of a Poet: The Last Days of Marina Tsvetaeva* by Irma Kudrova. She holds a BA from Stanford University and an MA in Slavic Languages and Literatures from the University of Michigan. She was an editor at Ardis Publishers in Ann Arbor and worked with the Ukrainian Research Institute at Harvard University.

Ken Frieden is the B. G. Rudolph Professor of Judaic Studies at Syracuse University, specializing in modern Hebrew and Yiddish literature. Since 1995 he has been series editor for *Judaic Traditions in Literature, Music, and Art*.

Select Titles in Judaic Traditions in Literature, Music, and Art

Café Shira: A Novel
David Ehrlich; Michael Swirsky, trans.

Diary of a Lonely Girl, or The Battle against Free Love
Miriam Karpilove; Jessica Kirzane, trans.

From a Distant Relation
Mikhah Yosef Berdichevsky; James Adam Redfield, ed. and trans.

Jewish Identity in American Art: A Golden Age since the 1970s
Matthew Baigell

The Odyssey of an Apple Thief
Moishe Rozenbaumas; Isabelle Rozenbaumas, ed.; Jonathan Layton, trans.

Paul Celan: The Romanian Dimension
Petre Solomon; Emanuela Tegla, trans.

The People of the Book and the Camera: Photography in the Hebrew Novel
Ofra Amihay

The Rivals and Other Stories
Jonah Rosenfeld; Rachel Mines, trans.

For a full list of titles in this series, visit:
https://press.syr.edu/supressbook-series
/judaic-traditions-in-literature-music-and-art/.